A PETAL IN THE CROWN

BOOK THREE OF THE MAGIC OF THE WILDFLOWERS TRILOGY

by Megan Shade

Published by: Shade Made Publishing LLC

First Edition

ISBN: 9798987832424

Editing by Sara Coombes: https://saracoombescom.wordpress.com/

Interior art by Lindsey Staton: @honeyy.fae on IG for commissions

Cover Art by SeventhStar Art Services https://www.seventhstarart.com/

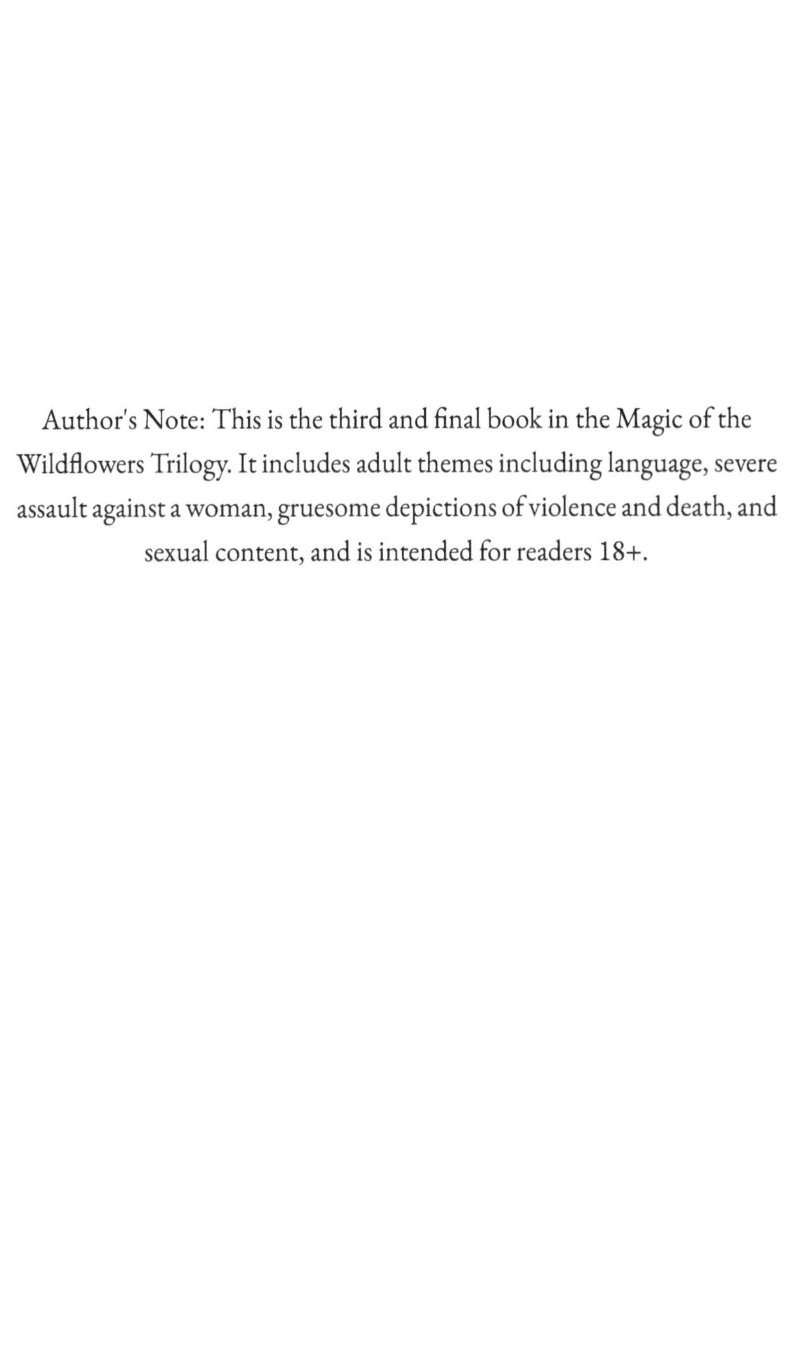

Author's Note: This is the third and final book in the Magic of the Wildflowers Trilogy. It includes adult themes including language, severe assault against a woman, gruesome depictions of violence and death, and sexual content, and is intended for readers 18+.

CONTENTS

To my readers,
You have no idea how much you have changed my life.
I love you all.

ÐESIA
Norwich
Pelar
Woodhurst
Auropera
Wicked
Wood
Bearswillow
Lupar
Santia
CALIR

BOOK I RECAP

Ever since her mother fell victim to the Lonely Death, Azalea (Lea) has tried to find a cure in the petals of the moonflowers. When a pack of fenrir attacks the town, Lea's friend, Thomas, uses his magic to save her, resulting in his arrest for hiding magic from the Black King. Lea is held prisoner by the commander of the Royal Army, Gray, while Thomas is put on trial.Lea falsely confesses to having magic and is sentenced along with Thomas to a lifetime of servitude. Gray and Lea travel to Auropera, and Lea learns that Gray is the son of the Black King—the Night Prince, Evander Nestruir.

After Alaric, Gray's older brother, nearly kills Lea in a brutal attack, Gray confesses his feelings for her. Thomas becomes angry about Lea's relationship with the Night Prince and admits that he is part of a rebellion led by the unknown Eclipsed King. Thomas tells Lea that the Lonely Death results from a spell that allows the Black King to take power from those who have died.

Gray reveals that he and Lea are mates, and decides that to keep her safe, they must marry. During the wedding, there's an explosion, and Gray forces Lea to flee to the dungeons where the rebellion awaits. Unbeknownst to the rebels kneeling in front of Vincent, Gray slips in the back and quietly confesses to Lea that he is the Eclipsed King and leader of the rebellion.

BOOK 2 RECAP

G ray, Lea, and the royal army flee Auropera, and a battle ensues. As they are escaping, Lea sees Alaric chanting between the trees, but he disappears. Gray and Lea travel South to Calir, while the rest of the army journeys to the cavern in the mountains surrounding Bearswillow. Lea becomes ill with the Lonely Death.

Emma senses something is wrong, and with Noah's help, they track and find them in time to marry Lea and Gray, making Lea a part of the Nestruir family and unable to be killed by the Black King's spell.

They travel through the Wicked Wood. Using his ability to freeze time, Lea's father, Henry, abducts her and takes her to an old cottage within the wood. There, she has a vision of Queen Emmaline's death, and somehow, she's able to keep death away from Emmaline's unborn baby long enough for it to be delivered. Lea finds out that Adelaide and Henry aren't her birth parents.

Once in Calir, Lea meets with Eudora, who tells her that to cure the Lonely Death, Nestruir blood must be spilled. In return for this information, Lea must retrieve an unknown object locked inside a cage in Auropera. Gray is told that to break the spell that prevents him from killing his family, he must make a sacrifice.

Lea learns that Emmaline's baby, Evangeline, was brought to Calir and grew up in the castle with King Tanad, but that she disappeared one day. She then returned with a baby in her arms (Azalea). She once again disappeared, and Tanad was told to take Lea to the healer in Bearswillow to keep her safe, and that the fate of their kingdoms depended on it.

Alaric kills the Black King and takes his power. Once back in Bearswillow, they prepare for battle. Lea fails again and again to grow the moonflowers. The rebel army is infected with the Lonely Death.

Alaric comes to Bearswillow, killing Noah. Emma takes a potion to connect her to the other side, allowing those who die in battle to fight even after death. Lea and Gray find Alaric and they battle, but Alaric has grown too strong. He stabs Gray in the chest. As Lea battles Alaric, attempting to steal his magic, Gray understands what the sacrifice Eudora spoke of must be.

He cuts the mate mark from his skin, allowing Lea to live on after he dies. Alaric, knowing he is about to be defeated, disappears, and Lea rushes back to Gray just as he takes his final breath.

CHAPTER I

LEA

The Earth itself was on fire. Not just the wildflowers and trees scattered across the massive hill Lea knelt upon. Not just the house she had grown up in, or the garden she'd spent years lovingly tending. Not just the well under the massive oak, or the small wooden marker Thomas had carved for her after her mother's death.

The Earth.

As if the very fabric of the universe had been set aflame by the god of the sun himself.

Fire rained down from the sky, trails and funnels of black flames soaring from the heavens and crashing into the ground—a ground that trembled as if trying to flee its own destruction.

The grass turned to nothing but ash and embers as the fire spread rapidly down the hill, but Lea didn't notice the flames as she leaned over her mate's lifeless body in a puddle of sticky, warm blood. A fist-sized chunk of bloody, jagged flesh marked with a solitary moonflower laid at her feet. Their mate bond.

Severed.

No longer attached to a body or a soul.

Where the gift of their bond had been inked and sealed—their promise of eternity—was only a gaping hole above where Gray's heart no longer beat, his lifeless body splayed open so violently that the broken bones of his ribcage protruded like gnarled fingers.

It was all Lea could see. All she would ever see again.

She was completely unaware of the storm clouds flashing furiously with lightning overhead, obscuring the moon and stars. Unaware of the rain pounding down in thick sheets that did absolutely nothing to extinguish the scorching inferno violently spreading around her. Nor did she hear her friends' screams—Erik and Janelle begging her to stop. Warning her that if she didn't rein in her magic, she was going to kill them all.

None of it reached her. She was too deep within her darkness, too overwhelmed by her grief and the horrific, pure power raging inside her, whispering into her marrow.

Destroy.

Destroy.

Destroy.

The command pounded with her heart's furious rhythm like a war drum, incessant in its demand. The floor that had once kept her primary magic tucked safely away had completely shattered, allowing the power of the gods, the immense magic that had been hidden inside her, to mix with her own.

Raw, primal magic reverberated through her chest and down her arms, tingling into the tips of her fingers and ringing in her ears. She was no longer in control. She was no longer Lea. Not without Gray. She never would be again.

In the span of a few heartbeats, the power of her primary magic seeped into every cell of her body, slowly burning through the good inside her—every bit of hope, everything about her that was *pure*. Lea was no longer the woman she'd been this morning.

No. All evidence of that girl had been seared from her being the moment her mate had taken his final breath. In an instant, she'd transformed into something new. Something completely and wholly devoid of hope and light.

As he'd traveled beyond the veil, so had Lea's soul.

Destroy.

Destroy.

Destroy.

Her vision turned red, her blood pumping furiously, death hovering around her shoulders like a shroud. Lea placed her palms on Gray's chest, searching with her magic for the reaper's cold fingers as she had the day she'd saved Queen Emmaline's baby. But where Gray's life should be, that thread of light nestled behind his ribs, there was *nothing*.

"You are *not* leaving this world," Lea growled as she ripped the vines from the ground that she had planted in Gray's blood. The ones she'd buried before he'd taken his final breath. The ones that, once again, hadn't worked.

It requires every drop... Gray had said just before he'd dug his blade beneath his skin, slicing through his own flesh as he'd cut the mate bond away.

Lea pushed a new handful of moonflower seeds into the dirt, plunging her hands into the blood-soaked soil and praying enough of Gray's blood had been spilled for them to grow—fast. "You are *not* dying," she insisted. "You are *not* going beyond the veil."

Even as she said the words, Lea knew he was already there. His chest no longer rose and fell—there wasn't even enough of his chest left to rise and fall—and his eyes were glassy with death. In them, Lea's reflection stared back at her, her own eyes completely black with shadows and her skin covered in deep, scarlet blood. Her mate's blood. Her blond hair had come undone from its braid and now flew about her face like a golden veil, accentuating her sharp jaw and flushed cheeks.

The fire crackling across the hill grew impossibly hotter, spreading rapidly toward town, where the royal soldiers were surely fleeing. The screams of grown men met her ears as the deadly blaze reached them in the distance, further fueling her rage.

Destroy. The voice became stronger, firmer—a slithering wickedness that didn't sound human at all.

Alaric might have disappeared, taking his magic along with him before she'd been able to sever it from his body, but those bastard soldiers that had chosen to fight with him remained. Even without looking away from Gray's unnaturally still form, Lea could *hear* them running—the thunderous rumble of feet pounding against the cobblestone roads of Bearswillow. Cowards desperate to escape with their lives after slaughtering gods knew how many innocent rebels.

Fuck them.

Lea shot her arms out, her eyes never leaving her mate. She pictured her shadows morphing into snakes—thousands of them. They slithered from her fingers like hungry cobras, lightning fast, fangs bared as they raced after the Royal Army.

Consume their hearts, Lea commanded them silently. *Every last one.*

There would be no chance for Alaric's men to repent or change sides. There would be no mercy. No redemption.

Not anymore.

Not ever again.

Raw power crackled across Lea's skin as she pushed her hands deeper into the ground, the cries of soldiers falling as her shadows ripped them apart, feeding her power. She commanded death like she was its master. A god on earth.

Magic that can create just as it can destroy. Tanad's words circled in her mind.

Destroy.

Destroy.

Destroy.

The voice continued to beg, a ceaseless plea surging through her blood and clattering around her skull.

But not yet. First, she had to *create*—even if it killed her. She needed the cure.

Then, and only then, would she give in to that voice demanding she destroy. And destroy she would. She would bring the world to its fucking knees.

"Grow," she hissed, her voice low and seething with desperate fury as she found a miniscule flicker of light that remained inside her and forced it into the soil.

As soon as Gray's blood saturated the seeds, they cracked open, vines furiously shooting up from the ground like fingers of the dead bursting from their graves. The puddle of blood she knelt in receded as the thirsty roots of the moonflowers drank in the thick, cooling liquid until, despite the rain still falling, the dirt around them was dry as bone.

In a haze of smoke, the black flames engulfing her burned away her clothing, draping her in a gown of undulating flames. The vines continued to spread across the hill, creeping up Lea's legs and torso and wrapping in spirals up her body until they surrounded her head like a crown. Her fire burned through the vines knotted at the back of her skull, creating a perfect, thorny diadem of moonflowers that rested just above her forehead and wound through her hair as if she had been born wearing it. As if she was and had always been the Queen of Death and Goddess of Destruction.

The dark fire continued to rage as the moonflowers opened. But as they grew and flourished, so did Lea's savagery. She'd waited for *years* for this moment, but even the sight of thousands of pristine white moonflowers beginning to unfurl did nothing to ease the poisonous need for vengeance inside her—to soothe the gory, scarred mess of muscle where her heart used to be.

Black, thorny vines crept, twisted, and swirled as they spread like poison oak, absorbing the flames as if they were water—as if the heat of the fire was giving them energy they needed to not only grow, but *thrive*. The flames had no effect on the delicate flowers—didn't singe or burn the thin, fragile edges of their petals. Instead, they cut clear pathways through the fire wherever they took root.

Lea could hardly find her light amongst the swirling void of darkness inside her, but she sought out a small ember, forcing it down her arms and through her fingers into the moonflowers, pouring it into the dirt until the final, tentative flicker of warmth extinguished completely. The tiny buds continued to open. Thousands of them—tens of thousands of blooming moonflowers. It was a choreographed symphony of *life*, of victory. And yet, Lea was completely unable to feel the joy of her success.

Focusing all her energy on a single flower in front of her, she demanded it to bloom fully. It listened, bursting open in a pop of pure white, a stark contrast to the black flames and thorny vines surrounding it. Hundreds more opened fully in sequence, as if all they had needed was for one to succeed for them to wake from their slumber.

Wait until they're ready, Wildflower. They must bloom fully... You'll know when to pick them. Picked by the right person with the right intentions, at the right time, the flowers from these seeds can stop death himself. Lea's mother's words echoed through the crackling of the fire. Had she somehow known what would be required for them to bloom? What Lea would have to lose to finally wield the magic of the wildflowers? Had she known that Alaric, The Black King's eldest son, would destroy not only her life, but the world as they knew it?

The wind picked up in a massive gust, pushing her arm toward the vines. Without hesitating, she ripped a flower from its stem, reaching out with her primary magic for any hint of death that may be lingering around the moonflowers, but death was nowhere to be found. The flower remained pristine as she stuffed a petal between Gray's lips and closed his jaw.

Lea froze, the blood roaring in her ears the only sound as she held her breath. The fire stopped popping and sizzling, and the flames halted—froze as if they were sentient beings waiting with bated breath to see what would happen next.

Lea wasn't exactly sure what she expected to happen—for Gray to take in a sudden, violent gasp of air and open his eyes, or for the color to slowly flush back into his pale skin.

But it wasn't for nothing to happen at all. Pain rocked through every inch of Lea's body, her chest and head throbbing and her lungs refusing to inhale. She gritted her teeth, pushing another petal into his mouth. It was impossible for him to be truly gone. Impossible that he was beyond her reach. But once again, he remained as still as stone.

Lea roared at the sky, the storm clouds flashing with savage silver-blue lightning. Cursing the gods above, she grabbed another flower, ripping off the petals and rolling one into a ball. She crushed it between her fingers until a small drop of liquid hung from the base, then dropped the juice onto Gray's tongue and closed the macerated petal inside his mouth.

This has to work. These flowers can defeat death himself. This has *to work.* There was no other option. No world in which she was willing to live without Gray. And yet, that's exactly what she was doing. Breathing in and out, heart beating, while her mate lay there, lifeless.

Tears streamed from Lea's eyes, evaporating into steam as they trailed down her cheeks. This wasn't how it was supposed to be. She had accepted the mate bond fully and whole-heartedly—every part of it.

They were never meant to be separated, whether in life or death. But Gray had stolen that certainty from her as he cut their bond from his flesh. He'd given her the gift of life. But what he'd done wasn't a gift—not without him here. Without him, it was nothing more than a curse.

"Lea!" a roar met her ears, and Lea twisted, her flames shooting outward on instinct.

"Please," a familiar voice begged. "She's dying, Lea. Look at her. Look at Emma."

CHAPTER 2

ERIK

*E**mma*. Somewhere within the fog of Lea's devastation, the word seemed to tug at her consciousness. *Yes,* Erik thought. Sweet, kind Emma, who had risked her life to help them win this battle. Emma, who Lea had promised—had *sworn*—she would save.

Emma. Who could see those who were no longer with us. Who was tethered to the world of the dead, allowing them to interact with the living.

Lea turned around in a haze.

Just behind Thomas, Emma laid on the ground, her face gray and clammy and her eyebrows creased as if in pain. Her heart still beat—Erik could see the pulse in her neck, could hear the swoosh of blood pumping through her veins.

Janelle knelt next to her, eyes flicking between Lea and Emma's short, rapid breaths.

Sweat poured down Erik's brow as he held his arms out, blocking the flames from reaching them. His face was red and his jaw clenched in concentration, allowing them a space only a few feet wide to stand in.

His stomach churned and his head swam, unable to process what was happening. He had to get them to Lea. Get them close enough to get through to her. He didn't care if he used every last drop of his magic keeping the flames away. If they didn't stop Lea, Emma would die. Their people would die. Clenching his jaw, he pushed the fire further away, bridging the space between them.

Lea's eyes roved over her friends, her grief and rage so thick it was as if she was looking at them through a piece of stained glass. Her eyes were dark, narrowed as if confused at how they'd fought their way through the flames to get to her. Or maybe suspicious that they were going to try to stop her from destroying the universe.

But even though the woman before him looked like Lea, she didn't *feel* like the friend he'd come to know and love. Erik was certain she loved them, too, but that love seemed hidden under a layer of sorrow and anger so dense, he wondered if she would ever break through it again.

Erik's eyes flicked around to the others, searching for any indication that they might have a plan, but they all seemed as lost as he was. Thomas's brown eyes were brimming with words he knew better than to say. His hands clenched and unclenched repeatedly at his sides, his fingers crusted with black ash from trying to pick the moonflowers for Emma himself.

And he had. Flower after flower, each one turning black and scattering into the wind as Lea's fire raged around them, oblivious to everything but Gray.

Only you can pick them, Eudora had told Lea. *They are owed to you, and to you alone.* Without Lea, there was no hope. No possibility any of them would survive. But how could he break through her grief and make her realize they were running out of time?

"Please," Thomas repeated, his voice cracking, the word bursting with desperation.

In another world, another time, Erik knew Lea would have picked a moonflower without hesitation. Would have done anything and everything she could to save her friend. She would have moved heaven and earth to bring her back—but this was no longer that world.

A distant, quiet part of Erik wished Emma could stay on the other side and allow Gray a moment with them to say goodbye. Maybe even to find a way back to them. But Erik wasn't a fool.

His friend was gone.

"Please, Lea," Thomas repeated. "You have to give her a moonflower before it's too late. She's barely hanging on."

"I need more time," Lea said, her voice oddly melodic at its core, but crackling with rage and ragged at its edges with sorrow. "What if Gray comes back to say goodbye? Maybe he just needs a few more minutes. If I could touch him, just one more time..." she trailed off, tilting her head to the side and narrowing her eyes.

Erik wanted to go to her. He knew Gray would ask him to take her far away from here and help her move forward and save their kingdom, but Lea raised her hands, and he paused.

Using her shadows, Lea picked four moonflower petals, her long trails of darkness floating through the air as they gently placed one at each of her friends' feet. Thomas picked up his petal and reached for Emma, but before he could touch her, Lea created a firm dome of shadows around her still unconscious body, blocking Thomas from touching her.

The color drained from his face, his posture going rigid. "Lea, please."

"A few minutes. That's all I'm asking for. Then you can save her." With trembling hands, Lea reached into her boot, pulling out a black vial that Erik recognized immediately as one of the potions she kept in that old box. The ones Gray had told him had been left by her mother.

"Lea, what are you doing?" Erik's eyes widened as she pulled the cork from the bottle with a *pop*. He stepped forward, the scent of the potion of death unmistakable, but Lea threw up a thick, waist-high wall of black fire.

"I'm getting him back," she said. She didn't scream. Didn't shout. But the sound of her voice made Erik pause—made Lea pause—only for a second. It sounded so unlike her. Hard. Sharp.

Wicked.

"You can't." Janelle pushed forward, pleading as she moved as close to Lea as possible, until her toes were up against the line of fire. "You have to know that. Please. *Please*, think about this."

Lea didn't answer, didn't seem to want to hear her own voice again as she lifted the vial, the sweet smell of death growing stronger. The wind tipped her hand up, pushing the bottle closer to her lips.

"Stop!" Janelle cried. "He's gone, Lea! He's *gone*! He's not here!"

"Then I will find him wherever he *is*." Lea pinned them with a stare, as if daring them to challenge her again.

"Do you want her to die?" Thomas pointed at Emma. "Only you can pick the petals. If you're not here... You'll kill everyone, Lea." Thomas's words sent a wave of grief across the hill, and Erik hoped Lea felt it through her haze. "Emma will die. The rebels. The sick. Every single one of them will die without the moonflowers. *Your* people will die." He was begging, groveling without shame, and it seemed to be working. Lea paused.

Erik nodded his head in agreement, his heart pounding. "Go on, Thomas," he whispered. Thomas knew exactly what he was doing. Playing on Lea's sense of obligation to her friends; her need to protect the people she loved. It had always been her greatest weakness, and right now, it was their best chance.

"You've worked so hard for this moment. To cure the Lonely Death." Thomas continued. "You can't let it slip away in your anger. You can't let everyone die trying to bring someone back who's already gone."

"I *won't* live without him," Lea hissed, unable to contain her rage as her flames and shadows exploded, the war inside her appearing to almost rip her in two.

Erik grimaced, grunting as he was forced to use more magic to protect them from Lea's flames.

"I won't take it, Lea," Janelle said, lifting her chin in defiance, as if sensing Lea's moment of weakness. She pulled her shoulders back, her eyes piercing and unyielding. Her throat bobbed as she swallowed, and her cheeks pinched inward in pain as a welt on her neck opened and began to weep. Erik's stomach dropped, but he didn't interrupt her.

Janelle stared Lea down. "If you're making stupid decisions, I'm going to make them right along with you."

"I won't either. *Hundreds* of our soldiers have the Lonely Death. They need you to pick petals for them, too. I'm not going to take the cure and leave the rest of our army to die," Thomas said firmly. "You can still change things. They need you. *We* need you."

The monster inside Lea seemed to pause, her wild, frantic eyes darting between the four of them as her chest heaved up and down. After several agonizing seconds, Lea corked the potion, but kept it fisted tightly in her palm.

"Fine," Lea relented, squeezing her eyes shut, a sob bursting from her throat as she pushed the vial back into her boot.

Without speaking and as quickly as possible, Lea grabbed a root from the ground and wrenched it free. She wrapped her fingers around the base of the vine, squeezing tight as she ripped it through her closed fist. The flowers tore from their stems; the thorns slicing through Lea's skin with ease. But she didn't care; hardly seemed to notice.

Blood streamed from her torn palms as she grabbed another root, her fire dimming slightly. She pulled the vine through her hand, then another and another, until she had a pile of moonflowers at her feet big enough to save the entire rebel army ten times over.

Lea collapsed, defeated, tears filling her eyes.

Janelle was at her side in an instant, soothing her as sobs wracked Lea's body. "I'm so sorry, Lea. I'm so, so sorry."

"I'm going to destroy Alaric for this," Lea sobbed, almost sounding like her old self. "I'm going to tear him limb from limb. I'll flay the skin from his bones. I'll—"

"We'll help you do it," Erik said, his voice thick with sorrow and unshed tears.

"Please," Lea trailed her trembling fingers across the black, bloody welts on Janelle's skin. "Eat the petal. All of you." Lea used her shadows to place one in each of her friends' hands. "I can't lose anyone else." Tears flowed down her cheeks, her emotions bubbling over until she could hardly breathe. Crawling over to Gray's body, she laid herself across him, running her hands through his hair. "I can't lose any of you."

Janelle narrowed her eyes. "Give me the potion," she demanded.

A shiver rushed down Erik's spine as he processed Janelle's accusation.

Lea jolted, her eyebrows creasing as a look of mock betrayal crossed her face.

"You don't trust me? After everything we've been through?" Lea's voice cracked.

Janelle stood firm, her arms crossed in front of her, unyielding.

Lea pulled the potion from her boot, throwing it at Janelle. "Here then. Just. Please—" she begged. "*Please*, eat the petal."

Erik's heart sank as he watched Lea beg for them to save themselves. She'd lost so much already. Her mate. The love of her life. "We'll take the cure," Erik said, placing a hand on Janelle's shoulder. "Right? We have the potion." His eyes skated across her skin, lingering on each welt. "You're getting worse," he said softly, just to Janelle, his chest growing tight.

Janelle continued to stare at Lea, her eyes sparkling with tears, her lips pressed together. For several agonizing seconds, she didn't answer. Erik's heart pounded as another welt opened, this time on her arm. "Please," he begged.

Her shoulders fell at the desperation in his voice, and she met his eyes. Janelle nodded, and together, they raised the flowers to their lips, placing them on their tongues and swallowing them whole.

This time, the moonflowers worked instantly. The black sores faded from Janelle's skin, not a single scar or blemish remaining, and Erik's bruises and cuts healed over, his pounding headache easing.

Lea's flames flickered around her as she turned her focus to Thomas. Thomas's shoulders fell, his eyes darting to Emma before finally following Erik and Janelle's lead. His throat bobbed as he swallowed, and Lea rocked back onto her heels.

Like the brisk snap of fingers, she turned off her tears, wiping them from her eyes and clearing her throat. Black fire wrapped around her body as she reached into her boot once again, pulling another potion from against her calf.

"What—" Janelle lunged forward, but Lea's fire grew again, forcing Erik to once more hold it back as it surged toward them. Erik's eyes flicked to the potion at Janelle's feet. Different from the one Lea now held, the vial longer and slimmer, with a black stopper rather than cork.

"The fire will die once I'm gone. Just please." She met Thomas's eyes. "*Please*, give me a few minutes. If Emma is connected to the other side, maybe the moonflowers can work. Maybe I can bring us both back. Just a few minutes, and if I'm still gone, you can save her," Lea said, pulling the stopper free. She brought the vial to her lips and closed her eyes, tilting her head back as she swallowed the potion in one gulp.

In less than three seconds, her limbs went limp, and she collapsed to the ground, her eyes rolling back into her head.

"I'm coming, Gray," she whispered—a sound Erik barely heard over the roaring in his ears—a smile flitting across Lea's lips as she fell into her mate's dead arms.

CHAPTER 3

GRAY

As the black haze faded from his vision, Gray groaned. Not from pain.

No, the pain was gone.

But in its place was a heaviness, weighing down his limbs and his spirit. His body felt strange in a way he couldn't identify—felt as if it didn't belong to him at all. Pulling himself to sit, he looked around the cool, endless void—not cold or uncomfortable, but somehow, soothing. A balm for his shredded soul.

There was nothing around him but a gentle, glowing white as far as he could see, except for two foggy glimpses into what he assumed were other worlds. Was this the in-between?

To his right, so far away he could barely see it, he could make out a patch of raging black fire and soot-filled smoke. *Lea*. His heart squeezed painfully. Not with regret. He'd made the right choice. Gray knew that. But seeing the consequences of his choice, his mate's grief, threatened to shatter him.

Gray forced himself to look to his left where a softly illuminated sky glowed with thousands of twinkling stars, hardly visible as the foreign constellations shifted and changed.

He wasn't sure how much time had passed. Minutes? Hours? All he was certain of was that he was dead. With slow, tentative movements, he trailed a hand along his chest, the skin smooth and unblemished, his black fighting leathers clean of the blood and gore that had soaked them as he'd cut the mate mark from his skin. He could breathe deeply without the torturous burning that had accompanied his final breaths. But the searing agony of what he'd done to Lea would linger for eternity.

A sacrifice, Eudora had said.

Gray's stomach twisted, and shame burned deep in his gut. He'd been a fool. How had he not considered that the sacrifice she'd demanded would be something like this? Something that would make his mate despise him. Something that would hurt her so deeply Gray wasn't sure that forgiveness would ever be possible, even once she won the war and joined him beyond the veil, far into the future. He wasn't sure there was any amount of time that would be enough to be granted forgiveness.

But what had been his other option? Bring her with him beyond the veil? End her tragically short life and doom every member of the rebellion to the same fate? Allow Alaric to continue to terrorize his kingdom unchecked, slaughtering the innocent and stealing their magic until there was no one left? It hadn't been a choice at all.

He'd done what was necessary—what had been required of him—to save their people. And he was certain that, had their roles been reversed, Lea would have made the same decision without hesitation.

She was already the most powerful among them, even if she hadn't yet fully mastered her powers. Without a doubt, Gray knew his mate was the key to ending the Lonely Death *and* his family's wicked reign. Everything she needed to defeat Alaric was already inside her.

Pride bloomed in his heart, but it quickly mixed with a misery so intense it made his bones ache. Gray had known what he was doing as he lay there dying—had known with sudden, devastating clarity that it was his blood Eudora had seen in her vision saturating the ground to allow the moonflowers to grow.

He'd also known that Lea would never forgive him for breaking their bond. How much losing it would hurt her.

Gray looked to his right, longing to go back to her, to where Emma still held open the door between worlds. He could touch her one more time, caress her face, and let her know that he was sorry. But he'd already said those words, and who knew how much time they had left?

A life for a life. That had been the deal—the key to breaking his father's curse and allowing the moonflowers to grow. All because of what Brennus had done hundreds of years ago. If he stayed, remained in the mortal realm rather than beyond the veil with whatever waited for him there, would the curse still be broken? Had he truly sacrificed his life if he could remain on earth and interact with Lea through Emma? If he could watch her?

No. He couldn't risk it.

A life for a life. He'd made the sacrifice. Done what had been required of him. What if he returned to his mate only to be stuck in the mortal realm? If the spell only worked once he was gone, *truly* gone, then there was only one decision to make.

He forced himself to his feet and pushed away the voice begging him to stay—to return to her. With heavy, tired footsteps, he walked toward the night sky in the distance. With every step, a sense of calm washed through him, dimming the despair threatening to consume him whole. As the nightscape grew closer and came into focus, Gray realized it looked quite a bit like the portal he'd destroyed in Calir—a shimmering wall of water standing between him and a completely different world.

On the other side of the wall was a soaring field, the tall grass waving in the wind as the land rose up to meet a sky that held more stars than he'd seen in his entire life. It was peaceful, and as he took a closer look, he realized he knew exactly where it was. Just on the inside of the Torres mountains was this same hill, one he could access from the cavern. He'd stood there a hundred times, looking out over the village and watching for threats, searching for a glimpse of his mate as she went about her life, completely unaware that he even existed.

It was peaceful, and a sliver of hope burrowed into his heart. With their bond broken, Lea would live a mortal life. Another seventy years, hopefully a little more. He would gladly sit on this hill and wait for her until her time in the realm of the living was up. He could fill his hours dreaming of the way her hair smelled, the sparkle in her blue eyes, and how he could make his death up to her. He could pray to the gods to keep her safe and happy. Pray she was successful in growing the moonflowers and killing Alaric.

He would wait the seventy years without complaint if it meant their kingdom would be saved. If it meant Lea was able to *live*. And he would do so without regretting the decisions he had made.

He would wait ten times that, a hundred times. He would wait forever if that was what he had to do to hold her again. Because they *would* be together again. And he *would* find a way to earn her forgiveness for the impossible and horrible choice he'd been forced to make.

Squaring his shoulders, Gray stepped through the portal. Shimmering magic brushed against his skin as he climbed up the hill toward those sparkling stars until he reached the top—so close to the sky he felt as if he could touch the clouds—and sat down to wait. With a deep breath of fresh air, his lungs filling fully, he bent his knees, resting his forearms atop them. The rustle of the breeze was soothing, and Gray tilted his head back toward the sky.

"I'll wait here, Little Flower. I'm sorry. I didn't want to do this. But I love you. Forever," Gray said, begging the wind silently to carry his words to her ears.

"Then why the *fuck* did you sever our bond?" a furious voice hissed from behind him.

CHAPTER 4

GRAY

Gray froze, the hairs on the back of his neck raising, the air ripping from his lungs so violently, he gasped.

It couldn't be Lea. Not yet. Not now. And yet, Gray knew that voice like he knew his very soul.

"Why the *fuck* did you sever our bond?" the voice repeated—his mate's voice.

It had to be a *dream. Or a trick. Some sort of test. Because if Lea's here...*

Gray turned his head. Slowly. Disbelieving. The peace and calm he'd felt just moments before as he'd settled in to wait for his mate turning to complete and utter shock.

"Little Flower. What—" he rose to his feet, his body numb with disbelief. "What have you done?" Gray's voice shook with fear as he took in his mate standing only feet away. She was breathtakingly stunning in a black dress made of flames, with hints of red, yellow, and orange glowing within the rippling fabric like the dying embers of a fire. A thorny crown of pristine moonflowers adorned her head, her long blonde hair blowing softly around her shoulders and back. But it wasn't her beauty that caused him to pause.

His mate looked *different*. Her features had sharpened, her jawline now angled and feline, and her cheekbones more prominent and rosy.

Her eyes were a blue so vibrant they matched the glittering sea outside Tanad's palace. Even her posture had changed—her shoulders back and her chin raised—and as she walked toward him, she moved with a grace he had only seen in those of his own kind.

Lea was no longer human. She was Fae.

Her softness was gone, as was any indication of her insecurity and self doubt. He didn't need the mate bond to feel that she had changed down to her core into something powerful—deadly. Tanad's words rang in his memory. *All I know, my friend, is that your mate has the power to become the Queen of Flame and Shadows, a kind and merciful ruler, but also a warrior. That queen changes the world for good. Restores peace and magic, and defeats the Black King. Or, she has the power to cast the world into darkness and destroy everything that we are fighting for.*

With impossible stealth, Lea stalked forward, her footfalls completely silent. "You made me a vow when you sealed the mate bond. Together in life and in death," she said, her words staccato as if she was trying to rein in her utter fury. "Life *and* death."

"It was the only way," Gray breathed, his voice almost a whisper. He reached out to her, unable to stop himself. All he wanted was to hold her, to pull her close and kiss her lips and scold her for the rash, foolish choice she'd made to follow him into death. But the furious glint in her eyes stopped him.

Lea looked at his hand like it was holding the knife that had stabbed her in the back, her lips pressed together as if she couldn't decide whether she wanted to embrace him or find a way to kill him even more permanently.

"I'm sorry, Lea," he said, breathless, his heart pounding. "You needed my blood for the moonflowers. And I couldn't let you die. You were supposed to live. To save our army—our people. You needed to *live*,

Lea." Gray's voice rose in pitch. "You shouldn't be here. What have you done?"

Gray's emotions warred inside him. She was here. With him, where she belonged, but where she shouldn't be.

"The moonflowers grew," Lea said, her voice suddenly soft and fragile. "Enough of them to save the rebels and hundreds more if we need them. And then these, to save you." She held her hand out in front of her where two bright white moonflowers rested on her open palm. "To save us." Her voice softened, just enough to make Gray almost drop to his knees in relief. She still loved him—even through her fury at his betrayal—and wanted to save him.

"Azalea," Gray breathed.

"The spell required your life. And you gave it. The petals worked on Janelle and Thomas. Emma is still tethered to the earth. These petals… Maybe they can save us, too."

Hope sparked in his chest, almost painful in its intensity.

"It cannot be done," a soft, sweet voice, heavy with sorrow, said from behind them, pulling on that fragile shred of hope until it stretched so tight, it threatened to shatter.

"His soul has been claimed by the veil. By the universe. He will stay. Now, and forever." This time, it was a man who spoke. Deep and commanding, his words making the ground rumble as they fell from his mouth.

Like dawn spreading across the horizon, a faint light glowed and brightened the night. Silver and gold together, it was both soothing and overwhelming, warm and cool at the same time, and carried with it was a power so immense it made Gray almost fall to his knees.

"I'm sorry, my daughter," the woman said again.

"The universe gets no say in the matter," Lea snapped, whipping her body around to face the voice. The fire making up her dress surged, the red and orange flickering inside it becoming more prominent as shadows slithered across the hill.

Lea narrowed her eyes and raised her chin, baring her teeth in a challenge. Gray followed Lea's glare, his jaw dropping at the sight of the god of the sun and the goddess of the moon standing only feet away, their eyes locked on him and Lea with an intensity that made his dead, unbeating heart shudder.

CHAPTER 5

GRAY

Gray watched with wide eyes, his heart pounding against his ribs, as the goddess drifted toward Lea. Every movement she made was like a whisper of the wind, her silver gown billowing around her like a cloud, its hem barely brushing the grass. The light from the moon seemed to bend toward her like a lover's touch, wrapping her in a ghostly glow as if the earth itself longed to be closer to her. Her silver-blonde hair flowed freely, weightless and wild, framing her face in an ethereal halo as her hand stretched out, trembling slightly, as if it ached to cradle Lea's cheek. Her eyes—the eyes that mirrored Lea's so perfectly—glistened with sorrow. But beneath the sadness lay something harder, more immovable.

Gray's breath hitched, and he took a hesitant step forward, instinctively positioning himself between Lea and the looming threat of the gods. How could he hope to protect her from the fury of gods so ancient and powerful? His fingers twitched, the urge to defend her warring with the knowledge of his own powerlessness.

"Do not coddle her," the sun god snapped, his voice like the crack of a whip. The harshness of it shattered the delicate moment, and the goddess flinched, pulling her hand back as if burned. Gray clenched his fists, his chest tightening as he watched the sun god's golden eyes fix on Lea.

On instinct, Gray reached for his sword, but his hand came up empty. His weapon lay somewhere far behind him, abandoned on the blood-soaked battlefield in the land of the living. Helplessness surged through him like a flood.

"You behaved rashly," the sun god spat, his voice brimming with disdain. "Impulsively. Selfishly." Molten red hair that glowed with the heat of a dying star hung around his shoulders, crackling with the white-hot embers of his rage. Standing at least eight feet tall, his skin flickered as if made from the sun itself—so bright, Gray could only stand to look directly at him for a few seconds at a time before his eyes began to water and burn. "You've doomed our people to death. And for what?"

"For love, my dear," the goddess of the moon said with the softness of a sweet dream. Her touch on the sun god's arm was a caress, and with it, the fire in him dimmed slightly, though it still burned hot beneath the surface. "People do irrational things when they're in love. It doesn't make them selfish. In fact, to sacrifice your life for another is the most selfless act of all. Don't you think?" Her voice, though gentle, carried a strength that could shatter stone, but Gray could see the ghost of grief in her eyes.

Gray met her gaze, a silent acknowledgment of the strange bond they seemed to share in their protectiveness of Lea. He lowered his head in a gesture of respect, but before he could move, a shadow—cold and shimmering—grabbed him by the chin. It wasn't violent, but firm, holding his head in place. His skin tingled beneath the shadow's hold, and a strange peace settled over him.

"You've done well," the goddess said, her smile kind and knowing. "You've protected her. Helped her find her power. You'll be rewarded for that here."

"We're not staying *here*." Lea's voice cut through the air like a blade, sharp and defiant. She grabbed Gray's sleeve and ripped him back from the goddess's shadows, and Gray's stomach twisted, the feeling of peace fading immediately as adrenaline pumped through his system. Lea was arguing with the *gods*. Acting as if they were the enemy she wanted to destroy. But could they hurt her here beyond the veil? Was there a punishment worse than death?

"The sacrifice required was made. Willingly. He will not return." The god of the sun's deep, booming voice made Gray's insides rumble. "The laws of the universe are no different here beyond the veil than they are on Earth. Balance is required. It is not he who must return. His sacrifice was made. *You* must sacrifice as well."

Gray's heart hammered in his chest. This was what he should want—for Lea to return and save their kingdom. She had to live, to lead, to fulfill her destiny. He would wait for her, no matter how long it took. But as he looked at her now, her hand gripping his arm as if desperate to tether herself to him, he realized he wasn't sure he could survive it again—the pain of losing her, of watching her slip away from him.

"I won't go back. Not if I have to leave him." Lea's nails dug into Gray's forearm, and he pulled her closer, trying to reassure her. Of what, he wasn't sure. But if Lea was going to go back, it had to be willingly. He wouldn't allow them to rip her away if that wasn't what she wanted of her own free will. Gray gathered his shadows in his chest, preparing for the worst and wondering how he could possibly defeat the gods, but knowing that he might have to, to keep Lea safe.

"But you *must*." The goddess moved forward, her steps so graceful it was as if she was hovering on top of the ground rather than treading on it. "*You* must be the one to sacrifice now. It was never you who was destined to die, my child. It was never your fate. The Prince of Fire lives. As long as he breathes, suffering will spread like a plague. He will destroy the world."

Lea's flames roared higher, darker, consuming everything around her with the force of her fury. "I've sacrificed everything!" she screamed, her voice raw with pain. "What more could you possibly want from me?"

"You've lost no more than others." The sun god threw out his own flames, attempting to smother Lea's. "How many in your kingdom have lost mothers? Husbands? You think you're special in your grief?"

Once again, the moon goddess laid her hand on the sun god's arm. His flames dimmed, but the tension in the air seemed to thicken.

She turned back to Lea. "My daughter. We know it is unfair. But is anything in this world fair? Equality in suffering isn't the goal. And your past trials do not change your fate. *You* have to defeat the Prince of Fire," she urged gently. "To save your people. To save *our* people. That's why you were born—to fulfill the prophecy. It's why we gifted you our magic. It is your duty. To us—to Desia."

"I'm not going without Gray." Lea raised her chin in defiance, her eyes narrowing.

"Only one may return. Even that is more than we should allow—even that will have repercussions." The god's booming voice caused the grass atop the hill to bend and bow.

"Repercussions?" Gray asked at the same time Lea said, "Fuck the repercussions."

Gray turned to her, placing a tender hand on her cheek and forcing her to meet his stare. "I'll wait here for as long as it takes. We *will* be together again, Little Flower. Please. You have to go back."

"I'm not their king. You are." Lea's jaw clenched. "*You* are the one who has planned for this war for a hundred years. *You* are the one who knows your brother better than anyone else, knows the castle and the land like the lines on your skin. *You* know your commanders and what they are capable of. I don't know how to lead a war." Lea turned and glared at the god of the sun. "Do you not understand? Together. *That* is how we defeat Alaric. That is how we stop the death and destruction coursing through the kingdom."

"It does no good to argue," the goddess interrupted. "Your friend grows weak. Her connection to this realm is fading. If you want to return, it *must* be now. This very moment."

Lea's lip trembled as she turned toward Gray, clutching at his hands as if trying to meld her skin to his.

"You have to go back," he urged, pulling their hands up and kissing her fingers. He pulled her into his arms, speaking into her hair. "I don't have the power to defeat him, but you do."

"I won't," she cried out. "I can't." Her voice broke.

"You *must,*" Gray said, his voice a broken whisper. "I will wait for you. No matter how long it takes. But you *have* to go back."

"And it must be now," the goddess said, her eyes glazing over as if seeing into a far away world. "You have *moments* until your friends give Emma the petal. Seconds before neither of you will be able to return."

Lea sniffled, clearing her throat as she stared down at the flower in her hand.

"Forever," Gray said, his eyes full of promises and a sincerity that made Lea's bones quake.

Lea nodded. Pressing her lips together, she plucked a single petal from the moonflower, dropping the rest to the ground.

The gods stood silently, the moon goddess wiping away a tear as the sun god clenched his jaw. His power thrummed in a mighty quake, the earth trembling beneath their feet.

Tenderly, Gray lifted Lea's hand. Without a word, he placed the petal in her mouth, watching for her throat to bob. She swallowed, then, leaning forward, pressed her lips to Gray's.

He opened for her immediately, needing to savor the last time they would share this kind of intimacy for gods knew how long like a drowning man needs air. Clinging to her desperately, his tongue caressed hers. Soft, then hard. Lea pulled back for a single moment before leaning back to Gray, but this time as their tongues met, it was with a moonflower between them.

So quickly Gray didn't have time to react, Lea pushed it between his teeth, pulling her mouth away as she used her shadows to clench his jaw shut.

His eyes widened in shocked disbelief as the petal was crushed between his molars, the sweet taste of sugar and earth and *life* coating his tongue.

"Lea, what—"

The moonflower's magic took hold, and in an instant, Gray faded away into nothing, Lea vanishing from his sight as he returned to the land of the living.

CHAPTER 6

ERIK

The silence was horrifying. Erik had expected for Janelle to sob or Thomas to scream, but instead, they just stood there. Frozen and in complete disbelief of what they had just witnessed.

Erik's heart pounded, his blood rushing in his ears. Maybe Janelle *had* sobbed and Thomas *had* screamed, because he couldn't hear anything past the rapid, thundering *whoosh* of his heartbeat.

Wake up. You have to wake up, he begged silently, unable to voice the words vibrating through his entire being. But neither of them moved, Lea's body draped across Gray's, her head resting on top of his body, her face relaxed as if sleeping. But the stillness was unnatural, so different from a peaceful slumber. Her chest didn't rise and fall, and her eyes remained still behind half-closed lids.

Emma squirmed on the ground as the fire surrounding her faded away. She cried out in a moan of pain, and the trance holding them still and silent snapped. Just as he'd suspected, a sob burst from Janelle's throat, and Thomas screamed so loud his voice went hoarse in an instant. But whether for Emma, or Lea—or both of them—Erik wasn't sure.

From his periphery, Erik saw Thomas press two shaking fingers to Emma's throat, but Erik didn't listen to what he said. He knew she was still alive. He could hear the blood rushing through her veins, the slow thump of her heart. Irregular and weak, but still *there*. And as long as it was there, they had time.

"What do we do?" Janelle dropped to her knees next to Lea and Gray, her shaking hands hovering over their still bodies as if she wanted to help, but didn't know where to start. "Erik! What do we do?"

"We wait." Erik ordered, crossing his arms and planting his feet, his heart still thundering furiously.

"There's no time!" Thomas's eyes darted between Emma and Lea, clearly torn between which woman to save. After a moment, a look of determination crossed his features, and he swallowed audibly as if choking down a mouthful of guilt and despair. "I'm saving Emma. I— If she dies, we lose them both. But I can still save her."

"A few more moments," Erik reiterated, never taking his eyes from his friends' corpses. All he needed to see was the twitch of a finger, the rise of a chest, or the fluttering of eyes, and Emma could have the petal. The cure. He just needed something to indicate they were coming back, because they *were* coming back. They had to.

Emma spasmed, her body going rigid and her eyes rolling back in her head.

"I'm doing it." Thomas began to pry Emma's mouth open, but Erik shot a blast of fire directly into his hand, burning it so severely the smell of human flesh wafted to his nose. With the moonflower in his system, the burn healed instantly, but the threat was clear. Thomas would not be the one to decide when to give up on Lea and Gray.

"You will *not*," Erik snapped.

Thomas hissed in pain as he fell backward, his face going red with anger. But Erik could still hear Emma's heart, the rasp of air as she inhaled and exhaled.

"Just a few more moments, Thomas," Janelle pleaded, crawling on her hands and knees over to Emma and placing a bloody hand against her forehead. "Thirty more seconds. We have to give them a chance." Janelle's voice shook.

A chance. A chance for his king and queen to return to them. A chance for them to win this war, to find Alaric and defeat him.

Thump...

Thump...

A pause, far too long.

Thump...

Froth dribbled from Emma's mouth along with another pause of her heart.

They were out of time. Vomit threatened to erupt from Erik's stomach, his lungs stiffening as if refusing to inhale. Understanding crashed over him.

He was Gray's second in command, a position he'd never wanted, but one he had agreed to, all the same. He'd made a vow to Gray, to this kingdom. He couldn't allow their mission to fail because of a shred of hope that Gray and Lea would find a way back. Alaric had to be defeated. And there was no more time to waste.

"Do it," Erik said, the words tiny razor blades slicing the muscles of his throat as he forced them out. His body felt heavy as he knelt next to his fallen brother, and with a shaking hand and a reverence he hoped Gray would feel beyond the veil, Erik slowly and gently closed Gray's eyes.

The pain was unspeakable, but he shoved down the guilt surging through his chest and wrapping around his heart. At least, he tried. But it felt like nothing other than a betrayal.

He was giving up on his family. His oldest friend. But he couldn't live with himself if Emma died, too. It would be a useless loss. A waste of life. Because if Emma was gone, so were Lea and Gray. He had given them time.

And they had failed.

Thomas didn't waste a single second, grabbing the petal and shoving it between Emma's lips. Erik watched intently, hoping that seeing the friend he *did* save would smooth the raw edges of his pain. He turned, but stopped suddenly. A cry left his throat as, out of the corner of his eye, he saw the abrupt clenching of Gray's jaw, the sudden gasp of air that caused his chest to rise.

A chest that was healing so rapidly, it almost looked as if it had never been injured at all. There was no evidence of a fatal wound except for the blood coating his torso, the tattered tunic falling off of his shoulders, and the brutal, jagged scar where the mate bond had once been.

Erik surged forward, attempting to move Lea so that Gray could sit, but his friend's arms wrapped around her tightly as a growl of primal rage rumbled from his throat. His eyes slowly opened, allowing tears to spill down his cheeks as he sat and then stood, holding onto Lea so tightly Erik wondered how she could even breathe. But...

The color drained from his face, and his joy evaporated as quickly as it had appeared at seeing his friend come back to life. While Gray's skin was flushed with blood, and his injuries had healed, Lea was ashen, her eyes closed and her chest still—so still, he knew without a doubt there was no hint of life within her body.

A series of coughs and a gasp sounded from behind Erik, but he couldn't pull his eyes away from his friend.

"You're okay," Thomas breathed, but his voice was shaky with sorrow and tears. "You're okay," he repeated.

The rustle of grass told Erik that Emma had sat up. That she had survived, but his eyes remained locked on his queen. On his king, who was holding onto his dead mate as if she were the only thing tethering him to this earth.

"Do you see her?" Gray rasped, his eyes locked on Emma, his voice shuddering with a pain so severe, Erik wondered if it would kill him all over again.

"See who?" Emma coughed, her voice weak.

Erik felt a stab of despair as he turned around. Emma's eyes scanned the hill, her brows creased in confusion. She didn't realize what Gray was asking. Didn't know what had transpired while she'd been halfway between worlds.

And if she didn't know who Gray was speaking of, then it looked like Gray had his answer. Gray had returned, but Lea had not followed him.

Gray's eyes darkened as the shadows of the night pulsed with a terrifying might.

Gods save us all, Erik thought, dropping to his knees.

Lea was gone.

CHAPTER 7

LEA

Lea felt with painful clarity the moment Emma ate the moonflower. Something snapped inside her, throwing her backward into the gently swaying grass. She scrambled to her feet, but for the first time since she died, she felt wholly untethered. Her feet touched the ground, but there was no weight to her body. She breathed in and out, but didn't feel the rush of oxygen through her lungs.

Instantly, she felt different—she no longer needed to swallow or blink, though she continued to do those basic movements out of habit. She had no heartbeat, no whoosh of blood in her veins. Only the crackling of fire still burning through every inch of her body.

A fire she knew with absolute certainty she would never be able to quell. Never be able to contain. From the moment she'd fully broken through the floor in her chest, she'd known it.

She was wrath. She was vengeance.

Destroy, that commanding voice inside her urged. The one laced with darkness and death. The one growing louder with every breath she took. Flames spread through her blood, her fire growing and her shadows coiling around her, begging her to listen.

Destroy.

Destroy.

Destroy.

But Lea knew she couldn't. No matter how much she wanted to end their eternal existence. It would only doom them all.

It was always about fucking balance.

Lea turned away from the gods. She didn't want to look at them, afraid seeing them would push her over the edge and sever whatever tiny thread of control she was hanging onto. They had betrayed her. Had demanded so much of her, all to allow her mate to be killed. They'd led them here, with no protection, as they'd battled Alaric.

Throwing her arms in the air, Lea built a wall of black fire behind herself in an attempt to block them off, furious at their inaction and afraid of their retaliation for the decision she'd made. Blazing heat exploded at her back, and a large, flaming hand wrapped around her bicep, stopping her in her tracks.

"You have doomed them all," the hand squeezed, whirling her around and sending agonizing pain shooting up her arm. "Our people. *Your* people," the god of the sun roared. A fiery haze surrounded his body, so bright Lea could barely stand to look at him.

But she forced herself to meet his eyes. "I just *saved* them all." Darkness grew around them, her shadows becoming solid as they twisted around his arm and ripped it from her own. "And you will not touch me without my consent."

The god froze, his fury *almost* matching Lea's. But she didn't care. *Couldn't* care. The fire inside her was too much. Too hot. The black, primary magic twisted and expanded, begging to be unleashed, her skin burning with the intensity of it trying to escape.

She couldn't hold it back. Didn't want to. She'd lost her mate—twice. Her friends. Her life. Her kingdom.

And so she allowed it to burst free from the swirling, raging pit of power in her chest. Just for a moment.

Darkness slammed into the god of the sun, sending him flying backward, and he roared in fury as black tendrils knocked him down, white-hot fire exploding in an arc toward her. Lea called on the wind, commanding it to whip furiously across the hill as a solid shield of air wrapped around her body.

The god's magic ripped against it, tore at the shield as it fought to get to her, but there was no way through. It was his own magic she wielded against him. His, *and* the goddesses. The magic they had gifted her, hoping she could purge the earth of evil, but instead leaving her wholly unprepared for how to control the might of what was inside her.

She held his furious stare, lifting her chin defiantly. "*You* are the one who did this to the world. *You* made me choose." Lea stabbed a finger at the god, unafraid. "One of us had to remain. You'd rather unleash *this* on your people?" Lea let go of the scrap of control she still held over her magic, and the hill beyond the veil exploded in flames. Black fire raced through the gently swaying grass, searing it into embers. The surge of power filled her with warmth, her fire shooting thousands of feet into the sky as her hair whipped furiously around her.

"You are unworthy of the power we gifted you." He lowered his chin, looking down at her with disdain, his lips curling in disgust. "The choice you made today will destroy everything. And only you will be to blame."

Lea raised her hands, her eyes darkening as she called her shadows and flames back into her fingertips. "Leave me," she ordered, lowering her chin. His mouth opened in shock and he threw up a shield, anticipating her attack. His fire grew brighter, his rage evident as he grabbed the moon goddess around the waist and pulled her closer, shielding her.

"You will regret this," he threatened, sparing only a brief look at Lea's inferno of rage before disappearing in a flash of white-hot light, leaving her alone, finally, to burn in peace.

The earth smoked beneath Lea where she sat on the hill, her knees pulled to her chest and her fingers swirling gently in the thick layer of ash coating the ground as far as her eyes could see. Her gaze remained locked on the patch of hill in the distance where her home should be. But even in the pitch-black night, with nothing but the twinkling stars overhead to illuminate the landscape, she knew there was no house to see. She was no longer in a world where home existed. Nothing was left but her grief, her rage, and the overwhelmingly violent power inside her.

A flicker of fury danced down her spine and into the ground, energizing the flames that draped her like a gown and spread across the earth. Of course, she couldn't watch her mate and friends. The universe was far too cruel to allow her even a sliver of peace in the afterlife.

It was her village she looked upon, but at the same time, it wasn't. The land was as unblemished as when the gods had first created it, not a rock or piece of stone out of place to indicate that man or Fae had ever been here at all.

The fire inside her continued to ripple and expand, and Lea attempted to tamp it down.

She'd done what she'd come here to do. Gray was alive, and she didn't regret her decision, even knowing it had infuriated the gods—that it would infuriate everyone who loved her.

History would call her a fool. But she was anything *but* foolish. In fact, she was the opposite. Her decision had been every bit as calculated as it was emotional. Gray was the one who knew the land of Desia like the back of his hand. Who knew every inch of the castle and every weakness of his brother. While Lea, on the other hand, knew very little of her kingdom. Only her little village, and the way through the Wicked Wood into Calir.

Gray knew every member of his army—had plans he'd been putting in place for a century. And though she might have more raw power brimming inside her, she didn't know how to control it. This power... It was something wicked and *dark,* simmering beneath her skin and threatening to consume her whole, something terrifying and vengeful—the ultimate reason she'd forced Gray to return instead of herself.

Yes. No matter how she would be remembered in history for the decision she'd made, in the end, it had been that dark magic coursing through Lea's veins and pumping through her body with every beat of her heart that had solidified her decision to slip the petal between his lips. The power inside her was *wrong*. Wicked and overwhelming in a way that made her worry if she were the one to return, that wrath and fury would grow so big, so terrible, that without Gray to help her contain it, she might *actually* destroy the entire world in her quest for revenge.

She couldn't protect her kingdom if she was too busy burning it to ruins.

A gentle breeze brushed against her cheeks, carrying with it the scent of honeysuckle, and Lea closed her eyes, inhaling deeply and trying desperately to find a hollow place inside to force her dark magic to hide. It was uncomfortable, the way it butted against her ribs and pushed them outward, as if the magnitude of the power might shatter her from the inside out.

Where her primary magic had once lived in her chest, there was only a massive gaping hole, and with nothing to hold the power back or lock it neatly in place, she couldn't stop the storm of rage and retribution threatening to consume her. Was this how she would spend the next thousand years? Burning from within from a power so awful, so horrifyingly omnipotent, that she'd be forced to spend every last second and minute and hour fighting the agony of its pull?

The wind blew again, and she leaned into its cool kiss. *Azalea*, she heard, the soft breeze carrying with it the sound of her name.

"Azalea." Her name again. But this time closer. And not the ghost of a voice, but her mother's voice. "Oh, my flower."

Lea's eyes sprung open, her head whipping around, praying it wasn't just the wind. Not this time.

Had Lea's heart still been beating, it would have stopped. Only feet away was her mother, exactly as Lea remembered. Her dark brown hair was in a messy, low bun, and her simple linen dress was covered by an apron stained with berries, herbs, and spices. She had soft wrinkles around her chocolate brown eyes and smile lines bracketing her mouth. It was as if she had been plucked straight from her memory and placed here, right in front of her.

Slowly, Lea rose to her feet. "Mom?" Her voice cracked, her lungs constricting with disbelief, but Lea was relieved to feel anything inside her body besides darkness and wrath.

"Oh, my flower," her mother repeated, rushing toward Lea and crushing her in an embrace so full of love that it almost broke through her fiery, black heart.

"Mom!" Lea cried, collapsing into her arms.

Adelaide cupped Lea's face tenderly, her eyes clouded with tears. "I'm so sorry. I'm *so* sorry I couldn't tell you more. That I *didn't* tell you more. I should have. I'm so very sorry I didn't prepare you."

"You couldn't have known," Lea's voice sounded foreign to her own ears. More melodic, but also sharper, and tinged with a fury that, days ago, she'd never have thought herself capable of feeling. Not at her mother. Never at her. But this anger was part of her marrow now, just as much a part of her as her own blood and bone. "I know you did all you could." Lea clung desperately to Adelaide, her touch a splash of cool water on her burning skin.

"I'm so proud of you, Azalea," her mother said. "For your strength and your courage."

Lea felt as if she might shatter at the words. She wasn't strong. Not strong enough to defeat Alaric, or to control the darkness inside her. Not strong enough to save Gray.

She'd failed. Not only herself, but her people. The thought made Lea's knees weak.

As if sensing her exhaustion, Adelaide grabbed Lea's hands and lowered them to the ground together, wrapping her in a warm hug as they faced out toward the black night.

They sat together in silence for a while, Adelaide stroking Lea's hair like a small child as the raging inferno inside her slowly calmed. As if it, too, needed rest. But even in slumber, its embers glowed white hot, ready to blaze again in the blink of an eye.

Lea forced away the thought. "Is this where you stayed?" she asked. "After you died, I mean?"

Adelaide patted her hand, the touch so familiar it made Lea's eyes burn. "No, my love. I didn't stay here. And you don't have to either, if it's not what you wish. Whatever your heart desires, wherever your heart desires, there's a way to find it here."

Lea's dead heart clenched. Whatever her heart desired. What she desired—*where* she desired—was Gray. The one thing that wasn't possible.

Adelaide continued. "I spend most of my time in a garden, with eternal sunshine and the richest soil. There are no bugs to eat away my plants, no diseases to rot their roots. No worries. Just the sun on my face and the soil beneath my fingernails."

Lea wondered what it would be like to join her there. To plunge her fingers into the cool dirt and forget, if only for a moment, but a fist of anxiety wrapped around Lea's throat at the thought of being further away from Bearswillow. Even if she couldn't see Gray or feel him on top of this hill, he was *here*. Unreachable, but nonetheless, *here*.

Lea shook her head. "I won't leave him." She looked back toward where she knew, in another world, another reality, Gray would be rising from the ground and beginning his quest for revenge.

Without hesitating, Adelaide squeezed Lea's hand and settled back onto her elbows. "Then I think I would like to stay with you. At least for a little while, if that's okay."

A bubble of gratitude settled behind Lea's breastbone. She wouldn't be alone. For now, at least. And the relief from that knowledge was enough to allow her a singular, shuddering breath.

Days passed slowly as they sat there together on the hill, the glow from the stars overhead and the fire dancing along Lea's skin the only source of light in the eternal night in which they waited. It was as if they were frozen in a moment in time, unable to move forward.

Adelaide told Lea everything she'd kept from her in life—about the day she'd found her lying beneath the sun all alone, and the joy she'd felt, mixed with the fear and terror that had flooded every fiber of her being the moment she saw the moonflower birthmark beneath her arm.

She told her of the journeys her father took trying to find her birth parents, trying to find *any* scrap of information that could prove who Lea really was. She told her that when Lea had turned three years old, it had become obvious that her magic was stronger than was usual. Her mother had given her the ice cold water from the stream that ran from the mountain, the same water that her father and the rest of the villagers drank whenever the royal army came to Bearswillow.

It was why so many with magic had chosen to dwell in their village. Even Adelaide hadn't understood it, but the water had somehow glamoured their appearance and hid their magic, so long as they didn't go more than a few months without drinking from the stream. But even the water hadn't been enough to hide Lea's power.

While she'd looked fully human after drinking it, within a few hours, her eyes would once again become unnaturally blue, and her features would sharpen. And so her mother had been forced to look for a more permanent solution. Adelaide cried true tears of regret and sorrow as she told Lea what she'd done. Told her how she'd created a potion that would permanently lock down her daughter's magic, so deep inside her that Lea would never be aware it was there at all.

Within Adelaide's eyes, Lea could see she was still struggling with the decision she'd made. She'd taken away her birthright. Her ability to protect herself. Her identity. But it had felt like the only way to keep her safe. And so she had given Lea the potion, so bitter that she'd had to sweeten it with two scoops of sugar for the toddler to take it willingly.

And then Adelaide had watched as her light dimmed, as the potion closed off everything magical about her forever. Or at least, until she'd met Gray, and it had once again awakened. Her magic had recognized its mate, its equal, and so her day and night magic had revealed themselves. Slowly, at first. But then, when Alaric and Lea had battled, her primary magic had shattered through the remaining floor holding down her magic.

Adelaide hadn't expected it. Hadn't expected for her to have a mate at all, let alone for that connection to overcome her potion's power and break its spell. She'd underestimated that true love was the most powerful force of all. Capable of anything. Capable of *everything*.

"I'm sorry," she said again, "for the mess I made for you. For making it so difficult. Maybe if I'd helped you learn to control your powers instead of taking them away, you would have been better equipped to fight against the Black King and Alaric."

"You did your best," Lea repeated, absolving her, because truly, Lea didn't blame Adelaide. She *had* done her best. Just as Lea had done her best by choosing to send Gray back in her place. And wasn't that what they were all trying to do?

"I have been with you," Adelaide said, smiling through the tears spilling over her eyelashes. "When you're in danger, I feel it. Here." She placed a hand on her chest, right above her sternum. "When you need me, I'm pulled to where you are—"

"The wind," Lea interrupted.

"Yes," Adelaide breathed. "The wind."

Lea's heart pinched. She had known, in some deep part of her, that it was her mother who had been guiding her. And while she hadn't been able to save her in her final moments on earth, Lea would be eternally grateful that she had met her here in her first moments in the afterlife.

CHAPTER 8

GRAY

Gray barely spoke. Barely looked anywhere other than his fallen mate's face. With quick, demanding sentences, he ordered Erik to gather the moonflower petals and bring them to the battlefield. He couldn't focus on anything else. There was no fire, or wind, or rain. There was no air in his lungs or stars overhead. There was nothing but grief and pain.

Gone.

She was *gone*.

She had deceived him. Fooled him. And now she waited beyond the veil, trapped and suffering beneath the weight of her own power.

Save their people, and return to Lea. That was all Gray could think about. He wouldn't let her sacrifice be for nothing—refused to let that sacrifice be in vain.

Forcing his feet forward, Gray kept his eyes on Lea's face. Her beautiful blue eyes—closed forever. Blood splattered through her hair. Her cheeks gaunt and sunken in.

The agony at seeing her this way was all-consuming, and so deep, he was sure it was tattooing itself on his bones. His heart felt heavy and dead, his soul in tatters, and every breath was like swallowing down shards of glass. Each inhale felt like a betrayal, because he shouldn't be breathing. Not when Lea wasn't.

One foot in front of the other. That was all he could do. Save his people. Find Alaric, and kill him. Slowly and agonizingly.

The battlefield appeared beyond the hill, and he forced his eyes from Lea's face to assess the damage. He needed to compartmentalize. Shut off the part of himself yearning to give in and burn down the world, and focus on saving his kingdom.

His soldiers went silent as he approached, turning one by one as they became aware of his presence. He stepped over the line of burned grass spanning the entire field, the evidence of the shield of fire Lea had placed around their army as they'd left to face Alaric.

He wished he'd made her stay behind, far away from Alaric and his crusade of death.

Painstakingly slowly, Gray knelt, lying his mate's body on the soft, unburned ground. He tenderly brushed her hair from her face, then tugged her shirt down to cover the sliver of midriff showing. His shadows floated around her, weeping as they brushed her skin, begging her to come back to them.

Gray lifted his chin, meeting Vincent's eyes for a long moment. His sorrow was palpable, despair hanging thickly in the air like a dense fog. Gray rose, taking a deep inhale and nodding to Janelle, who began handing out the petals. One for each soldier. His sacrifice, his mate's sacrifice, to heal and protect them.

In their tear-filled eyes and shaking hands, Gray could see they recognized what had been given in order to save them. What he had lost. It was clear in the way their throats bobbed and their gazes remained downcast. In the sniffles and red-rimmed eyes.

Minutes passed as Janelle finished handing out the cure to the Lonely Death—to the injuries for those who had survived. The field remained silent as every rebel ate their petal, whether injured or not. Color returned to cheeks and wounds disappeared from throats and arms and chests, lacerations closing over, broken limbs healing. It didn't cure what ailed them past the physical. Their hearts were scarred—would be forever. But his? It was eviscerated.

And nothing would ever be able to heal it.

Swallowing down the pain threatening to drag him back inside himself, he cleared his throat.

"Alaric is alive."

Sharp inhales and muttered curses spread throughout the soldiers.

"He's been weakened. Many of his soldiers slaughtered." And they had been. Nearly every one of them who had not fled in time now laid decimated throughout the streets of Bearswillow. As they'd walked from Lea's burned-down house, Gray had stepped over at least a hundred dead royal soldiers, their eyes wide and mouths open with black lines spider webbing from the bloody orifices. Gray wasn't sure exactly what Lea had done to them, or *how* she had done it. But whatever it was, it had been horrific, as if she had sent her darkness to eat them alive from the inside out.

"Your queen—" Gray's voice cracked, and he stopped speaking, closing his eyes and begging his body to hold it together. Just for now. Just until he was alone.

"Your queen sacrificed herself for the cure," Erik said, stepping forward. A rush of gratitude wrapped around Gray's tattered heart.

"We will not let that sacrifice be in vain," Gray found his voice again, a deep rumble brimming with rage and sorrow. "From this moment forward, every breath we take, every beat of our heart will be dedicated to one singular purpose. To defeat Alaric."

A battle cry sounded from a group of rebels to his left, raw and powerful.

"We will take back our kingdom. Take back your magic. We will lay down our lives, if that is what's required of us, as your queen did, to ensure a world free of terror and evil. We do not rest. We do not falter."

The stomping of feet and clanging of shields made Gray's heart pump faster, pushing his pain deeper into his marrow, but he refused to give in to it. Lea's death would be the kindling to invigorate their people, to cause them to burn with the fervor needed to fight. To win. Lea had known that when she'd made her choice.

"For her sacrifice," Erik knelt before Lea, his voice shaking as he plunged his sword into the bloody earth. "May the gods hold her in the light of day and serenity of night." His voice broke, and Janelle appeared at his side, kneeling next to him. "May the magic of the wind carry her, the kiss of rain cleanse her," dozens of voices chimed in, kneeling one by one as they lowered their heads and delved their weapons into the ground. "And may the promise of eternity soothe her weary soul, until beyond the veil we follow."

Gray dropped to his knees. "Until beyond the veil we follow," he repeated, trailing his fingers along Lea's cold cheek.

Thumbs tucked into hands as soldiers covered their hearts, the clanging of shields and pounding of feet growing louder. Except, there should be no pounding of feet. Not when the entire army knelt before him. Before Lea.

Someone's coming. Gray's shadows exploded outward at the same moment Erik realized they were no longer alone. Leaping up from the ground, he pulled his sword from the soil, shoving Janelle behind him as the rest of the army followed suit.

"Commander!" Time froze, the world and rebel army going utterly still, all except for Gray. Henry appeared, only yards away, followed by hundreds, maybe thousands of men and women, makeshift weapons in their hands and determination etched into their faces.

"We came as fast— No." Henry's eyes fell to Lea, and he dropped to his knees, his army faltering as he collapsed on the ground. "I saw the soldiers in the streets. I thought—" He bit his fist, trying and failing to hold back his sob.

White-hot anger boiled beneath Gray's skin. Thousands of rebels. Enough to have changed the tide of battle. And Henry's magic. Freezing time. He could have saved Lea. Could have saved them all.

He'd sent word, and they had not come. Not in time.

Henry's sobs became wails as he scrambled toward his daughter, but Gray threw up a shield, cutting him off.

"You're too late," Gray hissed, his shadows begging to be set free, to wrap around Henry's neck and squeeze until he begged for death. "She's gone."

Rays of sun peeked over the horizon, but Gray didn't move from where he still knelt next to Lea. Not when the rebels had slowly made their way back to the cavern, or when Erik had begged to let him help. He hadn't moved a muscle when Janelle had offered to sit with Lea while he made arrangements to prepare her body for burial, or to wash the blood from his tattered clothing.

He *couldn't* leave her. Not even for a moment. It was unfathomable for anyone to think he could leave this place, this ground, this town she'd grown up in. Leaving was too final. Too earth shattering. *Soul* shattering. Somewhere deep inside, Gray held onto hope that if he could just wait a little longer, Lea would suddenly sit up and take a deep breath, ready to scold him for sacrificing himself. For cutting away the mate mark.

He couldn't leave without being with her for a few more minutes. Not because he was too full of grief, but because she *had* to come back. He wasn't sure he'd be able to find a way to move forward without her.

Gray was so lost in thought, his hand resting on top of Lea's forehead and his eyes locked on her cold, still body, that his shadows exploded when someone placed a hand on his shoulder. His darkness wrapped around the arm, ripping it forward to his side and away from Lea.

Genevieve cried out in pain as she tried to pry herself away from the shadows.

Genevieve. His mother.

He released his hold immediately, guilt and shame pulsing in his chest alongside his agony.

"Mother, I'm so sorry."

"I'm fine," she said softly, absentmindedly rubbing her wrist as she looked upon Lea's body with sad eyes.

"I thought I was alone," Gray said, the only explanation he could give. There wasn't room in his head for more.

He hadn't seen his mother since *before*.

Before the death and destruction. Before his world had been taken away from him. Genevieve had come once the battle ended, after having remained in the cavern during the worst of the fighting in hopes that the injured and wounded could be brought to her and Elise for healing. Her magic was powerful, and Gray had hoped that, if nothing else, she could hold the Lonely Death at bay until they were successful in harvesting the moonflower petals.

"Everything is fine back in the cavern. Your rebels are healed and resting. But... we have to move her, Evander." With slow, tentative steps,

Genevieve walked toward him, once again placing her hand on his shoulder.

"I need more time," Gray's voice broke, his warrior exterior crumbling in the presence of his mother as if he were a child again.

"I know, my boy," she said. "There will never be enough time. There's never enough time to say goodbye the way we are meant to. The way we deserve. But still, we have to move forward."

A sob burst from Gray's throat, and Genevieve wrapped her arms around him, her small frame dwarfed by his broad shoulders, and yet he allowed her to cradle him like she was never able to as a child. "She's not coming back," he whispered finally, the words shattering something inside him. His hope. His optimism.

"No. She's not. But you are here. And you have to go on. Alaric will come to destroy everything you love. Dismantle everything that you and Lea built." His mother's sorrow joined his own, adding another layer to the pain and suffering of this war. Here she was, helping him—no, begging him—to find a way to kill her other son.

Gray cursed the gods again for the lot they had given him in this life.

"I don't know where to start," Gray said, allowing himself this moment of vulnerability. Later, in front of his soldiers, he would be strong. Confident and steadfast. A leader who could rally his army to lay down their lives, if that's what it took, to defeat his brother. But right now, right here, with only his mother, he allowed himself to express his doubt.

"Lea said she weakened him. That he was hurt. Now would be the time to strike, but I don't know where to even begin looking for him. He won't return to the castle, I don't think. He knows that will be the first place we go."

Genevieve nodded in understanding. "That's why I'm going back."

"Back?" Gray snapped.

"You need information. I am Alaric's mother, and I am still Queen of Desia, if only in title. That holds weight with our court. Puts me in a position of respect." She raised her chin. "You send your scouts throughout the villages to collect any information they can give you. I will return to the heart of Auropera and see what I can learn from within."

"He'll have you killed the second he finds out you've returned." Gray said, but the idea of having someone within the castle who could alert them immediately if Alaric did return, or if word came about where he was hiding, was tempting. It could change the tide of the war. Give them a huge advantage, if she could pull it off.

"I'll tell him you've gone mad, that losing your mate sent you into a rampage, and that I realized you could never rule the kingdom like he could. I can feed him false information."

"And if he doesn't believe you? If he kills you?" The thought made him sick. He'd just begun rebuilding his relationship with his mother. Had never really had a relationship with her at all, before now.

"Then I die knowing I helped my kingdom, and I will keep your mate company until you one day join us." She grabbed Gray's hand. "But I don't think he will kill me. His pride won't allow it. Not if I say I have abandoned your cause and wish to help him. He's always wanted my approval, has always possessed a deep need for me to choose him over you. He didn't get it from his father, and so he killed him. Stole his magic. But somewhere inside that wicked shell of a man is still a little boy who just wants to matter," Genevieve croaked, her voice as rough as sand.

Gray almost felt pity for his brother at that moment. Almost, but not quite. He would never be able to offer any emotion other than rage and hatred for the man who had taken so much from him. Gray knew that Genevieve had tried with Alaric, that she had shown them both love whenever possible, whenever their father hadn't been watching, ready to punish her *and* them for any sign of weakness. But despite her best effort, evil had taken root somewhere deep inside her eldest son, too deeply ingrained into his DNA to ever be changed or eradicated.

"If you sense danger, return to the cavern and send word. You'll be safe there." Gray paused, considering what his mother was offering. "It will be difficult, convincing him you have changed your mind. Even harder pretending to approve of what he does."

"We *all* must do hard things. Somehow, despite the odds, we find a way to survive."

Gray knew the meaning hiding beneath her words. There is a time to mourn, and a time to let your pain forge you into someone stronger. Into a weapon to be used for the greater good.

"It's time," she said. Softly. Gentle as the brush of a feather.

Gray somehow found the strength to nod, unable to speak. Lea wasn't coming back. He had to move forward, even if it killed him. Silently, he hoped that it would.

The wind blew gently as he bent down to pick up his mate's lifeless body, the melody of swaying grass and chirping birds a reminder that even in our darkest times, the world continues on.

They didn't speak, but Genevieve remained at Gray's side as he carried his mate back to the cavern to prepare for burial. To prepare for whatever comes after.

As he walked through the main corridor, his soldiers went silent, bowing their heads and whispering prayers as he carried Lea's body to their room, the one they'd shared so recently. Tears streamed down his face, and he allowed himself those final moments of surrendering to his sorrow. Sorrow he would find once again, in another time and another place—once Alaric was rotting in the ground, and the kingdom found peace.

CHAPTER 9

LEA

The rush of night magic washed across the land, the grass bowing to the immensity of the night's power, and the shimmering magic cascading like a wave from the horizon, making the sky appear darker. Lea pried her eyes away from the hill where, in another world, her house sat, burned to the ground. She wondered where her body was now. Where Gray was.

Where Alaric was.

The wind changed, and Adelaide gasped. With lightning speed, Lea whipped her head around, her night magic surging when she saw the moon goddess standing only feet away, her face far more stern and serious than Lea had ever seen before. Her usually smooth, tidy hair was frizzy around her face, her eyes wide and features uncharacteristically sharp.

Lea called on her magic, scrambling to her feet and scanning behind the goddess for the god of the sun. She'd been waiting for their return, mentally preparing for whatever punishment they would attempt for her disobedience.

"He's not here. Lower your hands," the moon goddess said in a hushed whisper. "And you shouldn't be either. You have to go." She rushed to Lea's side, grabbing her hands and squeezing.

"I'm not leaving here." Lea let the fire inside her grow impossibly hotter. *How dare she tell me where to go?* "Not until I'm with Gray again."

"You *are* leaving. Because you're going back." The goddess held out her hand, and instantly, as if her skin was made of soil, a moonflower bloomed in her palm. Perfect and pristine and white as snow.

Lea froze, a mixture of trepidation and disbelief wrapping between her ribs until she was breathless.

"You're letting me go back?" Lea's voice cracked, and for the first time since she died, some small glimmer of something other than anger and sorrow sprouted in her chest. The darkness inside her fought against it, trying to suffocate and smother it away, but Lea held on.

The goddess nodded, pulling her to stand. "Against my better judgment, I am. But you must go *now.*"

"But the god of the sun said there would be consequences. That—" Adelaide started.

"I know what he said," the goddess snapped, leading Lea down the hill and deeper into the shadowy night. "And he will be furious. With you, and with me. There *will* be consequences for allowing this, Azalea. With Emma no longer tethered to this side..."

The goddesses' hands shook, but she quickly clenched them into fists. "I am breaking a very sacred vow by giving you another chance at life." She paused, turning to Lea and staring at her with an intensity that made Lea feel truly frightened of her for the first time. "But I have no choice. You are the only one who can defeat Alaric. You must understand this. Please. *You* are our only hope. *You* must go back, and *you* must find him and kill him. And you must do so before hell descends upon earth."

"What do you mean?" Lea didn't really care what the consequences were. She would do absolutely anything to get back to Gray, to get back to earth, and help him defeat Alaric.

"The universe requires balance," the goddess said, echoing Eudora's words. "It will try to correct what I've done, but I don't know how. My husband will likely have his own punishment for you," she said, plucking a petal from the flower and pushing it into Lea's hands. "I can only grant you so much time. And a sacrifice will be required to allow you to return."

"Name it." Lea said, her skin buzzing and hands shaking.

The goddess traced the moonflower crown along Lea's head with a delicate finger. As she caressed the thorny vine, the flowers glowed, so bright, Lea was forced to squint against the light. A buzz of electricity flowed from the crown, down her neck and arms, through her torso and legs. As the sensation spread, Lea felt it dive beneath her skin, wrapping around her still heart and sinking into her blood.

"The moonflowers are a gift from nature. A mixture of my magic, and the magic of the earth. They do not live forever. You will have until the last petal falls from the crown to kill Alaric and restore peace to the kingdom. That is all the time I can give you."

"And if I don't kill him before the last petal falls?" Lea asked. She'd learned her lesson about not being specific enough with bargains with the universe. With sacrifices.

"If you fail, your heart will stop beating when the final petal turns to ash. You will be separated from your mate, even after death." The goddess's eyes were brimming with sorrow. "And it will not be undone."

Lea felt as if she might vomit, nausea churning deep in her stomach. She'd rather not exist at all than spend an eternity without Gray. Wasn't sure she could risk such a thing. But what other choice did she have? Leave him and her people to die a painful death and allow her kingdom to be destroyed in the process?

"There are other conditions," she continues, a heaviness in her tone. "It must be your hand that delivers the killing blow. The magic Alaric has stolen must be taken from him, as well as his own. What's happening now—Alaric holding so much power—it's... unnatural."

Lea nodded fervently, determined to succeed. "I can do that. I took his magic before."

"That was but a drop of what he holds inside him, Azalea. It will be different this time. You had your chance to kill him once—to take his magic. And you failed. To take it now..." the goddess trailed off. "The universe will not allow you another chance without consequence. To hold the enormity of his magic..." She met Lea's eyes, and her voice softened. "You will not be allowed to survive with that much power. It *must* be returned to the earth."

"How?" Lea's stomach dropped.

"I cannot say." The goddess shook her head.

Lea clenched her fists, fire wrapping up her arms. "So either way, I die?" Fury rose inside her, igniting her body from the inside out.

"That's not what I said. There is a way you succeed. A way you can defeat Alaric, return his magic to the universe, and still survive. But I can't say more. To do so would further upset the balance. This is your riddle to solve. Your battle to win."

Lea's nostrils flared as she exhaled sharply.

"This is how it has always been. By using the earth's magic to allow you to live, *everything* will be disrupted. I would not be surprised if the universe itself tries to destroy you until its power is returned. Succeed, and all will be right. But it must be *you* who corrects the imbalance. You must destroy him. But"—the goddess lifted Lea's chin—"do not destroy yourself in the process."

Lea's dark magic thrummed in her chest.

Destroy.

Destroy.

Destroy.

The begging—no, demanding—grew louder. But Lea pushed it down, using every bit of her strength to bring the darkness to heel. She could do this—had to do this. There would be a time to unleash this wild power, but only when Alaric was in front of her. Then, and only then, would she give in to its call.

"I agree," Lea said, turning to her mother. Adelaide placed a shaking hand over her mouth, her eyes flicking between the goddess and Lea.

"Please consider this," Adelaide begged. "The darkness inside you. I can feel it, Lea."

Lea squeezed her mother's hands. "I have to help him."

Adelaide swallowed, her brow creasing as she shook her head. "Then you must be careful, Lea. It will consume you whole, consume the world whole, if you allow it to. You must remember who you are. Who I raised you to be. The woman Gray fell in love with. Do not let the darkness win."

Lea tried to push it down, but it bubbled beneath her skin, pulsing and pounding to escape, so intense, she could only nod.

"Can you help me? Control it, I mean?" Lea asked the moon goddess.

"I'm afraid to interfere any more would only make things worse for you. All I can say is you *can* control it. And you can win. I wouldn't allow you to return if I wasn't certain."

Lea's throat bobbed, her primary magic rebelling inside her as if insulted. *Destroy.*

"You are destined for great things, my daughter. I will be with you," Adelaide said, throwing her arms around Lea and squeezing her tight.

"As will I," the goddess replied, looking over her shoulder. "Take the cure, before—"

The hills began to rumble, cracks forming and spreading beneath her feet like the earth itself was going to open up and swallow her whole. Light exploded around them in a white-hot flash of fury as the god of the sun appeared on the hill above them, his anger so bright, his entire being was hidden by flames.

Lea turned to run, placing the petal on her tongue and swallowing it as the goddess and her mother were thrown backward.

The sun god surged toward her, impossibly fast, but the magic of the moonflower was faster. In a fraction of a second, Lea was no longer on a hill in Bearswillow.

No. She was lying in a soft, familiar bed. Through her closed eyelids, warm light flickered from candles around the room. She shivered, a groan escaping her lips as feeling returned to her body. Every joint ached, and her head throbbed, but Lea welcomed the pain as her heart thundered its first strong beat. Gray's and Janelle's voices floated through the air, and she gasped, sucking oxygen back into her lungs.

A crash sounded from next to her, a chair being thrown backward, and Gray was suddenly at her side. "Lea," he cried, a plea. A prayer.

She opened her eyes.

CHAPTER 10

GRAY

A gasp—a deep inhale—and Gray's world stopped spinning. Lea's chest rose, and before he could even process what was happening, he lunged at her, his chair clattering to the stone floor with a crash. His hands cupped her cheeks, and his heart kicked into a furious rhythm as he found her skin warm and pink.

"Lea," he breathed, and as if his voice had called her home, her eyes opened. Her beautiful blue eyes that he had believed he would never look into again in this lifetime.

Gray cried out her name, his shadows wrapping around them as he pulled Lea into his arms and crushed her tired body against his. Countless questions ran through his mind, but all he could say was her name, again and again. She was here. She was home. She was *alive*.

"I'm here," she said, her voice weak as she inhaled deeply into the crook of his neck. She pulled back, running her fingers along the side of Gray's face. "I'm here," she repeated, her voice getting stronger with every word.

"How— How is this possible?" Janelle asked. Lea's eyes slid over to her friend, and just like when they'd both been beyond the veil, Gray was once again aware of how much Lea had changed. Her warmth was gone. There was no sparkle in her eye as she looked at her best friend, no hint of light within her at all.

It didn't matter. He would take her however she was, and would help her find her way back to herself. Of course, she was different. What she had been through... Gray's shadows pulsed at the memory.

"The goddess of the moon sent me back. She said if we are to defeat Alaric, she had no choice. The god of the sun—" Lea's voice hardened, her eyes darkening. "He was against it. There will be consequences."

The hair on Gray's arms stood on end as he took in Lea's words. If the goddess of the moon had acted against the sun god's wishes, they would be battling more than just Alaric. He hoped it wouldn't affect his magic, or Lea's. They needed every weapon at their disposal to win this war.

But he shoved down the thought. "Whatever the consequences are, we will handle them," Gray said. "Together."

Lea nodded, but her eyes remained haunted, unsure.

Gray's shadows caressed Lea from head to toe, prodding and assessing her for injuries as much as savoring the feeling of touching her warm skin. Making sure she was really *here*.

"Are you hurt?" he asked, no longer caring that Lea had forced him to return without her. He'd been so full of grief at losing her not once, but twice. It had been mixed with anger at what she'd done. At tricking him into returning without her. But not anymore. Now, he was filled with only joy and relief.

Lea nodded. "I'm fine. I'm..." she trailed off, clenching her jaw.

"Janelle, get Erik and Emma." Gray said without sparing a glance at Janelle, but the click of her shoes on the stone floor told him she was scurrying away to do what he'd asked.

The moment she was gone, Gray crushed his lips to Lea's, needing to feel her warmth seep into him. A growl left his throat as she opened her mouth and climbed onto his lap, straddling him, her tongue darting between his lips and her hands scraping down his back.

He pulled her flush against his front, needing to feel the erratic beat of her heart as he proved to himself that she was real with his hands and his lips and his cock.

Their kiss morphed into a clash of teeth and limbs, a groan leaving Gray's throat as he speared his fingers through her long, golden hair. His knuckles scraped on the thorny moonflower vines making up the crown on her head, but he hardly noticed as Lea's hands wrapped around his biceps, her fingernails digging into his arms. He welcomed the bite of pain, savored it, even.

It was proof that this was *real*, that she had somehow returned to him.

"You're really here..." Gray whispered, his lip still pressed to Lea's. She broke away, her chest heaving. As her eyes met his, Gray was once again struck by how utterly Fae she looked, how her human exterior had crumbled away once her primary magic had fully revealed itself, burning through the last bit of glamor from the potion her mother had given her to hide her true identity.

Lea didn't answer him, instead, placing a hand on his chest and firmly pushing him backward until he was flat on his back on the bed. Gray's shadows caressed her body, unable to stop touching her, even for a moment. They floated across her breast, driven by the need to feel her heartbeat, the steady, rhythmic rise and fall of her chest.

Lea wrapped her shadows around Gray's wrists, pinning them to his sides. Staring him directly in the eye, she grabbed the hem of her shirt, slowly lifting it up her torso and pulling it over her head. She tossed it to the floor, never breaking eye contact, and Gray's cock stiffened, the sight of her golden, freckled skin, flushed with color—with life—making him feral with need.

He tried to free his arms, pushing back against Lea's shadowy restraints, but she held them firm. Gray stilled, knowing he could break through them if he wanted, that he could have Lea in his arms in less than a second—her warm body under his as he made her moan with pleasure—but he stopped himself, sensing her need for control. She ripped open his shirt, revealing the puckered skin of his own scar, the jagged evidence of the chunk of flesh he'd cut from his own body.

"It's gone," Lea said, her voice cracking. "Gone."

Gray winced, the pain in her words as agonizing as Alaric's sword slicing through his sternum. Gray's eyes slid to just below her collarbone, to the faint scar where her own mate mark had once tattooed her chest.

"Forever, Gray. It's gone *forever*," she hissed, her shadows twisting tighter around his arms, pinning his legs in place against the bed so that he couldn't stand. There were no tears in her eyes, no hint of anything soft or gentle. There was only anger, dark and hard, and so intense, it made Gray's heart ache.

"I'd do it again," he said. There was no bite to his words, but she needed to know the truth. He hated that he'd been forced to sacrifice himself. Loathed the fact that they no longer had the mate bond between them, that Lea felt hurt and betrayed. But he didn't regret it. He couldn't. It had been the only way to grow the moonflowers, and it had saved their entire army.

It had saved her.

At least, until she'd recklessly and selflessly followed behind him and found a way to save them both. He would make the same choice now, even knowing what it had cost them. Because they were alive. They were together.

Lea's eyes darkened. "Never again," she said, her voice nearly a growl. "Never. Again." She was so angry. Absolutely furious. He wanted to rush to her, fold her in his arms and show her with his body how much he loved her, show her the grief he'd been feeling, the pain and despair that had consumed his every waking moment since he'd returned without her.

He thought again about forcing his way through her shadows, but instead, he just nodded. "Never again," he agreed. "I swear it."

Lea's breath rushed out in one fell swoop, and she closed her eyes, her shoulders falling slightly, but her shadowy chains didn't ease. She stalked forward, pulling her hair to the side as she knelt in front of him.

A memory flashed through his mind. *You serve no one, especially me,* he'd said after finding her on her knees scrubbing the floors of his hall. It had infuriated him. Made him want to rip out Alaric's throat for assigning her as his maid. But they had come so far since then. She was his queen. His equal, and the sight of her kneeling in front of him made the most primal depths of his soul crave more.

Placing her palms on his knees, Lea slid them upward, slowly, torturously, until they reached his waistband. A long trail of shadow floated from her fingers, unbuttoning his trousers and sliding down the zipper. Lea stared him in the eye, straight into his soul, and finally moved her hands, pulling his cock free from his pants.

He fell hard and thick in her hand, pulsing as her fingers danced across the sensitive skin. Gray's chest heaved with ragged breaths as she leaned down, never looking away from his eyes, and swirled her tongue around the tip of his cock. He groaned again, his hips bucking, needing more. Lea wrapped her fingers around the base of him, squeezing him gently and gliding up and down before sliding her tongue from base to tip, closing her lips around his thick length.

"Gods, Lea," Gray hissed as she moved faster, the warmth of her mouth and pressure of her tongue further igniting his need, almost driving him mad. Gray's shadows pulled her hair over her shoulder as he once again pushed against the restraints on his arms, desperate to thread his fingers through her hair, but Lea held him firmly in place.

"Let me touch you," he growled, the need to feel every inch of her body so intense it made his skin ache. He needed to kiss her, to hold her, to bury himself inside her until they were so entwined it would be impossible to separate them again. He'd thought he lost her forever, had broken her heart by breaking the bond. To have her kneeling before him, pleasuring him and not receiving anything in return? It didn't feel right.

Lea ignored his pleas, sliding her lips down again until he hit the back of her throat. His cock twitched as she worked him harder, faster. But this wasn't what he wanted. What he *needed*.

His heart thundered, his shadows mixing with Lea's and begging them to release their hold.

"How does it feel to have no control?" Lea asked, pulling back and rubbing her breasts against his legs.

"Never again," Gray repeated, forcing himself to not break through her shadows, even though the need to touch her was threatening to kill him. She needed the control. Needed to make her point. "I swear it to you, Lea. I will never," his shadows reached out, grabbing her chin and forcing her to meet his eyes. "I will never, ever leave you again. Not in life, or in death. I will not allow us to be separated. Never. Again." He reached forward, pushing against Lea's shadows once more, and this time, they relented, setting him free.

A growl ripped from his throat as he sank to the floor, grabbing her by the waist and throwing her onto her back on the bed. This time, he held *her* down with his shadows as he fumbled with her pants, ripping them off and spreading her legs open wide. Lea moaned as his tongue found her center, a rumble leaving his throat as he tasted her. No—*feasted* on her.

He splayed a palm over her stomach, holding her in place as she arched against him.

"More," she begged, her breaths ragged and her skin flushing. It was almost his undoing. He pressed a finger inside her, then two, his dick pulsing as he moved them in and out, her body squeezing against him tighter and tighter.

He leaned back to look at her, at his fingers claiming her, the way she writhed and bucked against him. Just the sight was enough to make him come, and he leaned back in, nipping at her thighs before once again finding her clit with his tongue.

It was as if he was starving. As if she was cold water after years in the desert. He pressed the pad of his tongue against her, hard, and Lea cried out, her body going taut beneath his hand. His shadows snaked around her thighs, holding them down as he worked her through her pleasure, her body spasming as her orgasm crashed over her in waves, his name a prayer on her beautiful, plump lips.

It was the most beautiful sight Gray had ever seen; her head thrown back and her body quivering as he fucked her with his fingers, and he was certain it was an image he would never forget as long as he lived.

It wasn't until she stilled beneath him that he pulled his fingers back, pressing kisses up her belly and neck until he was on top of her. He kicked off his pants and ripped off his shirt, unable to stand the thought of his skin not touching hers for another second. He was so hard it was painful, but he didn't want to rush. He needed to take his time, to feel and taste and worship every single inch of her.

Lea's hands trailed the lines of his back, pulling him closer, their hearts pounding in rhythm with one another as he dipped his head to her breast, swirling his tongue around her nipple. She squirmed against him, arching to push her breast deeper into his mouth as her shadows reached between them and positioned him at her opening.

Gray's chest rumbled, the feeling of her, warm and soft against him, driving him mad.

"Please," she begged, pulling him closer. "Please. I need to feel you."

And suddenly, the desire to go slow, to savor every moment, was crushed to bits.

He thrust inside her, gliding in as if his cock had been made just for her, and Lea cried out, her fingernails biting into his back. Gray reached the end of her and stilled, allowing her to adjust.

He could hardly breathe, the need to move so intense, it made his muscles shake. Lea wiggled beneath him, a silent plea for more, and he groaned, allowing himself to give in to the overwhelming need to claim her as his. To fuck her so deeply, so thoroughly, that even the gods would know she was his, and only his. That he would never again allow her to be taken away from him.

He began to move, his pleasure building unlike anything he'd ever felt before as he thrust again and again, harder and deeper, their need for one another driving them to the brink and holding them there for only a moment before they tumbled over the edge together. Lea screamed his name, and Gray growled hers as her walls pulsed around him, squeezing him as he spilled himself inside her.

It was ecstasy. Absolute euphoria.

"Mine," he rumbled into her mouth as he stilled, breaths ragged and heart thundering.

They laid there together, unable to part for gods knew how long. Gray pressed kisses to her forehead, her cheeks, her eyes and nose and jaw, and then finally, her lips before grabbing a wet cloth to clean Lea and himself. The sight of Lea's flushed skin was breathtaking, and his eyes lingered for several long moments before he finally pulled the blanket back over them and gathered her into his arms. His fingers caressed an absent trail up and down her arms as their breathing returned to normal.

"Gray," Lea said, her voice sounding somehow melodic and broken at the same time. "I still don't..." Lea trailed off, and even without the bond, Gray could tell what she was thinking.

"We lost one hundred and sixty-two brave men and women," he said, his voice low and somber. He'd forgotten that she had no clue what the outcome of the battle had been, other than their own deaths. "Your friends are alive. As is Vincent. All the fatal injuries were sustained in battle. The moonflowers worked, Lea. Not just for us, but for the sick and injured as well. There's no trace of the Lonely Death within the camp."

Lea sucked in a sharp inhale, her eyes glistening with unshed tears. It was the first moment since her death, both here and beyond the veil, that Gray saw a small bit of light within her. Of who she used to be. The soft, gentle woman she'd been before.

She nodded. "And Alaric?" Her words were tight, and within an instant, every hint of that softness was gone. Black flames danced along her skin, up her legs and around her hands.

Gray shook his head. "We don't know where he is. There's been no sign of him so far."

"He could be anywhere." Darkness flooded Lea's features, and it struck Gray how fierce she looked. Purely Fae, the flickering light of her fire accentuating her sharpened cheeks and jaw, the graceful way she turned her head.

"How many caves and small villages are there to hide in throughout the kingdom?" she asked.

"Hundreds," Gray answered. "But I know this land. No matter how long it takes, we *will* find him." He grabbed her face again, shaking gently to emphasize his promise.

Lea's hand drifted to her head, her fingers trailing the moonflower crown above her brow. "And what if we don't have time?" The desperation in Lea's voice made Gray pause. Fear flooded his veins, instant and overwhelming. He grabbed her chin and met her eyes.

"What do you mean? What aren't you telling me, Little Flower?" he asked, a shiver running down his spine.

The silence was thick and heavy as Lea swallowed, nodding absently, her eyes millions of miles away. Gray watched as she closed her eyes. Forced himself to remain still as she took a deep breath and commanded her flames and shadows to diminish, her nostrils flaring as she fought against her own power.

"The goddess said only I could end this. That I have to be the one to make the killing blow," Lea said. Gray's heart thundered against his ribs as he searched her gaze, but it wasn't pride or confidence he saw there. It was pure terror.

"This crown. I—" she paused, pressing her lips together. Gray somehow kept the dread and horror off his face as he grabbed Lea's hand and squeezed. He waited for her to continue, doing everything he could to make sure she knew she wasn't alone in whatever she was about to tell him.

"Until the last petal falls. That's how long we have to kill Alaric and return the magic he stole to the earth."

Gray sucked in a breath, his lungs constricting as he counted the flowers on her crown—forty-two tiny, pure white petals dispersed around crescent shaped seeds in between the dark thorns. "How often do they fall? How much time do we have?" he asked, needing to know the answer and afraid to hear it all at once.

"I don't know. I don't know anything, other than I have until this crown is bare to kill Alaric."

"And if it takes more time?" Gray swallowed, steeling himself for her answer.

A single tear rolled down Lea's cheek, a sliver of emotion betraying her stony exterior. "Then I return beyond the veil—"

Gray's veins flooded with fury, and he clenched his fists, his shadows writhing in his bloodstream. "No—"

Lea held up a hand, stopping him. "Then I return beyond the veil, and even in death, we will be separated."

Gray's vision went black with rage, and his shadows exploded outward, pressing against the walls as if needing to escape. He couldn't speak—his fury and terror wouldn't allow a single word to form in his throat. Every candle and torch within the room shrank, flickering until only tiny, soft halos of golden light illuminated the space.

"I must be the one to kill him, Gray. The goddess made that very clear. It must be my hand that delivers the killing blow. And I have to do it soon. I won't risk losing you again." Lea's voice was shaky. Unsteady and unsure. "Please listen to me. I know you. I know you will try to keep me out of harm's way. But you could be killed, too." She grabbed his hands, pulling them to her chest. "I *need* you to understand what the goddess said. You can't protect me from this."

Gray felt sick, his skin clammy and his heart racing as he thought about Lea facing Alaric again. What Alaric had done to him had been brutal. Horrific. He couldn't let her get close to him ever again. Refused to allow her within half a kingdom from him.

And yet, it seemed that was the only way.

Gray stood, pulling on his pants and pacing back and forth across the room. His fists clenched and unclenched at his sides as he tried to form a plan. "We'll find him, Lea. We'll start now. We'll find him, and we will kill him. *You* will kill him." Gray had never meant anything more. He wouldn't rest until they found him, and would do anything possible to help Lea fulfill her destiny. He had no choice. Because he refused to ever let her go again. There was no world, neither here nor beyond the veil, that he would allow them to be torn apart in. Not again.

Never again.

Lea sat up, wringing her hands together. "I'm afraid, Gray. Of who I am now. Of who I've become—or *could* become."

The confession took his breath away, making his heart ache. He forced himself to stop pacing and sat, pulling her into his arms. "You're the same woman I fell in love with. Everything you are now, it was always there. You've always been Fae. You've always had this magic. It was just hidden away."

She shook her head. "When I saw what Alaric had done to you, something broke inside me. This darkness, it's overwhelming me already." Small black flames danced along Lea's fingertips, her shadows writhing in a haze around her. "I tried to take Alaric's magic, and when he disappeared, when I watched you cut the mate bond from your skin and your eyes glaze over with death, I almost..." Lea's nostrils flared as she took a deep breath, several candles in the room extinguishing completely. The black flames along Lea's skin grew taller, hotter.

"I could have killed Erik for holding me back. Could have killed all of them—people I *love*—for trying to keep me from you. There's this voice inside me, telling me to kill. To destroy." She bit her lip, exhaling shakily. "I'm afraid that voice will win, Gray."

Lea finally looked up at him, the vulnerability in her eyes so shocking compared to the harsh planes of her face and determined set of her jaw.

Gray knelt before her, holding both of her hands firmly in his, steadying their shaking. "I know—as much as I know that I love you—that you can control it. You are strong. You are capable." He tucked a strand of hair behind her ear. "I will not allow the darkness to claim you, Lea. It will no more take you from me than the gods."

Lea exhaled slowly, nodding as she closed her eyes and forced her flames and shadows to recede. "There's something else we need to discuss. Something I've been thinking about since we went beyond the veil," she said, the moment of vulnerability fading as she lifted her chin. Fire still crackled around her, black and red and so hot, it burned just kneeling next to her.

"Many things," Gray agreed. "Your father is here—"

"Do you know how Alaric found us?" Lea interrupted, several more candles extinguishing. Gray's shadows surged in response, answering the call of Lea's darkness. Gray took a moment to examine her, her differences. It went beyond the physical changes that had occurred once her primary magic had been set free. There was a harshness to her eyes and a black haze surrounded her body, as if the shadows were so deeply a part of her they could never be separated.

But even more, Gray could *feel* the power inside her in a way he couldn't before, crashing and rolling like waves in the ocean that drag an unsuspecting swimmer into its depths to his death.

Lea's confession of her fear of that darkness echoed through his entire being. She didn't feel evil, but she did feel *dangerous*.

It changed nothing. This was who she was always meant to be. The strongest, bravest woman he knew. The only one with the power and resolve to defeat Alaric.

Gray tried to tug on the mate bond to see what Lea was feeling but found nothing to grab onto, no link to his mate to allow his magic to mix with hers. A lump formed in his throat as he realized he'd forgotten it was gone. How many times would he reach for her only to find the scarred remains of where their bond used to be?

What he wouldn't give to be able to read her thoughts again, her emotions and feelings. Maybe it could help him understand her better, and what she had become. Maybe it could allow him to find a way to help her control that which she was so afraid of.

"Vincent's been interrogating everyone. But no. As of now, we don't know who the traitor was."

Lea tilted her head, a cruel smile dancing across her lips. "Then that's where we begin. Bring me my sword," she said, her words as sharp as broken glass. "I think it's time we discover who betrayed us."

CHAPTER II

ERIK

The wreckage in Bearswillow was absolute. Chills ran down Erik's spine as he wandered the dark, cobblestone streets. They'd cleared the bodies they'd burned days ago, but the evidence that something wicked had occurred in this place remained.

Even in the dark, Erik could see the bloodstains throughout the village—the black, fingerlike scorch marks that trailed like spiderwebs everywhere the eye could see. Up the side of buildings, across the roads, over roofs, and through the meadows. Erik shuddered as a vision of Alaric's soldiers appeared in his mind. Their gaping black mouths would haunt him for the rest of his life.

Whatever Lea had done to them had been of pure might and darkness. And still, they hadn't won. Neither had Alaric, but he may as well have. Their queen was dead.

Their week of mourning was almost up, days full of nothing but grief and darkness. Gray had hardly left Lea's side since he'd placed her on his bed, and had needed to be reminded to eat and bathe. He took all his meetings in his room, his hand on Lea's chest, as if waiting for her heart to start again. It was morbid and wildly upsetting to some of Gray's advisors. But he would not be deterred.

Scorched earth crunched beneath Erik's feet as he continued his patrol through the village. He'd taken to walking the same path through it every day, needing to observe the horrors of what had transpired here, as if giving them space could undo some of the atrocities they'd endured. They'd lost too many. Far too much.

Erik made it to the base of the hill where Lea used to live, where she had taken her final breaths, sacrificing herself to bring Gray back. Where Noah had been killed. Where Emma had almost lost her life. Where Gray had taken his final breath.

He'd walked to this place every day, but hadn't been able to bring himself to go further. Every time he approached it, his heart would pound and sweat would erupt across his brow. His stomach would churn and his vision would go spotty, terrified that the moment his feet touched that cursed soil where the moon flowers still prospered, completely untouched by the flames, that everything would come rushing back even more vividly than they did in his nightmares every night.

But it was time. Because something wasn't right. It had been *days*, and Lea's body had shown no signs of decay. This wasn't completely unusual for the Fae, but Lea had been human. Or, at least, they'd thought she was partly human. But looking at her now, even in death, it was obvious this was yet another way her mother had tried to protect her. What was especially odd, though, was the wreath of moonflowers around her head. Gray hadn't allowed them to be removed, but even after days without water or sunlight, they remained pristine and perfect. White, almost iridescent.

Sometimes, when Gray needed to eat or sleep and Erik sat vigil with Lea, Erik swore he could see the vines moving. Just enough to make him wonder if he was losing his mind, or if they were still a living, growing thing.

With a deep breath, Erik pushed down his nausea, forcing his feet to trudge up the decimated hill. He was short of breath when he reached the top, and it felt a bit like panic as he struggled to force his heart to slow.

Guilt overwhelmed him as he looked at the spot where the moon-flower vines erupted from the earth. The spot where Gray had cut the mate bond from his skin as Erik held Lea back, allowing her to burn him in order to ensure that Gray could make the sacrifice required, not only to save their people, but to save Lea as well.

Erik hadn't allowed himself to be healed for days, needing the reminder that it was because of him that Lea was dead. He hadn't been able to save Gray, hadn't been there when Alaric had plunged the sword through his breastbone. He'd failed his friends, and it was something he would never forgive himself for. Not when he lived, and Lea didn't.

Erik turned toward where her house had once stood, the still smoldering remains crumbled into the backdrop of the hill. To the side was a crater, roughly the size of a wagon—the place where Alaric had disappeared into thin air like the coward he was.

A feeling of something *other* rubbed against Erik's skin, begging him to look closer, and he moved toward the crater, his eyes narrowed. In the middle of the massive hole was a perfect handprint. But that wasn't what had caught Erik's attention. It was the magic emanating from it. Embedded into the Earth like a beacon. It felt sinister, wrong in a way that sank into Erik's bones, begging him to turn around and leave this cursed place immediately. But he couldn't seem to look away.

All around the crater, the color had been leached from the ground. And while the rest of the hill was nothing but the scorched, ashy remains of grass, here it was simply black.

Ignoring his instincts, Erik moved even closer to the handprint, sweat now dripping down his spine. *Run,* his subconscious urged him. *You'll find nothing but danger here,* it said, but he couldn't turn away. Refused to fail his friends again. He wasn't sure exactly how, but this was a clue, a hint to what had happened to the false king.

He crouched down, now only inches away from the pulsing energy of the handprint as he reached out shaking fingers and placed his hand on top of it. The pain was instant, blinding, and Erik shouted in surprise as he pulled his hand away. An image flashed through his mind, there and gone in less than a second, but it didn't matter. As if Erik's subconscious had recognized the importance of the vision, it had committed the image to memory.

It *had* to be where Alaric had disappeared to, where his magic had somehow taken him. There was no other explanation Erik could think of. Even better, he *knew* the place he'd seen. On the far end of the castle grounds stood an old guard shack, one that had been unused for at least a hundred years. They'd played there as children, before Alaric's heart had turned completely black. Before it had withered and died in his quest for power.

Erik placed his hand back on the Earth, prepared for the pain this time, but no matter how long he left it there, the vision did not appear again.

"Erik," Janelle's voice made him jump, and before he even knew what he was doing, he stood and ran to her. She was crying, sobbing, and Erik's blood ran cold at the sound.

"What's wrong?" Erik asked, pulling her into his arms, shushing and soothing her as he rubbed her back.

"It's Lea," Janelle said, her legs giving out as she leaned into him.

He lifted her, supporting her weight fully. "I know. I know—"

"No," Janelle stopped him, lifting her head. Tears streamed from her red eyes, and his breath caught as she smiled. "Erik. She's alive."

CHAPTER 12

GRAY

A few soldier's stifled yawns or chatted amongst themselves as they gathered in the great hall. Between them were regular men and women looking around with anxious, darting glances. Gray wondered what they were thinking. They'd been roused from sleep in the early morning hours at Lea's insistence. She'd needed to know who betrayed them, and he didn't disagree. So long as a traitor was in their midst, none of them were safe.

Nothing could have prepared Gray for his army's reaction as their queen walked into the room. Within seconds of her appearing, roughly half of their army had dropped to their knees, pulling medals from beneath their tunics and chanting prayers. Others took weary steps back, or simply stood, slack-jawed and pale. Gray was fairly certain a woman near the back fainted, and the sound of gasps spread like a wave crashing upon the shore.

Lea's heels clicked against the stone floor, echoing through the chamber until she reached the front, lifting her chin as she scanned the crowd. There was no hint of what she was feeling on her sharp, angular face, not a single inkling of the thoughts running through her head evident as a makeshift throne was brought to the gathering room—an old wooden chair that was as unassuming as a daisy mixed into a field full of wildflowers. But somehow, when Lea sat in it, that is what it became. A throne.

As she lowered herself into the chair, the room quieted, the shocked gasps and muttered prayers turning to hushed whispers that rolled across Gray's skin like thunderclaps. Their surprise was palpable, bringing a fervent energy to the air that had been missing since the battle.

Gray had wanted to warn their army, but Lea had a plan and insisted that surprising them would be better. It would put the traitor on edge, and wouldn't allow them time to prepare for their mass interrogation—or worse, flee.

"Quiet," Lea said, her tone calm but commanding, and the whispers ceased completely. The tension in the room grew suffocating as her eyes raked over her rapt audience, Lea's shadows snaking out in long tendrils. Soldiers shuddered as the dark fingers of her magic wrapped up their torsos and caressed their cheeks, examining them before moving on to the next nervous rebel.

Lea's jaw remained set, her chin high. Once again, Gray wished he knew what she was thinking, longed for the mate bond to allow them to communicate silently. Could she tell who the traitor was through her magic? Or was it something more?

"You might be wondering how I'm here. How it's possible for me to be sitting before you when my body laid cold in Gray's arms only days ago," Lea finally said, her shadows continuing to thread throughout the crowd. "It was only by the goddess's mercy that I was granted this chance. Alaric must die. He must be defeated for the good of the kingdom. And he would have been, had one of you not betrayed our trust and disclosed our location."

A few rebels glanced around nervously, while others gasped. An older woman near the front looked as if she might vomit. Gray couldn't blame them. They were looking at a ghost. A queen risen from the dead with vengeance etched into every line of her body.

"I was shocked, too. As shocked as all of you," Lea continued. "But it does not change the facts. The only way Alaric could have found us is through one of you." She punctuated the final word with a snap of her fingers, her shadows thickening around them. "Because of one of you, we lost good men and women. We lost a battle that could have ended the war. And we lost this place." Lea gestured to the stone above them. "Alaric knows where we hide. It's not safe to remain here." Her calculating tone made Gray shiver. She was right, though. It *wasn't* safe to stay in the cavern. The thought made his stomach drop, but he forced the feeling away.

"This cavern has remained undetected for a hundred years. And yet, somehow, Alaric found us before Tanad and his army could arrive. Before we were fully prepared. It's too..." She tapped her chin, pretending to think, but Gray could tell she was buying time as her shadows continued to slide and slither throughout the men and women filling the chamber.

"You." Her head suddenly snapped to the right, her dark eyes locking on a young soldier, probably only nineteen or twenty years old. Alex.

The shadows still threaded throughout the crowd receded, wrapping firmly around Alex's body. "Come here," she ordered. His eyes widened and his face paled, but the boy had no choice but to obey as the shadows pulled him closer to their master, forcing him to his knees in front of her.

With the agility of a barn cat but the intensity of a lioness, Lea stood, stalking around him in a slow circle. Her shadows pulsed and puddled around her feet, so black they obscured the bottom of her dress, making it appear as if she was floating. And mixed within them was black fire. Crackling with an intensity that made Gray's shadows long to join it in a wave of destruction.

Lea drew the sword from her waist, its razor-sharp edge glinting in the torch flames. Gray's heart beat faster, his nerves squeezing his lungs as he watched Lea transform before his eyes. Her flames grew darker, her posture impossibly straighter and her demeanor more harsh. The call to destroy inside her was winning.

The darkness he'd sensed from her earlier grew, and Gray's muscles tensed as he prayed she wasn't planning on killing this young man in front of their entire army, traitor or not.

In private, it would be a different matter. But this was someone's son. Someone's brother. Without a trial or evidence, condemning him here and now was a risk.

The boy was sweating, his face completely drained of color and his hands shaking, making him appear even younger.

Lea stopped her prowling as she lifted the sword, examining it. As quick as lightning, she flipped it, the tip hitting the floor only inches from the boy's knees, with a clang that made those closest to them flinch."I suggest you answer honestly," Lea said, wrapping her fingers firmly around the hilt and squeezing. "Did you betray us? Was it you who tipped off Alaric of our location?"

"No! I swear!" the boy cried.

Lea's head snapped to where her skin touched the sword. She stared at it for several long, seemingly endless seconds, then clicked her tongue. "The *truth*. That was all I asked of you."

She lifted the sword, her shadows yanking the boy down so that his hands were pressed against the cold floor. Gray took a subtle step forward, sending his shadows to mix with Lea's. He didn't want to intervene, and knew deep down that no matter what Lea thought, she was capable of controlling the darkness inside her. But that didn't mean he wouldn't stop her if he had to. To kill one of their own, in front of everyone and without concrete proof, could cause a rift within their army. One they couldn't afford if they wanted to find Alaric and end this war before the final petal fell from her crown.

"It was an accident! Please!" Alex cried as Lea raised the sword higher, the back of his neck exposed as her shadows pulled his head even with the floor. "I swear. I'd never betray you." Lea paused, her eyes clearing of the darkness just a bit, and Gray ordered his shadows to pause.

"You already lied once." Lea lowered the sword a fraction. "You expect me to believe you now?"

"It's the truth. It was an accident. Just an accident," the boy sobbed.

Lea squeezed the hilt again, closing her eyes for a moment before the shadows holding Alex down loosened.

"Explain."

Alex looked up at her, taking a shuddering breath. "I was scouting a few weeks ago, about a day's ride from here. And I think..." Alex swallowed. "I think I was followed. When I was coming back, something felt wrong. But I was scared. And I wasn't positive. I thought I was being paranoid."

The sword remained poised several feet over the boy's neck, Lea's hands tight around the metal. She squeezed harder, and Gray wondered what her plan was. If she was fighting the darkness, or simply trying to make Alex sweat as a lesson to all the rebels that mistakes like this couldn't be made.

Put down the sword, he begged silently. It had been a fatal mistake, one that had cost them everything. But killing him now would do nothing but allow that immense, dark power inside her to grow even stronger. Gray sent his shadows closer, preparing to intervene should that sword start to arc downward, but praying that he wouldn't have to.

Lea met his eyes, turning her head so only he could see her face, and Gray sucked in a sharp breath. His fingers itched to reach toward her, his feet begging him to go to her.

This was not a lesson she was teaching their army. This was the very thing she feared most. Her jaw was clenched so tight he worried her teeth might crack, and her eyes were black, but tears threatened to spill over her eyelashes. Her forehead was scrunched as if she was in pain, her hands shaking with restraint.

"Gray," she whispered. A plea for help.

Without hesitation, he set his shadows free, slipping into the skin of Evander he had worn for so many years.

"Your decisions cost us greatly," Gray said. "Nearly cost me *everything*." Long tendrils of darkness lifted the sword from Lea's hand. Gray placed his palm against her lower back, pushing as much calming energy as he could beneath her skin. Lea sighed in relief as the sword left her fingers, floating through the air until it was firmly within his palm.

Gray brought the tip of the weapon beneath Alex's chin, forcing him to look up.

"He's telling the truth?" Gray asked, and Lea nodded, but the question was more for their audience than him. He already knew from the look in Lea's eye and the rage emanating off of her that if the sword had warmed in her hand to indicate that he was lying, he'd be dead right now.

"He told the truth. The *second* time I asked him." Lea's voice was dripping with venom, but she released her shadows, and Alex fell to the floor, shaking.

"Make no mistake," Gray said. "If my mate had been unable to return to me, your life would be over. But as she is here, I will be merciful. Vincent, take him away and decide his punishment. Whatever you see fit."

Alex scrambled to his feet as Vincent approached, sobbing in relief.

"Let this be a lesson," Gray said, handing the sword back to Lea, who swiftly returned the weapon to its sheath, in control once again. "We cannot afford to make mistakes. We cannot afford errors of judgment.

Alaric will not be deterred. He will not give up until either he is dead, or *we* are. Another mistake like this, and it could be the end of everything we've been fighting for."

"Another mistake like this," Lea said, turning and storming from the room, "and I bring the sword down."

CHAPTER 13

LEA

Lea's stomach rolled and her heart raced, her shadows bursting from her skin as she stormed from the massive chamber and down the hallway back to her room. She had almost killed him. Had been seconds away, maybe less, from bringing down her sword and severing the terrified boy's head from his body.

The thought made her want to vomit. She didn't enjoy killing. Didn't relish ending a life, whether deserved or not.

But her dark magic? It had begged her to do it—almost *forced* her to do it. The voice in her head had clouded her mind. *Destroy*, it had urged with each beat of her heart.

Destroy.

Destroy.

Destroy.

And oh, how she had wanted to. Except, somewhere deep inside her, she *hadn't* wanted to.

Not when the sword had remained cold in her hand. Not when she realized he was just a boy who'd made a terrible mistake out of fear. It hadn't been malicious. He hadn't been a traitor.

Kill him, her primary magic begged in her mind. *He is the reason your bond is gone. He is the reason you made the bargain with the goddess. Kill Alaric or be separated from Gray, even after death.*

Kill him.

Kill him.

Kill him.

Her magic had flooded from her chest and into her fingers, pushing her arm down with a desperate strength as she fought against it. It'd taken every bit of control she had to fight against what that dark power begged her to do.

This is exactly what she'd been afraid of, the reason that she'd sent Gray back instead of herself. And after what had just happened, Lea was more afraid than ever that she would succumb to the darkness. Had Gray not recognized her plea, had he not seen what was happening to her, she would've done it, unable to fight against that wicked power any longer.

"Lea," Gray called from behind her, but she didn't stop. He would catch up with her, but she needed to get to their room. Somewhere with a door between her and the rest of the army. "Lea!" he said again, finally reaching her side and stopping her with a hand on her arm.

She pulled away. "Not now. Please," she said, nodding down the hallway. She couldn't talk. Not here, where anyone could hear or see her. She was barely holding in her emotions, and knew that the moment she admitted out loud what she had almost done, how close she had actually come to killing that boy, she would lose the fight and her tears would come. She refused to fall apart anywhere other than the privacy of their room.

Seeming to understand, Gray took her hand and walked with her in silence until they reached the door. The moment it closed, Lea fell apart. Sobs wracked her body as she fought for breath, her chest tightening with panic.

Gray gathered her in his arms, carrying her to sit on the bed.

"It's okay," he said, rubbing his hand along her hair.

"It's not," Lea wiped at her tears. "I almost killed him. I *wanted* to kill him."

"But you didn't. And even if you'd tried, you were safe. I wouldn't have let you," he said. "I was ready."

Lea swallowed, desperately wanting to make the tears stop. But she hadn't cried yet. Not when the god and goddess had refused to let them both return, and not as she sat with her mother, the wind blowing across town from the top of the hill. She hadn't cried when she'd returned from the dead. Hadn't mourned the loss of their mate bond, or the death of who she used to be. At first she'd been too terrified, then too furious, her emotions too big and intense to allow her to feel anything other than fury.

But that one moment of control, of stopping herself from killing the boy, it was as if it had put her back in her own body, just a bit.

"I'm not who I used to be. I'm not the queen they all vowed to serve and protect. Not anymore," she admitted.

Gray looked at her without any hint of judgment or fear or disgust. "Death will change you," he said. "It changed me, too."

"It's not just that. Of course, that's part of it, but... It's this magic. I was never supposed to have it. I can feel it. It's wrong. When I—"Lea took a deep breath, thinking through what she wanted to say. "When my emotions get out of control, it's like my magic feeds on it. It takes over. I don't want to live this way. I don't trust myself around our people. Not if I can't control it."

"You *did* control it. You didn't kill him," Gray answered.

"Because *you* took the sword." Lea glanced at the hilt of her weapon, but Gray lifted her chin.

"Because you asked me to, and only because you fought against that darkness and won. You chose not to kill him."

Lea's shoulders dropped, and she sniffled. "But what happens next time? I don't want to be this person. I don't want to *want* to destroy and maim and kill."

Gray was silent, and Lea wondered if he agreed with her. If deep down, he knew she was no longer the girl filled with light that he had fallen in love with. Could he still love her if all the warmth inside her had been replaced by dark, cold power? The thought of losing his love was even more painful than her death. More painful than when Alaric had beat her, or when her mother died.

"What you think is darkness," Gray lifted her chin to meet his eyes. "It's just a weapon. One you can use for good. You *can* control it. Because you're the strongest woman I know. Because you are determined to protect the people you love. I have watched you try to sacrifice yourself again and again for your friends—for me. Even when it was misguided or foolish. You've always put others above yourself. This is no different. You'll find a way to control it, because that is what you have to do to protect the people you love. And however I can, I will help you. Because I love *you*. Every part of you. Darkness and all."

The words soothed the ache in her chest, just enough to take a deep breath.

"You can do this," Gray said, tucking her hair behind her ear. But as he said the words, a petal fell from Lea's crown. A warning.

And as it turned black and crumbled into dust before it even reached the ground, Lea realized... It wasn't a warning at all. It was a threat.

Lea held back a sob, a pain shooting through her heart as if it was shattering. Not just from her sorrow at seeing a petal fall, but her bone-weary exhaustion chipping away at every part of her—her heart, her lungs, and veins, and organs.

"Hey," Gray said, lifting her chin to meet his gaze. That same sadness and exhaustion were mirrored in his own eyes, every emotion she was feeling echoed on his face. His rough hand moved from her chin to her cheek, tucking his fingers behind her ear and into her hair. "We *will* figure this out," he breathed, leaning closer. "I swear it. And you know I don't break my promises."

He leaned his forehead to press against hers, their noses brushing together as Lea nodded. She couldn't speak. There was nothing left to say. No words that would make everything right or okay.

And so, when Gray closed the distance between their lips, she opened for him immediately, hoping she could tell him everything she was feeling with her lips and tongue. Gray crawled over her, the heavy weight of his body pressing into her and soothing her soul in a way that couldn't be replicated. It grounded her—reminded her that she was more than just a swirling mess of shadows, darkness, and fear.

Lea reached for the hem of Gray's shirt, pulling it over his head in one swift motion. She tried not to look at his scarred chest, but her eyes immediately moved to the jagged, puckered skin just below his collarbone. It was cruel that even after eating the moonflowers, the gods hadn't allowed *that* scar to heal. Every one of Gray's other injuries had vanished after consuming the petals. But not this one. It was as if they were destined to be reminded of their loss every moment of their lives.

It is a grave thing to break the mate bond, Emma had told her what felt like years ago. She'd been so naïve, hadn't wanted the bond that she felt had been forced upon her. But now? Lea would do anything to get it back, to be able to feel Gray's emotions that deeply again, to know his every thought and feeling.

Gray's scar disappeared from her sight as he pressed his chest against hers, dipping his head to kiss the curve of her neck as his strong fingers slowly unbuttoned the top of her dress. He pulled it over her head and tossed it to the floor, his eyes darkening as he took in every inch of her exposed skin.

His hand curved around her hip bone, and he leaned down to claim her mouth once again. His kisses were so different from the way he'd devoured her when she first returned from beyond the veil. Where before they had been animalistic in their intensity, now, they were soothing—long and slow—his steady pressure reassuring her that somehow, everything would be okay.

Lea gasped as his hand slid up to her breast, squeezing just above her heart. She reached between them, desperate to touch his velvety length, but a long trail of shadows snaked up her arm, pinning it above her head.

"Let me take care of you," he growled against her skin, nipping as he worked his way down to her breast. His hand slid between her legs, and Lea moaned, giving in to the warmth spreading through her body—Gray's touch making her feel comforted and loved and some-how...safe.

"So fucking beautiful," he rasped, pressing a finger inside her. Lea pressed down against him, needing to feel him deeper. "My queen," he continued. "My love. My life. My mate," he said, kissing her scar.

He pushed another finger inside, moving back up to kiss Lea's lips. "My mate," he repeated into her mouth, and tears burned the back of her eyes at his words, at his reminder that mark or no mark, she *was* his mate. His equal.

Gray pressed kisses to her throat as he lined up his thick, impossibly hard length against her entrance, staring into her eyes and pressing inside, so slow and tender it was *almost* painful. His shadows released the hold on her arms as he sank inside her, and Lea wrapped herself around him, her fingers tracing the muscles of his back as he began to move.

Slow and deep and rhythmic, he thrust into her, their bodies moving together as sweat built on her skin. Lea quivered as Gray changed the angle, just slightly, her pleasure building impossibly quick. Warmth spread through her body, her core turning molten as Gray's hands explored her body. Threading through her hair then trailing all the way to her toes, as if memorizing every small line and divot.

The pressure inside her continued to build, her breaths growing rapid and shallow as he thrust deeper, as if needing to mark her in some way to prove to the gods that she was his. That their missing mate mark meant nothing, because she *was* his. Forever. And the gods had absolutely no say in the matter.

At the thought, Lea shattered, her walls clenching around Gray as he followed her into his own release, wave after wave of pure ecstasy pulsing through every inch of their bodies.

Gray leaned down to kiss Lea again, slowly and thoroughly, and he stilled, as if making sure she understood what he was feeling. *No one can take you from me. We will find a way. You are mine, and mine alone.*

And Lea almost believed him. Would have, had another petal not fallen from her crown between their bodies as he pulled her into his arms, smearing black ash across their skin, and terror through Lea's blood.

CHAPTER 14

GRAY

Lea's panic at watching another petal fall had calmed by the time Erik banged on the door. "Gray!" he called, his voice urgent, and Lea sniffled, wiping her tears away with the heel of her hand. "It's Tanad," Erik said as Gray yanked open the door. "He's here."

"Let's go." Gray grabbed his sword, reaching out for Lea's hand, but Erik pushed past him, grabbing Lea in his arms and wrapping her in a bear hug. He lifted her off her feet, squeezing her so tight, Gray feared she wouldn't be able to breathe.

Lea hugged him back, the two of them embracing for so long it would have been awkward if it was anyone else. Erik exhaled and put her back on her feet, holding her at arm's length, examining her.

"You really burned me. Like, really bad," he said, a hint of mischief in his eyes.

Lea raised her chin, trying to hide a smile. "You really deserved it," she answered, and Erik laughed, his face bright with joy at seeing her again.

"Agree to disagree there," he said with a wink before turning and leading them toward the entrance of the cavern.

They walked in silence, Erik checking over his shoulder every few seconds as if he thought Lea might disappear again. Gray couldn't blame him. If her hand were not firmly within his own, he'd be doing the same.

It wasn't until they stepped through the shimmering magic and into the fresh mountain air, that Gray let go. And only because his heart nearly stopped when he saw what was waiting for him.

King Tanad had been very clear when they'd left Calir that he would not force any of his soldiers to join another kingdom's war. But looking at their sheer numbers now, Gray wondered if he'd changed his mind. Hundreds upon hundreds of men stood on the mountainside outside the cavern, if not thousands.

A wave of gratitude so potent it threatened to knock him over washed through Gray as King Tanad approached. That he'd convinced so many to risk their lives to help them was a remarkable testament to their friendship, as well as to what the relationship between their kingdoms could be like once his brother was overthrown.

Gray looked at the sky, wondering what time it was, and how long they'd been traveling. It was still dark, as pitch black as the middle of the night, and it concerned him that they'd risked scaling the mountain under these conditions.

"Commander," Tanad said, bowing his head slightly. Gray returned the gesture, a signal to their people that they were to be treated as equals, and not only that, but partners.

"Is there danger?" Gray asked, his voice hushed as he leaned forward to shake the foreign king's hand. "Did something happen to require you to travel through the night?" The terrain of the mountains was uneven—rocky and unstable in places. A single misstep on the wrong steep slope could cause a rockslide that would have devastated their entire army.

Tanad's eyebrows scrunched, and he inclined his head. "Have you not ventured outside? Has no one told you?"

Gray narrowed his eyes. "Told me what?"

Erik cleared his throat, stepping forward. "Between Lea returning and then dealing with Alex... Well. I was waiting for the right time."

"The right time for what?" Lea asked, squeezing her hands into tight fists. Gray could sense her trying to control her temper, could feel the heat emanating off her skin as she tried to quell her flames. One after another, she took deep, slow breaths, trying to master her emotions, but the crackling at her feet only grew louder.

"The sun did not rise this morning." Tanad said, turning his gaze to the sky where the moon glowed brightly overhead. Tanad seemed perplexed rather than worried, his eyebrows slightly raised and his hand out as if trying to sense what magic was responsible.

"It didn't— What?" Gray called on his night magic, pushing the clouds from the sky, but it remained just as dark as it had been seconds before.

"There will be consequences..." Lea whispered, her words pensive and soft as her expression turned haunted. "The god of the sun tried to stop me from returning, but the goddess sent me back, anyway. She said there would be consequences," Lea repeated, speaking directly to Tanad.

"I see," Tanad said. "Never a boring moment with you, is there, my dear girl?"

The sound of beating wings echoed around the rocky terrain, interrupting them. A steady flap that made Gray pause and Lea stiffen beside him, cursing under her breath.

She glared at Tanad.

"I'm going to prepare to search for Alaric," she said, turning on her heel, but Gray caught her arm.

"What's going on?" he asked, searching the sky again. Black flames sparked at Lea's fingers as she clenched her jaw.

"If I don't walk away now, I don't think I'll be able to stop myself from killing her," she said.

"Who?" Gray asked, not understanding. The flap of the bird's wings grew louder, the animal getting closer until an enormous blue heron appeared, floating over an outcropping of jagged rocks and morphing into a human woman before his eyes.

"Me," Eudora said, a sick smile spreading across her wrinkled face.

Lea stiffened. "How *dare* you come here," she hissed, fire billowing around her in a halo of vengeance. Gray took a subtle step forward, putting himself between Lea and the witch who had so thoroughly deceived them. Gray's own magic expanded, pounding beneath his skin to be set free. He'd gladly rip Eudora apart inch by inch, slowly and tediously, for what she'd put them through. But Tanad had brought them his own men, was willing to sacrifice their lives and his own to protect Desia.

"Yes, yes." Eudora waved a hand flippantly. "Get it all out, I suppose."

"You *knew* what you were sending us into," Lea seethed, "and you gave us no warning. No clues as to what we would face. You *knew* what Gray's sacrifice would be. What it would do to him. To us." Lea stabbed a finger at Eudora as her fire grew taller, black smoke rising and intertwining with her shadows.

"I did." Eudora nodded, not a single hint of regret or sorrow in her features. "And I would do it again. Without hesitation. Without regret."

Lea stalked toward Eudora with a feline stealth and grace that took Gray's breath away. Shadows shot from Lea's fingers, wrapping around the witch's neck. Tanad started forward, but Eudora waved a hand, the shadows dispersing into wisps.

"Leave," Lea ordered, baring her teeth.

"We made a deal," Eudora smiled, sickly and unnaturally sweet. "One *you* have not yet fulfilled."

Lea's shadows reached out again, hovering inches from Eudora's throat. "I remember our deal," Lea spat.

"Then you know you must keep your word, or there will be con-sequences far worse than a lack of sun," Eudora said, waving a hand over the ground. Cracks appeared beneath her feet, reaching toward Lea like long, spidery fingers. "The universe does not take kindly to broken bargains."

"Oh, I'll keep my word. I always do," Lea said, yanking Eudora closer with her shadows. "Here is my next promise for you, witch."

"I think you meant bitch," Janelle said from somewhere behind her, and Lea smiled, a cruel, amused smirk.

"She really is, isn't she?" Lea said over her shoulder to Janelle. "I'll get your precious object from Auropera. It's no bother to me. I'll even bring it to you. Deliver it right into your hands." Lea shoved Eudora backward, throwing her into the rocky ground.

Gray froze, his eyes bouncing between Tanad and Lea. The foreign king did not move, but his shoulders were tense and his gaze wary.

Without another look at Eudora, Lea turned, walking back toward the entrance to the cavern. "And then I will make you beg for death," she said, disappearing into the murky darkness.

CHAPTER 15

GRAY

Lea seemed to feel a little more like herself as she sat in Gray's office with the rest of their friends. It had taken Janelle some convincing to allow Eudora entrance to the cavern, and only after she'd exhausted an impressive list of unique and shockingly vulgar language. But she'd relented once Erik had convinced her that no one would allow the witch to come near them.

Janelle had no authority, really. No power to decide who entered the cavern, but Gray didn't have it in him to try to stop her. Really, he couldn't have warned the witch of the dangers of trying to harm them again better himself. If Eudora came within a hundred feet of Lea, Gray, too, would shove the sharpest rock he could find through her spine and out her asshole.

As Erik recounted the story, Lea had smiled for the first time. Not a timid smile or a smirk, but a genuine smile with crinkled, humor-filled eyes, and that brief glimpse of Lea's light had been enough to reassure Gray that she was still fighting.

Her reunion with her friends had seemed to pull another small piece of who Lea used to be back to the surface, the darkness inside her feeling a bit more tame, though he longed for the mate bond so he could know for sure.

Thomas had cried when he saw her—pulled her into a hug he imagined would feel like childhood and sunny days and skipping rocks, and Gray hoped it chased away a bit more of the fury churning in her gut.

Emma had simply told her she missed her and whispered in her ear that she was sorry she was struggling and that she would help her with the darkness in any way she could. But it was Janelle who had been the one to break through Lea's armor fully.

"You take this fucking potion back," she'd said, shoving the vial into Lea's hands. "If you ever pull anything like that again—" Janelle shoved her. Actually pushed her—someone with enough magic inside her to kill them all without even trying.

"I will fucking find a way to kill you even more permanently," Janelle continued, ignoring everyone's stares. "Like, kill you kill you. Here and wherever the hell you went after. Or I'll demand the goddess send you somewhere awful, like a place where you have to eat my mother's cooking every night for the rest of eternity. Or listen to Thomas's jokes. Do you understand me? I'll *never* forgive you. Not if you try to leave me behind again." Janelle's voice cracked, but no tears were shed.

Lea had studied her for a long moment before simply nodding and wrapping her in a hug.

"I'm sorry," she said, and Gray knew it was true. He also knew she would make the same decision again, even if it had almost doomed them all.

Gray stood, walking to where Lea stood next to Janelle and placing a hand on her lower back. He couldn't stand to not be touching her in some way. Even the time it had taken for her reunions with her friends had felt like far too long, and had made his heart race and nausea fill his stomach.

"Vincent, what have we learned?" Gray asked, his body relaxing now that he was close to Lea again.

"Actually," Erik said sheepishly. "I think I know where he went."

Gray's eyebrows shot up. "How? And why didn't you tell me this sooner?"

"I only learned of it just before Lea woke up. A lot's happened since then. You know, coming back from the dead, finding the traitor. Janelle's verbal sparring match with Eudora. The eternal night."

"Which you also didn't tell me about," Gray pointed out, but he wasn't able to force anger into his tone. He was grateful that Erik hadn't interrupted them. That he'd had the opportunity to be with Lea as she fell apart and pulled herself back together, ready to face what was to come.

"Sorry about that. But everyone's been a bit preoccupied since then... And rightly so."

"Where is he?" Lea said, the room darkening. Her hand drifted to the flowers in her crown. No more petals had fallen since the last one hours ago, but not knowing when the next would fall had them both on edge. Gray caught himself glancing toward the crown every few seconds, searching each one for flecks of black or ash.

"I went back to where—" Erik paused, a shadow of grief flitting across his features. Janelle's hand drifted to his shoulder, and he cleared his throat, giving her a small smile. "I went back to where Alaric disappeared. There's a crater right in the middle of the field there. The moonflowers Lea planted are growing around it, avoiding it as if the ground itself is poisoned."

Lea nodded. "I was stealing his magic, or trying to, at least. Then he slammed his hand into the ground and was just gone—vanished into thin air."

"There's a handprint in the scorched earth. I touched it, and when I did, I saw something. An image flashed in my mind." Erik's eyebrows lowered as if trying to relive a memory.

Hope sparked behind Gray's sternum. It was a clue. A way forward.

"Was it in Desia?" Gray asked, walking to the large map of the kingdom spread out across his desk. "Describe the landmarks. I'm sure we can figure—"

"I know exactly where it is. Back at the castle, the old guard shed we used to play in as children."

Gray's mouth cracked open in surprise. "It's not possible, is it?" Gray looked to Vincent, who shrugged, his brows furrowing.

"Would he go back there? Somewhere he could so easily be found?" Vincent asked.

"I think that's exactly where he would go," Lea said. "He was losing. He knew he was going to die and only had a moment to make a decision. He chose the first place that came to mind. Is that somewhere he would think of easily?"

Gray's jaw clenched, and he nodded. "We spent a lot of time there as kids. We'd hide there sometimes when my father was on a rampage and looking to punish someone."

"Even if he did go there," Vincent said, "he wouldn't stay. He has to know that would be the first place we'd look for him. Right?"

"But it's a start," Thomas said. "And if he left some piece of himself here that showed us where he went, maybe there's something there, too. A trail to follow."

"I'd like to see the crater myself," Gray told Erik.

"I can show you, but when I touched it a second time, nothing happened. I'm not sure there's anything to see anymore."

"I'd still like to try. Lea, you said you were stealing his magic. Can you feel him? Can you follow it?"

"No." Lea said. "I tried, when I woke up. But the magic I was taking? It didn't feel like his. I think I was taking his stolen magic. When I..." she trailed off, eyes drifting down. "When I died," she said, choosing the word carefully, "I searched for the magic I took from him. I could feel my own magic beyond the veil, but all the magic I'd taken and the magic I'd given to our soldiers was gone. I think it went back to the earth. Or wherever it came from." Lea said.

Gray nodded. "That would make sense. The goddess said you have to kill Alaric and allow the magic he's stolen to return back where it originated from. Back into the universe."

"If Lea can't feel him, then we have no choice but to follow the clues we do have," Erik said.

Gray considered their options, his mind already spinning. Was it possible he'd actually return to the castle? The very first place they'd look? Then again, he'd only had seconds to disappear. If Lea was right that she'd significantly wounded him, he'd only had one chance to escape. Gray nodded. "The castle is the logical place to start."

"When do we leave?" Thomas asked.

"Normally, I'd say at first light." Gray sighed, running a hand through his hair. Exhaustion pulled at his bones, his lips pursed and his eyes heavy and ringed with dark circles.

"Let's take a few hours to rest, to let our army prepare. They can't stay here without us, it's too easy of a target."

"I'll take care of the armies," Vincent said, standing.

"Have everyone bring everything they'll need. We won't be returning until Alaric is dead."

CHAPTER 16

THOMAS

The last time Thomas had traveled from Bearswillow to Auropera, it had been in handcuffs. He'd been a boy then. A child, so short-sighted and naïve.

So many things had changed since he'd made that journey. In fact, it would be easier to list the things that were the same.

While he still loved Lea, it was in a very different way. His heart belonged to someone else now. At least, he wanted it to. It was headed in that direction. He wouldn't necessarily say that he was in love with Emma, but now that he'd lived through what he had, he also wouldn't say he was ever actually in love with Lea. Not really.

A flicker of shame worked its way up his spine as he thought about the things he'd said to her in his anger. The way he'd stood by and watched Alaric torment her. Thomas had been so self-righteous. He'd had so many excuses for why his behavior was acceptable back then, had rationalized that he'd never have been strong enough to defeat Alaric and that Lea needed tough love to see the error of her ways.

An arrogant fool. That's *exactly* what he'd been. And now, more than ever, he was determined to make it right. He wouldn't repeat his past mistakes. Not with Emma.

A ghost of a smile crossed Thomas's lips as he thought about a future with her. He'd learned so much, and was excited for the possibilities of what a relationship with Emma could bring. But first, they had to survive. All of them. And for that to happen, he needed to help better prepare Emma and the rest of his friends for whatever else they would face before the war was through.

Thomas wasn't naïve enough to think he knew more than the others. Gray and Erik were far more experienced than he was at fighting. But weapons? *That* was something he could do to help. A new weapon for each of them, with as much magic as he could push inside to give them all the best chance at survival.

He'd started working on them the moment they'd returned to the cavern, and while he was exhausted in a way he'd never experienced before, he couldn't seem to stop and rest. It was an incessant need. A drive that kept him pulling more and more magic out of himself as the eternal night replenished it.

The forest was unnaturally dark tonight, and even though he was grateful for the boost it gave his magic, it was unsettling how the sun hadn't risen the past several days. But even though it was so pitch black Thomas couldn't see further than an arm's reach in front of him, the woods were brimming with the chirping of crickets and croaking of frogs, a sign that all was well.

Only about a day's ride stood between them and their arrival in Auropera, but even in the eternal night, Thomas couldn't sleep. And for once, Erik's snoring wasn't the reason.

The closer they got to Auropera, the more desperate Thomas felt to finish Emma's weapon. To give her a way to help protect herself.

Thomas had felt so helpless as the events of the battle in Bearswillow unfolded. Even though they'd planned and prepared, despite the fact that he and Emma had hidden away as far from the battle as possible, and they *still* hadn't been safe. It was a feeling Thomas never wanted to experience again. So he had started on a dagger for Emma—the most complicated one he'd ever attempted to make.

He pulled it from his pocket bag, creeping as quietly as possible toward the crackling fire. Stepping over Lea's sword laying beside her, he examined it for damage. It was the perfect weapon for Lea. Strong and powerful and fierce. But Emma needed something more delicate. She wasn't a warrior, not with weapons, at least. It was one of the things he loved most about her—her kindness and softness.

It wasn't a weakness. Not by a long shot. Emma was strong in a way Thomas had never witnessed before. It was awe-inspiring, and made pride swell in his chest every time she spoke to the dead, or used her powers and empathy to help someone else in pain. It took immense strength to open up her emotions to the world, to allow herself to feel the suffering of others. He was still in awe of the courage it had taken for her to take Eudora's potion and tether herself to the other side. It was the only reason Lea and Gray were still with them, and the reason so many had been saved on the battlefield. Everything about her was truly remarkable.

In the flickering light of the fire, Thomas twisted the blade of the dagger to inspect it. His skin buzzed with the power thrumming within the metal, but there was room for more.

His magic hummed in his chest, begging to be released as if it, too, needed to protect Emma. Focusing on his power, he funneled it into the hilt of the small dagger. Its gold blade sparkled as he pushed more and more of his power inside, projecting out the protections he wanted the weapon to provide.

Protection from being snuck up on. That was his priority. If this worked, Emma would never be caught unaware again. He'd teach her basic self defense. As long as Emma knew what threats were coming at her, he had no doubt she'd find a way to protect herself.

It'd taken so much magic, so much time and energy, for the weapon to start to do what he wanted. Not quite as long as Lea's sword had taken him, but still days and days where, before the sun had refused to rise, he'd drained himself completely, needing to wait until his magic replenished itself before he could resume working on it.

He *felt* with absolute clarity when his magic solidified in the dagger, clicking into place with a dull thump in his head. Thomas exhaled, relaxing as he twisted the beautiful weapon in the firelight. Finally, it was finished.

Emma whimpered in her sleep, and Thomas rushed to her side, placing the hilt of the dagger in her hand. He might have made the weapon to alert her of threats, but that wasn't the only power he had imbued inside it.

The dagger would also protect her from what happened to her in her dreams. Every night so far on their journey, Emma's sleep had been restless, and more than once she'd woken with tears in her eyes. Every time, he'd held her, whispering soothing words until one night she'd finally confided in him that something had changed while she'd been in her deep slumber. That the potion Eudora had given her had opened her up to the dead even more than before.

Her dreams were now full of those who had passed as well, the dead somehow finding her as she drifted throughout her subconscious. Some simply told her their stories, grateful for a kind ear to listen to them, while others begged for help.

But no matter how much she wanted to, she couldn't do anything for them. It had taken a toll on her. Dark circles laid heavy beneath her eyes, and her rich brown skin had lost its glow, becoming sallow and dull. But even worse was that her genuine, heart-stoppingly beautiful smiles often seemed forced after the battle.

Thomas closed her fingers around the dagger, and the moment the metal touched her skin, her face relaxed, an almost imperceptible smile crossing her lips as she sighed and rolled over. Emma burrowed herself deeper beneath the covers, and Thomas's shoulders lowered, the tension in his neck easing.

He found a piece of cloth, wrapping it around the blade and making a mental note that he'd need to find a more permanent solution for keeping her safe from the sharp edge of the metal while she slept. But for tonight, he simply laid down next to her, placing his hand on top of the weapon to keep it still and praying to the gods that Emma would be safe from what was to come.

That they'd *all* be safe, and that tomorrow they would find the information they needed to help them finally end this war once and for all. Because while it didn't feel fair to begin a love story he might not survive to see, Thomas knew that if they could end this war, he would finally settle into a love like he'd always wanted.

CHAPTER 17

LEA

The streets were completely silent except for the clop of their horses' hooves.

It was odd approaching the castle from the main gates rather than sneaking in after they had so brazenly escaped in a fiery explosion during their wedding. Stranger, even, to do so in the pitch black of night. Lea had been certain that should they ever need to return, it would be with the use of magic to hide themselves, scrambling over walls and through tunnels. But such lengths hadn't been necessary.

Gray had received word from his mother that while the majority of Alaric's army had returned to Auropera, *he* seemingly had not. But if that was the truth, what had Erik seen?

Gray and Vincent had spent hours discussing the best way to approach Auropera, but Lea had told them she was done hiding. She doubted Alaric's soldiers would be brave enough to try to harm them—not in his absence—and certainly not when he'd abandoned them with no direction during battle. But even if they did, Lea was confident they were no match for the power inside her. They had no idea what she was capable of. The only one with power that rivaled her own was Alaric, and with him hiding away and nursing his wounds, Lea wasn't worried.

Which is why Lea had suggested they approach the castle directly and out in the open—a show of confidence. A power move. If anyone was foolish enough to attack, she would kill them quickly and effortlessly, and—most important—publicly.

Images of the snakes Lea had sent out to kill the remaining soldiers back in Bearswillow flashed through her mind. Janelle had told her about the bodies, their mouths gaping open and eyes burned out, and she'd demanded to see them herself. Had wanted proof of what her magic was capable of. Erik and the others had burned the bodies of the fallen rebels, but Alaric's men? There hadn't been time to dispose of them yet, and so Lea had visited the mass grave, taking in the horror of their deaths before incinerating them all with a flick of her wrist.

Destroy, her power begged, feeding off the memory, but Lea shoved it down, down, down. *Not yet,* she told it, grappling with every ounce of her self control as darkness surged like a tidal wave inside her.

Her power hissed in response, and Lea wondered how long she would be able to contain her primary magic. The pressure beneath her skin increased, pain prickling like a thousand needles pressing out from inside her body.

"Let some of it go. Just a bit," Gray encouraged her, sensing her struggle. With a deep breath, Lea allowed the wickedest parts of her to slither through her veins, surrounding all of them in a thick, black aura. Almost like smoke, but so dark that even against the black of the night, it was visible. The difference was immediate, the pain in her chest lessening and the pressure easing.

Lea straightened in her saddle as they neared the gate, pulling back on the reins to stop her new horse, a majestic black mare named Luna. Her memory flicked to the day she'd learned of Gray's true identity right here at this very gate. Little did she know, walking through the portcullis would lead her to this. To a greater love than she could have ever imagined, and more pain and loss than she could even fathom.

She hopped off her horse, boots clicking on the dense wood of the bridge. The portcullis was lowered, the door blocking them off from the inside of the castle grounds, but it was of no consequence to Lea. As she threw up a shield of air around her friends, the black fog around her turned into flames. She didn't need to look back to make sure they were safe, allowing her darkness to map out her surroundings as she let the inferno grow, the flames licking up her skin and across the ground. Fire met the base of the door and spread upward, consuming the wood so quickly the soldiers on the other side had no time to even shout before it was burned away completely.

Through the smoke filled opening, Lea stalked forward, relishing in finally allowing her true nature to take over as she spread her flames even further into the courtyard.

Destroy.

Destroy.

Destroy.

The voice was stronger now, begging. No, demanding. It was a primal need, and Lea reveled in it as a chorus of screams echoed against the stone walls surrounding the castle. These soldiers saw what Alaric did and had still chosen to serve him. They didn't deserve her mercy, and so they wouldn't receive any. For the first time since she'd awoken, Lea didn't need to fight against the darkness inside her. She could become it.

As Lea made her way toward the front of the castle, she sent out snakes of darkness, the shadow monsters destroying and consuming whatever fell in their path. Of its own volition, her magic wrapped around a soldier's neck and dragged him backward into the flames, burning him alive as it snapped the neck of another. Her dark magic sighed in relief as it killed, dozens of soldiers taking final breaths full of smoke, their mouths frozen in screams of agony.

No one tried to stop her. Not Gray or Erik or even Emma. They knew better.

The main door to the castle loomed before them, beckoning. There would be more of Alaric's men inside. Hundreds. Maybe thousands.

She could end them, too, right here and now, before the few who had escaped were able to warn them. Before they could flee. Cowards just like their king.

Lifting her chin, Lea took a step forward.

Destroy.

Destroy.

Destroy.

But Gray's voice pulled her back.

"Lea." It wasn't an order. Not a plea or a proclamation of worry. It was simply a reminder. *You control the darkness. It does not control you. You've expended some of the power. That has to be enough for now.* She could almost hear his voice in her mind again, reassuring her as he'd done so many times since she'd awoken from beyond the veil. Clenching her jaw, Lea reluctantly reigned in her power, just enough to fade the haze of fury and revenge clouding her mind.

"Lead the way," she said, extending her arm and handing over the decision-making to Gray. It was better that way, right now. When she could barely hear herself think over the voice begging her to turn around and end more lives.

"Take the castle," Gray told Tanad, his eyes flicking toward the stone palace that had been his prison for so many years. Lea wondered if maybe his darkness was screaming for him to destroy it as well, if something inside him was begging him to bring that wicked place down stone by stone until nothing was left.

Tanad nodded, turning to his generals to give the order.

Gray didn't wait for him to finish, trusting Tanad to do his part. With long, confident strides, Gray stalked forward. Lea's primary magic rebelled as she followed behind him, surging in her chest with a swell so enormous it caused her ribs to expand painfully.

You're going the wrong way, the darkness seemed to say, begging her to turn around, but she forced her feet forward, gritting her teeth. The wind whistled through the courtyard, the bugs going silent as they passed. Lea's head remained on a swivel, scanning their surroundings for lurking threats. Secretly hoping she would find one to channel her magic into, something to eviscerate to soothe the sharp edge of need.

Thomas remained close to Emma, who held a new dagger in a white knuckle grip. Janelle was hand-in-hand with Erik, who stood slightly in front of her as if he could shield her from danger with his own body. But none of those things mattered. *She* would protect them.

As they rounded the back of the castle, a small shed came into view. A familiar tang of foreign magic hit Lea's nose, all the confirmation she needed to know Alaric had been here. She'd felt that very magic before, sensed it and smelled it and tasted it, but the trail was muted, as if the wind had carried the scent into the distance.

"You were right, Erik. But he's not here anymore," Lea said. Gray clenched his fists but nodded grimly, likely sensing the same thing. If Noah were here... A sharp stab of pain made Lea's breath catch.

Sweet Noah, with his tracking magic. Maybe if he were still here, they could follow his trail. The pain morphed into anger as the image of his skull bouncing down the hill replayed in her head.

"Let's go inside," Gray said, placing a hand on her lower back as if sensing where her mind had gone. "Maybe there's some hint to where he fled." With an order for Erik to stand outside, Gray kicked the door inward and disappeared into the shadows. Lea followed behind him, grumbling under her breath that she would have liked to kick the door in. It wouldn't help with her darkness, but it would have at least felt good to get some tension out of her body.

Lea choked on the dust kicked up by the door's movement, her vision adjusting to the complete darkness without the light of the moon to illuminate the windowless hut. The feeling of Alaric's magic was clearer here, like a fingerprint on a clean, washed window. Lea ran her fingers along the freezing stone walls, then the floor, hoping for some sort of vision like Erik had seen when he'd touched the battleground. But there was no crater here, no handprint seared into the ground. Wherever he had gone, it didn't appear that he'd used his magic to disappear, and Lea found comfort in that, hoping he was too wounded to have expended so much energy.

"Blood," Gray said, interrupting her thoughts. Lea's magic soared, rejoicing as her shadows slithered to where Gray squatted in a corner, his fingertips pressed against a dark irregular splotch in the dirt. He stood, following the trail of small red dots to the back exit, a wooden door with a bloody handprint on the latch.

Lea and Gray shared a tension filled look as Gray placed his calloused hand on top of the bloody handprint, and Lea held her breath, praying for some sort of clue, but his eyes remained clear.

"Nothing," he said, confirming Lea's suspicion that Alaric hadn't used magic to vanish this time. Gray pushed open the door, and Thomas jumped to attention outside.

"Dammit!" Gray hissed, the drops of blood disappearing into the long, unruly grass. Lea walked forward, trying to follow the trail of magic as it led away from the castle, but the farther she got from the shed, the more faint it became until it disappeared altogether. Lea had known Alaric wasn't there, but the fact that there wasn't a single clue to where he had gone caused fury to rise up her throat, hot enough that Lea feared speaking would cause it to shoot from her mouth and burn the hut to the ground. Black flames grew around her feet, gray smoke twirling into the sky. But a heavy hand fell on her shoulder, its calming effect instant.

"We knew it was unlikely we'd find anything." Gray squeezed her shoulder. "This changes nothing. We'll find him," he said.

Lea wanted to believe him, desperately. But it was as if the gods were taunting them. As he said the words, a petal fell from Lea's crown, floating down in front of her eyes and turning to ash in Lea's flames.

She sucked in a deep breath, her fingers raising toward the crown on her head, but she stopped herself. The gods *were* taunting her. Of that, she had no doubt. But she refused to let them see her fear. Lea clenched her jaw and turned on her heel, ignoring the shocked silence of her friends and their panicked stares, and stormed back toward the castle.

She didn't bother arguing with him, didn't have the energy or patience. But Gray was wrong in saying it changed nothing. Their lack of finding any hint or clue to guide them changed everything. Without a way forward, and with time running out, they were doomed.

CHAPTER 18

GRAY

Nothing could have prepared Gray for what he'd see once he walked into the castle, but it wasn't his mate's shadows or her searing black fire that made him stop in his tracks. What made him pause was that the castle was in utter ruin. The once grand chandelier lay smashed on the stone floor, a million sharp, sparkling pieces scattered like diamonds across the blood-stained rug. The rich, ancient tapestries that had hung proudly in the great hall for hundreds of years had been torn to ribbons and now swayed gently in the breeze coming in through the shattered windows. Dust and debris were everywhere, a thick layer of glass and stone that crunched under his boots as he turned in a slow circle, taking in the damage.

Not a single one of Alaric's soldiers were inside, but Gray wasn't sure if that was because Tanad had taken care of them while they'd searched the hut, or if they had simply fled upon their arrival. His mother had told him in her letters that their home had fallen into disrepair, but this was far more than a neglected building. It was a battlefield, destroyed by a madman in a wretched push for power. The desperation was evident in every piece of glass and stone and cloth.

"You." Gray pointed to the eldest of a group of young maids cowering in the corner. Lea drew her sword and Gray stiffened, watching out of the corner of his eye. He could feel Lea's need to fight—to use her power. He could only imagine that seeing the evidence of whatever evil had taken place here was only fueling her primary magic and worsening her need to destroy. But as far as they knew, these girls were innocent.

Gritting her teeth, Lea squeezed the hilt of the sword, then nodded for him to continue. Gray's breath loosened, his heart slowing. She was only discerning the truth. For now, she had control of her darkness.

"How did this happen?" Gray asked the oldest girl, reeling in his shadows. Her shoulders lowered a fraction as the shadows receded from the room.

"Alaric. He…" she trailed off, her eyes filling with tears. "We've done our best to clean the mess, but he killed so many, we haven't made much progress. Anyone with magic, all his advisors…"

"Our sister," one of the younger girls said, her voice breaking.

Emma took a deep breath and stepped forward, wrapping an arm around the terrified girl's shoulders. She began to lead her from the room, but Gray stopped them.

"When did this happen?" he asked.

"Weeks ago, before the army left."

"And has he returned?" Gray asked. "My brother?"

The girl shook her head furiously. "We haven't seen him, thank the gods. Many of his soldiers returned. Those with nowhere else to go."

"Where are those who returned?" Erik asked, standing straighter.

The girl's eyes darted sideways. "The king—the foreign one—he took them to the dungeons."

"What about my mother? Queen Genevieve? Did she return as well?" Gray's heart skipped a beat as he asked the question. There was every chance Alaric's soldiers would have killed her on sight.

"No. I haven't seen her since before she fled."

Gray's stomach twisted into knots and he ran a hand through his chestnut hair, unsure if it was a good or bad sign that she hadn't been seen. He paused, examining the girls. They were trembling, clinging to one another as if afraid he was just as wicked as his father and brother.

"Do you support Alaric's cause?" Gray asked. "Any of you?" He met each girl's eyes, lifting his chin as if daring them to lie.

"No!" The eldest girl swallowed. "Like I said, this is our home. We had nowhere else to go."

"Very well," said Lea, confirming that they were telling the truth. She sheathed her sword.

Gray sighed, rubbing the back of his neck with his hand. Exhaustion weighed down his movements. They were getting nowhere, still had no clue as to the whereabouts of his brother. "You may stay," Gray said, and the girl relaxed, sagging into Emma's arms.

"Thank you," she said. "We'll do anything we can to help. We can keep cleaning—"

Gray held up a hand, stopping her. "For now, rest. Then maybe you can begin to prepare some food. Find Elise. She's likely in the kitchens already. It's been some time since we've had a proper meal, and many more will be arriving to eat soon."

"Of course," she said, allowing Emma to lead her from the room. They seemed familiar with one another, and Gray realized it was likely they had worked together before the rebels had left. Guilt gnawed at his gut as he realized how young and unprepared for war they were. Could he have done something to get them out? But he shook away the thought. Guilt wouldn't help them find Alaric or change the past.

He turned to Erik with a curt nod. "Have our men clear the debris. There should be enough rooms between the barracks and both wings to house our armies. We'll set up base camp here."

"On it," Erik said, turning on his heel to leave.

"Thomas," Gray said. "We'll need more weapons."

"Of course," Thomas said, dipping his chin.

Gray finally turned back to Lea, and his tone softened. "You should rest," he said, his thumbs tracing the dark circles below her eyes.

But Lea's jaw clenched. "I don't need rest," she said. "Show me to the king's dungeons. I have a bargain to fulfill."

CHAPTER 19

ERIK

The main dungeon had never been so full. At least, not to Erik's knowledge. Sure, there had been times over the years when the cells were doubled—tripled, even. But those occasions had been *nothing* like this. Each cell contained at least fifteen men, packed so tightly he wasn't sure they would be able to lie down to sleep.

At least three hundred royal soldiers were crammed into the stuffy, windowless chamber. Three hundred men pleading for Erik to let them go, begging on their knees for mercy. The ones who could manage to get to their knees, at least.

"They haven't stopped since my men rounded them up. Each one of them claims they had no choice, that they want to join our side," Tanad said, coming to stand by Erik.

"Of course they're saying that now," Erik said, crossing his arms as his eyes skipped across the prisoners. He didn't know exactly what he was looking for, though he did know who. It had been on his mind ever since Janelle had told him about her past. Had been hanging over his head and heavy on his shoulders every moment of every day.

Erik wondered if he would know the bastard when he saw him. If he'd be able to identify the man who had hurt Janelle.

"We took their weapons," Tanad said, mistaking Erik's reason for his attention on the prisoners. But, even though he had countless things he should be doing, including ensuring the prisoners were unarmed and safely behind bars, he wasn't here on official business. Certainly wasn't here to make sure they had been properly disarmed.

"Don't trust a word they say," Erik told Tanad, lifting his chin. "None of them are to be released without Gray's orders." Tanad nodded, likely already coming to that conclusion on his own. It probably went without saying, but these were the men who hadn't been deemed worthy of joining the rebellion. So loyal to the king and Alaric that they'd known it was either a lost cause or an unnecessary risk to try to sway them.

Erik and Gray would have to discuss how to handle these prisoners, now that they'd taken back control of Auropera. He was certain that many of them did despise Alaric, especially after he had abandoned them in a ruined castle with no guidance or protection. But there were too many variables to simply let these prisoners pledge their allegiance to the cause and trust that they wouldn't turn on them once the time was right.

"Thank you for handling it," Erik said.

"Of course. Shall we reconvene with Gray to determine our next steps?" Tanad asked.

"Soon," Erik said. "I have something rather important I must see to first."

Tanad leaned back, narrowing his eyes, but he didn't say a word. With a knowing look and a nod, he left, and Erik followed behind, making sure the door was firmly shut behind him.

A buzz of magic brushed against Erik's neck, pulling his head toward the door, and all sound from outside the dungeons suddenly ceased. As if sensing whatever Erik was planning was likely private, and possibly loud, Tanad seemed to have placed an enchantment to block out whatever screams would come of what he was planning to do next.

Erik couldn't help but smile. He'd always liked that guy.

The prisoners shouted, begging for anyone to free them, but it was of no use. No one would hear them, thanks to Tanad.

"Quiet," Erik said, his voice low. Lethal. The men around him instantly stopped their pleading, silence spreading throughout the entire dungeon like a plague. Fire crackled off his skin as he let his rage feed his magic, the stone beneath his feet charring. Erik continued to search each face, some of them familiar, some of them strangers, hoping that somehow, he would know when he saw Stefan and Jakob.

"I'm looking for someone," he said as he slowly stepped forward, the heels of his boots clicking on the damp floor. "A man named Jakob." Hushed whispers bounced off the domed ceilings, but no one stepped forward. Not a single soldier.

"Then I'm looking for a man—any man—who knows a Jakob."

Shuffling sounded from the back corner, followed by a "Shut up!" Erik's head snapped toward the noise, bringing fire to his fingertips. "Tell me what you know. *Now*."

The silence was deafening, and rage churned through Erik's blood. He called fire to his fingertips, allowing it to drip from his hands like lava. "It would be a shame for the whole lot of you to die to protect one lowlife. Trust me, the man I'm looking for isn't worthy of your protection." He pushed more fire through his hands, causing the dungeons to glow a vibrant orange. "*Or* your death."

More hushed whispers. Erik lowered his chin and raised his hands.

"Wait—" A voice called from the back cell, the men inside parting around a young boy as he stepped forward. A boy who couldn't be more than eighteen years old. Tears shined in his eyes, his throat bobbing as he walked.

"I'm Jakob," he said, his voice so small and terrified Erik wondered if he was even younger than seventeen.

"Don't lie to me, boy. Don't take the fall for someone else."

"I'm not lying, I swear it."

Erik wished Lea was with him with her sword in her hand to discern the truth.

"It's not you who I'm looking for. His name is Jakob. His brother is named Stefan." Erik's blood heated, just uttering their names. "Them, and their group of friends."

The young boy cleared his throat, his shoulders visibly relaxing. "There is another with the same name. I don't know him well. He's older than I am, but I believe he has a brother."

"Where is he?" Erik asked, believing him.

The boy blanched, turning white. "I don't know."

"Where is he?" Erik roared to the entire dungeon, spinning in a circle and shooting fire from his hands, so hot it singed the uniforms of the nearby soldiers.

"We don't know! None of us know." A man stepped forward, one Erik knew well. Colin.

A soldier he and Gray had very specifically *not* recruited to join their cause. "Even if we did, why would we give his location away to a traitor like you?" he hissed, spitting at Erik's feet.

Erik froze, and the men around Colin backed away, as if sensing the charge crackling in the air. "I hope he finds you," Colin continued. "And I hope he kills you for what you've done to us. For betraying our king."

"If anyone's memory is triggered," Erik said, ignoring Colin's words as he stalked past him, "and you remember Jakob's location, you'll be rewarded. Lead me to him *or* his brother, and I will promise you won't meet the same fate as your brother in arms," Erik said, raising his hand and sending a steady stream of fire directly into Colin's chest.

Colin hardly had time to scream before he collapsed into a pile of smoldering ash. The silence somehow felt even louder this time, the only sound the pop of smoldering embers.

Erik turned to leave, waving away the smell of singed flesh.

"What did he do? What is Jakob's crime?" a soldier called out, and Erik froze in the doorway, not bothering to turn around.

"He hurt the woman I love," Erik said, slamming the door shut firmly behind him.

CHAPTER 20

LEA

Lea had expected the door to the dungeons beneath the Black King's wing to be as unassuming as any other she'd walked through in this castle. Because if whatever was inside was so important that Eudora wanted it so desperately, it would stand to reason that he would have hidden it among the hundreds of wooden doors everywhere else. But the door to Brennus's private dungeons was *anything* but unassuming.

It was a beacon of danger. Made of pure, polished iron, its condition was impeccable, the metal almost unnaturally shiny and buzzing with that familiar tang of magic that held what Lea now recognized as the imprint of the Black King. She steeled herself against the waves of power thrumming off the door, though she wasn't sure if it actually came from the door itself or from whatever hid behind it.

Or even if it came from simply being in this part of the castle. A place she'd never visited before, had never *wanted* to visit before.

It looked no different from Gray's wing, with walls and floors built from large cuts of stone, paintings and tapestries adorning the halls. It was dark and cold, with only the occasional window to brighten up the space, and the feeling of distress and savagery that hung in the air and spread into her lungs with every breath made her uneasy. The longer she remained, the more her magic pulsed and shouted.

Destroy.

Destroy.

Destroy.

And that was Lea's plan. Whatever was within the cage was so heavily protected, not even Eudora knew how to get it out. Lea imagined a monster with black eyes and dozens of clawed hands reaching toward her and raking at her skin, and she shivered, pushing the unwelcome image away. Though it would be unwise to trust Eudora, she couldn't help but think that whatever was inside the cage couldn't, or wouldn't, hurt her.

If the witch's visions were true, she was destined to defeat Alaric. And even if Eudora was an evil bitch, she clearly held some sentiment toward King Tanad. To allow Desia to fall to Alaric would be to hand Calir over on a silver platter, and Lea simply couldn't make herself believe that Eudora would do that. Allowing Tanad to be harmed seemed to be the one line she wasn't willing to cross.

It was a feeling she understood. She would rather die than allow Gray to be harmed. As if he heard his name in her thoughts, he turned to her, eyes assessing. Even without the mate bond, Lea could feel the tension rolling off of his shoulders. She didn't miss the way his fingers clenched and unclenched at his sides, his knuckles turning white. But he remained silent, simply standing beside her until she was ready to enter and face whatever it was Eudora couldn't face herself.

Lea lifted her chin, indicating to Gray that she was ready, and he swung the door inward, moving out of the way as Lea's shadows spread throughout the room, mapping it out in the way Erik had taught her what seemed like years ago. Gray's shadows intermingled with hers as he did the same, and the feeling of his darkness wrapping around hers brought her comfort as, together, they stepped forward.

The room was so very different from the one she'd trained at in Calir. Instead of a large triangular space, her shadows slipped down cold stone stairs and wrapped around old, crumbling columns that rose at least sixty feet toward enormous arched ceilings.

Her shadows continued onward, branching off into different rooms that opened up along the side walls. In some alcoves, they slipped inside easily, scraping through the shattered remains of what used to be wooden doors. At some of the entryways, her darkness was forced to slide through cracks, their doors still in place and firmly shut. Chains and manacles hung from the walls, some spaces filled with torture devices that Lea didn't allow herself to examine too closely.

As her shadows prodded every corner of the dungeons, she could *feel* the vibrations of the pain of its past victims, echoes of agony that made her stomach churn and her dark magic rejoice all in the same measure. Scowling at the immense depravity and inhumanity etched into the foundation, she tried to push the feeling down. *You control the darkness,* Gray's voice said in her head. Not through the mate bond, but instead from somewhere inside her—the mantra he'd repeated every day as he watched her struggle with controlling the power inside her.

She pushed her shadows even deeper, until—there. A box. An exact replica of the one she'd seen in Calir.

Lea stepped further into the chamber, covering her nose at the stench permeating the space. Sweat and excrement and despair soaked into every inch of stone, and Lea wondered where the Black King's prisoners had been taken once he'd been killed. Had they been disposed of before Alaric had gone mad? Or set free once he'd fled?

Small, firm pieces of debris crunched beneath her boot as she navigated the darkness, but it wasn't gravel or rock. It crackled like splinters of wood, but harder. Bone, if she had to guess. A shiver ran down her spine at the image, nausea bubbling in her stomach as she waded deeper into the fog of emotions thickening the air around her. It wasn't just pain and suffering and agony. It wasn't simple destruction and wreckage.

It was sadness. Grief so thick it stole the air from her lungs as it crashed over her in waves, and the further they traveled into the dungeon, the more intense the feeling became. Neither she nor Gray said a word as they approached the cage, but she could sense his shadows intermingling with hers as they explored every inch of it, mapping it out in their mind's eye.

Lea moved closer, her shadows prodding the thick, impenetrable metal of the box. They slithered along every inch, exploring every lock, every obstacle to opening the cage. Eight locks adorned the cage in total, some of them as simple as a chain that only needed to be slid along a groove and out of the large divot at the end.

There was a combination lock, a keyhole, a padlock, plus several other locks she had never seen before. A soft orange glow washed over the cage as Lea called on her flames, and she approached the first lock. The easiest one. She grabbed the knob to the chain, sliding it out into the little pocket that would allow it to fall free, but just before she pulled it out of the notch, she paused.

Something dark and dangerous buzzed from the metal, causing the hair on her arms to stand on end. Lea's own magic recoiled in response, and she stepped away.

"Move back," Lea ordered, her voice sharp. Gray narrowed his eyes but listened, stepping away, and Lea followed, the foreboding buzz of magic easing slightly as she stepped back. No longer within view of the cage, Lea reached out with a long trail of darkness, flicking the lock free.

The castle shuttered and rumbled as if it were a beast waking from a deep slumber. A flash of light bolted through the chamber, a brief bang that lit up the pitch black of the dungeons illuminating the horrific machines used for gods knew what torture that had occurred there. She forced the images of blades and chains and ropes from her mind, peeking around the corner.

Where she'd been standing only moments before was a hole in the stone floor at least two feet wide and eight inches deep. Gray's head snapped toward her, but she ignored his fiery stare. His hand twitched as if he wanted to pull her out of the dungeon altogether, but instead he clenched it, stopping himself, and Lea's shoulders lowered a fraction in relief.

She was standing on the edge of a blade, the fury growing in her chest so potent, she worried she was about to explode. Of course, it wouldn't be as simple as opening the locks. She'd known that already, deep down, but it didn't change that she'd wished that just once, something would just be straightforward and simple.

Lea moved forward with tentative steps to examine the cage, hovering her fingers just above a padlock. The same dark energy radiated into her skin, making her own magic twist uncomfortably. "Dammit!" Lea cursed, pulling her hand back despite her sudden urge to smash her fist against the cage. "They're spelled. Every one of them."

Gray cursed under his breath, his jaw going tight before inching forward. "Maybe I can open it," he said. "Maybe someone of my bloodline—"

"No," Lea snapped, holding up a hand. "You will *not* sacrifice yourself again." She narrowed her eyes, giving him a look that would have killed a lesser man.

Gray's eyes softened, but he didn't argue. Tentatively, Lea prodded the cage again with her magic. Seven more locks. Seven locks enchanted with who knows what spells that would detonate once they were opened. She spread out her darkness, sliding them across every inch of the cage. If she couldn't go through the locks, she would have to find another way.

Closing her eyes, she focused on the seams of the box, testing the smooth metal with as much force as she could muster until—there. A tiny crack. Lea's heart swelled, her darkness rejoicing as she pushed against the smallest sliver at the very top back corner of the cage. A fissure that couldn't be more than a centimeter long where it felt like the welding had been incomplete.

"Out," Lea said. "All the way, this time."

"I'm not leaving," Gray said. "If you need my help—"

"I can do this on my own." Lea didn't even look at him. "But I can't if I'm worrying about you."

"Azalea—"

"Do you not trust me?" Lea asked, finally swinging her head to stare him down. "Do you not think I'm capable?"

"Of course I do."

"Then, let me do this," she growled, refusing to back down. Lea knew she was being controlling. That if the roles were reversed, she would never leave his side. But she didn't care. Not when she'd already watched the life drain from his eyes once before. This was already their second chance. There would not be a third.

Gray hesitated, his shoulders tight. It took several moments, but Lea could tell when he relented. He reached out and cupped her cheek, touching her for just a moment longer than a casual goodbye before sighing and leaving the room.

With a hard click, the door shut firmly behind him, and Lea finally exhaled. She pulled the sword on her hip from its sheath, squeezing the hilt tightly as she followed the thread of magic that connected the sword's powers to her own. With a slow exhale, she pulled its magic inside her, bending it to her will to create an impermeable shield of air around her body and sending a gust of wind to hold the door firmly shut.

Without giving herself time to falter or second guess her plan, she allowed her shadows to seep through the tiny crack in the cage, forcing them inside until they filled every inch of space. All except for the small mound that lay curled in the back right corner. Whatever it was, it was alive, its back rising and falling with deep, even breaths as if it were asleep. Lea prodded the pile of cloth and skin. Human, she realized as she mapped out the shape. It was curled up in a ball, its knees pulled to its chest and its head tucked beneath thin, frail arms.

Even though it was only her shadows touching the person, Lea's stomach rolled at the filth it was living in. The person's hair was matted and long, its skin caked with dirt and who knew what else.

A chill ran down Lea's spine. How horrible must the person inside be to be forced to live this way? Were they a monster in human clothes? Or were they simply so powerful, the king hadn't been comfortable with allowing them to roam the dungeons freely?

Lea forced down her revulsion and spread a shield of air, along with her shadows, placing it firmly around the form to protect it. Whoever it was, whatever they had done, Lea was certain that her deal with Eudora wouldn't be complete unless it survived her breaking it free.

Once she was certain that both she and the figure were protected, she pulled away the shield around her primary magic, allowing it the freedom to escape. Like the click of a lock of a different kind, she opened that door inside her, power exploding in a spectacular display of black flames and shadows.

Destroy.

Destroy.

Destroy.

Lea sighed, the pressure in her chest easing as she funneled it through that crack, pushing more and more of her power inside until the seams groaned and the iron buckled outward. She threw her head back, letting the magic expand and explore. Now that her raw power was free, she closed her eyes, savoring the sweet feeling of relief—but it was short-lived.

Far too soon, the cage exploded outward, the metal buckling and breaking into jagged, deadly fragments and crashing throughout the dungeon. Lea ducked as a piece embedded itself into the wall just behind her head, another several bouncing off her shield and shattering into smaller pieces.

Her magic swelled, building and straining as debris rained down around her. It pushed out further, snaking through the dungeons. The ceiling creaked, small pebbles joining the ash now floating down like snow.

Destroy.

Lea sucked in a sharp breath as too much magic escaped, cracks forming beneath her feet.

Destroy.

"Azalea!" Gray banged on the door, and she shuddered, biting her lip as she tried to control the magic.

Destroy.

"Lea! Open the door!" Gray shouted again, and she wanted to. But the magic overwhelmed her, fire spreading along the cracks and climbing the walls. Her chest hurt, a searing pain that made her worry the skin was being ripped from her bones as the darkness burst outward.

A guttural groan ripped from her throat.

"Come back to me, Lea!" Gray roared, his fists beating the door with an unrelenting rhythm.

Gray. Her husband. Her mate. *You control the darkness,* his voice said in her head, drowning out the constant call to destroy.

With every ounce of her strength, Lea demanded the darkness return back into her chest. It fought back against her, but she refused to let it win. A dribble of blood dripped from her nose, as she grit her teeth and closed off her primary magic. It roared in fury, raking long nails against her ribs and throat, but she allowed Gray to become the mantra in her head.

You control the darkness.

You.

You.

You.

Finally, her shadows receded and her flames dimmed, the agony in her body easing to a dull throb.

She wiped her bloody nose on her sleeve as a figure walked forward through the smoke—a woman holding a hand out in front of her—barely visible through the thick haze of ash and muttering under her breath.

Lea allowed the door to unlock, and Gray burst inside, spinning her around as his hands traced her face, then her arms and her torso, looking for injuries, but Lea didn't look at him. She was too focused on the woman now emerging from the shrapnel that had only moments before been her cage.

Lea pulled back her flames to better see her, a pang of pity settling in her stomach. She was small and frail, and her ribs protruded even through her thin shift. Her bones looked as if a strong breeze could snap them with ease, her elbows the largest part of her arms. But even her emaciated appearance wasn't what caused Lea's stomach to roll and her skin to break out in goosebumps.

No. It was the woman's eyes. Eyes that had been so horribly disfigured they were completely scarred closed.

"My father's witch," Gray said, pulling Lea behind him. "That's what Eudora wanted."

"What? Why would she want her?" Lea asked, goosebumps creeping up her arms.

"Because *she* is the one who was helping him strengthen the spell for the Lonely Death."

CHAPTER 21

GRAY

The witch now waited in a cell of a different kind. Not a cage, per se, but a locked room with no way out except a regular wooden door. One Gray now stood in front of, arms crossed and magic ready. He had called on his shadows immediately once he realized who'd been inside the cage, a jolt of fear and anger buzzing along his skin at seeing her scarred face again.

Gray remembered the first time he'd seen the witch, her horrible, disfigured eyes seared into his brain for eternity. She hadn't been the first witch who'd lived within the palace, but she was by far the most tormented. Gray had wondered on more than one occasion why the king beat and burned her, and then he realized. *This* witch was strong willed. Had not been as easily broken as the witch before her—a tiny thing who'd been so afraid of Brennus's might, she'd agreed to his every whim, including creating the Lonely Death. She'd been only a shell of a woman when she died, and his father had been determined for his new, shiny witch to become the same.

Gray wondered if she had. Years and years in a cage could break you, but it could also make you go mad, and if that was the case, Gray would not be caught unprepared. But instead of showing any sort of aggression, the woman had simply crossed her arms around her emaciated stomach and asked who was there and if she could have a glass of water.

As Gray had walked toward her to check for weapons, she'd flinched at the first sound of his heeled boot hitting the stone. A jolt of pity settled in his chest, surprising him. This was all her fault, after all. Even if his father had lied about her temperament, at a minimum, she'd been complicit in his plans. Without her, the Lonely Death wouldn't be nearly as strong. It wouldn't have spread to Calir through the portal.

But Gray had seen morally strong men give in to his father before. Could he fault her if years of torture at his hands had made her give in to his wicked demands?

His stomach twisted.

Yes, he could. But could he also allow himself to feel pity for the clearly broken woman? It appeared, to his ire, the answer was yes.

Once they'd returned upstairs, Gray had asked Elise to get some of the maids to bring a bath for the filthy witch. Blood and dirt caked her skin, making the scars across her eyes appear all the more gruesome. He wasn't sure what Eudora had planned for this woman, but the bargain had been made all the same, and the least Gray could do was allow the woman some dignity before handing her over to a witch even more evil than herself.

Lea stood against the wall as they waited, using a dagger to pick the dirt from beneath her fingernails. She hadn't said much since they'd discovered the witch, but the sharp edge of her tension and anger seemed to have dulled. The tight lines of her jaw had relaxed a bit, as had the tension in her shoulders.

"What are you thinking?" Gray asked, anger bubbling up his spine at the missing mate bond and his inability to sense her thoughts and emotions.

"I'm wondering what happened to her eyes," Lea said plainly. "Why, if she helped the Black King, he would harm her so horribly?"

"My father could be very convincing," Gray said wryly, fighting off a shiver as a memory of him holding a courtier's head under water until he submitted to his will flashing through his mind.

"She must not have done it willingly," Lea said, pretending to examine her nails. It wasn't pity Gray heard in her voice, just a plain statement of fact. He could practically see the wheels turning in her mind, trying to piece together what had happened.

"Maybe there was something he didn't want her to see?" Gray said.

"Or maybe she'd seen too much," Lea answered, finally meeting his eyes, her brows drawing together.

The door at the end of the hallway swung open, and a cold breeze swept through the corridor and rustled the tapestries. Gray bristled at the immediate way the air seemed to thicken with ill intent.

Eudora, come to collect her prize.

Gray's shadows begged him to set them free. To block off the witch. To keep her from ever coming close to Lea again. It didn't matter to him that Tanad was fond of Eudora. In fact, he didn't understand it at all. She'd done nothing but trick him for her own self-serving purposes for *years*, and he was certain this was no different.

"Where is she?" Eudora wasted no time asking.

"What do you want with her?" Lea sheathed her dagger and straightened from where she leaned against the wall. Eudora's answering smile was taunting, and she flipped her long white hair behind her shoulders.

"I don't think that information was part of our deal." Eudora strode forward, her movements far too graceful for the supposed age of her body. "But I'm feeling kind today. Show her to me, and I'll consider telling you."

Lea's chin lifted slightly, defiance etched to the tight lines around her eyes. "Or maybe I'll kill you now and be done with it," Lea said, her eyes flashing black. The two women stared each other down, and Gray watched, hesitating. Lea couldn't kill Eudora. Surely she knew that. Not if they wanted Tanad's help with this war. They needed his forces. His army provided even more men and women than their own for the cause.

Was this a tactic to get information? Or was that darkness inside her truly threatening to kill the witch and destroy their relationship with Tanad, the best ally they had.

"Considering you weren't exactly forthright with your deal with Gray—you know, that *little* sacrifice that you failed to mention would cause us to lose our mate bond and both of our lives—I think you can forgive me for wanting a little something out of this exchange, too."

Eudora narrowed her eyes, her smile faltering. "The terms of the deal were set. My end was fulfilled. Let me have her."

"No." Lea walked forward with slow, deliberate steps, pulling her sword from its sheath and wrapping her fingers tightly around the hilt. "If she was capable of helping the Black King with the Lonely Death, then she's capable of far more. Her magic combined with yours could destroy the world. So I'll ask one more time. Why do you want her? Who is she?"

Eudora's smile twisted cruelly, and Gray's stomach dropped, absolutely certain that whatever was about to come out of her mouth was going to hurt Lea somehow.

"Who she is is another question altogether, my sweet girl. You should've just asked that to begin with," Eudora said with mock sympathy.

"Enough with the games," Gray snapped, his shadows rolling across the floor. He was tired of the witch and her puzzles and half answers.

"So testy, all of you." Eudora rolled her eyes, unbothered. She looked down at her hands, brushing a smudge off her ring finger.

"Get the fuck on with it, Eudora," Gray demanded. His heart pounded, his fingers tensing at his sides. "Or I'll—"

"As to why I want her," Eudora interrupted, as if Gray hadn't been speaking at all, "I will tell you once I see proof that you did, in fact, retrieve who I asked for without harming her. As a kindness, and a show of good faith that I am, in fact, not the horrible bitch you and your purple-haired friend believe me to be. But as far as who she is, well, I'm surprised you don't know. The resemblance is uncanny, don't you think, Evander?"

Gray pictured the frail witch in his mind. Her scarred, disfigured face was so mutilated, it would be impossible to tell if there was a resemblance to anyone beneath all those scars. Lea tensed beside him, her jaw going tight. Her eyes cut to his, searching, and he shook his head, confirming that he wasn't sure what Eudora was talking about, either.

"You still don't know?" Eudora's eyes lit up with delight, and Gray braced himself for whatever she was about to say, preparing for the chaos or despair her confession would cause.

Eudora grinned, a sickly sweet smile that made Gray's blood run cold. "Why Azalea, I'm shocked. You don't even recognize your own birth mother?"

CHAPTER 22

EMMA

"**A**gain," Thomas urged. "Harder this time."

Emma sighed. She could feel Thomas's frustration radiating off him like a sunburn—could feel that he knew he was being hard on her, maybe a little *too* hard.

She couldn't blame him. Life *was* hard. War was harder. And it was coming again, whether Emma was prepared or not.

Thomas had changed after the battle in Bearswillow. He hadn't said as much, but she had a feeling part of the shift inside him came from having to watch as Emma nearly didn't survive being tethered to the other side.

He had a desperation about him now that hadn't been there before. His work on their weapons was relentless. Hours and hours every day, pouring his time and his magic into daggers and swords and shields. He'd finished one for Janelle—a small hand dagger similar to Emma's. She hadn't asked what power it held. It seemed too personal, but she was grateful all the same that her friend was protected.

But along with that gratitude was churning worry for Thomas. He didn't sleep. Couldn't seem to rest. He barely even ate. Not unless Emma brought him something, and even then it was hurried and left unfinished.

He only took breaks to train her—like now. The dagger Thomas had created especially for Emma was firmly in her hand, and just as he'd asked of her, she always kept it with her. But it appeared the dagger had only been a small part of his plan to protect her. Even with a weapon, he still wanted her to know how to defend herself.

The notion seemed to be consuming his every waking thought, and the constant terror radiating from his chest made Emma want to cry. To feel that much worry... It was a burden she desperately wanted to help lighten. So even though she still had absolutely no intention of taking anyone's life, she'd agreed to his fighting lessons.

Emma stabbed her dagger into the makeshift punching bag hanging from the ceiling, the one Thomas had set up in her room when she'd been too nervous to train in the main hall with the soldiers. He hadn't argued the point, but instead, had shown up at her door with a length of rope and a twenty-pound bag of flour, ready to train.

The blade barely poked in, a tiny puff of white dissipating into the air, and Thomas sighed. A mix of failure and grief churned in Emma's stomach, and her face fell.

"Hey," he said gently, placing a hand on her shoulder, "I know it's hard. But you're doing great, and your form is good. You just need more strength behind it. You won't even puncture through clothing with a stab like that."

"I can't do it," Emma finally admitted, dropping her arms to her sides in exhaustion. "I'm trying, I really am, but before I push the blade in I imagine it's a person, and my arm just stops. It's like my body won't let me."

"I know you don't want to kill anyone," Thomas said, obviously trying to keep his tone as understanding as possible. "I don't want that for you either. Hopefully, you'll never even have to use this dagger. This is just preparing for the worst-case scenario."

Emma shook her head. Agreeing to Thomas's lessons had been a mistake. She'd known she wouldn't kill, but she'd wanted so badly to give him some relief from his worry. "This *is* the worst-case scenario for me. Killing someone and then having to watch their soul realize they're dead. That *I* killed them." She cringed at the thought.

Thomas reached up as if to push her curly black hair behind her ears—to tilt her head back and force her to look in his eyes instead of over his shoulder or at the ceiling. But he held himself back, and Emma was grateful. She was on edge enough already.

"Why don't we take a break," he suggested instead, holding out his hand. Emma's face softened, her shoulders falling in relief.

"A walk, maybe?" she asked, only hesitating for a moment before taking his hand.

"Of course." Thomas smiled warmly, leading Emma out of the room and past the blood red tapestries lining the hall. She didn't miss the way his eyes stalled on the third one on the right, behind which a door was hidden to the small secret room Thomas had met Vincent in several times when he'd first learned of the Eclipsed King and his plans. He'd told her all about it once they'd fled Auropera—about how he'd come to join the rebellion. Emma could feel the visceral reaction rising within him, the memory of the excitement and thrill he'd felt when he learned there was a way to fight back against the Black King and had decided to join those planning it.

Even with so many memories tying them there, and even though it had been her home her entire life, it was strange being back in the castle. Stranger to see Thomas openly creating weapons for the rebellion instead of sneaking around dark passageways and having meetings in the middle of the night.

So much had changed. There was no more sneaking. No more secrets. Here they were in the middle of the day, hand in hand, walking through the Black King's castle after training to defeat Alaric. It was progress.

And there was no longer a need to hide. Brennus was dead. And Alaric, wherever he was, already knew they'd be coming for him.

They stepped through the main entrance of the castle into the courtyard, the large doors wide open, and she felt the way Thomas's heart sank as his feet touched the dark grass outside. He had to have expected it, of course, but the pitch black of night during what should have been the middle of the day was startling all the same. How long had it been since they'd seen the sun? Had it really only been just over a week?

"I don't mind the eternal night," Emma said, wondering if it ever bothered him that she could read his emotions so well, it was as if she was reading his mind. "It's calming, I think. Seeing the stars when I wake, hearing the frogs croaking throughout the day."

Thomas looked down at her intently, assessing her face. He was always looking at her. Sneaking glances every chance he could, as if *she* was the sunrise they were all waiting for.

"I miss the sun. But I don't mind its absence quite so much when I'm walking under the stars with you," Thomas said, squeezing her hand. Emma blushed, her cheeks turning a deep red that was visible even in the black of night. She didn't answer. She couldn't.

She was fully aware Thomas longed to know what was going through her mind, and once again, she couldn't blame him. He'd been more than open about his feelings for her. Always a gentleman. Always honest. But as good as Emma was at empathizing with other people's emotions, she seemed to struggle with expressing her own.

Thomas didn't press her, though, in tune with her emotions enough that he sensed her need for silence. And Emma was glad he could be content with just being here with her, both of them safe and alive and well.

They continued on, the soft, squishy grass springy beneath their shoes as they headed toward town.

"I don't always hate my gift, you know," Emma finally broke the silence. Thomas's eyes widened, his eyebrows raising. "I'm starting to appreciate it. Even when it's hard." She ducked her head, her hair falling from behind her ear. Thomas's fingers wiggled as if wanting to push it back, but his hand remained at his side. "I've always felt different. But having this gift? It confirms it, I guess. That I was different. *Am* different. Not just weird or quiet or shy."

Thomas stayed silent, allowing her to get the feelings off her chest, but Emma could tell he was holding back his reassurances. That her ever feeling those things hurt him.

"It's difficult. Painful sometimes, even," Emma continued. "But helping people get closure? I kind of like that part of it. If I were to lose someone I loved, I'd want that closure. Wouldn't you?"

Thomas pressed his lips into a thin, grim line, pulling her to a stop. He finally lifted his hand and tucked her hair back behind her ear, and Emma felt the tingle all the way in her toes.

"I think what you can do is a gift to those families. But it's not one I hope you'll ever have to use for me. For any of us."

Emma's answering smile was sad. "I wish I'd never have to use it again. But if people have to die, then I will try to view my gift as a way to help. *That* is my role in this war, Thomas. It's not killing. Even to defend myself. I can't do it. I don't know if it's my magic stopping me from taking that killing blow, or if I'm not supposed to cause death but connect with it in a different way..." She rubbed her forehead. "I don't know what it is. I don't want you to be disappointed in me, but I won't be able to take a life, even if you train me every day until the final battle comes. It's not who I am."

This level of honesty was terrifying for Emma, and she tried to block out the disappointment in Thomas's eyes she knew would follow her words, but they never came. He tilted her head up to meet his gaze, caressing her cheek with his thumb.

"I hear you, and I'm sorry. I just—" He cleared his throat. "You don't have to worry about fighting. I'll fight for you," he said, never breaking eye contact. Emma's mouth popped open, and she sucked in a deep breath, ready to argue, but he continued. "If you don't think you can defend yourself, I will. With my own body if I have to."

"That's not— Why would you do that?" Emma's voice was breathless, her pupils dilating as he leaned closer.

"I care about you. You know that. All this time we're spending together? It's not just—" The ringing of a bell from the castle tower sounded, interrupting his confession.

"Fire!" a guard shouted from somewhere behind them, and Thomas swung his head toward the castle where a faint orange glow was spreading inside the courtyard. Emma's stomach dropped, guilt gnawing in her chest at the fact that she was more disappointed that he hadn't leaned in to kiss her than the fact that there was a fire that needed to be contained.

"Fire!" The warning sounded again, but this time as she looked up toward the courtyard, it made Emma's blood run cold. The fire was too bright, spreading too fast. As the bright orange and white flames danced toward the sky, it was clear that this wasn't just any fire. The way it was spreading. The height. The color. It was unnatural.

Emma didn't know how it was possible in the dead of night, but this was day magic. The strongest she had ever seen.

CHAPTER 23

LEA

"**M**y mot—" Lea didn't even have time to finish the word as a blast of heat pulsed through the ceiling, the temperature so unbearably hot it burned her skin. "Fuck!" she shouted, taking off in a sprint, Gray right on her heels. They burst out of the stairwell and into the great hall.

"Your Majesty," a maid choked out, soot smeared across her face.

"What is it?"

"Fire," she coughed, clutching her chest. "Near your chambers."

"Get everyone outside the castle walls and down to the village," Lea ordered, running straight toward their rooms. Throwing out her magic, she searched the air for any hint of Alaric. An explosion so big she could feel the blast so far from Gray's wing shouldn't be possible, not without the sun to recharge day magic. Alaric was the only explanation, and yet she couldn't feel him, couldn't sense him or his dark energy.

"He has to be here," Gray said, and Lea clenched her jaw. Something didn't feel right.

"I don't understand," she mumbled, the uneasiness swirling in her chest growing stronger the closer they got to their chambers. The heat grew more intense with every step until it was so hot, sweat dripped down her back and legs. But there was no time to stop. Instead, she picked up her pace, flinging herself around the corner and stumbling when she saw that it wasn't only their rooms that were on fire, but the entire wing of the castle.

Bright orange and yellow fire billowed from floor to ceiling, turning the stone black with soot. Lea grabbed her sword, harnessing all the power she could. Somewhere within the blade was the ability to move air—she'd used it before to create an impenetrable shield when battling Alaric—but would it be enough? Digging her heels into the floor, she searched for a way to suck the air out of the hall.

As she pulled the oxygen around them toward her, the fire calmed, but not enough to stop the spread. It continued onward, inching towards her feet until Lea was forced to take a step back, the heat too much. She wiped her brow with her sleeve, sweat dripping into her eyes and her hair sticking to the back of her neck. Gritting her teeth, she pulled more oxygen from the air, her lungs burning as she struggled to breathe, but it was worth it.

With the final pull of oxygen, the flames finally receded enough for Lea to move deeper into the hallway to search for the cause of the fire. She forced a bubble of air around herself, taking several quick, deep breaths, but the further she got into the hallway, the harder breathing became.

"Lea!" Gray called from behind her. The world went hazy, her vision dotted with black spots, and her chest ached. She sucked in several breaths, coughing on the smoke. Her lungs burned and her head swam, and she dropped to her knees. The sword clattered to the ground with a resounding clank. She scrambled for the weapon, but it was too late. The moment the sword left her hand, the magic she had been wielding through it snapped. Instantly, the fire surged, long tendrils reaching toward Lea as if trying to boil the very blood in her veins.

Gray darted forward, scooping her up and running as fast as he could to escape the fire coming for them. Shadows branched out around them, suffocating what they could of the fire, until they were far enough down the hallway to take a breath. Lea's tunnel vision lessened, her lungs finally filling with oxygen, still burning from where the smoke had seared their insides. She sent healing energy down her throat, healing herself from within.

"What do we do?" Lea asked, her eyes frantic.

"We can't fight this." He gestured to the hall behind them where the fire was quickly spreading up the walls and ceiling, creeping further toward them. "We need to get outside. Make sure everyone is accounted for."

Lea wanted to argue, desperately. The castle couldn't go up in flames. They had just arrived here. Just set up Auropera as their army's camp, but Gray was right.

This fire was unnatural. Magical. And she didn't know how to fight it without putting them in unnecessary danger. Lea nodded, turning to follow Gray out, but paused when she heard the click of heels coming toward them. Lea's heart thundered as the footsteps approached, and she coiled her magic tightly in her chest, ready to explode it outward at the first sign of danger. *Who would be approaching rather than fleeing, if not whoever created the fire?*

Destroy.

Destroy.

Destroy.

Her primary magic was shouting now, but she forced herself to hold back.

Through the smoke, the scarred witch stepped forward—her birth mother, Evangeline—hair blowing around her as her body glowed a deep purple.

A haze of black surrounded her thin frame, the darkness far more dense than Lea's own shadows. They seemed to buzz rather than slither and writhe—far less wild than the ones emanating from Lea's own body. With graceful, controlled movements, Evangeline lifted her hands in front of her, her darkness funneling from her fingers and consuming the fire like a drop of water in the ocean.

As if her shadows were a thick blanket, they suffocated the flames in an instant, filling the hallway until it was so dark Lea couldn't see her own fingers.

But she did not feel afraid. The darkness welcomed her like an old friend, and her magic surged. The smoke grew thicker, and Lea called on her own magic, sending a gust of air to blow the smoke away. The change in heat was instant, the flames no longer even embers.

"The god of the sun," Evangeline said, her arms still outstretched. "He is angry. This will not be his last warning." Evangeline shook her arms, tilting her head side to side, a grimace of pain spreading across her face for a brief moment before she wiped it clean.

Lea had the feeling that had she been able to see her eyes, they would have been black—as dark as the shadows now gently floating back up the hallway as they returned to Evangeline's body. Jealousy coiled in Lea's stomach at Evangeline's ability to command her darkness rather than let it taunt and consume her. But as quickly as her envy had appeared, fury replaced it—fiery hot anger that she was jealous of a woman who had abandoned her to help the Black King.

As the last of the flames disappeared, Evangeline dropped her arms and hung her head, her breaths ragged and irregular. She turned, her hand finding Lea's cheek. Lea couldn't move. Couldn't even breathe. She wanted to fight her. To demand answers. To tell her to go away and never return, but her curiosity got the better of her.

"How did you stop it?" Lea asked, her voice hoarse from the smoke, but Evangeline ignored her question.

"Are you the one I've heard of? The Daughter of the Sun and Stars?" Evangeline's voice was soft and melodic, familiar and breathless.

Lea's heart shattered as she stared into the witch's face. The curve of her jaw and the narrow bridge of her nose a mirror to her own.

"I am," Lea said, her voice coming out a whisper.

The woman's chin trembled, and she took a step forward, her other hand wiping the soot from Lea's cheek.

"Then you are not only their daughter," she said, her voice cracking. "You're mine, too." Tears slid from the corners of her scarred eyes, her whole body shaking. "You're alive. You're alive," she said again, pulling Lea into a bone-crushing hug. "Gods forgive me for what I did, but you're alive."

CHAPTER 24

GRAY

They would have gathered in Gray's study, except that his study was now nothing more than charred, smoking stone and ruins. Miraculously, no one had been harmed in the fire. The fire the sun god had lit as punishment for Lea's disobedience, if Evangeline was to be believed, seemed to have been more for destruction than to cause death. A warning for them all that they were navigating a dangerous path.

Gray had suggested using his father's study, but Lea had refused, admitting that her dark magic felt too hard to control in his part of the castle. Her voice had been strained as she'd said the words, and Gray could tell it was hard for her to admit that weakness to him. Knew that she was still trying to pretend as if she had everything under control. Watching her struggle made Gray feel like he couldn't breathe, like his lungs couldn't expand enough to allow him a single shallow breath. But what could he do? He had no more experience with controlling the magic of the gods than she did.

He had no advice, other than what he'd already offered to her, so he simply stayed nearby. Always touching her, rubbing her back or running his fingers up and down her arm. It didn't seem to give her any relief from the turmoil inside her, but he hoped that it at least helped remind her that she wasn't alone.

"Someone better fucking explain what's happening," Gray said as he took his seat, his temper growing shorter by the minute. They sat around the table in the grand dining hall, Gray and Lea both at the head, Erik to Gray's left, and Eudora and Tanad seated at the other end.

Even in the worst of times, Tanad normally had a twinkle in his eye that betrayed his serious demeanor, his deep-seated belief that everything would be okay, eventually. But today, his eyes were cold and calculating. Hard in a way Gray had never seen before.

Before anyone had the chance to answer, Tanad stood abruptly, his chair scraping against the stone floor, almost tipping backward. He stalked behind Eudora, his arms crossed over his chest and his lips pressed into a tight line. Gray watched him closely, trying to determine if Tanad had known about Evangeline. If she truly was Lea's mother, and he had known all this time, Gray would never be able to forgive him. He'd certainly never feel comfortable trusting him again. But based on the tension in his posture and the furious glint in his eye, Gray guessed that he was as surprised as the rest of them.

"I agree," Tanad said. "Explain. Now."

For the first time, Eudora looked sheepish. Maybe even regretful, but Gray knew better than to trust what he saw and heard when it came to that vile witch.

"I love her, too." Eudora's voice was almost pleading as she twisted to look at Tanad.

"Don't." He held up a hand. "Do not speak to me of loving her. Have you *seen* her? Her—" He swallowed, bringing a hand to his mouth. "What was done to her is abhorrent!"

"I didn't know he had tortured her. The cage she was in blocked my visions. I *couldn't* see what was happening to her." Eudora tilted her head and furrowed her brows, as if not concretely knowing Evangline had been tortured should absolve her of their ire.

"Does it matter?" Tanad snapped. "You knew she was in the hands of the most evil Fae who has ever lived, and you did *nothing*!" He slammed his palms on the table, and Eudora flinched. "We could have saved her. I would have found a way! She was like a child to us. We raised that girl!"

"It's really her then?" Lea asked Tanad, not bothering to look at Eudora. "That woman... She's my birth mother?"

Tanad's eyes softened for the first time since he'd entered the room, his shoulders falling. He held his palms out to her. "You have to believe I didn't know, my dear. She was just gone one day. I searched for her, but—" He stopped, taking a deep breath. "Yes, the witch you rescued from the cage is Evangeline. Your birth mother."

"How could my mother be a witch?" she asked. Gray's stomach twisted into knots. It wasn't adding up. Tanad had told him about Evangeline, and she *hadn't* been a witch. Her magic had allowed her to keep death at bay, and she'd been a seer, but her parents weren't witches. Queen Emmaline and her mate were both fully fae.

"Speak," Tanad's tone sharpened again as he spoke to Eudora. There was no kindness or compassion in his voice, and Eudora curled her shoulders inward, but lifted her chin. A surge of rage sped through Gray's veins at the complacency on her face, and Gray wondered what Tanad would do if he were to wring her neck. If there was ever to be a time he could get away with it and keep their alliance intact, this was likely it, based on the wrath emanating from Tanad's expression.

Eudora sighed. "Evangeline knew the king would eventually find out about her, and by extension, you." Eudora's eyes snapped to Lea. "You should be honored, really. She did it to protect you. You're the reason she's lived in that cage for the past twenty-three years." Her words weren't accusatory, but matter of fact. Gray searched her tone for any hint of remorse. Any hint of regret, but it simply wasn't there. She spoke as if discussing the weather outside.

Gray wanted to strangle her, but Lea beat him to his feet. "You're a fucking bitch," Lea said, stalking toward her. Her hand trembled, her fingers extended as if she wanted to slap Eudora's insincere smile off her face. "Why should I believe anything coming out of your mouth? All you've done is lie."

"But I have no reason to lie *now*," Eudora said, holding out her arms as if confused why they weren't believing her. As if her statement was fact. "Not now that you've retrieved her for me."

It made Gray's blood boil. "My patience is running thin, Eudora," he said, the wood creaking beneath his fingers where he gripped his chair.

"As is mine," Tanad snapped, beginning to pace.

Eudora sighed, rubbing her forehead as she settled back in her chair. "The Black King was hunting Evangeline." She met Lea's eyes. "And she was afraid. Not for herself, but for *you*. The more powerful Brennus became, the more he could feel Evangeline's magic. The gods' magic. Though hers isn't quite as strong as yours, it's still stronger than most. Strong enough for the king to sense someone out there in his kingdom with so much power, he could almost taste it. Evangeline knew he wouldn't rest until he found her."

Tanad's face turned grim. "We hid her well. She was safe with us."

"It was foreseen," Eudora said. "It was her own vision that prompted her to ask for my help."

"She's a seer?" Gray asked, his fingers trailing up and down Lea's back. She was stiff beneath his hand, but the way she leaned into his touch told him she needed his support more than she wanted anyone to know.

"She is. One almost as powerful as I. She started seeing glimpses of the future as a child. She rarely spoke of it, though. Not until she began having visions of the king finding Lea. Of her death. First, she tried fleeing, hiding. But every time she moved, he found her in her dreams. Her visions changed, sure, but her death still occurred one way or another. So she came to me, and we made a plan."

"You should've told me," Tanad hissed, but Eudora turned her head away, ignoring him.

"The Lonely Death may be the only way to steal magic for a Fae, but it isn't so with witches."

"What do you mean?" Gray asked, a dull throb forming at the base of his skull. He wanted to shake her. To throttle her and force her to just get to the damn point, but he knew there was no use. If anything, it'd make her less likely to give them information, purely out of spite.

"Witches are the guardians of magic here on Earth. It is our sacred duty to maintain balance. A witch may give her magic away, so long as it's done so freely and willingly. We also have the ability to take magic, but to do so is the gravest offense to nature."

Eudora looked around, meeting each of their eyes. "Evangeline wasn't a witch, and no matter how powerful she was in her own right, she would never have been able to defeat the Black King, alone. So I gave her some of my magic. She would take you to Bearswillow, where the old palace healer lived. You would be safe there. I knew the rumors of the stream from the mountains that protected those with magic from detection were true. You would be hidden, and your mother could return for you once the king was dead. As soon as the decision was made, I saw you growing up, a beautiful young girl at the fire night celebration, dancing in the flames as a certain commander watched. It allowed you two to meet, you know—"

"You're saying witches can be created," Gray interrupted her, ignoring her insinuation she'd known of their future together before he'd even met Lea. He hated to think of her having a hand in their love story in any way. Refused to feel gratitude to the vile woman who had deceived them so thoroughly. Gray clenched his jaw, forcing the thought away.

"In a sense. They can wield the power of the witch who gifted them their magic. But they cannot create another, and they can't grow in their power. A technicality, I suppose. A witch in ability, but not in name or nature."

"You expect us to believe you gifted Evangeline some of your precious magic out of the goodness of your heart? What was in it for you?" Lea asked, her hands fisted as if physically restraining herself from launching at Eudora.

"You don't think I simply wanted to help her? Help *you*?" Eudora held her hands out as if offering an apology, and Gray had the sudden urge to cut them off.

Lea's skin warmed against his arm, and Gray could sense her trying to keep her black flames at bay.

"No. I don't," Lea said, the words sharp as a dagger's edge.

Eudora sighed dramatically, rolling her eyes. "I did want to help Evangeline. As Tanad said, I loved her dearly. But yes, I did require something in return." She crossed one leg over the other. "It's all about balance, is it not? The king stole something of mine. My niece, Seraphine. Kidnapped her from her own bed in the dead of night. I am duty and honor bound to protect my blood. So I agreed to help her, with one single condition. Our deal was simple. She wouldn't be able to kill him with the magic she was born with. As you remember, she could hold death at bay—but she couldn't command it. She had no special abilities to heal or create weapons. But I could give Evangeline some of my magic, strengthening her own seeing abilities, and I could give her the ability to create a potion strong enough to kill the king. A single drop. That's all it would take, undetectable by even the strongest of magic. She was to kill the king, and bring my family home to me."

"Which isn't what happened. So what went wrong?" Tanad asked.

Eudora shrugged. "*That*, I do not know. Evangeline never returned. And when I tried to see her, to find her, all I saw was that damn cage. Just the sight of it in my visions made me physically ill, spelled somehow against my family's magic. The king must have known I would come for her and made it so I'd be unable to retrieve her."

"So you just left her there, rotting away?" Tanad's voice cracked, and his eyes suddenly appeared so very tired.

"What was I to do?" Eudora asked him, the first bit of humanity entering her voice as she stared at Tanad, silently begging for his forgiveness.

"You should have told him what you saw," Gray snapped. Eudora swallowed, then shrugged, the movement so flippant Gray considered decapitating her right then and there. After he cut off her hands, of course. The thought made him smile.

"Leave," Lea said, her voice so low and full of fury, it made Gray's hair stand on end.

"Not until—"

Lea stood in one swift motion, drawing her sword. "Another word, a single syllable, and I will run my blade through your heart until the life fades from your old, decrepit body."

Eudora's eyes flew open in shock, her smug smile disappearing as she turned to Tanad.

"Are you going to—"

Tanad held up his hand, stopping her. "Speak again, and I will allow it. Go."

Eudora tilted her head as if weighing her options. A slow, knowing smile spread across her lips as her eyes went white, her head falling back. A vision. Nobody moved until the witch's eyes cleared.

She looked around, meeting Tanad's eyes for a long moment before nodding slowly. Sadly. She stood, the chair scraping on the floor the only sound. Eudora looked to Tanad one more time, and he held her gaze, anger hardening his features.

"So it will be," Eudora said, the whisper of a smile crossing her lips. Lea surged forward, but in the blink of an eye, Eudora shifted into a great blue heron and disappeared through the open window and into the black of night.

Tanad hung his head. "I'm sorry—"

Lea held up a hand. "I can no more blame you for Eudora's deceitful actions than I can blame Gray for being related to Alaric." She cleared her throat, clenching her fists as her shadows fought to follow Eudora. "If you'll excuse me," she said, not bothering to look behind at either of them before striding from the room, ripping her shadows out with her.

CHAPTER 25

GRAY

A black haze surrounded Lea, so thick and dark Gray could barely make out the anger in her features. She was overwhelmed. Had been since the moment she'd returned from beyond the veil, but even more now that she knew of Eudora's lies. It crushed him that he hadn't been able to take that burden away. At least a hundred times a day he found himself reaching for the absent mate bond, wanting so desperately to feel what she was feeling and ease whatever pain he could.

The rage that pounded through him each time he felt nothing but blood and sinew and bone, when his magic slid straight past where the bond used to rest, was enough to bring mountains crumbling down. He wanted to fight, to unleash his own magic and take out his need for vengeance, his own rage, but he stayed at Lea's side instead, and he would continue to do so as long as she allowed it.

Lea's hands clenched and unclenched as she stormed through secret passages and stairwells in the quickest route out of the castle. That was one thing that hadn't changed—her need for fresh air when her emotions grew too big.

Gray knew she missed the sun, and he wondered if maybe the everlasting night was only making her primary magic even more powerful—more difficult to control. Maybe just a few hours of sunlight would chase away some of the darkness she was constantly fighting against. But wondering didn't help the matter. Not when the god of the sun was still punishing them for her disobedience.

Lea flew forward onto the grass, her shadows expanding the moment she cleared the doorway, black fire turning the grass to embers wherever she stepped. Shadows and flames overtook the courtyard in seconds, stretching and twisting until they reached the tall stone walls surrounding the castle. Lea bit her lip, closing her eyes and taking several deep, steadying breaths. Gray waited, knowing she was trying to work her emotions out in her mind before speaking.

"How could Eudora do this?" she finally asked. "How could she keep this from us? From Tanad? How could she allow Evangeline to suffer the way she did? And how the fuck do I forgive Evangeline for helping the king?" Lea took a deep breath and closed her eyes. "Have I not lost enough?" she croaked, her voice breaking.

"You've lost more than enough." Gray walked to her, forcing himself through her thick shadows to wrap his arms tightly around her tiny, shaking body. His heart clenched, and his own shadows pushed against his skin. "Evangeline, right or wrong, was trying to protect you. That's a feeling I can understand," Gray said gently. "There's nothing I wouldn't do to keep you safe. Nothing I wouldn't have done to keep my father from discovering who and what you were."

Lea didn't argue. "I can't do this anymore, Gray. The more I find out, the more emotional I get, the harder this darkness is to control. I feel like I'm going to explode." Lea's fingers squeezed the fabric of his shirt, pulling him against her as if wishing she could somehow get closer to him.

Gray stood up straight, the beginning of an idea forming in his mind. He pulled himself back to look into Lea's eyes as he tucked her hair behind her ears. "Then we need to find a way to let you explode without taking half the kingdom out with you," he said, pulling her toward the stables. Obsidian whinnied as he opened the door, sauntering over to his stall gate and kicking it as if he knew Lea was suffering and wanted to be near her. Gray opened the door and Obsidian pushed through, rubbing his nose against Lea's chest. The ghost of a smile crossed her lips as her hand came up to pat his mane.

Gray hoisted Lea on top of Obsidian, climbing swiftly up behind her.

"Where are we going?" Lea asked, her voice so exhausted it made Gray's heart stutter. "We don't have time for a ride." Her hand rose to her head, her fingers subconsciously tracing across her moonflower crown.

"If you don't get this magic out, you won't make it long enough to lose all the petals, Lea. You can't go on like this." He kicked Obsidian's side, leading him toward the forest, and hopefully, a way to help Lea find relief.

The cave was exactly where he remembered it to be—an opening carved into the side of a waterfall, hours from any village or town. They were completely and truly alone out here, exactly what he needed to help Lea expend some of her magic. Erik and Gray had found the cave as children one day long ago when they'd stolen horses from the stables and rode off in search of adventure. Back before he'd realized how evil the world was. How evil his father was.

Gray led Obsidian to the base of the waterfall, patting his neck as he slid off. He pulled Lea down effortlessly, keeping a hand on her back as he led her forward. Her skin practically vibrated with the intensity of the emotions still coursing through her, the painful ferocity of the primary magic demanding she destroy the world.

That pain had become a part of her, as she fought against that raw, immense power, the darkness she was convinced would destroy her. And if Gray was being honest, it was. It was too vast and insistent, and controlling it seemed to be taking a toll on Lea in a way that made Gray's shadows writhe. He was desperate to soothe her, to find a way to help her release that magic out of her body safely.

Grabbing her hand, Gray tugged Lea behind him through the waterfall, and she begrudgingly followed. She thought this was useless. He could feel it in her posture, in the way her feet were half a step slower than his. But he continued pulling her forward, neither of them speaking as they traveled further into the cave. Lea called on her fire to light the way, but Gray didn't need it, his long-ago memories leading them twisting through narrow pathways, scrambling over rocks and ducking under stalactites until a vast chamber opened up before them.

Water dripped from the ceiling, and crystals embedded within the cave walls shimmered in the firelight from Lea's hand. Another waterfall, a far smaller one than the one outside, ran down the far right corner of the angular, irregularly shaped chamber. As soon as they entered, their footsteps echoed throughout the space. Memories of sparring with Erik flashed through his mind, bringing a tiny smile to his lips. They were many of the few happy memories of his childhood, the days they'd been able to sneak away to come here and just be children.

Erik had enchanted it long ago to withstand their magical battles. Pinning the rocks in place with spears of magic, creating a thin, invisible barrier between them and the stalactites for their magic to bounce off of.

The space wasn't perfect. It had cost them a half day's ride and taken them away from their army, but Lea needed to release her magic, and this was the best he could think of.

Lea flicked her wrist, and a small black fire appeared on the ground, giving her just enough light to the space to examine it. She turned in a slow circle as she took in the chamber, her eyes narrowing slightly.

"It's safe here, Little Flower. Let go," Gray said.

"What? Here?" She gestured to the large rocky formations all throughout the room.

"It'll hold. Trust me." Gray reached out and cupped Lea's cheek. "This magic will eat you alive, Lea. It's already doing it. I'm seeing it happen in front of my eyes, and I can't watch you struggle anymore." His words came out as a growl. He tried to rein in his frustration, the desperation so clearly bursting from every word. Every fiber of his being, every cell within his body, was begging him to find a way to force her to let the magic out. It was almost as if they were newly mated again, his protective instincts animalistic in their intensity.

But he also knew Lea. Knew her to her core, and he was more than aware that there was no forcing her to do anything. She wouldn't release her magic until she was absolutely certain he'd be safe.

"Let go," he said again, exploding his shadows outward until they hit the walls and ceiling, careening outward with as much force as he could muster. He wrapped a tendril around a stalactite and pulled, but it remained firm. Unmoving. Gathering his storm clouds overhead, he crashed lightning into the rocky walls and ground, but the cave didn't so much as shake.

Lea didn't say a word as she watched, her lips pressed together as if still not convinced she could truly release her magic and be safe within these walls.

"You have to let go," Gray said again, his voice gruff as it rumbled from his chest. "Let go." His shadows snaked up her body, loosening the ties of her dress and pulling her hair from its braid.

I think I will enjoy watching the wind through it as we ride... A memory. So sweet and bitter at once. He stepped forward, pulling the collar of Lea's dress over her shoulder. His shadows continued trailing up her legs, brushing and kissing, begging for her to let her guard down. Gray leaned down, pressing a kiss to the hollow of her neck, sucking and biting as he worked his way up to her ear.

"Let go," he rasped. As his shadows reached her breast, whisper soft against her skin, Lea leaned her head back. Gray's chest warmed at the crack in her armor, and he reached a hand around her back, undoing the laces of her dress. It fell to the floor as he lifted her, his hands cupping her ass as he carried her toward the wall. His shadows never stopped, pinching and brushing and teasing relentlessly.

Lea's darkness radiated outward, the black fire now behind them growing and spreading toward them, but he wasn't worried. Lea would never let him be harmed. She would rather die than allow him to be injured. Subconsciously, her magic would protect him, just as his would for her.

He pressed her back against the rock wall, her breath coming out in short, shallow spurts as he claimed her mouth. His hands found her breasts, and she arched against him as his thumbs rolled across her nipples. Gray stepped back, removing his shirt before leaning down and replacing his fingers with his tongue. Lea gasped, but still, Gray could feel her reserve. She was holding back, the shadows and fire streaming from her body only a whisper of what she was capable of.

"Let go," he said again. Dropping to his knees, he pinned Lea's arms above her head with long trails of darkness, holding her in place as he pulled her leg over his shoulder. He wasted no time. There was no teasing, no gentle touches. He simply devoured her, his tongue circling in an unrelenting rhythm as he pressed two fingers inside her. She fought against his restraints, but he held them firm.

"More," she begged. And he listened, the shadows squeezing her breasts, caressing between her thighs as his tongue and fingers continued their assault. Her body went rigid, her back arching as she began to cry out, and as quickly as he had started, Gray pulled back, her orgasm dying off abruptly.

It nearly killed him to do it, to step away and remove his touch in every way but the shadows still pinning her in place. But this release... It wasn't the one she needed. He just had to get her to a place where she could no longer hold back. Lea's eyes darkened with anger as she opened her mouth, panting, gasping for air. She started to speak, but Gray cut her off.

"Let go," he said again. An order. A command. His voice was nothing but a growl, far darker and more controlling than he'd ever spoken to her. But she *had* to listen, *had* to release some of her magic or she was going to explode. For all Gray knew, it would kill her if she didn't. Kill other people. He slowly stepped forward, rising to stand as he slid his hands up her body. She arched into his touch, his hands gliding up until they once again found her nipples. He rolled them between his thumb and finger, pinching, squeezing as his shadows began teasing between her legs again. Gradually building her back up into a haze of pleasure.

He lifted her, moving her to a boulder-like rock nearby and laying her backward as if on a table, her legs hanging down. Once again, he pinned her down, teasing, and brushing and pinching until she was begging for more.

"I need..."

"I know what you need," Gray said, unbuttoning his pants and pulling his cock free. He was so hard it was painful, but this wasn't for him. It was for Lea. Always for Lea. "Let go," Gray ordered, lining himself up with her entrance and agonizingly slowly, pressing inside, just a fraction. It was torture. Blinding torment. Not only for Lea, but for Gray. His shadows begged him to slam inside, his muscles bunching with the need, but still, he held back.

"I can't," she gasped. "Please, Gray." She tried to wiggle against him, but he kept her pinned down, not allowing her to move even an inch to get some relief from the ache building inside her.

"You *have* to let go," he said again, pushing in, just another inch. Lea cried out as her back arched, her need growing more desperate.

"Fuck you!" she snarled, her shadows trailing from her flushed body and grabbing his ass, trying to push him further inside. Gray resisted, barely able to overcome the strength with which she pulled. Fire spread from her limbs, across the stone and toward the walls surrounding them, washing them in a flickering, black and orange light. He pushed in deeper, torturously slow, and Lea cried out in a guttural moan of need.

"Please," she begged, pulling on him with her shadows again.

"Let go," Gray whispered this time, his voice nothing but gravel and desperation. Lea wasn't the only one begging. He needed this just as much as her, but first, she had to let her guard down.

Her words became nonsensical as her need took over. "I can't, I don't—"

Gray pushed inside her with one hard thrust, hitting the end of her so hard Lea screamed. And that was all it took. Like the crack of thunder, the room exploded in shadows and fire, a deadly mixture of magic—light and dark, crackling together in a lethal display of power.

Gray began to pump, hard and fast, driving Lea further away from the scraps of control she still held.

"Yes!" Lea cried out as she broke free from his shadowy restraints. "Oh gods, Gray! More!" she begged. And Gray was happy to oblige. He tilted her hips, reaching for that spot inside her that drove her mad. There was nothing gentle about the way he fucked her, nothing soft or slow or tender. His touches were bruising, full of nothing but pure desire.

Lea dug her fingernails into his back and down his arms, and Gray was certain she was drawing blood. It didn't matter, he would bear those marks like badges of honor. Would refuse to heal them. He *wanted* to see the evidence of their lust. Of their bodies' pure, uncontrollable demand to get closer. Deeper.

Fire flew from Lea's hands as she threw them to the side, grasping at the rocks, trying to find some purchase. Her shadows threaded around his body, grabbing the back of his head and forcing his mouth to her breast. His tongue circled her nipple, biting, sucking as he continued his steady rhythm in and out. In and out.

Lea's moans built, her body once again going taut , but this time, Gray didn't stop. He fucked her through each wave of her orgasm until she was moaning his name again and again, a puddle in his hands. And once every ounce of pleasure had been wrung from her flaming body, he flipped her over, her breasts pressed against the rough stone as he thrust inside her once more.

He roared as the position allowed him deeper inside her, pleasure unlike anything he'd ever felt before ripping through his body. The fire grew hotter, impossibly so, sweat dripping down his back and from his brow.

"Yes," he growled. "You're so fucking beautiful. So wet for me. I love you. Come for me again. Let me feel you come around my cock. Gods, Lea." Words tumbled from his mouth, praise and adoration and affection mixed with all the dirty thoughts racing through his mind. Gray continued touching and kissing and thrusting until she was so full of him—his cock, his words, his love, his need—that there was no room for that dark, terrifying power inside her anymore.

The cave began to tremble as Lea's fire and shadows grew, and Gray built a shield of shadows above them, as thick as he could make them. Because he was not going to stop. Not until her magic was drained and her body stopped quivering. Lea's breast scraped against the rough stone as she cried out, a gurgle of nonsensical words and begging.

"Yes! More... Uhhgg. Fuck! Harder!" He pulled her backward, his hand wrapping around the space between her shoulder and neck for more leverage as he pounded into her with everything he had. So deep, he felt every inch of her warmth. Pebbles rained from overhead against his shield, the cave trembling as Lea's fire exploded out with a crash, blindingly hot as she screamed, pushing back against him, a violent orgasm ripping through her. Stalactites severed from the ceiling, but Gray's shield held, the cave shaking, rocks crashing, but he didn't care. She needed this release, and pride swelled in his chest knowing he was the one to give it to her.

Only once Lea's body went slack did Gray allow himself to still inside her, a growl ripping from his throat as he found his own release. Her name pouring from his lips like the sweetest song. The rumbling beneath their feet faded away, the creaking and groaning of rocks shifting coming to a stop as Lea's fire and shadows diminished.

But not completely. The fire still crackled in her eyes and her darkness swirled above her skin, but finally, Lea didn't seem like she was about to shatter under the pressure of her magic. Finally, she seemed whole again.

He pulled himself out, lifting her gently and carrying her limp, relaxed body to the waterfall. The cool water washed over their skin, beating against his back, and he held her tight as it washed away the tiny bits of rock and dirt stuck to their sweaty skin. Lea lifted her chin, her eyes meeting Gray's, and she smiled. A small, but real, breathtakingly, beautiful smile.

Gray's heart swelled as she lifted a hand to his cheek. "Thank you," she said, exhaling deeply now that the crushing weight of her primary magic had eased. She laid her head back against his chest, and he rocked her beneath the water until her breaths grew even and deep, her body spent and her mind finally at rest.

She didn't wake as he dressed her, as he climbed on top of Obsidian with her sleeping body still in his arms. She didn't wake as Obsidian carried them back toward Auropera, and Gray was grateful. He didn't know how long her relief would last, how quickly that dark magic would build up inside her again, but for now, she was at peace. And Gray would do his best to make sure she stayed that way as long as possible.

But as he raced back toward the castle, the ground trembled beneath him. An ominous rumble from deep within the earth's crust. It felt like a warning, like the gods had heard his thoughts and were telling him that until Alaric was dead, there would be no peace.

CHAPTER 26 ·

LEA

Lea placed another crescent shaped seed into the moist ground, row after row of them, dirt caking her fingernails and staining her dress at the knees. Seeing her mother—her *birth* mother—had been too much. It was cruel the universe had taken Adelaide away—allowed her to believe Evangeline to be dead as well, only to reveal that she was the one who had been helping the king spread the Lonely Death further throughout the kingdom.

Gray was right. Lea couldn't blame her, not really. She surely hadn't known the scale or size of what the king was planning, hadn't known that by serving him and doing his bidding, she had contributed to the devastation that plagued their kingdom. Evangeline had simply been trying to protect her daughter and biding her time, convinced there would come a day she would be able to kill the king herself.

Still, it felt like too much. Too much information. Too many moving pieces. She'd almost lost control earlier with Eudora. Could have easily killed her if she hadn't morphed into her heron form and disappeared into the sky. Part of her wished she'd just done it—set her darkness free and allowed it to tear the witch apart limb from limb.

But the other half was relieved she'd held herself back. It was for the best that she hadn't unleashed her magic in the middle of the dining hall, where she could have brought the entire castle down on their heads. Her magic was still overwhelming her. Even though Gray had helped her release it, she could feel it slowly building again, somehow angrier than before.

But here, planting her moonflowers outside in the eternal darkness, she felt—not calm exactly—but at least useful. The moonflowers flourished, blooming and creeping across the small plot of dirt Gray had taken her to so long ago to tend to. In what felt like a different lifetime. When she was a naïve girl with nothing but hope and optimism for the future. A girl who didn't have the magic of the gods threatening to eat her alive from inside.

She wasn't any closer to controlling her magic now than she had been a month ago, and frankly, she was surprised she hadn't lashed out and killed Eudora before she'd even had a chance to speak.

Lea's shadows surged at the thought, and she clenched her jaw, forcing them to return to her side.

"You must follow the darkness."

Lea froze, her eyes lifting from the soil to where Evangeline stood several yards away, her long blond hair unbound and blowing gently in the wind. Behind the scars, beneath the horrors that she had endured, she was beautiful. But noticing the similarities in their features cut into Lea's heart like a finely honed blade, carving the already mangled mass of muscle into a bloody, pumping mess.

"So I've heard." Lea looked down at the flowers, funneling as much magic as she could into them. They would be leaving soon. To where, she didn't know. But they were running out of time, and staying here would help nothing. Alaric surely wouldn't be coming to them. But Lea felt responsible for providing enough moonflowers to keep their army safe and wasn't comfortable leaving until they had a store ten times the amount they might need.

"Gray can't help me harvest the petals," Lea said flatly. "And if you haven't noticed, it doesn't seem like the darkness is ever going to end. I have no choice but to embrace it." Without taking her eyes off the vines, Lea lifted a hand and waved it to the dark sky. She tried to keep the bite out of her words, knowing deep down that she would have made the same choices as Evangeline to protect those she loved most, but some part of her was unable to let go of the anger she felt at the situation it had put them all in.

"That's not what I'm referring to. Your magic, the magic of *our* ancestors." Evangeline sighed, lifting a foot as if to step closer, but pausing. "May I?"

Lea shrugged, and Evangeline moved forward. It made Lea shiver, knowing that the witch had been able to feel her agreement without her saying a word. Evangeline didn't touch her as she settled down into the dirt, crossing her ankles over one another to sit sideways. Her fingers trailed absently in the soil, the flowers closest to her growing even faster, sprouting off multiple buds and splitting. They worked in silence for a moment, in tandem, until the entirety of the land around them was covered in pristine, *living* flowers. It took Lea's breath away.

"What do you mean?" Lea finally asked, still refusing to look at Evangeline.

"I know how it feels to hold magic different from your own."

"The gods?" Lea finally looked up.

"Not as much as they gifted to you, but yes. A bit of their magic. But I'm mostly referring to Seraphine's," Evangeline admitted.

"Eudora's niece?" A ripple of disgust spread through Lea's stomach at the thought of the traitorous bitch who had deceived them.

Evangeline nodded. "It's how I was able to help the Black King. Eudora only gave me enough magic to strengthen my seeing abilities and to make a potion that would kill Brennus. But Seraphine? She gave it all—every last drop—in exchange for death." Evangeline pressed a hand to her chest. "It felt like it would rot me from the inside, like all it wanted was to escape from beneath my skin. It almost killed me. For *years*, I fought against it. It wasn't until I embraced it, made it a part of myself, that I was able to control it fully." Evangeline inhaled deeply through her nose. "It was like taking my first breath of fresh air after eons underwater. That darkness you're feeling? You need to follow it. Embrace it."

Lea's heart pounded, picking up in rhythm at the idea of pulling her primary magic even deeper inside. All she'd done since the floor had broken during her battle with Alaric was try to compartmentalize it, attempt to make it as small as possible and hide it away. Lea thought she might throw up at the notion of doing the opposite.

"That's not who I want to be. The woman I am when the magic takes over. When I slip, everything else is gone. Every bit of anything good or kind," Lea admitted. "That's not who I want to be," she said again, louder, her heart racing at the thought that the only way to control that dark magic was to become it.

"But that *is* who you are. You are both of those things. You're good and light, *and* you are vengeance and darkness. They're both a part of you as much as your blood and bone. We cannot change what is inside us, as much as we may wish," Evangeline said, her lips tipping down. She reached out, placing a hand on top of Lea's. Lea froze, tears threatening to spill over her lashes, but she swallowed them down. She didn't want to cry.

Never again. She was weak enough already. Too out of control.

"There's no shame in being who you were born to be. In embracing every piece that makes you who you are—even the parts the world may find disagreeable. Because they're not. Every facet of you has a purpose. Especially the ones that scare you."

Lea fought back tears with shaking breaths. "And what if it destroys me?" she whispered, looking away, uncomfortable with this moment of vulnerability with a woman she didn't even know.

"The gods wouldn't have given their power to you if it would destroy you. If they didn't know for certain you could claim it as your own, control it, and use it for good. You're the kingdom's only hope, and they knew that. *You* know that."

Her words were gentle and soft, but still caused Lea's heart to pound. She knew Evangeline was right. Had known for some time that mastering her primary magic would require her to give into it, at least a bit.

"Your own magic. What you were born with. What is it like?" Lea asked, and Evangeline went back to digging in the dirt, pressing another seed into the soft ground.

"Not nearly so powerful as yours. I don't have both day and night magic, but my gift was unique. I was a seer, even before Seraphine. And I can—"

"Hold death at bay," Lea said, remembering Eudora describing her powers.

"Yes. I think it was my relationship with death that allowed me to assist the Black King with his spell. I tried to stop him. To only give him enough help to placate him, keep him from looking for you until I could escape the cage and kill him myself." Evangeline pressed her lips together. "I know I've caused a lot of harm. Truly, I was trying to protect you, but maybe I can help somehow."

Lea's mind flicked to Emma. How she'd connected the worlds to allow the dead to fight. But with Eudora gone, there was no way to get more of the potion that had allowed it. But maybe it wouldn't be needed. Maybe Evangeline could keep death from coming for their army at all.

"I'm sure Gray and I can find a place for you." Lea rose to her feet, suddenly exhausted. "It's late. We can discuss it more tomorrow."

Evangeline nodded, twisting her hands in her lap. "I'd like to speak more, another time. If that's okay with you, I mean. About your life. What I missed."

Lea stiffened at the reminder of what she'd lost by not having Evangeline present the last twenty-three years. Grief worked its way up her throat, but she held it down, nodding.

"I love you, Azalea," Evangeline said.

Lea's soul felt as if it was going to shatter. "Please, stop." Her voice broke. "I can't. Not right now. I know you were tortured. I know you thought you had no choice, and that you lived through things so horrible I will never understand. But please. If I have to forgive one more person, listen to one more excuse for why I didn't get a mother, why I lost my mother—" She stopped to take a deep breath. "I'm barely holding it together."

Evangeline's answering smile was sad. "Of course. When you're ready, then," she said. Lea nodded. And once again, she could tell that even without her sight, Evangeline had sensed her agreement, but whether it was from mother's intuition or from her powers as a seer, Lea was too broken to ask.

Lea turned on her heel, but stopped when Evangeline fell to her knees, her head thrown back and her hands gripping the dirt. Her face scrunched as if in pain, and Lea wondered if behind Evangeline's scarred skin, her eyes were turning the same milky white Eudora's did when she had a vision. Lea rushed to her, desperate to help even though there was nothing to do but wait for the vision to pass.

Her stomach dropped as she took in the pain etched into every line on Evangeline's face. Her lips twisted in a grimace, and a choked moan burst from her throat as if the vision was ripping her apart from the inside.

With a trembling hand, Lea reached out to comfort her, placing her palm on Evangeline's shoulder. For what felt like minutes, Lea simply knelt there, hoping Evangeline knew she wasn't alone, until she let out a deep breath and sank back onto her heels.

"Does it hurt? When you have visions, I mean? You looked as if you were in pain."

Evangeline's fingers drifted absently to the scars on her face. "I'm used to it." She cleared her throat, tucking her hair back behind her ears. "It's nothing I can't handle."

Lea heard what she didn't say—*it's nothing compared to what the Black King did to me.* The pain that she'd allowed him to inflict upon her to keep her only daughter safe.

"What did you see?" Lea asked, pushing down the surge of emotion rising up her throat. Evangeline scrunched her eyebrows, her mouth pinching in.

"I'm not sure. A large body of water with a rocky edge. There's a forest around it with odd trees. Bare except for the very tops, and full of bird nests. I heard..." Evangeline tilted her head as if trying to summon the sound. "I heard breathing, I think. Wet breathing, like someone was injured, maybe? There's a village on the other edge of the water. A small one. Maybe twelve houses? Do you know where it is?"

Lea racked her brain, but it didn't sound familiar, though she'd never been north of Auropera. "Gray will know. Did you see anything else?"

"A single phrase before I was pulled back. *Quisque occidere...*"

"What does it mean?" Lea asked, breathless, her heart pounding and her palms sweating.

"A spell..." Evangeline looked away, her hands shaking and her lips trembling. "It's the beginning of the spell for the Lonely Death."

Lea's shadows exploded, fear churning in her gut and spreading like wildfire through her veins. "It's Alaric. It has to be. I injured him during the battle. It makes sense—the breathing, the darkness I forced inside him. He's trying to gain more power to heal. We have to tell Gray." She scrambled to her feet, taking Evangeline's hand to quickly lead her back to the castle.

But it seemed they couldn't move fast enough. As they climbed the stairs to the front hall, a single petal fell from Lea's crown, turning into black ash that danced away in the wind behind her, reminding her that even if this was a clue, time was not on her side.

CHAPTER 27

EMMA

Emma slept deeply, her dagger clenched in her hand beneath her pillow. She never slept without it now—how could she? It was her only defense, her only weapon against the horrors that relentlessly haunted her dreams. Every night, the dead came. Faces twisted with pain, begging for her help. Their voices were relentless and their hands cold as they reached for her, their pleas ringing in her ears and breaking her heart.

She'd become used to seeing them while awake. Or as used to it as she could be. But when she was asleep? She was defenseless. Trapped, and unable to escape.

A sharp pounding at the door jolted Emma awake, her dagger clattering to the ground. Even half-awake, she was instantly grateful Thomas had fashioned a hard case to clip around the blade at night to protect her from sudden movements like this.

"Wake up, Emma. We're leaving in ten minutes. Gather whatever you need. We might not be back," Erik ordered through the door.

The urgency in Erik's voice sent a ripple of dread down her spine, but Emma forced herself to move, swinging her legs out of bed. The icy stone floor bit into her skin, the cold creeping up her bones. She shivered, wishing she could curl back under the covers and escape back into her dreamless slumber. But this was war. She would rest once Alaric was dead.

"I'll be out soon," she called, voice steady despite the whirlwind of emotions stirring inside her. She quickly pulled on a riding dress, its fabric familiar and worn, and slid her feet into her soft, weathered boots. They, too, had seen their share of journeys.

But hopefully that would change soon. Emma wanted nothing more than to stay in one place for a while, close to her friends, and, most importantly, safe. She grabbed her satchel—the one she'd kept packed and sitting by the door since they'd arrived at the castle.

Emma hadn't been able to shake the idea that they might have to leave at a moment's notice, and so she'd prepared, her paranoia and anxiety paying off.

She glanced around her room, eyes sweeping over the few things she would leave behind—books on the windowsill, too heavy to carry, and clothes that would be of no use on the road. There was no room for sentiment. A light pack would reduce her burden as they traveled. Though she couldn't help but hope her things would be waiting for her if they returned.

When we return, she reminded herself, turning and throwing open the door.

"Shit!" Emma said, nearly jumping out of her skin when she found Thomas standing just on the other side, fist raised and ready to knock.

"Sorry!"

"Thomas! Gods, you scared me!"

His expression softened, and he lowered his hand. "I— Um... Do you need any help?"

Emma shook her head, but his eyes latched onto the satchel. It was light, easy to carry, but she could feel from Thomas that he needed to do something. Help in some way, so she held it out to him. "Do you know what's going on? Where are we going?" she asked.

"I'm not sure." He took the satchel and slung it over his shoulder. "Do you have your dagger?"

"In there." Emma pointed to the bag.

"Perfect. Ready?" Thomas held out his hand, and Emma took it. It warmed her chest the way his face relaxed at her contact, and together, they hurried toward the main gates.

As they moved quickly through the hallways, Emma's mind raced. "Do you think they found him?" she asked softly, her voice so fragile it reminded Emma of glass.

"I hope so," Thomas gave her a sideways look, his steps slowing as they approached Lea and Gray sitting atop their horses.

"Has something happened?" Thomas asked.

Gray nodded. "Evangeline had a vision. We're leaving for Howen. We think Alaric might be there."

Emma's stomach dropped at the thought. Of course, they needed to find Alaric. It was the only way to end this war. But going after him so brazenly made her pause. As if sensing her discomfort, Thomas squeezed her hand.

"It'll be okay," he promised, leading her toward two unoccupied horses, already saddled and ready. With a boost beneath her feet, Emma plopped onto the saddle and settled in, stifling a yawn.

"I'm so fucking tired," Janelle said from beside her where she sat with Erik on top of Cinnamon, her eyes heavy as if she, too, had been woken from a deep slumber.

Emma looked at the dark sky, wondering what time it was, guessing that it was the early morning hours before what should be sunrise. Would they be able to find their way in the dark? Anticipation and anxiety grew in Emma's chest as she watched Vincent speaking with Gray and Tanad in hushed tones.

Gray turned to Thomas. "You brought weapons?"

"All that I could carry," he said, gesturing to the bag now hooked to his saddle. "Daggers mostly."

"That should be enough. Are we ready?" Gray asked Lea, sitting up straighter, and she nodded.

Another bolt of anxiety worked its way through Emma's chest, wrapping around her heart and threading through her ribs.

Gray turned to Vincent. "This is a reconnaissance mission, to start. Once we're certain where Alaric is, we'll send for the rest of the troops in their entirety. Every last one of them."

"We'll be ready," Vincent answered, tucking his thumb inside his fist and placing it over his heart. Gray returned the gesture, then turned Obsidian to face the portcullis. Lea moved to his side, and they shared a look, so full of fear and passion and fury that Emma had to look away.

Erik led Cinnamon over to them, positioning himself and Jenelle to Thomas's left.

"Evangeline had a vision? And Alaric's there?" Thomas asked.

Erik pressed his lips together. "That's what she thinks."

Thomas's nostrils flared as he took a deep breath, looking at Emma as if assessing if she was prepared for what the next few days might hold.

"Your dagger?" he asked again, and Emma nodded, grateful for the reminder. Holding it would ground her. Calm her mind and give her something to focus on.

"Yes." She opened her shoulder bag and rooted around, her shoulders relaxing as her fingers found the hilt.

"Keep it touching your skin," Thomas reminded her, not unkindly. "Remember, it will warn you of danger."

With a grateful smile, Emma nodded, moving to clip her bag back to the saddle. She paused as a glint of silver caught her eye from within the bag.

"What's that?" Thomas asked, leaning over to peek inside.

"I don't—" Emma shoved her hand in the bag, her face paling as her fingers found what had caught Thomas's attention. A vial. Her heart picked up in rhythm, thumping furiously against her sternum. She'd packed this bag herself, had checked it nearly every day since, just in case something had fallen out or she'd forgotten something important. "I don't know how this got in here." Emma pulled the vial from her bag, a twin to the one Eudora had made for her that would tether her to the Earth.

"You didn't put that in there?" Thomas asked, and Erik stiffened.

Emma shook her head. "No. I haven't seen or spoken to Eudora since we left Bearswillow," she said, her breaths growing shallow. Panic bubbled inside her chest, and Emma worried she was going to hyperventilate and faint.

"Hey." Thomas leaned over, placing his hand on her lower back. "It's okay. We already know we can't trust the witch. She's just playing with us. Trying to keep us on edge."

"Lea and Gray banished her earlier today," Erik chimed in. "She must have slipped it into your bag before she left."

Emma's breathing grew even more ragged.

"It's nothing," Thomas repeated, rubbing slow circles on her back. "It means nothing."

Struggling to slow her breath, Emma nodded. "Okay," she said. "Okay. She probably had extra, right?"

"I'm sure that's all this is," Thomas said, handing Emma's reins back to her and leaning over to give her a peck on the cheek before they started moving. Blood rushed into Emma's cheeks as she kicked her own horse's sides to cause her to trot forward, but even as she tried to convince herself that there wasn't a deeper meaning to the potion being snuck into her bag the very day they left to go after Alaric, Emma couldn't shake the feeling that something horrible was coming.

After all, Eudora could see the future. Did she know that they would need the potion again, and soon? Did she not realize that Emma almost hadn't survived the last time? It was all she could think about as they rode in silence—what Eudora's intentions had been. What tricks she could be playing now, or what mind games. Emma turned it over and over and, analyzing it from every angle, not even paying attention to where they were.

Her horse simply followed along, cantering when Obsidian cantered, galloping across fields when he galloped. And stopping when Obsidian stopped suddenly, his ears folding back and his eyes darting around nervously.

"What's wrong, boy?" Gray asked the clearly unsettled animal. The magnificent black stallion pawed at the ground. He was nervous, but why?

Gray's shadows shot outward, Lea's following closely behind as they searched for whatever threat Obsidian was detecting. Erik drew his sword, whispering in Janelle's ear.

"Do you sense anything?" Thomas asked Emma, but she just shook her head, no. "Then what—"not even a second later, a surge of magic rushed across the land, throwing their hair back and causing the horses to jolt backward. A pink and red haze grew from the horizon, magic still flowing past them, shimmering and bending the grass and branches with immense force.

Emma's jaw dropped, her breath escaping in a whoosh of awe.

The sun was rising.

Erik tilted his head back as the first rays of light met his skin, the dark circles beneath his eyes fading as his magic replenished itself. Lea and Gray shared another loaded look, one that echoed Emma's own feelings. Seeing the sun after weeks of night should be nothing but joyful. But it wasn't joyful.

It was terrifying.

The sun no longer looked like the sun. It was at least five times its usual size, burning orange and red, and so hot, Emma had the sudden urge to take off her jacket. But that wasn't even the most unusual part. As the sun rose, the black sky faded away, turning a deep, blood red.

Thomas once again reached for Emma. And once again, she was grateful for his need to be close to her in moments of uncertainty. Because this? It seemed like an omen.

But an omen of what? Terrible things to come? Without night, Thomas would no longer be able to make his weapons. Gray's magic would take some time to weaken, but if the day lasted long enough, it could leave them vulnerable and without his full ability to protect them.

The thought made her want to throw up.

"This changes nothing. Let's go," Gray said, his voice sharp and his shadows pulsing as he dug in his heels and led them toward the bloody, flaming horizon.

CHAPTER 28

ERIK

The city of Howen appeared in the distance, the intense, red glow of the sun illuminating it from behind in a way that made it look like the entrance to hell. Shadows lengthened from its buildings, creeping toward them like long fingers ready to pluck them from their horses and pull them into the darkness. Erik shifted, subconsciously pulling Janelle closer, his arm wrapping tightly around her middle.

Obsidian paused, stomping his feet as Gray turned to look at Lea. A silent conversation passed between them, and despite the stifling heat and the heavy, thick atmosphere of uncertainty, Erik smiled. He'd spoken to Gray several times about his frustration with the lack of mate bond, with the fact that he and Lea could no longer communicate without words spoken aloud or prying ears listening in.

But what Gray didn't seem to realize was that even without the physical bond marking their skin, or the auditory sound of her voice in his head, they were still deeply in tune with one another, always communicating with small shakes of the head or shrugs of the shoulder. Always touching, searching for each other's eyes.

Not for the first time, Erik wished for a bond like that with Janelle. He'd considered trying. Just a few days ago he'd been thinking of private spots beneath the sun where he could—

"Stop it," Janelle snapped. "Stop thinking about that. Now's not the time."

"Hey!" His hands flew in the air. "I'm not thinking about anything!" he protested. "I would *never*."

"Tell that to little Erik digging into my back," Janelle fired back, and Erik laughed. He shrugged. There was no use denying it. She could obviously feel the evidence of his desire for her. It wasn't her fault. His need for her was constant, almost insatiable. Erik was considering his retort when Gray motioned him forward.

The tension in his shoulders and sadness in Lea's eyes caused Erik's body to turn off immediately, switching from desire and need to adrenaline and alertness.

"What's going on?" Erik asked. "Is he here?" Erik peered through the trees as if squinting would somehow make Alaric appear.

"Lea feels his presence, but it's gone stale."

"It's older. Days. A week, maybe," Lea added.

"Do you want me to follow it?" Erik asked. "I can try to track him while you investigate here."

"I think we need all hands in the village," Lea said, her shadows floating down onto the ground and between the long blades of grass like fog rolling in at dawn. "Alaric isn't the only thing I can feel."

"What do you mean?" Janelle asked, and Gray's lips tipped downward.

"Death. The air is thick with death." His voice was almost a whisper, and Erik turned on instinct to find Emma. Maybe she knew something that could prepare them for what they faced.

He regretted it immediately. Emma's face had gone ashen, a shaking hand covering her mouth and tears welling in her eyes.

"So much death..." she whispered.

Thomas moved to her side, grabbing her reins and pulling their horses closer together. "What do you need from me? What do we need to do?" he asked, his voice gentle and warm.

Emma cleared her throat as she tried to push away the tears choking back her words. She looked around, her eyes settling on empty air all around them, and the familiar eerie feeling of knowing the dead were near and though he couldn't see them settled on Erik's shoulders. He subconsciously pulled Janelle closer.

"They want to be laid to rest," Emma finally said.

"Then that's what we'll do," Thomas soothed. He turned to Gray. "Right?"

Gray and Lea shared another one of their looks, and Lea nodded, her hands squeezing tighter around her own reins. Black flames cascaded down the side of her horse, sinking onto the ground and singeing the grass. Her shadows trailed outward, intertwining with the flames and twisting, almost violently, and Erik looked away, giving her privacy to fight her inner demons.

Lea cleared her throat. "Let's go, then," she said, sliding off Luna and tying her off to a tree. The others followed suit. Erik and Janelle joined hands, as did Emma and Thomas, and as one, they moved forward, the heat growing almost unbearable as they walked through the tall grass on foot. Erik's heart pounded in a combination of heat and anticipation.

Emma was used to death, or being close to it anyway, so what had she sensed that had been so horrible it'd taken the color from her face and brought tears to her eyes? It was a tiny village, after all, but after only a few yards, Erik sensed what both Lea and Emma had felt.

Death *did* hang heavy in the air, the scent of decaying bodies so pungent and suffocating, it made his eyes water. Lea and Gray remained stoic as Emma began to sob, and Erik's heart sank for her. It was bad enough walking into the village knowing what waited for them. But to *feel* it? To see the dead and hear their pleas? It made Erik shiver.

Thomas pulled her closer and helped her continue forward, as if the only way they would make it further was if their feet never stopped moving. It was only a few more yards before Janelle coughed, her non-Fae senses finally allowing her to smell what the rest of them already had.

"He's not here," Lea confirmed, speaking under her breath to Gray.

"Are you certain?" he asked.

Lea nodded. "His magic, I can't feel it. Not like I would if he were hiding here somewhere."

"My dagger isn't alerting me to danger," Emma said, sniffling as they stopped at the entrance to the village—an old, rickety wooden gate hanging slightly off its hinges.

With a sigh, Gray turned to the others, his shadows already floating toward the village. Erik knew what he was going to say before he even opened his mouth. "No one is required to follow me. I've seen this before—what a village decimated by my father's magic looks like. I will never unsee it. It haunts my dreams. I will not fault you, *any* of you, if you want to stay behind."

One at a time, Gray looked to Emma, then Thomas, then Janelle, and Erik was grateful Gray had the sense to know he wouldn't be dissuaded. "Whatever waits for us inside this town... it will likely be worse than anything you've seen before."

"The dead might be able to help us," Emma said.

A sad, proud smile darted across Thomas's face as he looked down at Emma. "Thank you for your concern, Gray, but I will be joining as well."

"Janelle?" Erik asked, leaning down to speak in her ear. "No one will blame you for not wanting to see—"

"Where you go, I go," she said, cutting him off. "You should fucking know that by now." A surge of gratitude and pride filled Erik's chest at Janelle's words. So brave. So honest.

"Of course," he said, squeezing her hand tighter. Janelle was his, and he was hers, and he would no more allow someone to separate them than the gods would allow the sun to set.

"Then it's decided," Lea said, straightening her shoulders and lifting her chin. "No turning back now."

CHAPTER 29

LEA

The absolute destruction they stumbled upon was so much worse than Lea could ever have imagined. She *felt* the wreckage and death in a way she'd never experienced before, every shallow, ragged breath pulling it deeper into her very marrow. The moment the village had come into view, Lea had known that what they'd find inside would be tragic. She'd sensed the lingering pain of the horrific suffering that had occurred here, and somehow, she still hadn't been prepared for it.

Bodies. Men, women, and children. Babies. Spread throughout the village square carelessly and haphazardly, as if they were nothing more than sacks of horse feed.

Lea's darkness grew and grew, her power expanding painfully in her chest, so big Lea worried her ribs would crack from the pressure of it begging for release. It wanted to destroy, craved suffering like a drug, but not like this. It took no joy from the suffering of the innocent.

Find him, the voice said.

Destroy.

Destroy.

Destroy.

The command pounded like a drum in her brain, a vibrating rhythm that repeated again and again and again. The pain became overwhelming and her vision blackened, her flames rising several feet above her head.

Find him, and destroy him. Destroy them all.

A command. An order she had to heed. And yet, she had to control it. Couldn't let that darkness win. Lea's ears rang, her throat closing and her breaths growing more shallow. She tried to push her primary magic down, the anger and rage and wrath threatening to eat her alive. It wasn't helpful. Not when it could cause her to lose herself.

Her friends shouted her name from somewhere through the blackness, but Lea couldn't see them. They were gone. Out of sight. It was simply her, the bodies, and the black fire around her.

Destroy.

She had to find something, anything, to help her release her magic. Just enough so she didn't explode and hurt the people she loved. Lea walked toward the circle of the town square. If nothing else, she could burn the bodies. Give them a burial by fire. Emma had said the spirits needed to be at rest. And the blood bath in front of her? There would be no rest until the bodies had been respectfully disposed of.

Disgust crept up her throat, coating her tongue in bile. No one deserved this. This... horror. Her eyes flicked to a man with his intestines hanging out, throat slashed. Nearby lay an arm ripped from a torso, and nearby, teeth scattered across the pavement like dice that had been abandoned mid-game.

Alaric hadn't just killed these people, he had slaughtered them, magic or not. Infected the village with the Lonely Death, and either tortured them until they were weak enough for him to steal their power, or brutally murdered them just because he could.

Emma's head suddenly swung to Lea, her mouth opening to shout, but the moment Lea's feet moved from the cobblestone road to the larger, flat stones of the courtyard, an explosion rocked the Earth. Lea stumbled, her eyes snapping up to search for the cause. Her rage grew even more fierce, black flames and shadows branching out in every direction.

"Alaric!" she hissed, pulling herself upright and swinging her head around until her eyes found the church, a tiny chapel, only large enough to fit maybe twenty people inside, and it was going up in flames. Screams of agony punched through the fog of darkness around her. Cries of "Help me!" and "Please, gods!" made Lea's darkness surge even more.

"My daughter! Help her!" Lea pushed down the wave of nausea in her stomach at hearing a mother screaming for her child's life. She didn't know how many people were in the church, but she'd had enough. Enough death. Enough suffering. Gray and Erik ran toward the flaming chapel, but Lea knew there was nothing they could do. Not against *this* magic. Alaric's magic.

The magic of thousands of Fae. Stolen and wielded by a madman.

It'd all been a trap, just like the one surrounding the cage inside the castle, the one that had held her mother hostage for decades.

Enough. Enough of the games. The death. Enough of the fighting and losing. Enough suffering. Lea's flames grew taller, mixing with the fire around the church, making it grow hotter and burn faster.

"No!" she screamed. Or, at least, she thought she did, but Lea wasn't sure.

You must become the darkness, Evangeline's voice circled in her mind, and Lea's heart stuttered, pounding furiously out of rhythm. She *couldn't* become the darkness. It would kill her. But if she didn't, they would all die. Every single person screaming for their life right now inside that church. Every innocent villager—her own people. Sweat broke out on her neck, panic surging up her throat, but she forced it down.

She'd watched helplessly as Gray's eyes had glazed over with death. Never again would she allow it to claim one of her own. She was their fucking queen.

Not a coward.

Not a slave to the gods' power.

She was a warrior.

No one had fought for her. Not until Gray. Not really. Her parents had lied. Her birth mother had abandoned her. But she'd felt love now. Real, sacrificial love. *That* was the kind of queen she wanted to be. A loving one. A brave one. One willing to risk it all for the people who depended on her.

Lea closed her eyes and shoved away her terror, reaching inside and allowing the darkness to claim her—to seep into her marrow and wrap around her bones, merging with her own flesh until it was coursing through her bloodstream with every beat of her heart. Her head flew back as she opened herself up to it, calling it home, begging it to fill her—to change her.

A flicker of fire ignited in her chest, and instantly, the inferno consuming the church began to pull back, climbing up Lea's body and wrapping around her in a blazing tornado of flames. Agony, unlike anything she'd ever experienced before, spread through her veins and arteries. Through her capillaries and into her organs and across her skin. She screamed again, falling to her knees, her voice sounding miles away as she screamed until her voice was raw and her throat bled.

And *just* as the pain became too much, the moment Lea was certain she was going to die, her agony disappeared into nothing. The pain was gone, as was the inner turmoil she'd been battling since returning from the dead.

Lea shot out a hand, forcing shadows from her fingertips in the direction of the church. Enormous storm clouds of darkness flew forward and shrouded everything in black. Emma shrieked and Gray shouted her name, but she couldn't focus on them. There were lives at stake.

Striding forward through the black smoke, Lea pulled a moonflower seed from her pocket and shoved it into the ground at the base of the steps to the church. She felt the last flicker of fire extinguish within the building, then grabbed her sword, pulled the magic of the sword inside her, and forced a gust of wind to blow the smoke away. The windows to the chapel shattered outward and thick black smoke poured out between the remaining pieces of jagged glass.

Lea pulled her shadows back into herself, sighing in relief as they nestled back behind her breastbone. The brilliant red sun was blindingly bright now that her shadows weren't blocking it, and she squinted as she stumbled up the stone stairs to the still smoking church. She grabbed the old wrought iron handle of the door, pushing and pulling, but the door remained shut. Lea gritted her teeth, rage bubbling inside her as she lifted a hand to burn the door away, but Gray was at her side in an instant, kicking the door inward, splinters of wood flying through the air from the impact of it hitting the inside wall.

The cries of pain and agony from those inside grew louder. So intense, the sound made Lea dizzy. She wasted no time, jumping off the stairs and kneeling on the ashy ground as she pulled a handful of moonflower seeds from her pocket.

"Bring them out here!" Lea ordered as she shoved her fingers into the dirt and funneled her magic into the soil. The moonflowers responded instantly, threading across the ground and blooming into pristine white flowers within seconds. Her heart thundered as she plucked them, reveling in the way they remained white—almost glowing.

She held her palm out to the side, not bothering to stop picking petals with the other, and Janelle took them from her, distributing them to the men and women being carried through the doors.

Oozing, charred skin faded to red, then pink as wounds healed over, the color returning to the faces of those still unconscious. Lea held her breath as she waited, watching for them to wake up.

"It's the smoke, I think. Their lungs," Emma said, tilting her head to the side and closing her eyes. "They were near death, but I can still feel them. Stronger now. I think they'll wake soon." She placed a hand on Lea's arm. "You saved them."

Lea didn't have the time to feel relief.

"Who did this to you?" she asked a young woman coughing in the grass next to her. A child clung to her waist, soot coating his cheeks and throat.

"The King. Alaric. His soldiers rounded us up. All of us who didn't fall to the Lonely Death. He locked us inside and just left us there."

Lea's vision dotted with black as her fury grew. "How long were you in there?" she asked.

"Four days, I think." The woman scrunched her forehead as if she couldn't quite remember. "Maybe more?"

"Where did he go?" Gray dropped to Lea's side, having finished evacuating all the villagers from inside the church. Sweat dripped from his brow, and he rubbed it away with the sleeve of his forearm, smearing black ash across his forehead.

"I don't know. He looked sick. Terrifying. His veins were black, and his eyes..." The woman shivered. "I picture them every time my eyes close. Any time I even blink. He was furious when more of us didn't contract the Lonely Death. He said he needed more. More. More. More. He just kept screaming it."

Lea's darkness roared, black fire bursting from her skin, but Gray's shadows trailed up Lea's back, a silent reminder he was with her.

"What does he want? What did we do to deserve this?" the woman asked.

"Nothing," Lea said, pushing off the ground to stand. "You did *nothing*. You *didn't* deserve this. Alaric is nothing but evil." Even now, she could feel the vile fingerprint of the wicked false king.

She looked to the woods—toward that tiny trail of magic reminding her that Alaric had been here and fled.

"Go," Gray said, nodding at her. "See if you can track him. Maybe if we know the direction he fled, we can follow behind. We'll take care of the villagers. They've all taken the cure."

Lea turned, her stomach twisting as she realized why Gray wasn't insisting he come along. Alaric was long gone. They all knew it. There was no danger. No risk.

"And Lea," Gray said, stopping her with a hand on her arm. He reached out and cupped her cheek. "I'm proud of you. For accepting the darkness. You saved them." He tilted his head to the villagers, all now awake and recovering.

Lea couldn't speak as she choked back tears. Not because Gray was proud of her. He was always proud of her, whether she deserved it or not. And someday, when the war was over, she would find the words to tell him how much it meant to have his unwavering and unquestionable trust and love and support.

But the emotions churning inside her weren't because of anyone else. She was simply proud of herself, too. Proud of herself for making the choice she did, for embracing the darkness when it had been the last thing she'd wanted to do. It was her greatest fear. Lea had thought she'd lose herself if she gave in to it. That she'd become as evil and wicked as Alaric. But she'd been so wrong.

She didn't feel evil or wicked. She still felt the need for vengeance—sharp and bitter in the back of her throat. But unlike before, she now felt like she could handle the emotions that had threatened to consume her.

Lea closed her eyes, trusting her shadows to alert her to obstacles as she focused on Alaric's trail. The glimmer of his magic and essence. Now that she'd embraced her primary magic, her senses seemed sharper, her understanding of Alaric deeper. On the backs of her eyelids, his movements played out like a movie. His magic felt weak at the entrance to the town, then stronger at the church from when he walked away.

She pictured him reciting the spell for the Lonely Death, ensuring that everyone with magic was infected before slaughtering them mercilessly to take it. She could see him walking inside the church, enchanting it to explode when Lea neared it. But to kill the villagers or taunt her, she wasn't sure. The spell igniting the fire in the church hadn't killed anyone. Hadn't even managed to kill those within the church. Had it been a miscalculation on Alaric's part?

Or had he wanted her to know he was one step ahead of them.?That his callous disregard for life had only grown since their last encounter. Was he trying to show her she couldn't defeat him?

The wind blew at Lea's back, pushing her further north. Sweat dripped down her spine as the sun burned her skin. She called clouds into the sky, but within seconds they evaporated, the sun god's magic too hot and too powerful for her to overcome it. Not even her shadows could find relief from the heat.

Lea walked on, Alaric's trail becoming more sparse and harder to follow until she reached a stream where it washed away completely, disappearing as if he had never been there to begin with. Lea waded into the stream, the hem of her riding dress pulling at her legs as water filled her boots.

She spread out her shadows, searching for where the trail might pick back up again, but it was simply gone. Her heart sank, her body suddenly heavy. She closed her eyes, begging the goddess of the moon to help her, to give her some sort of clue as to where he may have gone.

But there was only complete silence. Until a branch snapped to her left. Lea startled, drawing her sword and summoning her shadows into her hands.

There was no voice begging her to destroy. Not anymore.

She *was* destruction, and gods help whoever was trying to sneak up on her from the forest beyond. Lea wasn't afraid as she coiled her shadows into a dense ball in her hand, ready to explode them outward at the first sign of danger, but she stopped when a familiar voice met her ears.

"Lea?"

The white tips of a horse's ears appeared through the trees, the head and body following as they pushed through the dense brush. And on top of the horse was a witch with horrible, scarred eyes.

"Lea? I know you're there. And I think you need my help."

CHAPTER 30

GRAY

The bodies would need to be burned. While burial was traditional in Desia, Gray was unwilling to risk the chance the Lonely Death could spread to other unsuspecting, innocent civilians. The spell had morphed and changed since his father had created it, expanded in a way he hadn't foreseen and hadn't been prepared for. But if there was even a chance that trodding upon the ground of those infected could cause the disease to spread, it wasn't something Gray was willing to risk.

What if a nearby town came to check on their neighbors? What if Tanad sent soldiers behind them to help and Lea wasn't here to plant and pick the moonflowers? They didn't know what Alaric, or the spell, was capable of. Not anymore.

Gray lifted a body into his arms—an older woman with a kind face and blood coagulated around a slit in her throat. It was sickening, but he refused to look away, determined to honor the deceased by, if nothing else, acknowledging their suffering. One by one, Gray, Erik, and Thomas gathered the bodies. They moved them from where they'd been haphazardly discarded like spoiled meat and lined them up in neat rows in front of the half-burned church.

As the men who'd been inside the church recovered, they joined them, picking up those they loved and fixing their clothing, covering them with whatever cloth they could find. Emma closed their eyes as she passed by the bodies one by one, reciting a prayer before turning to look into the blank air. Tears streamed down her face as she held space for each of those who had passed. She spoke to the dead, soft enough that Gray couldn't hear her words, and Gray worried about the toll this would take on her. It was one thing to see those who had passed long before, or passed in battle, but this had been nothing short of cold-blooded murder.

Fighting to control his shadows, his anger, he turned away from Emma only to find Janelle, her eyes red and mouth pinched in as if she might be sick. A pinch of guilt shot between his ribs. He couldn't help but feel like he was failing. These villagers had lost their lives, and all he could do was burn them. Couldn't even protect his friends from having to see the horrific destruction his brother had caused.

Gray looked to the tree line, searching for Lea. How far had she been able to track Alaric's magic? His chest tightened with the sinking suspicion that whatever trail she had found wouldn't lead them anywhere, just like the hut at the back of the castle grounds. But still, he could hope. He *would* hope.

Just as he had hoped that Lea would find a way to control her primary magic. He'd never doubted she was capable, but he hadn't known how to help her. Day after day, he'd watched her struggle. Encouraging her while guilt ate him alive. Loving her through her pain, but dying inside because he was unable to help bear the burden.

Gray's heart had nearly stopped when he'd watched Lea pull the darkness inside her, certain it would kill her. Instead, she'd found a way to take control of the power it had been holding over her. She'd made a choice that terrified her—becoming the darkness. But in the end, it had allowed her to master that raw, dark primary magic. It was as much a part of her as her light, and he loved both sides of her completely and equally. Pride surged in his heart at her strength and bravery, as well as relief that she would no longer be suffering as she tried to fight against the magic of the gods.

As the final piece of cloth was draped over the twenty-third body, the sound of hooves made Gray pause. His adrenaline kicked in as he twisted toward the sound, commanding his shadows to search for the approaching horse and its rider, but he pulled them back when he was met with Lea's energy. She was returning, but where she found a horse, Gray didn't know.

"Erik," he said, and Erik met his gaze. "Will you interview the survivors, please? Find out anything you can. How Alaric got here. How long he stayed, and how long the Lonely Death took to take effect. Any information you can glean from them, no matter how small. We don't know what piece of intel could be the key to finding him."

"On it," Erik said, moving immediately toward the decimated church as Gray returned his attention back to the forest, his eyes widening and his head tilting as Lea appeared, holding the reins to a horse with Evangeline sitting on top.

Lea's eyes were hard, and Gray couldn't discern what emotions her birth mother's appearance had dredged up inside her. Was it anger? Sadness? Her face betrayed nothing—stony and hard. But he couldn't fault her. Gray was sure his face echoed her own. Could they trust Evangeline? They'd left her behind, and yet, she had found them.

As Evangeline approached, she sucked in a sharp breath, her hand flying up to cover her mouth. Gray wondered how she knew what she had walked up on. What they'd been forced to witness here—this act of his brother's depravity that would haunt them all for a very long time.

She couldn't see the lines of bodies or the burned out church. Not after what the Black King had done to her. Was it simply the death hanging heavy in the air that had alerted her to the monstrosities that had occurred here? The scent of decay and burned wood? Or was it something more?

"Evangeline saw us in a vision," Lea said by way of explanation as they neared. "She said we need her help."

Gray crossed his arms. "Then thank you for coming," he said, still not completely positive he trusted her. "What did you see?"

Evangeline turned toward him, her scarred eye sockets facing him as if she could see into his soul.

"Many things. I'm sure you know the future changes constantly. There are so many outcomes. Too many." Evangeline touched her forehead as if in pain. "I saw the fire, then Alaric disappearing. Someone was helping him, but I couldn't see who it was. I saw cities of death. A final battle, and Lea on her knees. There's so much that needs to be done to keep her safe."

Gray's stomach churned, his shadows instantly finding Lea and wrapping around her body as if they could protect her from the horrors of Evangeline's visions. "Why was she on her knees?" he demanded.

"She was taking Alaric's power, but it was too much."

Lea crossed her arms defensively. "The goddess says there's a way."

Gray's voice deepened. "Don't you remember what happened when you tried to take my magic? It nearly killed you."

Evangeline interrupted him. "But it *has* worked. You took Genevieve's power. It can be done. I've seen you victorious. That means somehow, you *can* drain his magic, return it to the earth, and still live."

"Then we'll practice. We'll figure it out," Lea said, and Gray turned to her, his face lined with worry and his shadows pulsing. He reached out to cup her cheek, and a petal fell from her crown. His heart skipped a beat as it crumbled into ash, tiny black flecks scattering across the skin of his hand.

A lump formed in his throat—a fist-sized ball of fury and pain and fear that made it hard to breathe. The flowers were nearly half gone, sporadically falling at the most random times. He's seen petals fall only minutes apart, others hours, even days. There seemed to be no rhyme or reason to when they would fall—as if the universe didn't want them to know how much time they had left. A cruel trick of the gods to keep them on edge.

Pushing down his worry, Gray pulled Lea into his side, and she melted against him. Even without the mate bond, her uncertainty and self-doubt pushed through her skin and into his, causing his shadows to tremble, desperate to soothe her. But she couldn't be soothed. Not really. Not until Alaric was dead, and to do that, she had to drain his magic.

"If it's the only way, and that's what you want, Little Flower, then we'll try again. We'll practice as much as it takes," Gray said. "You said the goddess thinks you can do it. That there's a way to take his magic without it hurting you. She said you could defeat him. Evangeline says she's seen the same. Then there must be a way to take his power. We just have to figure out how to do it. *Safely*." He lowered his chin, growling out the last word.

Lea's jaw tightened, but she didn't argue.

"I think I can help find Alaric," Evangeline said. "If I can pick up the trail of his magic..." she trailed off, leaning down to brush her fingers through the grass, searching.

"We'll take you where he was. What would be most helpful?" Gray asked. "Figuring out his final moments? Walking through what happened when he arrived?"

"I'm not sure." She shook her head.

"Then we'll try both. Erik is interviewing the survivors. Why don't you join him? See what you can learn, and if it triggers anything." Evangeline bowed her head slightly, but whether in a sign of respect or simple agreement, Gray wasn't sure. It didn't matter to him. He didn't need her respect. All he needed was to find Alaric in time to save Lea and his people.

"Are you okay?" Gray asked, pulling Lea close and rubbing small circles on her lower back.

"I'll be fine," she said, leaning back to meet his eyes. "The trail disappeared at the river. It's just—" Lea's fist clenched. "He's always one step ahead of us. How can he disappear with no trace?"

He has help, a small voice said inside Gray's head. An unwelcome thought. But Lea was right. Alaric was always one step ahead of them, as if he knew their next move at all times. Was it possible there was another traitor? Someone Gray trusted who was deceiving them all?

The thought made him sick, but he pushed it away. "We'll find him. I promise you, we will find him, and we will end this."

Lea's eyes raised to the line of bodies covered in patchwork quilts and children's blankets. Sheets and coats.

"We'll have to burn them," Lea said, her face falling.

"I know," Gray said, frowning. "So do their loved ones. Emma has already helped them say their goodbyes."

Lea nodded, her shoulders falling as she stepped out of Gray's arms. Her movements were sluggish, tired, and Gray once again worried about the toll this war was taking on her. Not just her body and her mind, but her soul.

Clearing her throat, Lea raised her hands and closed her eyes. "May the magic of the wind carry them, the kiss of rain cleanse them, and the promise of eternity soothe their weary souls," Lea whispered as fire expanded around her, enormous, deep black flames that flickered through the grass as they spread across the ground toward the bodies. They caught fire, and Lea dropped to her knees, her arms still outstretched. "Until beyond the veil we follow."

A single tear rolled down her cheek, evaporating off her skin before it could fall to the ground. "I'm so sorry." Her voice softened, so low Gray could barely hear her. "I will keep your families safe." Lea promised them, finally dropping her arms as the blanket on the last body caught fire. "And I will avenge you. If it's the last thing I ever do, I will avenge you."

CHAPTER 31

LEA

The others joined Lea and Gray as the fire crackled away into embers, the bodies crumbling to ash, and even then, being consumed until nothing remained but twenty-three scorched patches of stone. Gray knelt next to his wife, a steadying hand on her back until the last flicker died off, and only then did they turn their eyes away from the makeshift graves of the victims.

It was done.

Lea's body felt heavy as she turned to Emma, who gave her a sad smile. Her face had relaxed a fraction, the lines around her eyes less pronounced. Emma nodded in confirmation. The dead were at rest. It was all they could do.

She finally stood when Erik cleared his throat behind her.

"Did you find anything that would help?" she asked.

"Not yet." Evangeline shook her head. "Most of the villagers said they never saw Alaric. That they were too lost in the chaos to notice him, but a few said he was here..."

"Ordering his men to round up those without the Lonely Death to put them in the church." Erik finished for her, his tone grim.

Lea's chest felt tight with anxiety. Nothing. All of this, and they were no closer to finding him than before they'd left the castle.

"Did you learn anything else?" Gray asked, and Lea didn't miss the hint of desperation in his voice.

"Just that he has a group of royal guards with him. The villagers estimated about thirty-five."

A crack rang out as the back corner of the church crumbled, and Evangeline's head snapped to the burned-out building. Lea froze, watching in rapt silence as her birth-mother moved toward it as if under a spell. She was nearly floating, one hand extended out in front of her as her graceful steps carried her forward. Her forehead scrunched again, that familiar look of pain etching into her features as Lea followed behind her. Was it a vision? A premonition?

Lea hurried after her, placing a hand on Evangeline's shoulder as if keeping her close would allow her to see or feel whatever was causing Evangeline to move as if hypnotized.

The witch's long fingers trailed the remains of the outer wall, and she sucked in a sharp breath. Lea watched intensely, barely breathing as her heart thundered and her blood roared in her ears. The wind blew softly, pushing her hair back from her face. It was soothing, comforting, but it also seemed to speak to her. *Pay attention*, it said. *Something is happening. Something important.*

Gray opened his mouth to speak, but Lea held up a hand, stopping him. Evangeline shuffled sideways toward the door, moving up the stone steps and rolling her neck from side to side.

In a second, Evangeline's demeanor shifted. Her soft, gentle movements became rigid, and her lips twisted into a smile that looked...wrong. Crooked and gleeful and sick.

With strength far more powerful than her weak, starved body should have allowed, Evangeline slammed the door shut, latching the large bolt into the iron slot. Evangeline laughed a horrible, wicked laugh, and began to mutter. Tears burned Lea's eyes, and her stomach flipped as she realized what she was watching.

Evangeline was acting out what Alaric had done like she was possessed. She was no longer looking at her mother's face, but Alaric's, twisted with excitement. Her fingers tapped against her side in exhilaration, and her posture tall and confident. But what truly made Lea's stomach fill with bile was the absolute joy on Evangeline's face—Alaric's expression as he'd locked all those people inside, knowing what was going to happen to them. Knowing that he would enchant the church to be engulfed in flames the moment someone stepped within the town center.

Women.

Children.

Clutching her chest, Lea forced herself to breathe. Evangeline waved a hand in the air as if enchanting the church herself, then threw her head back and laughed again—a sick horrifying cackle that made Lea's magic revolt.

It was as if she had become him. The man they hated. The man they hunted.

Evangeline turned, a spry skip in her step as she walked the same path Lea had followed when she'd picked up on Alaric's magic. Her movements were so different from her usual, elegant grace—eerily similar to Alaric's pompous posture and arrogant stride. Gray and Erik followed behind them, none of them speaking as Evangeline began to whistle.

It made Lea physically ill, seeing how Alaric had been so lighthearted as he'd walked away from the destruction he caused. As if it was a relief to finally unburden himself and the kingdom of this village.

Evangeline reached the rushing river and paused, twisting her head side to side as she searched for something. But what? She reminded Lea of an owl, her head turning so far it was unnatural as she looked all around her periphery.

She stepped forward until her dress was soaked to just above her knees, then bent down and splashed the cold water on her face. She lowered her head, cupping her hands and drinking from the stream. She suddenly seemed agitated, her joy evaporating as she kicked at the water, and she wiped her mouth with her forearm, looking back up to the sky impatiently.

The rush of murdering the townspeople was completely gone, her smile falling and her eyebrows scrunching in annoyance.

Evangeline scowled, crossing her arms over her chest.

"There you are," she finally said, still looking at the sky. "Fucking witches," she muttered under her breath.

Lea and Gray looked at one another, dread creeping across her skin. Her arms turned to gooseflesh, and she couldn't help but look over her shoulder, the hair on the back of her neck rising.

Evangeline stared at the empty air in front of her for several more seconds, then suddenly her head was thrown backward, her arms spread out to the sides as her back arched.

The woods went silent as she screamed out in pain, and Lea rushed forward, grabbing her around the waist before she could collapse into the water. Gray was at her side in an instant, helping bring her back to shore.

Evangeline rolled over, vomiting onto the rocky shoreline, heaving again and again until there was nothing left.

She took several ragged breaths, lying her head on her hands as if the effort of keeping her head up was unfathomable.

"Eudora," she said, spitting the name out as if it was ingested poison. "It was Eudora who helped him escape..."

CHAPTER 32

LEA

"**O**f fucking course it was Eudora. It's always that bit—hey!" Janelle hissed as Erik jabbed her in the side of the ribs, and he gave her an apologetic grimace.

"What do you mean, Eudora helped him?" Gray asked, and Evangeline rubbed her forehead between her eyes. Something she seemed to be doing more often, and Lea wondered if it was pain that caused her to repeat the gesture again and again.

Evangeline's eyebrows scrunched. "Well, I think it was Eudora. It *felt* like her, at least," she said.

A wave of confusion crashed over Lea. Evangeline and Eudora had met before. Surely she would know what she looks like. "Start at the beginning. What did you see?" Lea urged, her mind reeling. There were very few things that Lea felt she knew about Eudora with complete certainty, but the one thing she felt wholly confident about was that she would never betray Tanad. That only he held her loyalty.

"Alaric closed the door and locked everyone away in the church. He was happy. Thrilled, actually. But something was wrong with him. He looked ill—felt weakened. His face was gaunt and pale, and his skin looked like it was sliding down his bones with veins like black spiderwebs creeping across his skin."

Lea shivered. Alaric was terrifying enough without his veins turning black and his skin sagging. But if he was weakened, maybe taking his magic would be easier.

Evangeline continued. "Then, when he got to the stream, well, I wasn't sure at first what was happening. But he was waiting for something. Looking to the sky."

"Eudora?"

Evangeline nodded. "I think so. It felt like her. Had the same energy. But she looked completely different. Much younger. Beautiful and vibrant."

Lea's brain spun. She remembered thinking on more than one occasion that Eudora had characteristics of a woman far younger than she was. The way she'd climbed the stairs in her tower. The smooth skin on her hands that Lea had thought she imagined just before Eudora had poured a vial into her tea. The potion Lea had swiped from her that very day but hadn't tested, not knowing what it was or what it would do. Lea's fire flickered in her chest, furious that she hadn't put the pieces together sooner.

"If she makes herself older, frail and aged, it would make sense," Gray said. "She can get people to underestimate her, and they'll be far less likely to push back against her wishes."

"You're absolutely sure it was her?" Lea asked, hoping to the gods Evangeline was wrong. If they didn't know Eudora's true appearance, she could be anywhere. She could have been in their army, gathering information without their knowledge. She could be pretending to be *anyone*.

"My magic felt her. The magic Eudora gifted me. It recognized its own blood." Evangeline nodded firmly. "Yes, I'm certain. It's the only explanation," she said.

"What did she do once she saw Alaric?" Lea asked. "Did he recognize her?"

"He did. He's clearly known her for some time. It was like they were lovers. She caressed his chest, trailed a finger down his cheek."

Lea pushed down a wave of nausea. "Why? Why would she do this? How does this make any sense at all? She caressed his chest and then disappeared? To where? And why would she help him at all when she claims to love Tanad?"

"Because Tanad sent her away. It could be revenge," Erik suggested.

"Because she's a vindictive bitch," Janelle said at the same time.

Lea lowered her eyebrows, her jaw clenching. "Tanad didn't banish her until a few days ago. What if this was her plan all along? What if she wants power, just like Alaric? She can help him defeat us. With her seeing abilities, she'll know our every move. Can warn him if we're coming, or give away our location if he decides to come after us."

Gray rubbed a hand across his scruffy chin as he paced. "There must be something we can do," he said, his shadows trailing out in all directions. "The goddess *said* Lea can defeat him. There has to be a way around this."

"We can confuse her visions," Evangeline said, her voice soft. Gray froze, and Lea's stomach twisted.

"Eudora will be watching you and Lea closely, I suspect. Neither of you can be the ones to make decisions. Not the same ones, at least. Not together. There must be too many possibilities for her to be certain of the outcome."

"You're saying if we don't have a concrete plan, she won't know which possibilities are our *actual* intentions?" Lea asked.

"Exactly. If everyone is acting independently, if decisions are never settled upon as a group, her visions will show all the possible outcomes.

It's only once the choice has been made that those of us with the sight can see what the actual outcome of the future will be."

"Then how do we move forward? How do we know where to go next if Gray and I can't decide?" Lea asked.

Evangeline bit her lip. "I saw a place. But I'm hesitant to even describe it to you. Even that could tip her off that we're coming."

"Do *you* know where it is?" Erik asked, scrunching his brows, and Lea had the urge to ask what he was planning.

Evangeline shook her head. "No. I can only describe it."

"If you don't know where it is, and you can't tell us what it looks like without tipping off Eudora, how are we supposed to get there?" Gray asked, every word brimming with tension.

"I don't believe Eudora will be watching me. At least, it's far less likely than her searching for you all. She'll expect me to stay behind. I can't fight. I can't even see. I'm a liability in battle. And let us be honest. After years with the Black King, I would bet she's counting on Gray not trusting me to be near Lea until he can be certain of where my loyalties lie."

"She has a good point," Gray said under his breath before turning to face Evangeline. "How do we know you're telling the truth?"

Evangeline lifted her chin, shaking her head slightly. "You don't. But all the bad things I've done, any help I gave the king, it was to keep your mate, my daughter, alive. That is all I have cared about from the moment she was born. I don't regret the choices I made to keep her safe. I *can't*."

Lea's eyes burned, and her face turned red. Her mind flashed back to when she had saved Evangeline in the womb. To the twisted threads of fate that had ripped them apart and pushed them back together. The goddess herself had told Lea to save the baby. Maybe it was all leading them here, to this moment. "I trust her," Lea said, realizing as she spoke the words that it was true. Even if there was lingering anger and resentment over the choices Evangeline had made, it was obvious she loved her. That she truly had only wanted to protect her.

Gray looked into Lea's eyes for a long moment before nodding. "What do you suggest?" Gray asked Evangeline.

"I think I can start us in the right direction," she said. "The geography is typical of—" she stopped herself, taking a deep breath. "Let's prepare to leave. I will get us as close as I'm able before I tell you more. Even if Eudora sees you coming, maybe this will allow us to make some headway. The more ground we can cover before they flee, the stronger the trail should be when we arrive."

"It's worth a try," Lea said, looking to Gray. "The only other option is to—"

"Separate," he finished for her, his eyes darkening. "Absolutely not."

Erik stepped forward, placing a hand on Gray's shoulder. "Let's feed and water the horses. And ourselves. I'll describe some towns and landmarks to Evangeline. Maybe it will help her get us closer without needing to give us more information."

"Do you think this will work?" Lea asked Evangeline honestly.

"Your guess is as good as mine. But I'm certain it's less likely she'll be focusing on me in her visions. She'll be far more focused on you two. Maybe your friends. The more possibilities, the better. I'd like you all to consider what you think the best plans are. What towns you would have us travel toward. Focus on them; make them a reality in your mind."

"You decide when we leave, Evangeline. The rest of us will follow behind you. Close enough to track, but far enough that we're not all together. Maybe not deciding to leave until the last moment will give us even more time.

Evangeline nodded, rubbing her forehead again.

"Are you okay?" Lea asked.

"Just fine," she said.

"You seem like you're in pain," Lea prodded, moving closer.

"Truly, it's nothing." Evangeline waved her off. "Just a headache. When I use Eudora and the Seraphine's powers, it's... uncomfortable. But it's nothing I can't handle."

Lea swallowed, not sure how to respond. She didn't believe Evangeline for a second. She knew pain, had seen far more of it than anyone should ever have to see.

"I promise, I'm fine," Evangeline said, once again reading Lea's mind. "Don't worry about me. You need to rest and focus on yourself. On what must be done."

"That's all I've focused on since I returned," Lea said, a bit more harshly than she'd intended.

"I know, my dear girl. But even if the future isn't written in stone, one thing is certain. Finding Alaric is of no use unless you learn to take his magic. I've seen his strength. And it only grows. With Eudora at his side..."

Evangeline trailed off, but Lea didn't need her to finish her thought. She already knew. With Eudora at his side, this war just had just become a lot more difficult. And certainly, far more deadly.

CHAPTER 33

LEA

Lea struggled to keep her eyes open, fatigue pulling at her bones as she stripped down to her underclothes. The heat was stifling, even in the shade, so she wandered to the stream, praying to the goddess it would give her some much-needed relief.

She didn't bother including the god of the sun in her prayers. He obviously hated her with the fiery passion of a *thousand* suns. It was obvious, based on his intense and unrelenting punishment. Lea had hoped that maybe after a few days his temper would dim. That he would realize she and the goddess had made the right decision. One meant to save the people he claimed to love. His people. *Their* people. But no. Every day just seemed to get hotter, each passing hour bringing them closer and closer to incineration.

Pulling off her socks, Lea dipped her feet into the stream, groaning as the water washed over her skin. She waded further, goosebumps popping up all over her body at the stark contrast between the heat of the red sun and the chill of the water. Once she was about knee deep, Lea sat, relishing in her body temperature cooling as the water gently rushed around her shoulders. Tilting her head back, Lea undid her braid and positioned herself so that the water pulled her hair out behind her in a long golden trail.

It was the most human she'd felt in days, but even the relief from the unending sun did nothing to soothe her frazzled nerves. Eudora had been deceiving them this whole time—for who knows how long. A tiny pang of pity settled in her stomach as she thought about King Tanad. He'd certainly been fooled even worse than the rest of them.

And for what? Power? Riches? Lea wondered what Eudora's plan had been. Had she been searching for a way to take Alaric's power for herself? Would she come for Tanad's power next? Or had she truly cared about him until he'd stood in the way of what she wanted most?

But to deceive him so thoroughly and completely... It was still the most surprising piece of the puzzle. After all, what was the point of holding all the power in the world if you couldn't use it for good? If you couldn't help the people you loved? If there was nobody left to love you back?

"There you are."

Lea snapped her head up as Gray plopped down on the rocky shoreline, pulling off his shoes and rolling up his trousers. He leaned closer to hand Lea a tin plate—dried meat, stale bread, and hard cheese. Her stomach clenched in protest, practically begging her not to eat. She was too anxious. Too overwhelmed.

But Gray wouldn't be deterred, nodding at the plate and raising his eyebrows. His shadows floated forward as if they weren't above force feeding her. Lea rolled her eyes, but grabbed a piece of bread and took an obligatory bite. It tasted like tree bark, but she swallowed it down anyway and bit off another chunk. It wouldn't have mattered even if he'd brought her the most decadent quadruple chocolate cake with fresh berries and caramel. Even the richest, sweetest treat would taste like paper right now.

Lea's stomach protested, but she kept chewing, forcing herself to swallow and eat some cheese. Who knew when they would have the time to eat again? And she needed her strength more than ever.

"Have *you* eaten?" she asked Gray, noticing he hadn't brought anything for himself.

"I ate mine on the walk over here," he said, splashing water on the back of his neck. "Tasted like dirt." He smirked, and Lea couldn't help but smile. Even without the mate bond, he could read her so well. "Still finished it, though," he said pointedly.

"I'm going to eat it," Lea said, taking an exaggerated bite.

Gray pushed a thick cloud of shadows over their heads, blocking out a tiny portion of the other worldly bright light. Lea added her own shadows, forcing down a piece of dried meat.

"I don't like this, Gray," she finally said. "Not knowing where we're going. *When* we're going. Not knowing what we're going to find when we get to whatever secret location we're searching for."

"I don't either," Gray agreed. "Maybe we should rethink this." He tilted his head and clenched his jaw, his fingers cutting into his palms as he squeezed his hands into fists. He was more nervous than she'd seen him in some time, likely because of his lack of control of the situation, but Lea couldn't blame him. She felt the same.

"We don't have time to waste on rethinking things," Lea said, forcing her hands to remain at her sides rather than floating up to touch her flower crown.

Gray sighed. "I thought we were ready for anything. I planned for a hundred years. For every contingency. But what I didn't expect was Eudora helping Alaric."

Lea took another bite, chewing mechanically.

"I was thinking more about what Evangeline said. About you taking Alaric's power..."

Lea swallowed, handing her plate back to Gray. He narrowed his eyes at the few pieces of meat remaining, but didn't say anything.

"And?" Lea asked, already certain of what Gray was going to say.

"I think it's a bad idea."

"Gray—"

He held up his hands. "I know. I know I said I think you can do it. I'm sure with enough time, you could. But what if it's another trap? Or a trick. Don't you remember the last time? I thought it was going to kill you."

"What other choice do we have?" Lea asked, frustration pounding in her head like a drum. "We have no other options. The goddess herself said it's the only way. I have to take Alaric's magic, and return it to the earth."

Gray opened his mouth, but Lea cut him off. "I know what you're going to say. That it's not safe. That we're missing something. But right now, it's the only chance we have. Evangeline has seen us winning, Gray. And the goddess herself said there's a way for me to take his magic without it hurting me."

"Without it *killing* you," Gray growled, his shadows expanding, but Lea ignored him.

"There *is* a way. We just have to keep searching for it. I know you don't completely trust Evangeline, but we're blind without her. She can help us find Alaric. We *have* to find him, Gray. And soon."

Gray's eyes flicked to her moonflower crown, and Lea let the moment linger, thick and heavy.

"We either trust her and *maybe* die, or we don't listen to her and *definitely* die. I at least want to die with my feet moving," Lea said.

"We're not going to be defeated. We just need more time to find him. More time for you to learn how to steal his magic without it hurting you, or worse."

"We can't just chase him through the kingdom until the last petal falls. We don't have time to spare trying to figure every last detail out before I try again. Once these petals are gone, so am I. Forever. I have faith I'll find a way to take his magic, but to do that, I *have* to practice."

Gray's forehead creased, his lips turning down and his jaw tightening, but Lea saw the moment he relented. He had no other choice. Because she was right. They had no other information. No other clues.

Evangeline had no reason to lie. Not unless she herself was searching for power like Alaric and Eudora. But she'd been abused by the Black King. Had allowed herself to be tortured and tormented for years without giving away Lea's identity or even her existence.

Evangeline's visions were their only lead, and unless something changed, she was their only chance of finding Alaric. Once again, Lea forced her hands to stay in the water. Didn't allow them to trail across the moonflower vine around her head. She already knew they were running out of time, and didn't need to touch the crown to remind herself.

"Come here," Lea said, motioning for Gray to come into the water. He looked exhausted, his face drawn and flushed from the heat, and his eyes bruised with dark circles. But he stood, removing his trousers and shirt before wading in to sit next to her. Even with Alaric's absence and the clock looming over their heads, ticking down on the end of their lives, the sight of his muscular body still left Lea breathless.

His bare chest had become even more defined over the last few weeks, and his skin was bronzed from the intensity of the sun. Lea lifted a hand and placed it over Gray's heart. Over his scar, the place he had cut the mate bond from his flesh. The sacrifice he had made to save her life.

"This can't all be for nothing. What you've done, what *I've* done. I know you're afraid of me taking magic again—"

"Because it almost killed you last time."

"No." She stopped him. Guilt gnawed at her stomach. She knew very well that taking Alaric's magic could kill her. Likely would. The goddess had said as much. But she'd also said it was possible for her to take it, and still survive. She just had to figure out how.

"Trying to take your magic was painful, but after everything we've learned about the universe, would you expect it to be easy? Remember what Eudora said? Witches can gift their magic to others, but if they take it? It kills them. It's the gravest sin to take another's magic. The universe demands balance. Have we not been told that time and time again? Eudora, the goddess, the god of the sun even said it. If stealing magic were easy, if it didn't demand some sort of sacrifice, there wouldn't be balance. If I could just take other people's magic, I'd be no better than Alaric."

Lea paused, taking a deep breath and allowing her words to sink in. "I am the Daughter of Suns and Stars." Lea pushed her shadows outward, sending her fire following behind until it bubbled away into steam in the water.

"Queen of Flames. Queen of Shadows. *My* queen," Gray said, reaching out to cup her face. He sighed. "I know all those things. I don't doubt your strength. But watching you in pain? I'd prefer death."

Lea rolled her eyes. "So dramatic. Wasn't it horrible enough the first time?"

Gray grumbled something under his breath, his shadows pulling her closer.

"Look. If it's so hard to watch, then don't. I'll practice on Janelle. Or Erik."

"No," Gray pulled her into his arms, twisting her so her back was pressed against his front. She settled between his legs and leaned her head back onto his shoulder.

"If you insist this is the only way, then you'll practice with me." His voice was gruff. "I can handle it."

"Now?" Lea asked. Gray's arms tightened around her, just a fraction, and he nodded.

"You're right. We don't have time to waste. So, yes. Now."

Lea closed her eyes, taking a deep breath and exhaling slowly as she pushed her magic outward. She was grateful to be in the water, certain she wouldn't be able to focus if she was fighting off the heat.

Picturing her magic as roots, Lea spread them outward and wrapped them around Gray's skin, trying to force them through. She was met with resistance, a hard layer like stone pushing back against her, but she pushed harder, leaning back into Gray as if more physical contact might help get her through his shields. She grit her teeth, then with a firm shove, commanded her magic through the stoney barrier and into Gray's body.

She sighed in relief as she recognized the feel of Gray's magic, a tiny echo of what she'd felt when they'd been connected through the bond. After allowing herself a moment to revel in the comfort of their connection, and with another slow inhale, she wrapped her powers around Gray's magic, isolating a small tendril of shadows. His magic resisted immediately, pulling back against her with a sharp tug, but Lea refused to let go.

A stab of pain exploded behind her sternum, and she whimpered, pulling harder as she clenched her fist and jaw and scrunched her eyes. Gray's magic went taught as she tore at it, and agony exploded behind her eyes, spreading outward until it seared into her temples and down her throat.

"Lea," Gray growled, a warning. But she pulled harder. She *had* to. What was her other option? If she couldn't take Gray's magic, even a tiny sliver, she certainly wouldn't be able to take Alaric's. Gray wasn't even resisting.

She clenched her jaw and pulled harder, the roots of her magic twisting and ripping at Gray's with all their strength. She honed them into a blade, attempting to sever them from their master.

His magic screamed in response, vibrating along the thread of her magic and roaring until her teeth rattled.

Or maybe it wasn't her teeth rattling. She was thrown sideways as the earth trembled beneath them, rocks tumbling from the hill down into the stream.

"Stop, Lea!" Gray snapped, trying to pull away, but she wrapped him in her shadows, refusing to give even an inch. She had to do this. Had no other choice. They were running out of time.

She cried out as she pulled more magic from her chest—her primary magic, pushing deeper and harder and wrapping tighter, tangling her magic with Grays more firmly—and yanked backwards.

"Stop!" Gray yelled, but she couldn't. Wouldn't.

"Lea!"

Stars dotted her vision as her lungs twisted closed. She couldn't breathe, her heart pounding so rapidly she could feel her pulse in her throat and her temples. But still, she hung on, pulling with everything she had.

Something wet dripped from her nose, and her vision faded, but the last thing she saw as she fell into black, quiet unconsciousness was a river of blood floating from her face and down the stream. A crimson reminder that she would never be strong enough. That the universe hated her, and that if she couldn't find a way to take Alaric's magic, they were all doomed.

CHAPTER 34

JANELLE

For the first time in two days, the harsh light of the sun dimmed, though only a fraction. It hadn't set, but the furious storm clouds and lightning in the distance blocked enough of it out to allow the temperature to drop a few degrees.

"Here we go," Erik said with a sigh, dropping his plate on the ground and standing. He brushed off the knees of his trousers, then turned to face the oncoming storm and crossed his arms.

"What do you think's happening?" Janelle asked, identifying the tell-tale gray lightning that meant their fearless king and her best friend's husband was furious about something.

"Who knows these days? There's no clear way forward anymore. All Gray wants to do is protect this kingdom, and especially, Lea. I worry his temper will only rise the longer this takes."

"And the closer the last petal is to falling," Janelle added softly.

Erik faced back toward the storm, and sure enough, within moments, the clouds rolled over their heads, following behind Gray as he stormed back into Howen. The storm was even more furious as it neared, lightning crashing dangerously close and Gray's shadows billowing in all directions. In his arms was a visibly frustrated Lea, her face red and her eyes narrowed as she hissed something at Gray under her breath. They were both soaking wet, and Janelle gave her best friend a mental high five for what she imagined had happened—a fight that led to Lea shoving Gray in the water, then jumping in after him to dunk his head under for good measure.

Fae men were so intense in their emotions. *Too* intense. Even Erik, sometimes. She loved him more than she'd ever loved anyone or anything. She could admit that now, even though it made her feel a confusing mix of being vulnerable and sappy. But the things that came out of *their* mouth sometimes? Way over the top.

Neither Gray nor Erik were going to burn the entire world down for any reason, no matter how many times they threatened it. It just wasn't possible.

"Where. Is. Evangeline?" Gray snapped, placing Lea down on the ground to lean up against what used to be the town bakery.

"Over by the church, going through everything again with the survivors. She's worried we're missing something," Erik said.

"So am I," Gray growled, storming toward the burned-out building. Lea attempted to rise to her feet, but Gray spun around, pointing at her and pinning her with a look. "Sit. Eat. Hydrate. For the love of the gods, hydrate. This can't happen again, Lea. You can't weaken yourself like that. Especially if we *do* find Alaric in the next town we come to."

Lea rolled her eyes, but sat down, and Gray's shoulders relaxed. "Thank you," he said, his eyes softening for just a moment before narrowing again as he stomped off toward the church.

"Wanna tell me why there's blood coming out of your nose?" Janelle asked, settling next to Lea against the wall. She knew better than to actually be worried about her. Her face still had color, and Gray would never have left her if she was actually injured or at risk of injury.

Lea wiped at her bloody nose with the back of her hand. "I still haven't found a way to take Alaric's magic. Only Genevieve's, and I don't know why it worked that time. Maybe because I was in a vision?" She rubbed at her forehead. "I don't know. I tried again just now..."

"And got a headache and bloody nose and fainted?" Janelle finished for her.

"Explains the clouds," Erik said, shaking his head as he turned to watch Gray in a heated discussion with the blind witch.

"Evangeline said it's the only way. What else am I supposed to do? We know it's possible. The goddess said I could defeat him. I just need to practice more."

Erik laughed. "Good luck with that." he leaned against the wall, pointing up towards the storm clouds.

"I don't have a choice." Lea turned to Janelle and tilted her head. "Erik, close your ears," she ordered.

"Not happening."

"Then don't blame me for what you're about to hear." She waved him off and grabbed Janelle's hands. "I have a tiny, basically insignificant favor to ask you," Lea said, her voice sweet and calm.

Erik straightened. "No. The two of you scheming is *never* a good thing. Not once has it ended well. Do you remember the trial? That's stupid satchel you had her sneak in?"

"We're running out of time, Erik, and you know it." Lea snapped, pointing to her crown. "I'm not trying to save Thomas with some half assed plan. I'm not a stupid, naive girl anymore. I'm a woman—a queen—put in an impossible situation, working with the only thing I have. I'm desperately trying to save our people the only way Evangeline sees us winning." She stopped, taking a deep breath. "Alaric's magic has to be diminished, and until we can find another way to make that happen, we have no choice. I have to learn how to take his magic, even if it hurts me."

"Sounds reasonable to me." Janelle shrugged. "You can practice on me."

"No. She will not," Erik said, his chest puffing out. Janelle held up a hand.

"Not your decision," she quipped, winking at him. "That territorial Fae shit? It doesn't work on me."

Erik sighed heavily, running his hand up his face and through his hair. "Gods above. Maybe you two need to take Alaric out together. You'll kill him out of sheer frustration."

"That's an idea. We're open to any and all reasonable suggestions that don't involve Lea not practicing on me," Janelle said, and Erik glared at her.

"Listen," Lea said, standing. Janelle chuckled, knowing Erik was dying to tell her to sit back down, just as Gray had, but choosing to keep his mouth shut.

"Smart man," she whispered to him, but he ignored her, the only indication he'd heard her at all the slight tipping up of his lips.

"Gray is too blind with fear trying to keep me safe. I love him, but at this point, I don't know if he can make unbiased decisions. And you know it, too. If we fail, we die anyway. I'm not going beyond the veil again without knowing that I did everything I could to save us. I'm doing this, and as your queen *and* your friend, I'm asking you not to tell Gray."

"Fuck me," Erik said, huffing and shifting from side to side. Janelle opened her mouth, a joke on the very tip of her tongue.

"Not now." His eyes flashed with heat.

"Later," Janelle mouthed, and Erik couldn't help but laugh. Booming, bubbly laughter, that made a few nearby villagers turn.

"I'm so sorry," he said to them, his face turning red.

"Can you not take anything seriously?" Lea asked Janelle, but there was no anger or bite to her words.

Janelle tilted her head. "I mean, you're the one saying we're all proba-bly gonna die. If that's the case, I wanna get laid as much as I can before we go."

"Gods, I don't *think* we're all gonna die. That's what I'm trying to prevent. And I can only do that if I practice. Okay?" Lea quirked an eyebrow at Erik, and his demeanor turned serious again.

"If anything goes wrong, you need to tell me. And if it becomes too much, you have to promise me you'll stop. We'll keep searching for another way to end this." He sighed. "But you're right. If Evangeline thinks it's the only way, then this might be our only hope."

CHAPTER 35

LEA

Just as they'd discussed, Evangeline surprised them all when it was time to leave. They spread out their departures, just by a minute or so, in hopes that it would confuse Eudora were she to try to see what their plans were. But Evangeline wasn't the only one with a secret.

Lea had the beginnings of one herself. Her own plan. A way that she could maybe take Alaric's magic without it killing her. Or, at least, to keep death from coming for her until she had taken every last drop and stabbed a blade through his heart.

And the first step in that plan was speaking to Evangeline. Lea volunteered to leave after her birth mother, knowing Gray would take the tail of the caravan to ensure no one was left behind. It was the perfect opportunity for a private conversation, and one she might not get again anytime soon.

They traveled northeast, through tall, skinny trees with fat pinecones and long, spindly leaves. But Lea tried not to focus on where they were going as she urged her horse forward, moving next to Evangeline.

"Do you mind if I ride next to you for a while?" Lea asked, and a bright smile spread across Evangeline's face, her shoulders loosening.

"I would like that very much," she said, moving her horse over to the left to allow them a bit more room. They rode in silence for a while, Lea wondering how she was able to navigate the forest without her eyesight, and unsure how to have the conversation with her that she needed to. Lea shared her own blood and bone with this woman, but knew virtually nothing about her, and she was at a complete loss for what her life had been like. Where she'd traveled and what she'd experienced. Why she'd been so afraid the Black King would find her.

"What would you like to ask me? I have no secrets." Evangeline's voice was kind and warm, soft and melodic.

Lea cleared her throat. "Why did you do it? Why'd you help the king? Why not just hide us both? Tanad would've kept us safe. Did you not trust him? Or was it Eudora you didn't trust?" Evangeline's smile turned sad.

"Eudora," she echoed, and Lea's gut churned. "It's hard to know, now that she's working with Alaric, what was the truth and what was deceit. We knew of her prophecy, of course. The Daughter of Suns and Stars would come to save the kingdom. She warned me to never get pregnant. Said whatever child I conceived would never be safe from the Black King. That her power would call to him. Power immense enough to change *everything*, to save the world or destroy it."

Evangeline looked at her as if she could actually see her face. "I told her she was foolish, that I had no plans to have a child. I didn't want to raise a child outside of my kingdom, and I knew to do so within it wasn't safe. And then, I met Ryland."

"Is he..." Lea didn't know what she wanted to ask. Her father? Alive? A good man?

"Your father, yes." Evangeline reached out as if to touch Lea's arm, but stopped herself.

"What happened to him?" Lea's voice was soft. Hesitant. Did she even want to know?

Evangeline's shoulders fell, and suddenly, she seemed exhausted. "The Black King happened, just like with everything else. We were happy. So happy, but the king found out about me. Had heard that the queen's child had been taken from her womb. He was paranoid, certain I was out there somewhere, plotting his demise." Her bottom lip trembled. "I wasn't. I just wanted to live on my own soil, in my own kingdom. We built a home, a garden, right in the Wicked Wood. The demons stayed away, as if we were blessed by the goddess herself. Maybe we were."

Lea pictured the house her father had brought her to. The very garden that she'd had her vision in.

"I shielded it, and every day I added to the shield's strength. But it still wasn't enough."

"How did you escape?"

"I was out gathering herbs when I heard Ryland's scream. The pain in that scream..." Evangeline quieted, swallowing several times before continuing. "I *felt* his pain. There was no way he would have survived whatever had been done to him." Her hand drifted to her stomach. "I'd just found out about you. Hadn't even had the chance to tell Ryland yet. But when I heard that scream, I knew they would kill me if I returned, and therefore, kill you. So I fled. I left him behind."

Her voice broke, and she raised her fist, biting down on a knuckle to stop the tears. The tears she couldn't cry, but certainly felt.

"I'm sorry," Lea said, the word feeling so small and insignificant.

Evangeline shook her head. "No. It was the right decision. I wouldn't change it. And I certainly don't regret it. I hid, hoping I could eventually return home, but it never felt safe. Once you were born, I fled south, back to Calir. To Tanad. I knew they would protect you, just like I knew I had to try to kill Brennus. Eudora came and made a bargain with me. She would give me some of her magic—magic that would allow me to make a potion to slip into the king's food or drink that would kill him instantly and was undetectable. It would target only him, even if he had poison testers. I didn't have his strength, or his power, and it seemed like the only way. In exchange, I would bring home Eudora's niece, Seraphine."

"The witch he kept captive before you. The one who created the Lonely Death," Lea said.

"Yes. I know you judge her—and me. And we deserve that. But the things the king did to us..." Evangeline shivered. "She begged for death, but he wouldn't grant her pleas. The pain. The torture. The way he cracked into our minds. When I was caught, when the king realized who I was, he *almost* broke me. He knew I wasn't the daughter of suns and stars, that I didn't have both day and night magic. So he had me examined. It was—"

She stopped, taking a deep breath. "When his healer told him I had given birth before, I think he saw an opportunity. Eudora's niece was nothing but a shell of who she'd once been. She was almost comatose, sitting in an empty room day in and day out with her head hung and her eyes glazed over. He couldn't get her to do magic anymore, even with the most horrific punishments. But he knew I would do *anything* to protect you. He told Seraphine that if she would give all her magic to me, he would grant her death. She did it freely. Willingly and desperately. Every last drop, and I had no choice but to accept it."

Lea pondered this for a minute. "The king gave up on finding me that easily?"

"No. He searched for you everywhere. He tortured me daily. The one thing I have done right in this life is enduring it all to protect you." Evangeline's lower lip trembled. "I'm sorry I missed your childhood. I knew that Adelaide and Henry would be good to you. That they would protect you. It was the only way I'd been able to leave at all. Eudora promised me Tanad wouldn't leave you unless you were protected.

"I was protected, and very well loved." A jolt of sorrow stabbed between Lea's ribs at the memory of her mother.

"You must hate me for this mess I put us in."

"Of course I don't hate you. We've all made mistakes and errors in judgment. If Brennus had found me, this war would've been over before it even started. It was foretold that it would end up this way."

"Thank you," Evangeline said. "I don't deserve your forgiveness, anyone's forgiveness, but I will take it." She patted Lea's hand, quickly and tentatively, and Lea allowed it. A lump formed in her throat as they rode on, the silence far more comfortable this time as Lea let Evangeline's confessions sink in.

She truly had loved her. Had been trying to keep her safe all along, and even though Gray was worried she had ulterior motives, Lea knew somewhere deep inside her that for once, there were none. Evangeline was simply a mother who loved her daughter and hadn't known what else to do.

"Tanad said something about your magic that I've been thinking about," Lea said.

Evangeline stayed silent, waiting for Lea to continue, but she sucked in a sharp breath. "He said you could hold death at bay. I did that, once," Lea said, "but I don't know *how* I did it. I just kind of..." Lea trailed off, trying to figure out how to put what she'd felt that night into words. "I could feel death, and I fought it off. But I've never felt it again."

Evangeline nodded. "It's an eerie feeling, isn't it? Finding death's cold fingers grasping for something. Someone," she corrected herself. "It took some time for me to figure out what it was. Death... He's not often brazen and bold. His presence is subtle. Sneaky. He doesn't want himself to be known, so he hides. Once I learned how to tell when he was lurking, though, he became easier to fight."

"What does he feel like?" Lea asked, a cold dread spreading through her stomach.

Evangeline shivered. "A chill. Like you need a sweater. Not cold enough to make your teeth chatter or your nose run. Just enough to turn the skin on your arms to gooseflesh. That was always my first sign that death was approaching. And then, if you pay attention, really focus, you'll feel him. It's as if he's standing over your shoulder, watching you. You'll never see him, but you'll know he's there, waiting for the moment he can reach out and pluck your soul away; take it to wherever we go before we enter the veil."

"How did you hold him off?" Lea asked, her heart picking up in rhythm. This was it. The information she needed to know if her plan could work.

Evangeline tucked her hair behind her ear. "I'd hoped this vision wouldn't come true." Her words were sad. "That you would find another way."

"There is no other way." This time it was Lea who reached out and touched Evangeline, placing her hand on her mother's forearm. "Please," she begged.

Evangeline looked down to where their skin touched, then nodded sadly. "I would simply push my magic outward as hard as I could, like I was trying to drain every bit from my body. It created a shield death couldn't get through. Not when I channeled every good thought I had into it. Fortified it with every bit of love and laughter and joy I had ever felt. I would think of you. Of Ryland." She cleared her throat. "I couldn't hold death off forever, of course. I would weaken, eventually, but in most cases, I could maintain the shield long enough to allow time to get a healer for whoever had been injured or ill."

"Our magic comes from the same place," Lea said. "Do you think—"she stopped, clearing her throat. "Do you think I could do it? Again, I mean?"

"I think you can do anything."

"Because you're my mother?" Lea said, the first time she'd actually admitted those words out loud in front of her.

"No. Because I've *seen* it. I haven't seen the how of it all, but I've seen flashes of the world with Alaric dead, you and Gray ruling a peaceful kingdom, magic restored to its rightful state... So that's really your plan, then?" Evangeline asked. "To try to hold death at bay as you steal Alaric's magic? Because to get so close to death, to really know and understand what and who he is, Lea—it changes you. He never really leaves you again. Once you find him—feel him—he'll lurk over your shoulder until the day he finally takes you."

A shiver ran down Lea's spine, but even if the idea terrified her, it didn't matter. She was running out of time and running out of options. The goddess had been clear that she wouldn't be able to take Alaric's magic and survive with it. That the universe wouldn't allow anyone to hold that much power ever again. But if she could hold off death, maybe she could find a way to get rid of the magic. To return it to the earth, though she still didn't know how that was possible without her death. At the very least, she would be able to hold death at bay long enough to stab Alaric through his heart.

"Why did you say you'd hoped this vision wouldn't come true?" Lea asked, her words shaky.

Evangeline's shoulders fell, and she pressed her lips together. "Because you don't survive in it, Lea. My magic cannot hold off death forever. Neither can yours. This solution... He will still come for you."

"I know," Lea said. "I don't need forever." She left it there, riding next to Evangeline in heavy silence for several moments.

"I've spent my life trying to protect you," Evangeline finally said. "I don't know if I can be part of your plans to sacrifice yourself. You must keep searching for the answer. There's a way for you to take his magic and not let it kill you. I've seen it. I just can't see *how*."

Lea bit her lip, holding back her retort. She was exhausted—tired of saying the same things again and again. If Alaric wasn't defeated, they would all die. Every last one of them. And worse, Lea would lose the chance to be with Gray beyond the veil.

"I know you've spent your life trying to protect me," Lea finally said. "And I'm grateful for it. I will keep trying to find another way, but please, understand I have people I love, too. It's my turn to protect them. Gray, Janelle, Erik, Thomas, Emma. My father, Nora, Elise. You..."

Evangeline choked back a sob, but Lea pushed forward.

"I will keep searching for another way. I don't *want* to die. I don't *want* to sacrifice myself. But I won't be separated from Gray forever. I *will* kill Alaric before the final petal falls, even if it kills me, too. Can't you understand that?"

Evangeline's answering smile was sad. "I can. I would do anything to be with Ryland again..." Evangeline sniffled, wiping her nose on her sleeve before clearing her throat and straightening in her saddle. "I will help you. I won't allow you to be separated from him, either. If it comes to it, I will help hold off death, and teach you to do the same. You have my word, as long as you promise me you'll continue to search for another way."

"I swear it. Thank you," Lea's words came out in a whoosh of emotion, and suddenly, she felt lighter. It wasn't the perfect solution, but it was a solution. And for now, that had to be enough.

"Have you seen a way to get Gray to agree to this?" Lea asked, only half joking. He didn't want to be separated after death any more than she did, but she knew Gray. Knew that he wouldn't be able to see past her death in this life. She couldn't imagine a scenario where he would allow her to sacrifice herself again, even if it meant killing Alaric.

"Lea, Gray can't know." Evangeline pulled back on the reins, pulling her horse to a stop just short of a sparkling waterfall.

"What? I can't hide this from him. Not again. Not after what happened before." Lea's chest tightened, her breaths becoming shallow with panic. She didn't want to leave this life with secrets and regret. Didn't want Gray to resent her. There had to be a way to make him understand. To get him to agree that unless they could find another way, this was their only option.

Evangeline shook her head. "Gray can't know any of this. He can't be with you when you battle Alaric. If he finds out your plan, he *will* follow you. I've seen it again and again. He will never allow you to sacrifice yourself."

"I can get through to him—"

"No. I'm sorry, my daughter. But you can't. I promised you I wouldn't allow you to be separated from Gray after death. Your bargain with the goddess is the only reason I'm agreeing to any of this—because I know you would suffer for eternity if you fail to kill Alaric." Evangeline paused, and she reached out to grab Lea's hand. "I need you to listen carefully. Really listen, and understand what I'm saying. Gray can't know of your plans, under any circumstance."

"Why? Why can't he know?" Lea asked, her heart in shreds as she realized she already knew the answer.

"Because in every single vision where Gray is with you—in every single vision where he follows you—you fail."

CHAPTER 36

LEA

The waterfall roared as it rushed down the rocks and into the churning stream as they waited for the others to catch up. Lea couldn't swallow down the knot in her throat or the nausea swirling in her stomach.

She would have to lie to Gray. Would have to hide her plans from him. And it would destroy him.

The sound of horses approaching met Lea's ears, and she forced the sorrowful feeling from the air, donning a smile. She could hope all she wanted that she'd find another way, would even try her best to do it, but *this* was a plan that could actually work—that could allow for Alaric to be defeated *and* for her and Gray to not be separated after death. It was something concrete she could hold on to as she searched for another answer.

But only if Gray didn't suspect it. If Evangeline's visions were correct, he'd never allow her to sacrifice herself again. Not for him or anyone else.

Never mind the fact that he'd done so before. He'd understood the reasons, the necessity of selfless acts in war. And truthfully, her plan wasn't completely selfless. Lea would rather die winning the war to protect their people and have eternity beyond the veil with Gray, than to waste time coming up with another plan, fail, and have to endure the gods' and goddesses' punishment of being separated forever.

It wasn't even a choice. Lea knew in her bones that this was the path forward, no matter what Gray, or Evangeline, or anyone else said.

The sound of hooves picked up in rhythm a moment before Gray appeared, Obsidian trotting straight to the stream to drink. Gray narrowed his eyes at Lea as he approached, always so perceptive, and for the first time, she was thankful for their lack of mate bond. She'd never be able to hide her plans from him were he capable of feeling the way her heart was racing and her palms were sweating.

Knowing she needed to deflect his attention, Lea frowned, looking at her mother and shaking her head slightly, as if it was simply painful to be around her. Gray's shadows reached toward her, wrapping up her arm and gently caressing her cheek.

"I don't know where to go from here," Evangeline said. "I've taken us as far as I can."

"What did you see in your vision?" Gray asked, wasting no time.

"A cliff. With a rocky outcropping shaped like an owl."

"Aynor," Erik said, and Gray nodded, shifting Obsidian slightly west.

"It's only about an hour from here. Maybe less."

"Then let's go," Lea urged, adrenaline pumping in her blood. One hour. They were so close. But the longer they waited, the more time Eudora had to sense them coming. The more time they had to flee like the cowards they were.

Gray took the lead as they galloped forward as one. Now that the decision of where they were going had been made, it didn't matter whether they were together or not. All that mattered was that they got to Aynor, and fast.

Lea's back ached as she bounced in the saddle, but she refused to focus on the pain. Instead, she waited for a chill. For death's presence.

Evangeline had said it was subtle, and so she tuned out everything else. The sound of the horses' hooves and the rustle of crunching leaves beneath them. The hot air blowing across her face and the way her muscles burned.

She didn't allow herself to notice the way the trees began to thin, or the enormous red sun still staring at them in the sky. She simply allowed Luna to carry her forward and waited for a chill to wash over her skin.

Twenty minutes. Thirty. She focused, but nothing came.

Did that mean they were going to make it before Alaric could kill the villagers? Or was she missing something? Maybe they weren't close enough. Or maybe, this was it. They were going to find him.

Suddenly, Lea knew with perfect clarity that Aynor was just beyond the treeline, but it wasn't the sound of life within the small village, or death's cold kiss that warned her that they had arrived, but smoke.

Black, billowing smoke that blocked out portions of the red sky in a way that made it appear as if demons themselves were descending from the heavens.

Gray cursed under his breath, pulling back on Obsidian's reins as they reached the top of the hill. It wasn't until then that she felt death. Unmistakable and terrifying.

A shiver ran down her spine as she looked at the burning buildings, the charred bodies in the street already taken by death lying among the ruins of what must have once been a pleasant, thriving town.

"Dammit!" Gray shouted, his shadows racing toward the village to smother the flames, but it was too late. The villagers were gone, as were Alaric and Eudora, but this time, Alaric hadn't bothered to set a trap. He'd simply stolen what magic he could, and then killed every last one of them.

CHAPTER 37

LEA

"What can you see?" Gray jumped off Obsidian, following Evangeline to where she now stood in front of the horses, facing toward Aynor. Her hands were out, her forehead scrunched as if closing her eyes. She took a step forward, then another, nearing the edge of a rock that jutted out from the top of the hill. Her head fell backward, a gasp of pain leaving her throat as she clenched her teeth.

She dropped to her knees, but Gray caught her before she could tumble off the rock and down the hill, holding her steady. It only took a moment. The vision passed just as quickly as it had started, Evangeline sucking in a sharp inhale and holding her head.

Lea started toward her, but Evangeline held up a hand. "I'm fine." She brushed off Gray, who was still holding her upright, and settled down to sit sideways. "Alaric looks stronger. Much stronger. The magic he's taking... It seems to be healing him."

Lea's heart pounded erratically, terror pulsing through her blood with every beat. They needed Alaric weakened, not stronger. The more magic she had to take... *No. Don't go there right now,* her subconscious ordered. Lea forced away the thought. "What *exactly* did you see?" she asked Evangeline, needing more information.

"I saw Eudora and Alaric together. I don't think they brought their men this time. Their army must be somewhere else. It was just the two of them. And they stood right here. Right where I'm standing, staring down at the village as it burned."

"Did they say anything?"

Evangeline shook her head. "They were silent. Completely silent, just staring at the smoke. Smiling. They're sick. It's—"

"How many people do you think lived here?" Erik interrupted, turning to Gray.

"No more than fifty."

"And how many with magic?" Erik asked.

"Three, that I knew of. So you agree with what I'm thinking?"

Lea's eyes bounced between Gray and Erik, her stomach sinking as she connected the dots along with them.

Erik's face was grim as he nodded. "Eight at the last village. Three here. If he looked as bad as everyone said, the magic of eleven people shouldn't be enough to make that much of a difference."

"What are you saying?" Thomas asked, his voice hard and sharp.

"That we're missing something," Gray said, jumping up onto Obsidian. "We have to go."

"But the bodies. Their souls want to be put to rest." Emma's voice was desperate, and Lea wished for a moment that they had time to spare. That they could give the departed the rest they craved. The rest they deserved.

But it would have to wait.

"We'll come back," Gray said. "I swear it. But we can't risk the living for the sake of the dead."

CHAPTER 38

GRAY

The village of Illyn was nothing but ruins. A tiny village. Maybe five families who had once called it home. Gray didn't even stop his horse as they passed, leading them to the next closest town. Another hour of riding that dragged on as they fought against time. They'd known before they'd even cleared the hill that it, too, had been decimated and was now nothing more than the smoldering carcass of the community that had once called it home.

This village had been larger, maybe ninety people, and it had been reduced to ashes just like the others.

Gray jumped off his horse, frantically searching for survivors within the rubble. "How is this possible?" he asked, flipping a beam lying across the street to allow the others to pass through. No one answered, because surely, they were all asking themselves the same question.

How quickly was the Lonely Death taking effect, and how many villages had been infected? Fury pounded in Gray's blood, so hot he thought maybe he could create flames, even without day magic.

"Ride on Erik," he ordered. "To Coombes. Warn them to leave. To go south to Calir if Alaric hasn't attacked yet."

Erik didn't even respond, kicking Cinnamon's sides and racing away with Janelle.

"Evangeline," Gray said, desperation clawing at his throat. "Please. What can you see? What do we do?" Shame burned the back of his neck at the panic and fear in his voice, but what were they to do? It made no sense—how could Alaric work so quickly? How could he be so far ahead of them? Based on the stages of embers, he didn't even seem to be going in order by location. Was he choosing villages at random? How many in their kingdom had already been killed? How much magic had been stolen? How many of his people were even left to save?

Evangeline rubbed her forehead, focusing. "I think there's another to the north. Yes. At the very north end of the kingdom. But that one," she scrunched her forehead. "I think it's been a while. I don't know. I don't know," she said again, frazzled. "I don't think I'm seeing things in order. I don't know if it's Eudora scrambling my visions, or if I'm just seeing different possibilities. Maybe I'm seeing them out of order... I don't— I'm sorry."

"I'll kill her," Gray said. "I'm going to fucking kill her."

"We have to find her first," Lea said, her fingers trailing her crown absently.

"He said he's playing with you," Emma said, nodding to the air. "Yes, thank you. I'll tell him." She turned to Gray, her face pale. "It's a game. The dead said he's returning to his army now. He wants you on edge, wondering where he'll go next. He thinks lying low will make you even more anxious, just waiting for his next attack. They heard him speaking to Eudora."

"So we have time?" Gray asked.

"Some, it appears."

Through his rage, a tiny flicker of gratitude ignited in his chest. It wasn't much, but knowing they had time to make a plan felt like a miracle.

"What do we do next?" Thomas asked.

"Evangeline," Gray said. "Can you see where Alaric's army is?" Evangeline shook her head.

His mind spun in circles. Calculating. Assessing. "Keep trying," he said, turning toward where Erik and Janelle had ridden north. Should they follow behind? Stop at the villages along the way to make sure Evangeline's visions weren't missing anything?

"We need to get back to the castle," Lea said, interrupting his thoughts.

Gray turned to her, tilting his head in confusion. His heart skipped a beat, hope pounding against his ribs that she had a plan.

"I need to plant enough moon flowers to send throughout the kingdom. A bag for each village. And have our army distribute them as quickly as possible. It's the only way to save their lives. We don't know how long Alaric will be lying low. But it gives us some time. If we can get moonflowers to them, they'll be immune if Alaric does start stealing magic again. We need to keep him from getting stronger. Our army can search for him as they distribute the flowers."

Gray rubbed the back of his neck, sorting through the options in his mind. It made sense, after all. At the castle they were surrounded by a wall, with an entire army at their disposal. Here they were, running blind, unable to discern Alaric's next move. It didn't matter where they were, not when it appeared Eudora could transport Alaric wherever they wished with the snap of her fingers. Maybe, in this case, preventing Alaric from being able to steal more magic was their best chance at defeating him.

"You're right. Maybe mobilizing our army throughout Desia will help us find him faster. He can't hide if we flood the entire kingdom with soldiers. *Someone* will know something. Even if Alaric himself isn't spotted, his guards should be easy to break."

For the first time since they'd found Howen destroyed, Gray felt a surge of hope. This war was going to end one way or another. But chasing after Alaric was playing his game. Giving him the control. They had to take it back, and keeping him from stealing more magic was their best move.

Suddenly, he couldn't return to the castle soon enough. "Let's find Erik, and get back."

Gray didn't wait, kicking Obsidian's sides and leading them along the route Erik would've taken. Obsidian moved like the wind, jumping over fallen logs and dodging between trees, his mane whipping behind him as if he understood every word they'd said and knew the importance of finding Erik as quickly as possible. Leaning down, Gray patted his neck.

"Good," he said. "Find them."

Obsidian suddenly halted, almost throwing Gray to the ground as he tried to avoid a small patch of flames spreading across the grass.

"Woah, boy," Gray soothed. He sent his shadows out behind him, finding Lea and wrapping around her protectively as he whipped his head around to look for the cause. The flames spread rapidly, growing taller by the second, but there was no sign of Alaric anywhere. No sign of anyone at all.

Lea pulled Luna up next to him, holding out her hands to suffocate the fire that had spooked Obsidian with her own shadows.

"Can you feel him?" Gray asked, still searching for what could have caused the fire.

Lea shook her head. "No. He's not here."

"Then what—" Gray stopped as another pillar of smoke rose in front of them. Just on the other side of the flames Lea had put out, another small patch of dry grass sparked, the fire moving quickly toward the trees. His stomach dropped as another fire started only feet away. "It's not Alaric. It's the sun. This heat." Gray said, putting out a section of flames with a burst of shadows while Lea attended to a larger fire several yards away. Within seconds, small fires ignited all around them, the air growing thick with smoke.

"Wildfires," Lea said, swiveling her head around as if trying to decide which one to fight next.

Before she could choose, Evangeline's head flew back, a strangled cry leaving her throat.

"We have to find Erik," Thomas said, his eyes darting between the fires and Evangeline.

"No, you don't. Neither you nor Emma can fight the flames. Get back to the castle. Warn Vincent. We'll find them and be right behind you," Gray said.

Emma didn't protest, turning her horse and racing forward. Thomas's jaw tightened, but he nodded, following behind her, and Gray was grateful. They'd be no help against the fires. Not without any sort of elemental magic. He couldn't worry about them when they needed to find Erik and Janelle.

Evangeline shuddered as she came out of her trance, grabbing her head with both hands and grimacing. "It's the god of the sun. He's causing these fires. There will be more, all throughout the kingdom," she said.

Gray threw up his hands, his magic raging inside him at the thought of his kingdom going up in flames. "But why? Why would he not want us to succeed in killing my bastard brother? Why make it so much harder?" Gray growled, throwing his shadows out in a net as far as he could to push down the flames.

"Balance," Evangeline said, looking at Lea with sad eyes and nodding slowly. And even without her saying more, Gray knew what Evangeline meant. Lea wasn't supposed to be here, saving the people of the kingdom. She'd had that chance before and failed. There was nothing balanced about her defying death to come back and kill another—no matter how evil Alaric was.

This was the god of the sun balancing the scales, creating chaos and destruction as Lea fought to save them all. It filled him with fury. What was balanced about Alaric taking other people's magic? Why had he not been punished for the crimes he'd committed against the universe?

But even through his fury, Gray knew the answer: it was because Alaric hadn't been killed. Hadn't been defeated. It was himself and Lea who had failed already once before, now using a second chance the universe hadn't wanted to give them, and Gray couldn't help but wonder, after all was said and done, what the universe would demand as repayment for the time they had stolen.

CHAPTER 39

ERIK

"Where's the smoke coming from?" Janelle coughed, covering her mouth with her sleeve. "We're still too far from Coombes for it to be coming from there, aren't we? Are there more villages between here and there?"

Erik shook his head, his heart racing. The smoke was getting thicker by the second, floating above the ground and billowing into the sky above them. Janelle coughed again, harder this time, and Erik pulled on Cinnamon's reins, turning her around. "We're turning back. Something's wrong. This isn't safe."

Janelle nodded, unable to speak as she choked on the smoke, her eyes watering. Erik reached down and ripped off a piece of his shirt, thin and worn, but better than nothing. "Breathe through this," he said, handing it to her while urging Cinnamon forward. He hadn't completed his mission, but Gray would have to understand. None of the other villages had been smoking like this—like the fire was consuming the ground, coming from within it—and Erik didn't feel prepared to face whatever was causing it alone.

Sensing the danger, Cinnamon increased her speed as she raced around a large tree trunk, skidding to a halt at a waist-high line of fire spreading in front of them. "Dammit!" Erik hissed, throwing out his hand and smothering some of the flames as he forced Cinnamon through. He'd been correct that the smoke wasn't from a village burning.

It was a wildfire.

The extreme heat from the relentless sun had dried out the grass and twigs until they were nothing but kindling. And now, he and the woman he loved most were in the middle of that kindling, a strike of flint away from being burned alive.

"Take the reins," Erik demanded, needing both hands to fight off the fire.

Sweat poured down his neck as the flames rose taller, orange and red flickering and growing in every direction. Within moments, the fire grew so high that its fingers blended in with the blood-orange sky. Erik gritted his teeth and pulled the flames inside himself, shooting a stream out behind them and suffocating what he could.

Janelle led Cinnamon to the left, towards a small pocket of forest yet to be burned, her face tense with fear. To the left and right were more lines of fire—spreading slowly and tauntingly, consuming the grass as they inched across the ground to block their path.

It was almost as if the fire was sentient, moving to block their way, to consume them as well.

"They're getting closer, Erik!" Janelle shouted, her voice choked with fear. Sweat dripped into Erik's eyes as he focused on the lines of fire getting closer to trapping them. He commanded the flames to turn around and retreat, but they fought against him, surging and fighting to survive.

It didn't matter; it was enough for him to buy them time to race through the remaining gap. The air became slightly less smoky as they galloped forward, and Erik sucked in a deep breath. But his relief was short-lived. How long would they be able to breathe without smoke burning their lungs when fires were popping up every few feet? They had to get out of the forest, somewhere with rocks or stone where there was less fuel to feed the flames.

Erik placed a hand on Janelle's chest, sending healing energy rushing into her lungs as she struggled through another coughing fit. "Hang on," he soothed. "I'll get us out of here."

Cinnamon began to slow, the smoke taking its toll. Erik sent healing energy into the horse's body, too, his magic pulling taut as he expended more and more of it. "Just a bit further, girl," he urged as she dug deeper and picked up speed. The fire had to stop at some point. The wind was behind them now, and Cinnamon was running faster than he'd ever seen her run before, but as they drew closer to where they'd left Lea and Gray, the flames only seemed to grow stronger.

Cinnamon halted, planting her feet into the ground as Erik swung his head around, desperately looking for an escape. His heart pounded in his ears as he tried to force a path through the fire, but they were surrounded. Flames, almost as tall as the trees themselves, billowed and danced around them, taunting them.

"No," Janelle gasped, her voice raw. "No! This can't be the end."

Erik pulled her more firmly against him, focusing his magic ahead of them, digging into the dregs of his power for every last bit to suffocate the flames, but they were so strong. Too strong.

"Erik!"

Erik's head snapped to the left at the sound of Gray's voice.

"Over here!" he shouted, relief flooding through him unlike anything he'd ever felt before.

Erik pushed Cinnamon to move toward Gray's voice, promising her that if she could just get them out of here, he'd give her nothing but apples and sugar for the rest of her life.

An enormous wave of shadows, immeasurable in its intensity, punched through the fire, Lea's hands outstretched before her as darkness funneled in an arc. The flames extinguished instantly, revealing a path ahead of them like a burned out, cobblestone road to paradise.

"Hurry!" Lea ordered, shouting over the crackling of the fire behind them. Cinnamon responded before Erik could even command her to, leaping onto the road made of ash. Lea twisted her shadows out, spreading them out to clear the way as their horses raced forward.

The darkness coming from Lea's hands grew, a tidal wave crashing around them in every direction, putting out the fires as far as Erik could see. But even then, once the smoke had cleared and the only orange in the sky was the reminder of the sun god's fury, they didn't stop to rest—not for hours.

Not until Cinnamon couldn't run any further, and Erik forced them all to stop so he could heal her.

None of them spoke about the fires, or how narrowly they had escaped them. Maybe they were too exhausted. Or maybe it was because acknowledging what had happened would mean admitting that it wasn't just time that wasn't on their side, but the universe itself.

CHAPTER 40

GRAY

Lea jumped off Luna before she'd even stopped moving, asking Janelle to gather more moonflower seeds as she pulled the ones she'd carried with her from her pocket and shoved them into the dry dirt. Soot stained her face and coated her hair, and her eyes were bloodshot from the smoke and lack of sleep, but she barely blinked as she funneled magic into the ground.

They had rushed back to the castle, racing against time to mobilize their army—to send help to the villages being ravaged by wildfires and to distribute the moonflower petals to protect them from Alaric.

Tiny shoots peeked out of the ground as Lea dug her fingers deeper, closing her eyes and pushing her light into the soil. The first white flower popped open, and Lea exhaled, her shoulders relaxing.

Vincent rushed from the front gate as Gray launched off Obsidian.

"Anyone with water or wind magic, gather them immediately!" Gray ordered.

"What's happening?" Vincent asked, his voice tight with urgency. "Thomas said there was a fire."

"Fires. They're everywhere," Gray replied, his face grim. "The earth is so damn dry from the relentless sun that the grass is nothing more than kindling. They're spreading fast."

"What about Alaric?" Vincent asked.

"We still don't know where he is," Gray said, shaking his head. "Only that Eudora is helping him. She's been at his side for days."

Vincent's eyes widened in shock, but Gray continued, his voice hard and determined.

"He's moving from village to village, taking all the magic he can and killing the rest."

"Gods above," Vincent breathed. "How do we fight this?"

Gray glanced over his shoulder at the moonflowers, now sprouting in a thirty-foot radius around them. Fingernail-sized white petals unfurled before their eyes as they spread out in every direction. "We need to get petals to every village. Every town and settlement."

Vincent rubbed his temples, clearly uncertain. "Do we even know how many small groupings of families are scattered across the kingdom?"

"No. But we have to find them. Everyone should be evacuated toward bodies of water." Gray said.

Vincent frowned. "He's making us spread out our army. Weakening us."

"What choice do we have?" Gray countered. "We won't have a kingdom left to fight for if we leave them unprotected. Send them now. Tell them to report back with what they find, and to look for Alaric. He's out there somewhere."

"Yes, sir," Vincent said. Bowing his head, he turned and disappeared back into the castle to carry out Gray's orders.

It wasn't until Vincent left that Gray noticed the figure standing in the shadows of the doorway. His breath caught as he met Tanad's familiar eyes, so joyless and dark. It had been a long time since Gray had last seen him look this grim, and it only worsened the pit in his stomach.

In just the few days they'd been gone, Tanad had aged significantly. The twinkle in his eyes had dimmed, and his once shiny silver hair was now brittle and dry. Wrinkles lined his forehead and bracketed his mouth, and he looked like he hadn't eaten in days—but then, none of them had, really. How could anyone have an appetite when the world was falling apart so thoroughly?

"It's true then?" Tanad asked quietly. "She really is as deceptive as you always claimed her to be?"

Gray stepped forward until he was within arm's reach. He'd always wondered if Tanad had truly loved and trusted Eudora, but looking at the man now, it was clear. He *had* truly loved the witch, and she had betrayed him in the worst way.

"I'm sorry," Gray said softly. "She's helping Alaric—helping him steal magic and burn villages to the ground. She's the reason we haven't found him yet."

Tanad's voice was low and filled with sorrow. "Was she with him before? Before I banished her?"

"We don't know," Gray replied, his heart heavy for his friend. "But this isn't your fault. None of it. If anything, I should have anticipated something like this happening. I knew she wasn't trustworthy."

Tanad shook his head, his expression resolute. "I didn't," he said, straightening his shoulders. "And I should have. I will bear that burden until my dying breath." He swallowed. "Tell me what to do. I— I need to do something to help."

"We need men and women to fight the wildfires," Gray said. "Your kingdom is near the sea. You must have many soldiers with water magic."

"I'll gather them immediately," Tanad said brusquely, walking away before Gray had the chance to offer any more platitudes.

A sense of dread swirled in Gray's stomach as Tanad disappeared, a wave of nausea washing over him. The heat, the stress—it was all too much. They had to find Alaric, but how? And even worse, how much time did they have left?

As if the universe was answering his question, Gray turned just in time to watch another petal fall from Lea's crown, turning to ash and floating away in the wind.

CHAPTER 41

GRAY

Two soldiers were to be sent to each town. It was all they could spare, and hopefully, with the majority of them possessing magic that lent itself toward moving water or air, it would be enough. Aside from those days that Lea had been beyond the veil, these had been the worst hours of Gray's life, but pride swelled inside him as his and Tanad's men lined up to depart.

Each soldier grabbed a satchel of moonflower petals from Lea as they prepared to leave, and one by one, she gave them a bit of her magic—enough that she could see through their eyes. If Alaric was spotted, she would know, and they could act.

Gray tried not to think about what the toll of giving away so much magic would be on Lea—the hundreds of ties she now had to monitor. Ties that would stretch thinner as the soldiers holding them traveled further and further away. But as Lea had told him repeatedly, they were out of options. There was nothing left to do but wait until they knew more. And to know more, she needed to be able to communicate with the soldiers scattering throughout the kingdom.

Once the last soldier cleared the gate, Lea sighed, her shoulders slumping and her head falling back in exhaustion. She turned around, jumping when she saw Gray watching her.

"Gods!" She put a hand on her chest. "Sorry. I didn't realize you were there," she said, her voice crackly with fatigue.

Gray opened his arms, and she walked into them without hesitation, melting against him like she was returning home. His own chest loosened at the contact. "This has to work. It will work. Right?" she whispered.

"It will work," Gray soothed, rubbing her back in rhythmic circles.

Lea didn't respond, as if she knew his words were nothing but hopes and empty promises. Shadows darkened beneath her eyes, and Gray rubbed the bruised skin gingerly. "You need to sleep," he said. "What we've been through so far is nothing compared to what's coming. You won't make it if you're exhausted."

"I know," Lea said, nestling her face into his chest. "I know that, rationally, but my body can't seem to relax enough to fall asleep. I just lie there, thinking about what could happen... What we're missing."

Gray's heart sank, and he squeezed her tighter. "We're doing everything we can. You're doing more than anyone has the right to ask of you," he said.

Lea forced a smile, clearly uncomfortable with his praise. He knew she felt like she was falling short, like she was letting people down. But frankly, the notion was ridiculous.

"Come on, Little Flower," he said, pulling her toward their quarters, determined to find a way to help her rest.

He had chosen a room several floors above his old, and now destroyed, wing of the castle, knowing Lea didn't like being anywhere near where the Black King had resided. The room he'd picked was small, much less extravagant than his former suite of rooms, but Gray knew Lea didn't care, and neither did he. As long as there was a comfortable bed and a place to bathe, it was enough for the both of them.

They entered the bathroom, and Lea's eyes softened as she noticed he'd already arranged for warm water to be brought to their bathtub.

"You shouldn't have," she scolded, but there was no bite in her tone. "Wasting people's energy carrying buckets up all these stairs—"

"They wanted to help," Gray said gently. "They *asked* how they could contribute. They're grateful to you, for your sacrifice."

Lea covered her face with her hands. "I don't want people feeling indebted to me."

"I know," Gray said, pulling her hands away to look into her eyes. He trailed his fingers down her arms. "But it doesn't change that they still feel that way. And for good reason. Now, would you like to get cleaned up?"

Lea nodded. With slow, reverent movements, Gray slid her arms from their sleeves, pushing her shirt down around her waist. He dropped to his knees, unbuckling her pants and sword belt before gently wiggling them down her legs. He held her hand as she stepped out of her clothes into the tub and sank down into the warm water. The ripple echoed around the bathing chamber as Lea submerged up to her neck and tipped her head back against the lip of the basin, letting out a soft sigh.

Immediately, gritty pieces of ash drifted off her skin, turning the water a murky gray with soot leftover from the fire. They swirled around her like snowflakes dancing in the air, sinking to the bottom as Lea's breaths evened out and the water stilled.

Picking up a bar of soap from next to the tub, Gray slowly smoothed it up and down her arms, then her torso. Her breasts and her legs. Slowly, as to not disturb the water and stir up the ash.

Desire surged through him as he looked upon Lea's bare body, and his mind flashed back to a time that felt so long ago, when he'd helped untangle her hair after bathing on the road—the first time he'd allowed himself to give in to the constant yearning inside him.

But tonight, he forced down his longing. His need. Because what Lea needed right now was to recover from the past few days. The past few weeks. She needed to feel safe and taken care of. And he needed to give that to her.

He gently washed her hair, massaging her scalp until her eyelids closed and her breathing became deeper and more even. The sweet scent of jasmine filled the bathing chamber as he worked an amber oil into the ends of her long golden hair and untangled it, her chest now steadily rising and falling in the rhythm of sleep. Slowly, he rinsed the oil out with warm water, then rocked back onto his heels.

Gray's own breathing relaxed as he savored the peace in her features. Her face looked softer, her lips parted and the lines around her eyes nearly gone. Finally, she was resting.

Gray watched her until he worried the water would cool, then grabbed a fluffy, warm towel from next to the fire. As he lifted her from the tub, Lea's eyelids fluttered, and she forced them open.

"Shhhh," he urged, carrying her to the bed.

"There's no time," she protested, fighting a yawn.

"Rest," Gray urged, helping her lie down and pulling the covers over her. "Just for a little while."

Lea's eyes closed again as she snuggled into the pillow. "Just for a few minutes," she murmured. "Wake me if anything happens. Promise?"

"Of course," Gray said, knowing full well he wouldn't wake her. There was nothing they could do until they got more information from their soldiers. So instead, he simply sat beside her, holding her close as the hours passed and memorizing the steady, rhythmic beat of her heart, the gentle rise and fall of her chest, and the small smile that graced her lips.

And then, before he joined her in sleep, he whispered his love to her—love that even death hadn't been able, and would never be able, to take away.

CHAPTER 42

ERIK

There had been a moment, as the fire surrounded them, when Erik was certain he and Janelle were going to die. He'd never been afraid of death before—not really. He had resigned himself long ago—the moment he and Gray had taken their oath—to the fact that this war might lead to his death. But since meeting Janelle, everything in his life had changed in the most spectacular, immense way.

Now, he had a reason to *live*. A reason so much bigger than defeating Alaric. But along with his renewed purpose came more reasons to be afraid, too.

Erik washed quickly after helping to organize the armies, cleaning the soot from his skin and relishing the cold water. He wondered where Janelle had gone. It felt wrong not knowing where she was. And every moment away from her seemed like far too many.

He checked their room, searched the main hall, then the courtyard. But it wasn't until he made it to the kitchens that he found her, flour dusted across her cheeks and her hair up in a messy bun.

He walked up and put his arms around her waist, kissing the top of her head.

"Gods dammit, you ill-timed sugar-sniffing bloodhound. You ruined my surprise," she said, her smile betraying her pretend anger.

"And that surprise is?" Erik asked, looking down at the globs of half-baked dough she had just pulled from the oven.

"Cookies?" she said, raising her eyebrows.

Erik chuckled, grabbing one of the under-baked cookies and shoving it into his mouth.

Chocolate exploded on his tongue, and he moaned. "They're the best thing I've ever tasted," he said around a mouthful. "Other than you."

Janelle laughed as he flipped her around and kissed her cheek. She wrapped her arms around his neck, looking up at him with eyes so full of love it could have made him cry. It probably would have, if their love for each other hadn't been the entire reason he'd come to find her in the first place.

Erik grabbed another cookie, then tugged on her hand. "Come with me," he said. "There's something I've been wanting to try."

Janelle laughed, wiggling her eyebrows. "Anywhere, anytime. We've been through this before, haven't we?" she teased.

"I never get tired of hearing it."

"I never get tired of saying it. Where are we going?"

"You'll see," Erik replied, lifting her into his arms. Janelle squealed as he carried her around the back of the castle toward the armory. Thomas could only work at night, and the other soldiers working there had already left for the evening. Erik was positive the place would be deserted, and the line of trees behind them would provide extra cover for what he had planned.

Once they reached the armory, he set her down, immediately feeling a rush of heat as he pressed her against the stone wall and her body curled into his. He swept his tongue inside her mouth, and his fingers tangled in her hair.

Janelle moaned, deepening the kiss. "If this is what you wanted, you could've just told me," she said, catching her breath. She grabbed his hand and tugged him toward the back door of the building.

Erik dug his heels in, not budging. "No. Right here," he said, pressing her back up against the wall and pinning her with his hips.

He grabbed Janelle's hands, then let go with one to tilt her chin up toward him. "I'm going to say some very sappy things," Erik started, "and I need you to not throw up. For the sake of my manhood. If you love me, you'll keep your mouth shut, and just listen to what I have to say without gagging."

"Oh my God, you're ridiculous," Janelle swatted at him.

"No, I'm serious." He looked around as if searching for eavesdroppers. "I want to talk about my... feelings."

Janelle rolled her eyes. "Oh my God. Get on with it already!"

"If you insist." Erik cupped her cheek, pausing until he was certain she was listening to him. *Really* listening. "Until I met you, I was living my life for only one thing—this war. Gray was my brother, my only family. He was all I had, and that was enough. Then you and Lea came here, and everything changed. All of a sudden, I wanted to win this war for so much more than just revenge against my father. I wanted to win it for you. For us. We don't know what's going to happen or what we'll be able to accomplish, but I need you to know how I feel." He pressed a soft kiss to her lips. "No matter what happens, Janelle, you're mine."

He took her hand and placed it over his chest where his heart pounded beneath her palm. "Mine forever. Win or lose, our souls are bound."

Janelle placed her hand over Erik's, tears welling in her eyes as she looked up at the sun. Erik smiled as he watched understanding wash over her face, her mouth popping open and her eyebrows raising. "You really think... You think it could be possible for more than just Lea and Gray?" she asked, her voice soft.

"I don't know," Erik said. "Not for sure. But I know that if there were ever to be another pair of mates, it's us."

"Okay," she whispered, leaning forward and raising her hands to his buttons.

"Wait, I'm not done," Erik said, dropping to one knee. "I want you to marry me. Please. Because no matter what happens once we try to seal the bond, it doesn't matter. You're mine, and a mark on our chests isn't what proves that. Our love—our commitment—that's what's going to make this last."

A sob burst from Janelle's throat, and Erik kissed her cheek. "Hey, you promised," he said with a grin.

"I promised I wouldn't gag, not that I wouldn't cry," she laughed through her tears, throwing herself into his arms. "I would marry you this second. I would marry you every day, no matter what the gods say about it."

"Tonight then? You'll marry me?" His eyes sparkled with joy. "Do you really mean it?"

Janelle's smile grew wide, almost matching Erik's. His entire body warmed, and his heart pounded with a happiness he hadn't felt in ages.

She leaned up on her tiptoes, throwing her arms around Erik's neck. She kissed him in response, her tongue molding against his in a resounding yes. He looked overhead to make sure there wasn't a single branch or cloud between them and the celestial body that ruled their magic.

Erik reached for Janelle's tunic, still dusted with flour, and pulled it over her head. His eyes raked over her pale skin, taking his time memorizing every inch of her body. He called fire into his hands as he cupped her breasts, burning away the thin fabric with ease, taking special care to avoid burning Janelle's skin.

Dropping to his knees, Erik pressed his lips to her navel as his fingers went to the waist of her pants. Janelle kicked off her shoes, her hands coming to rest on the top of Erik's shoulders. His scruff tickled her stomach as he pressed kisses to one hip bone, then the other, wiggling her pants off until she stood completely bare before him.

Flames licked up Erik's arms as he slowly stood, already thick and hard in his trousers. He wasted no time, pulling his shirt over his head and stepping out of his own pants. He lifted Janelle in his arms, laying her down into the soft grass and crawling over her, pressing kisses as he went. The inside of her calf. Her thigh. Her waist and breast, then her lips. He groaned as she speared her fingers into his hair, pulling him closer until every inch of their bodies aligned.

It was ecstasy, just the contact of their skin, and Erik slid a hand between them, craving more. More touching. More kissing. Just *more*. He slid a single finger through her folds, teasing as he explored her slowly. Savoring every moment with this woman who was to become his wife.

The word made his cock jolt, and unable to stop himself, he pressed a finger inside her, slowly stretching her as she moaned out. Their kiss deepened, their tongues saying everything they needed too, sharing each other's air. Erik pressed in a second finger, then turned his hand to use his thumb to circle her clit.

Janelle broke their kiss as a gasp escaped her throat, her fingers digging into Erik's shoulders. She bucked on his fingers, and he leaned back to watch, the sight nearly driving him mad. He pulled back, desperate to taste her, but Janelle put a hand to his chest and pushed him onto his back.

She climbed on top of him, a wicked glint in her eyes as she grabbed him in her hand. She raised up on her knees, holding him at her entrance and sliding his thick length back and forth, wetting him and then, in the most glorious display of earth-shattering beauty he'd ever seen, Janelle threw her head back as she sank down on his shaft inch by inch until he was fully sheathed inside her.

Grabbing her hips, he pinned her down against him, circling his hips as she adjusted to the fullness. Janelle bit her lip as she lifted herself up, then slid down again, faster this time. She leaned forward, changing the angle and driving him impossibly deeper as she began to truly ride him, using his body for her own pleasure.

The sight made him almost come, the pure rapture in her hooded eyes and her open mouth. Erik met her every movement, thrusting whenever she rocked back, his hands pulling her down harder and harder.

Their speed increased, Janelle moaning with every thrust of his hips. Her fingernails dug into his chest as they climbed together, higher and higher until Janelle's movements became less rhythmic, her walls pulsing around him as she cried out.

Erik flipped her over, settling between her thighs as she continued to cry out beneath him. He pushed his fingers through her hair, tilting her head back and claiming her mouth, swallowing his name on her lips.

Lifting her leg, he thrust again and again, Janelle's orgasm continuing on as he pounded into her, his rhythm becoming frantic as he found his own release.

"I love you," he said, pressing his forehead against Janelle's and thrusting one more time, whispering praises as he found his own release.

Erik stilled, tasting Janelle's lips once more. "Marry me?" he asked again, their foreheads still pressed together.

"You think amazing sex would make me change my mind?" she asked, biting his bottom lip, and Erik laughed as he pulled out of her, nipping back at her jawline.

"I want to hear it," he said, tucking her hair behind her ear.

"I'll marry you," Janelle said, her face softening as she pulled back slightly, her eyes searching Erik's skin. The disappointment he saw there was heavy, so obvious Erik didn't need to look to know what she was, or *wasn't*, seeing. There was no mate mark. But surprisingly, he wasn't sad. Not even a little.

Erik cupped her face between his hands. "So beautiful," he murmured, gazing at her smooth, unmarked skin. He'd expected disappointment if the bond didn't snap into place, but in reality, all he felt was gratitude. He was lucky. Happy. Regardless of what the gods thought, Janelle was still the love of his life, mate or not.

The gods may not have blessed them, but he hoped they would have no mercy on anyone who tried to tear them apart.

CHAPTER 43

LEA

Gray was meeting with Vincent, but for how long, Lea had no idea. He'd let her sleep for several hours, many more than she'd planned on when she'd curled up on the soft bed and allowed her eyes to close. She wanted to be angry Gray hadn't woken her, but gods, she'd needed the rest. Those hours asleep had helped more than she could have ever expected, and for the first time in who knows how long, she felt energized. Hopeful.

At least, *almost* hopeful.

There hadn't been any tugs on her magic yet to let her know Alaric had been spotted, but she had to believe it was coming. The pieces of their plan were falling into place. Now, if she could only find Janelle while Gray was preoccupied so she could practice taking her magic. If Gray wasn't going to let her practice on him, she needed to do it during one of the rare times he wasn't by her side.

Lea was about to go search the courtyard when Janelle and Erik wandered through the door hand-in-hand, their faces flushed and eyes bright.

Lea's heart skipped with excitement. Maybe, for once, the gods were on her side. "There you are! I've been looking for you," Lea said.

"I was just coming to find you, too, actually," Janelle answered, stretching up to whisper something in Erik's ear. He smiled down at her so warmly, it gave Lea the sudden urge to cry. Somehow, even with all the terrible things going on in their lives, there were still moments full of genuine love and joy, and witnessing them was a privilege she'd never again take for granted.

"Fine. I'll see you both later, then," Erik said, leaning down to kiss Janelle. Deeply and slowly, with so much passion Lea felt the need to turn away until they broke apart. Janelle hurried over to her, looping their arms together and leading them toward her and Erik's room.

"Actually," Lea said. "Can we go outside? I wanted to talk to you about something... you know, in private."

Janelle shrugged, narrowing her eyes slightly and allowing Lea to lead her toward the courtyard. "I mean, it's hot as balls out there, but sure."

She didn't say much as they walked, hurrying around the side of the castle to the old guard shack, but as Lea examined her friend's face, she couldn't remember a time she'd seen Janelle look so happy. Her eyes sparkled and her cheeks were pink and tilted up with a smile.

"What's going on with you?" Lea asked, raising an eyebrow. "Did you just get laid or something?"

"Obviously," Janelle rolled her eyes, pulling her arm from Lea's as she settled down in the shade of a tree behind the hut. "Oh. And Erik and I are getting married. Tonight."

The floor fell from beneath Lea's feet. "You are?" she squealed, jumping up and down like a teenager. It wasn't queenly, and it certainly wasn't poised, but it was genuine. Janelle and Lea had talked as children about their weddings—granted, Lea had talked far more about it than Janelle ever had—but it'd always been something they'd known about their futures. They would stand by each other as they pledged themselves to the one who made their hearts soar.

Lea plopped to the ground and embraced her friend, almost forgetting about the sense of dread looming over their heads every minute of every day. "I'm so happy for you," she said, squeezing Janelle so tight she squirmed. "There's no one better for you than Erik. And I just want you to know—"

Janelle pulled back, wiggling out of the embrace. "Gods. All right, enough hugging," she said. "You know how I feel about that."

"I do, and I don't care." Lea sniffled, pulling her close again. "You're getting married. Let me hug you!"

Janelle sighed, stiffly and begrudgingly wrapping her arms around Lea and allowing one more very brief hug. "Anyway, that's my news. What were you wanting to find me for?"

Lea waved her off. "It doesn't matter. We can talk about it later."

"No. Please tell me. I can't handle secrets."

Lea cracked a smile. Janelle had always been like that. She simply couldn't stand knowing there was information out there that she wasn't aware of. "I wanted to talk about practicing..." she paused, narrowing her eyes and preparing to gauge Janelle's reaction, "taking your magic."

Janelle waved a hand at her dismissively, as if Lea had just told her the lamest secret of all time. "Oh. Gray's occupied, then?" she laughed, seeing right through her.

"He is. But it can wait."

"Why?" Janelle twisted to face her. "I've got about eight hours to kill until my wedding. Let's do it."

Lea tilted her head, her heart picking up in rhythm. "Really? Don't you want to, I don't know, get ready? I'm sure we can find you a pretty dress somewhere in the castle."

"All I want is to get married, and then to have years of happiness with my husband. I want us to live. I want to survive." Janelle turned away, hugging a pillow to her chest. Always hiding her emotions—her fear. "So," she clapped her hands together, "steal my magic, bitch."

"I mean, if you insist," Lea said.

"Insist we live?" Janelle raised her eyebrows. "Absolutely, I do. "How do you want to do this? We don't have to hold hands, do we?" She pretended to gag, clearly having had enough physical affection for the day.

"It might help, but I think it's better if we don't. It's not likely I'll be able to touch Alaric as I'm taking his magic. I need to figure out how to do it without contact."

"Thank the gods," Janelle said, scooting back a few inches. "Okay then. Ready when you are."

Lea wasted no time, closing her eyes and isolating her magic in her chest.

Carefully and cautiously, Lea reached out with her power, the dark, finger-like roots of her magic floating from her body and wrapping around Janelle's arms and legs, cascading down her torso and back until it covered her fully like a blanket. With a deep breath, she forced her power inside Janelle's chest, searching for her magic.

It took longer than finding Gray's, but there, tucked right next to her heart, was a small pocket of power—mischievous and stubborn—and so very different from anything she'd ever felt before. It was easier to isolate, much more solid and compact than Gray's magic.

It was difficult, keeping half of her mind on figuring out how to take Janelle's magic and the other half on alert for death's presence. She forced her breaths to remain even as she pictured the dark tendrils of her magic as a hand and a blade. Holding Janelle's power firmly in place, she used the blade to dig into the shell of Janelle's power, pushing firmly enough until she pierced it with a *crack* that made Lea's teeth rattle.

Janelle gasped, and Lea paused, not pushing any further. "You alright?" she asked, keeping her eyes shut and her consciousness on alert. "I can stop."

"No, I'm fine. It was just startling. Go on," Janelle urged, her voice high pitched and breathy with excitement.

Slowly, Lea dug the blade deeper, carving away a little of the magic seeping out, careful not to take too much. The moment she cut the first thread tethering Janelle's magic to its home, a shiver ran down her spine. She'd been waiting for it, but the feeling was unsettling, all the same.

The hairs on the back of her neck stood on end as the sensation of someone watching her skated across her body. Now that she'd felt it, it was unmistakable, and she wondered how she'd missed it before. It was sickening, cold and dreadful, but she kept going.

Lea tugged at Janelle's magic more firmly, and just as she suspected, pain burst behind her eyes, and a dribble of something wet trickled from her nose.

Blood.

Janelle gasped, but Lea ignored her, forcing her breaths to remain steady. Her chest squeezed, her heart thundering, and she swore she felt death smile. A sickly, slimy feeling that forced the chill into her bones. Death thought he was winning, but she had prepared for this. Lea had held death back before, and she was determined to do it again.

As quickly as she was able without dropping her hold on Janelle's magic, Lea formed a shield of shadows around her, as thick as the stone walls of the castle and black as the everlasting night had been, blocking herself from death's sight. She pulled at her friend's power, cutting another tiny tether away, swiftly and efficiently.

The cold washing down her arms told her death was searching through her shadows, desperately trying to find her soul and rip it from her body, but she refused to be afraid. With a burst of power, she yanked Janelle's magic backward, pulling until the final thread holding it back snapped. Lea wrapped the foreign magic in her shadows, tugging it close as she pulled it into her chest and nestled it next to her own power.

Her ears rang with death's roar of rage, but before it could find her again, she disconnected her magic from Janelle, severing the connection she'd built and closing it off completely.

In an instant, death was gone.

Interesting, Lea thought, considering that it seemed to be the act of taking someone's magic that allowed death to find her, rather than holding it inside her.

Lea exhaled, using her forearm to wipe the blood from her nose.

"You did it!" Janelle said, beaming at her. "You did it, didn't you? I can feel it—like a piece is missing. You *fucking* did it!" Janelle jumped to her feet. "What was different? How did you figure it out?"

"Evangeline helped me," Lea said. "I had to keep death from getting to me."

"Lea, do you know what this means?" Janelle asked, her voice stuffed with hope. Lea's heart sank. Sure, she'd taken a little of Janelle's magic, and that alone was a feat. But that had been only the tiniest bit, and it had still allowed death an opening.

"This means we can win!" Janelle hugged her, and Lea laughed, shoving down her sadness. Her fear and uncertainty.

"You're actually initiating physical touch with me?" Lea teased.

"I'm just so proud of you," Janelle said, not even trying to hide that she was tearing up. "You didn't give up. You did it. You took my power, and it didn't kill you, and now you can take Alaric's power. We get more time. All of us."

Tears filled Lea's eyes, but not because she was full of joy and hope like Janelle. Her tears were drops of sorrow. Guilt. Lea didn't want to lie to her best friend. Didn't want to give her hope that they would all live happily ever after. But no matter how she looked at it, she couldn't convince herself that there was a way she'd survive taking Alaric's power.

Even taking the tiniest bit from Janelle had left her feeling nauseous and weak, her head still throbbing and blood crusting her nostrils.

Not to mention the goddess had been clear. She would never be allowed to live taking such a massive amount of power. Even if she survived taking all of Alaric's magic, it would be impossible to hold it all inside of her. She *had* to return it to the universe. To the earth. But how?

She funneled her magic into the ground all the time growing the moonflowers, but it never drained her. And every time she tried to give a piece of her magic to the earth, it returned to her like water evaporating back into the sky on a sunny day. No matter how many times she tried, she couldn't give her magic to the universe. It was as if the power needed a living soul to tether to, like when she gave magic to their soldiers to see through their eyes.

She had only been successful in returning magic to the earth through death.

Lea's hands shook as she isolated Janelle's magic and tried to push it back out into the air. She directed it away from Janelle, pushing it outward until it grew taut, and severed it with a blade of shadows. But it didn't matter. The magic came back to her like a magnet, thumping back into place in her chest.

She grabbed it again, this time pushing it into the grass beneath her feet, but once again, it returned, locking back into place with an almost painful snap.

Her heart sank, but she smiled anyway. She would just have to keep searching for another way to return Alaric's magic to the earth. The goddess had said it was possible. That she could find a way to live. But for now, this was their best option. A way to save their people. If she and Evangeline could keep death away long enough to take Alaric's magic and allow her to plunge her sword through his heart—if she could give everyone else more time before they joined her beyond the veil—it would be worth it.

"Well... you're welcome," Lea forced a laugh. "Now you'll get all those years with Erik."

Janelle jumped up. "Erik! Right." She blushed. "Maybe I do want to find a dress. Not that it matters to *me,* of course, but, you know, I want Erik to have the perfect wedding. For him."

"Of course," Lea said, grabbing Janelle's hand and squeezing. "Let's go find you that dress. For Erik."

Janelle bumped Lea's shoulder as they walked back to the castle. "Hey," Janelle said, stopping and turning to her. "About that magic—it's amazing that you can take it and all, and I'm thrilled you figured it out. Really. But I don't really have much. Do you think I can have it back?"

CHAPTER 44

EMMA

Emma pinned the last curl in place on Janelle's head, creating soft, cascading waves that swept over her shoulders into a low, loose bun. Soft purple tendrils framed her face, and her eyes and lips had been painted a delicate shimmering pink. Janelle had insisted on the makeup when she asked Emma to do her hair, saying it was only fair since Erik deserved for her to look her best. But Emma could feel the yearning emanating from beneath her carefree exterior. She acted tough, as if she didn't care, but deep down, she wanted to feel beautiful on her wedding day, and Emma was determined to help make that happen.

Emma held up the mirror, and Janelle's mouth popped open in surprise. Her hand rose to touch her cheeks and the hair hanging loosely around her face. For the first time in Emma's memory, Janelle appeared speechless, her arm falling to her lap.

"Emma, it's—"

"You're beautiful," Emma said, squeezing her shoulder before grabbing Janelle's dress, a beautiful, deep purple gown that accented her hair. Janelle held the mirror back up, turning her head from side to side.

"No crying, or your makeup will run," Emma warned.

"I don't cry," Janelle insisted, but her voice was choked. She coughed, then met Emma's eyes. "Thank you. For everything."

The door swung open with a squeak, and Lea walked in, stunning in a sparkling silver gown, a bottle of wine in hand. "A toast before we put on the dress?" she suggested.

"Hell yeah!" Janelle exclaimed, hopping to her feet and grabbing three glasses. Janelle placed them on the table as Lea opened the bottle with a *pop*, pouring them each several fingers worth of sweet pink wine.

"To the best friends anyone could ask for," Lea said, looking at Janelle, then Emma, "and the men who will forever have to put up with us."

"Cheers!" Emma smiled as she took a sip, her heart warming. Not even a year ago, she hadn't even met either of these women, and now she couldn't imagine her life without them—without any of them.

"To your happiness," Emma said softly, avoiding their eyes. The moment felt intense, making her skin buzz uncomfortably, but she didn't want to miss it. She would remember these big moments in their friendship for as long as she lived.

Janelle raised her glass. "To Lea, for never giving up so we can have the chance to live and love for a very long time... and for giving Emma the time to find that love."

They clinked their glasses and drank deeply. Emma blushed, thinking about Thomas—the way he wanted to protect her, but wasn't controlling. The way his touches never seemed to overwhelm her the way other people's did, and how he always seemed to know what she needed without her having to say it out loud. Emma knew without a doubt that if she suggested it, he would rush her far away from here, that he was desperate to do so. But he respected her enough to allow her to make her own choices.

"Maybe I already have," Emma admitted, her stomach warm from the wine.

"Holy shit, really?" Janelle asked, while Lea beamed at her. Emma waved them off as a knock sounded at the door.

"Are we ready?" Thomas called.

"We were just talking about you!" Janelle said, but Lea cut her off with an elbow to the ribs.

"What's that?" he asked.

"Um. Nothing. Give us just a minute. We need to get Janelle dressed," Emma said through the door, a blush creeping down her neck.

Avoiding her friend's eyes, Emma removed Janelle's dress from its hanger, opening up the back to allow her to step inside. She laced it tightly and tied it with an elegant bow as Lea adjusted the straps. They both stepped back, and Janelle spun in a circle, suddenly appearing nervous.

"Well?" she asked.

"Come on in!" Emma called to Thomas, her voice light, a smile plastered on her face. He walked straight in, stopping short when he saw Janelle.

Thomas placed a hand on his chest. "You look so beautiful," he said, moving forward to hug his friend. "Who knew the girl who used to throw mud at me could look like such a lady?" he joked.

Janelle shoved him, the emotional moment over. "Asshole!"

"No, really," Thomas said, holding his hands up in apology. "You look beautiful."

And really, she did—her deep purple dress hugged her body like it was made for her, with delicate straps wrapping from the bodice around her back to form an intricate pattern before meeting back together and making a train.

"Shall we?" Thomas offered his arm, and Janelle took it, nodding.

"We'll see you in there," Lea said. Emma fixed a curl on Janelle's head, then turned to follow Lea out, but Thomas stopped her.

"You look stunning," he said, making Emma blush again as she looked down at her feet. "Promise you'll save me a dance?"

"Of course," Emma said, suddenly feeling warm and itchy all over. She hurried after Lea, unable to look Thomas in the eye. The feelings he stirred inside her were so strong—overwhelming and wonderful and terrible all at once.

Lea was waiting for her just outside the door, her silver dress shimmering, as ethereal as the moon. "So... Thomas? It's getting serious, then?" Lea smiled, and Emma grimaced.

"We don't have to talk about it," Lea said, reaching out to touch her arm. "But just know I'm happy for you. You bring out the best in him."

Emma nodded as they walked into the dining hall, grateful that Lea seemed to understand she wasn't ready to talk more about her feelings for Thomas. Not yet. Not here.

The thick velvet curtains of the hall had all been closed, with a roaring fire in the hearth providing a gentle orange glow instead of the harsh, bright sun. Lea had constructed a shield of air to push the heat up the chimney, and was swirling air through the room in an attempt to keep it cool. The candles on the mantle and across the long table flickered in the breeze, creating an intimate coziness in what was normally a massive, overstimulating space.

In front of the fire, Erik and Gray stood together—Erik beaming and Gray actually looking somewhat not angry and terrifying for once. He smiled when he saw Lea, who rushed over to him, folding herself into his arms as if the few moments they'd been apart had been far too long. Emma closed her eyes and basked in the joy and love emanating from everyone around her. The past few months had been difficult, to say the least. Waves of anxiety pounding against her skin from every person she walked past. Anger and sorrow. Pain and terror.

But right now, all she felt was warmth and gratitude and unconditional love, and she pulled it inside her, memorizing the sensation so she could remember it the next time she was bombarded with others' suffering.

"Is it time?" Erik asked as Emma moved to stand to his right, his cheeks flushed with excitement. "What's taking so long?"

Erik's energy washed through the space, so overwhelming that Emma couldn't help but smile. It was infectious, and the way he loved Janelle so deeply was palpable.

"She's coming," Emma said. "She looks beautiful."

"She always looks beautiful," Erik replied, shifting from side to side impatiently. "I'm sure she looked just as beautiful ten minutes ago. Maybe go get her?"

The doors at the end of the hall opened, and Janelle appeared, with the purest, most uninhibited smile Emma had ever seen on her face. Erik stepped forward immediately, as if desperate to run to her, but he stopped himself.

Emma's eyes were drawn to Thomas, his arm extended to Janelle. He looked handsome, freshly shaven and dressed in all black, a sword on his hip. He found her immediately, and Emma's stomach warmed as their gazes locked, butterflies flapping their delicate wings in a way that made her need to fidget. His eyes never left Emma's as he escorted Janelle to where Erik stood in front of the fire, handing her off and silently moving to join Emma.

His hand found her lower back and Emma's skin ignited, but this time, she leaned into his touch, looking around at the people she loved most in the world. It was fitting that only the six of them were there to witness Erik and Janelle's vows to one another, though Emma guessed that the other person she loved most, her mother, Elise, was likely spying through a crack in one of the doors. They'd been through so much together, and still, there was so much more to come.

Uninhibited tears streamed down Erik's cheeks, his eyes red as he stared at Janelle with complete adoration. Emma had expected Janelle to make a joke, but instead, she gently caressed Erik's tears away, allowing him to lean into her touch.

"I love you," she said, accepting him just as he was—tears, big emotions, and all.

It struck Emma that these two people couldn't be more different: Erik, boisterous and outwardly affectionate and loving, a man who felt things deeply and honestly; and Janelle, a woman who kept her secrets close and her friends closer, hiding behind her emotions with humor and sarcasm. Together, they were the best of both worlds.

Gray stepped forward, taking a length of rope and wrapping it around Erik and Janelle's joined hands and sealing it with a tight knot. "Erik, do you bind yourself—body, mind, and soul—to this woman? Do you promise to love and protect her until your last breath leaves your tired body?"

"I vow it to you, with the gods as my witness," Erik said, his voice thick and scratchy. A single tear escaped from Janelle's eye.

"Janelle, do you bind yourself—body, mind, and soul—to this man? Do you promise to love and protect him until your last breath leaves your tired body?"

Janelle took a moment, clearing her throat and swallowing before speaking. "I vow it to you," her voice cracked. "Dammit." She sniffled, but continued. "I vow it to you, with the gods as my witness," she said, her voice heavy with emotion, too.

"I told you she'd cry," Emma leaned over and whispered to Thomas. He smiled at her, taking her hand. Tingles ran from her fingers up her arm and into her chest, and she wondered if it would always feel like this. If Thomas's touch would always make her feel alive in a way that terrified her in the best, most exciting way. If maybe someday they would find what Janelle and Erik had, and stand before these same people and make vows to bind themselves together for eternity.

"Then, as a child of the gods, here to witness your vows in truth, and of your own free will, I declare you husband and wife," Gray said, his own voice shaking. "From this moment on, nothing shall separate you, whether here on earth or beyond the veil."

"And may the gods annihilate any who try," Erik added, burning away the rope around their wrists and pulling Janelle into his arms. As they shared their first kiss as husband and wife, Emma sent her own prayer to the gods—the same one Gray had just spoken.

Please, gods, do not allow anyone to tear them apart. But even with her prayer, Emma knew it was out of their hands. Alaric would try to pull them all apart, and she had a sinking feeling in her gut that he would be doing it soon.

CHAPTER 45

LEA

There was something exceedingly odd about celebrating in the midst of chaos. Wildfires still sparked throughout the kingdom, and their armies were spread to every village to fight them and distribute the moonflowers. She'd been alerted by several tugs on her magic since the soldiers had left, showing her more villages attacked by Alaric. None of those visions had shown him, but somewhere, Alaric was out there, still hidden away and biding his time.

Yet here they were, warm from the wine and dancing, finding joy amidst the chaos. While the ceremony itself had been intimate with only the six of them, they'd invited several others to a reception following Erik and Janelle's vows. Vincent was there, along with Elise and several of Erik's closer friends.

Lea drank wine and ate sweets and smiled—some of which were even genuine—but an undercurrent of worry clouded the festivities. At any moment, everything could change.

While she was somewhat comforted by the fact that she'd been able to take a tiny sliver of Janelle's magic, she still wasn't confident she'd be able to take Alaric's before it killed her. Sorrow settled beneath her breastbone.

Would Gray forgive her for hiding her plan from him? She had no choice. Evangeline had seen their future—seen them fail each and every time Gray found out what she was going to do. She *couldn't* tell him, but the guilt still gnawed at her gut, relentless and agonizing. Even if he were to somehow agree to allow her to sacrifice herself, even if he conceded to staying behind, telling him would give Eudora the chance to see what she was planning. Keeping their options open, the possibilities endless, would give her an edge that they couldn't afford to lose.

They needed every advantage they could find, and so even though it made her constantly feel like she was going to throw up, she had to continue to hide her plan from everyone—Gray, Janelle, Emma...

Emma. Who, as the party went on, seemed to sense that something was troubling her. Every few minutes, Lea's skin prickled from the sensation of eyes on her. Emma hid her stare when Lea turned around, her brow creased with concern and her cheeks turning red as she realized she'd been caught. But even with her concerned looks and questioning eyes, she didn't pry. Never asked what was troubling her so deeply, as if she knew that their survival hinged on Lea keeping her troubles to herself.

Once again, she was painfully aware of her lack of mate bond with Gray, but in this instance, she was grateful. If he'd been able to feel what she was feeling, it would destroy him. Tears burned the back of her eyes as she realized these might be her final few days with him for quite a long time, but she pushed them down. Those thoughts weren't helpful or productive. They wouldn't change anything. But what she could do was make sure she spent as much time with him as possible before she set her plan in motion.

Scanning the room, she found him speaking with Vincent. A single violin played out a slow, soothing ballad that rang out high and clear, making goosebumps freckle her skin. As soon as she found him, Gray's eyes snapped to hers, and he paused his conversation with Vincent, turning and holding out a hand toward her.

They needed no words, their magnetic pull bringing them together in a choreographed embrace. They met in the middle, Lea taking Gray's hand as he gathered her into his arms, placing one hand on the back of her head and wrapping the other arm around her waist as they began to sway.

"You look like the brightest star on the clearest, darkest night," Gray said. "Absolutely stunning."

Lea smiled against his chest. "As you've said several times tonight. But thank you."

"I'll tell you a hundred more times. A thousand, if you'll let me."

"I wasn't complaining. You can tell me until your tongue falls out, if that's what you'd like." She breathed in his scent, the wind that carries in a rainstorm, committing it to memory. "Is that the most beautiful thing you can think of? Stars?"

"Besides you?" A tendril of shadows reached up and pulled her hair off her shoulder. "It used to be the sunset. But I'd give anything to see the stars right now," Gray said, pulling back and spinning her in a slow circle, the skirt of her dress flaring out around her legs. "I'd do anything for relief from this heat."

"Taking off our clothes might help," Lea teased, pretending to reach toward the top of her dress, and a growl ripped from Gray's throat.

"Later," he said, pulling her cap sleeve back up over her shoulder, and Lea laughed at the absurdity of his protectiveness.

From her periphery, Lea saw a shadow swoop outside through a tiny gap between the curtains. Lea turned to look harder, but Gray tipped her chin up, forcing her to meet his eyes.

"You enjoy torturing me, don't you?" he asked, his shadows teasing as they slid against her skin.

"I enjoy everything about you—torturing you." She reached up on her tiptoes and pressed her lips to Gray's throat. "Kissing you... loving you."

Gray's eyes darkened as he trailed a thumb down her cheek.

"You loving me," she added.

Emotion bubbled up her throat along with the urge to tell Gray everything about her love for him, to make it entirely clear how she felt, but there weren't words big enough for the feeling. Not words her tongue could speak out loud.

Gray looked down at her, the absolute adoration in his eyes making her knees weak. A shadow darted again between the small sliver of curtains, catching Lea's eye, but she ignored it.

"There was never a choice but to love you," he said, leaning down and brushing a kiss across her lips.

"But there was. You could've chosen to focus on saving your kingdom without the added complications of loving someone. You could've kept your secrets; it would've been easier. But even when I was at my worst, when I was fighting for air and didn't know who I was, you were there for me. I can't tell you how much your love has changed my life."

Gray rested his chin on the top of her head, his swaying slowing until he stopped, pulling back to look at her. "Why does it feel like you're saying goodbye to me?"

Lea's stomach clenched, tears working their way up her throat.

"We're going to win, Lea. We're going to defeat Alaric. There's no other option. I won't allow it."

"I know," she sniffled. "I know. We *have* to win. I just needed to say it. I love you, Gray. Forever."

"And even after that," Gray said, his expression suddenly serious. He cleared his throat, opening his mouth to speak, but Vincent appeared, interrupting his thought.

Gray stiffened at the intrusion. "Has something happened?" he asked, his voice low.

Vincent shook his head. "Not here. It's about… the soldiers from Hampstead have returned."

"Right," Gray said sadly, rubbing the back of his neck. "I'd like to speak to them. Lea?"

"I think I'll stay here," Lea said, looking over at Janelle, who was beaming up at Erik, who was somehow smiling even harder than her. Gray cupped Lea's cheek, his eyes full of understanding.

"I'll be back soon, then," he said, kissing her softly before following Vincent out of the dining hall.

Pushing the images of another burned village from her mind, and suddenly exhausted, Lea went to find a glass of water. As she neared the window, a shadow once again darkened the crack between curtains, darting back and forth again and again. Whatever it was seemed to be taunting her, waiting for her. It settled on the ledge outside, and Lea squinted again, trying to determine what it could be. It was small, no more than a foot tall—a bird of some sort?

Tap, tap, tap. The shadow knocked on the window.

Lea shook her head. Probably just an animal trying to escape the blistering heat outside. She turned away, but the bird tapped more firmly. *Tap, tap, tap, tap, tap.* A prickle of magic dusted against Lea's skin, and she paused, looking around to make sure no one was watching before slipping toward the window and peeling the curtain back. Only a few inches, not wanting to let more light into the room and bring attention to herself.

Outside on the stone ledge perched a hawk. It was smaller than any hawk she'd ever seen before, with reddish markings on its wings and black circles around its eyes.

Lea bent down to look closer, and it tilted its head at her, meeting her eyes. Once the bird saw her, a small roll of parchment appeared in its beak.

Lea's heart skipped a beat as it tapped the glass again, and with shaking hands, she cracked the window open, just enough to reach outside. The heat was stifling as the bird dropped the parchment into her open palm.

It was rough; the edges frayed as if ripped from a larger piece, and she turned it over to look for a seal or something to identify the sender, but there was none. Lea looked back to the bird, searching for any indication of who might be responsible for its presence, but before she could search for clues, it opened its wings and took off, gone in an instant as if it had never been there at all.

She moved to close the window, but before it latched shut, a gust of wind blew, slipping under the edge of the parchment and unfolding it in Lea's hand. Her stomach clenched as her mother's words clanged around her skull with an intensity that made her breaths quicken. *The wind will guide you.*

With a quick look over her shoulder to make sure nobody was looking, she snapped the window closed and hurried to the far side of the room by the fireplace, hiding behind the table of small cakes and candies Elise had prepared for the reception.

Lea turned to face the fire, pretending to admire the ornate swirling decorations on the mantle as she peeled open the note.

Lea,

It is at great risk that I write this letter, but I do so in hopes this message can be delivered to you, and to you alone. I met Alaric on the road as he was leaving the palace, and with Gray's advice, groveled for his forgiveness. The things I had to say about Gray—about you—to convince him of my loyalty still sit thick in my throat, threatening to choke me. But Gray was right. Somewhere inside Alaric is a small boy who has always wanted his parents' approval and affection.

I am safe. At least, for now.

Please listen carefully. Eudora has joined Alaric, and they are watching you closely. But for some reason, thank the goddess, Eudora cannot see you. From what I have gathered, you are blocked from her visions, but only you. It is a small mercy, and I hope it buys you time.

Alaric grows stronger by the day. He hides inside the Wicked Wood, just south of the town of Pontor. Even the demons flee from him, and I fear if you do not act soon, he will find a way to use them against you.

You must separate yourself from the others and find him; use any excuse you can, but you must go alone. As long as you tell no one of your plans, Eudora and Alaric will be caught unaware. Burn this note.

And please, hurry.

Genevieve.

Lea's blood turned to ice as a heavy blanket of emotions settled over her—terror that the time was coming, mixed with relief that one way or another, this would soon be over. Sorrow that she would have to deceive her friends and her mate, mixed with the resolve to do what she had to do to save their kingdom.

Is this why Evangeline's visions had shown her failing when Gray knew of her plans? Because Eudora wouldn't see her coming if she acted alone?

The goddess had been very clear; she was the only one who could end this war. It was her destiny to do so. Surely, it was the goddess protecting her now by blocking her from Eudora's visions.

Or was this simply another trap? Maybe she could tell Gray. Maybe the god of the sun was punishing them, trying to separate them. Lea's sword warmed on her hip as if telling her she was lying to herself.

She knew the truth. It wasn't a trap at all. *This* was the way forward. Alone.

Before anyone could see what she held, she crumpled the letter into a ball and forced it through the shield of air into the fire, allowing the flames to consume the words that had changed absolutely everything.

She'd been working on her plan, but now she had a location. It was time to act.

As if the goddess was listening to her thoughts, another petal fell. Confirmation that the clock was ticking down.

Lea straightened her pristine dress and turned around, plastering a smile on her face as her eyes found Erik and Janelle. She would excuse herself soon; would need to rest for the journey ahead. But she could give them one night of happiness, one night to enjoy each other without the threat of death looming over them. Because tomorrow, everything would change.

A hand on her shoulder made her jump, and Lea turned to find Gray looking down at her, his eyebrows creased in concern.

"Everything okay?"

Lea leaned into him, desperate to feel his touch for as long as she could.

"Fine," she said. "Another petal fell while you were gone," she said. His lips pressed into a grim line as his eyes skated across her crown.

"Soldier's arrived back from Hampstead. It was as you saw—burned to the ground. The same as the other villages."

"They found nothing new at all?"

"No. Not about Alaric, at least. But the wildfires are somewhat contained at the moment, and they confirmed that several royal army outposts have been identified."

Lea nodded, grateful that the soldiers had returned to confirm what she'd seen through their army's eyes. It was one thing to be able to see what they saw, but without the context, it was hard to have the full picture. They still didn't know how many soldiers were at each outpost. Or what the closest towns to them were.

"Then that's where we start," Lea said, her plan falling perfectly into place.

"What are you thinking?" he asked.

Lea sighed, pulling him out of earshot of the others. "We split up. We can go scout the army outposts. Surely, Alaric is at least somewhere nearby one of them. Erik and Janelle can go to one, Thomas another. Once we find out more, we can mobilize the army to join us. Emma can come, bring the potion and take it again, if she's willing. I think Vincent should go, too. Maybe he can convince some of Alaric's army to join us. And Tanad. He knows Eudora so well. Maybe he can help us find her. And if we find her..."

Lea trailed off, the seeds planted. Guilt sat heavy on Lea's shoulders, but it was what had to be done. The more outcomes that were possible, the more confused Eudora would be. Spreading out across the kingdom would muddle her visions, and hopefully, keep her from realizing that Lea now knew where they were.

"We find Alaric." Gray finished for her, shadows rolling around his feet.

Lea nodded in agreement. "We know where his armies are. That's so much more information than we had before. He has to be close to one of his battalions. And with the wildfires more contained, we should be safe to travel."

"Tomorrow then," Gray said, nodding. "I'll let the others know."

Lea reached out and put a hand on his arm, stopping him. "Wait. Give them a few more minutes," she said, her heart throbbing with pain. "Who knows the next time we'll all be together again?"

CHAPTER 46

EMMA

Emma's head pounded from the intensity of the emotions swirling around her in the room. The air was thick with fear and worry, both spoken and unspoken, and it made it difficult for her to breathe. Her hands flapped at her sides, and she bounced on her toes, desperate to expel the weight of everyone else's feelings, but it was like trying to shake off a heavy cloak.

Thomas moved to her side, somehow sensing her need for space without touching her, as if he was the one with the gift of empathy.

It wasn't that she didn't enjoy his touch. He would often casually graze her arm or hold her hand, and his physical contact usually brought her peace. But in this moment, it felt as if he understood that having to process any more sensory information might cause her to explode. His presence next to her was a steadying force, calming her amidst the onslaught of feelings radiating off the others.

No one argued with the plan as Gray and Lea presented it, but still, an undercurrent of anxiety and uncertainty swirled through the group like the wildfires still sparking throughout the kingdom.

"Emma, I'd like you to stay here with the rest of the army. When Alaric is found and we mobilize our armies, you can join them. If you're willing to take the potion, that is. I hope you will consider it. We don't know what advantage could tip us over the edge to victory."

The gravity of Gray's words weighed on her, but she nodded, agreeing even though she was terrified. It didn't sound like they were going anywhere that would have spirits to speak to and gather information. She couldn't fight. *Wouldn't* fight. But taking the potion, especially knowing the moonflowers could bring her back? That was something she could do.

"Thomas," Gray started, but Thomas cut him off.

"I'd like to stay here with Emma." Thomas lifted his chin, almost as if in a challenge, then took a deep breath. "Please. If I'm needed somewhere else..." he trailed off, his internal struggle pinging off Emma's skin. She could feel the battle within him, a fierce desire to protect her butting up against his need to serve the rebellion.

Gray shared a look with Lea, understanding passing silently between them.

"That's fine," Lea said, her voice steady, and Thomas visibly relaxed, his shoulders easing as a sigh of relief escaped his lips.

"Thank you. I'll work from here. Continue to strengthen our weapons and make sure our army is as prepared as possible."

Lea nodded, her determination shining through her fear. "That leaves Vincent, Tanad, Erik, Gray, and myself. What are our options?"

"What are your thoughts, Tanad?" Gray asked.

"There were a few places Eudora was particularly fond of within Desia. Maybe there's an outpost close by? What are the nearest towns to Alaric's army?"

"Longdal, Wolfpine, Pontor, Alnwick," Erik chimed in, his eyes narrowed as if picturing a map of Desia in his mind.

Janelle sucked in a sharp breath, her hand coming up to her chest. Waves of apprehension washed over her, making Emma's stomach churn. Erik leaned down, whispering in her ear. She only nodded, and his eyes turned fiery with resolve. "If there are no objections, we will go to Alnwick," he said.

Gray's eyes flicked to Tanad. "I don't know that name. I think it's safe to say Eudora would be more likely in Pontor. She's mentioned it before."

"Then we'll take Pontor," Gray said. "The sooner Lea can get to him, the better."

Emma felt Lea's disappointment, there and gone in a second. She tried to meet her eye, but Lea continued on without missing a beat.

"That leaves Longdal to Vincent," she said.

Gray put a hand on Lea's shoulder. "Then we're all in agreement?" Gray asked.

"I think each group should take a few soldiers with them. Safety in numbers. I'd like to bring Henry, Daniel, Patrick, and Cole." Lea said firmly, her voice cutting through the tension like a blade. Gray tilted his head, and Emma could feel his confusion at her choices, but he didn't argue.

"Okay. Everyone choose your men, and let them know that we'll leave in the morning. Rest tonight," Gray ordered. "Who knows when we'll get the chance again."

Everyone nodded, the mood growing somber now that the plan had been put into place. All except for Lea. Yes, there was a sorrow within her, a heavy weight pressing down on her heart. But mixed with it was a powerful sense of relief and unwavering resolve. Emma stared at her for a moment too long, until Lea's eyes flicked up, meeting Emma's gaze. She shook her head, almost imperceptibly, but Emma knew exactly what she was saying: *I know you feel what I'm feeling. But please, don't say a word.*

So, Emma simply turned, grabbing Thomas's hand to lead him from the room. But as Emma walked away, the uncertainty of what lay ahead gnawed at her insides, leaving her feeling hollow and yet, somehow, hopeful.

CHAPTER 47

LEA

Lea wasted no time stripping out of her dress the moment they returned to their quarters to sleep. She knew he didn't blame her; the heat was absolutely stifling. Lea almost longed for the sun to set as much as she longed for Alaric's demise. She put on a thin shift before turning around. Her heart raced as she met Gray's eyes, silently begging him to hold her. To make her forget everything that was happening, just for a few moments.

She stepped forward into his arms, and he placed his chin on the crown of her head, inhaling deeply. Eight petals remained. She was certain he was counting them, calculating how long they had before the gods' threat came true, but it was no use. The petals fell as they pleased, without any distinguishable pattern or timeframe. Did they have days left? A week? Surely, they weren't out of time yet. The thought made Lea's shadows expand and her lungs squeeze.

"Are you okay?" Gray asked, as if sensing the turmoil inside her. She was sure it was an echo of his own, that they were both terrified of what would happen next.

"Fine. As good as I can be, I guess," Lea said, and Gray squeezed her tighter. She wished he could keep his arms around her forever, holding her together in the way only he seemed to be able to do. If she asked, she was certain he'd do it. Simply hold her until they found Alaric and ended this whole cursed war.

"We should rest," Gray said, stroking her hair. Always trying to take care of her, even when it wasn't what his body wanted. She knew what he needed—could feel his yearning for her thick and hard against her stomach as they embraced.

"We will," Lea said, slowly trailing a hand up his chest. She cupped his cheek and met his eyes again. The longing and devotion inside them made Lea breathless. Nearly weightless. He wouldn't deny her what she was asking for, even if they needed to sleep—needed their strength for what lay ahead. Because they needed this just as much.

Gray led her by the hand to the bed, pulling her nightgown over her head and pulling back the covers. Lea slid in, the cool kiss of soft sheets awakening her body. Lea heard the rough scratch of a zipper, the heavy thud as Gray's sword belt dropped to the floor. He climbed in behind her, tucking her firmly against his front, his warm body cocooning her from behind.

Lea wiggled backward against him, and he grabbed her hip, his thumb caressing the arch of the bone as his fingers crept closer to her center. "Are you sure you don't want to sleep?" Gray asked. Lea didn't answer, instead grabbing his hand and sliding it up to cup her breasts. Her skin was on fire, her flesh craving his closeness, and her shadows sneaking out and wrapping around them like a cocoon. Gray had dipped down to her neck, and he pressed soft kisses against the hollow of her throat, his fingers dancing across her nipples, moving from one to the other with a reverence that made her core turn molten.

Reaching back, Lea cupped the back of his head as she enjoyed the sensation of his strong fingers teasing her, his lithe muscles supporting her, and the magnitude of his love wrapping around her. His hand dipped between her legs, and he slipped a finger inside, but Lea needed more. Needed to be as close to him as possible.

"I need to feel you inside me," she begged, her voice a low whisper of need.

Gray's chest rumbled as he bent her knees further, lining himself up with her entrance and slowly pushing inside. He filled her immediately, and Lea moaned his name. His fingers trailed up her leg, slowly, until he reached her hip and held her in place, steadily increasing his pace as he pumped in and out, their pleasure slowly building

It wasn't rushed, but a slow worshiping of each other's bodies. The end of the war was coming, and so much was uncertain. But this? Their love for one another? It was their only constant. The only thing Lea could truly depend upon.

Lea's body went taut, tensing as a pleasure built from her toes and spread up her legs.

"I love you," she moaned, ecstasy coursing through her blood, her breaths becoming shallow and her heart pounding until she exploded, crying out Gray's name as he did the same. He buried himself deep inside her as he came, reminding her of all the ways he loved her.

And once everything had been said, they laid there together, panting and intertwined, unable to move from each other's embrace. Unwilling to break apart. They didn't speak the words, but it was clear from the way they held tight that they both knew this could be the last time in a very long time they would be together like this. And so they simply laid there, savoring each other's closeness until they drifted off to sleep.

CHAPTER 48

LEA

Lea only had a few moments to spare as she hurried down the stone corridor toward Evangeline's room. Her heels clicked in a rapid rhythm, a steady metronome to remind her how little time she had left. Gray was busy with last-minute plans—ensuring the horses were being readied and packed, briefing his generals on the plan to mobilize the army if and when Alaric was found... If she was going to speak with Evangeline, now was her only chance.

Before her feet even caught up with her body, Lea leaned forward and rapped her knuckles on the door. She waited two seconds, then pushed inside. There was no time for manners.

"Who's there? Lea? Is that you?" Evangeline asked from where she stood by the window, and once again, Lea felt the odd sensation of awe that her mother knew who she was and what she was doing, even without her sight.

"It's me," Lea confirmed, closing the door behind her. "I don't have long."

"It's time then?" Evangeline asked.

"Our men confirmed Alaric has at least four outposts, all of them surrounding the Wicked Wood's border. He has to be somewhere in that area. We're splitting up," Lea explained.

"Good," Evangeline said. "That must be why I've been unable to see much in the next few days. There are too many variables. I'll pack my things—"

"No," Lea interrupted. "If I bring you along, Gray will be suspicious."

"But you'll need me there with you—to hold death back so you can kill Alaric."

"I know," Lea said. "But I have an idea. I know you created the portal for the king to enter Calir," Lea said.

Evangeline's cheeks flushed, the red hue creeping down her neck with what Lea assumed was shame.

"There's no time for regret. Could you do it again?"

Evangeline nodded. "If I start preparing now. It would take some time, but yes. Where will this portal lead?"

"The outposts all surround the border of the Wicked Wood. If I had to guess, he's somewhere in there," Lea said, avoiding giving her too much information in case it could tip off Eudora or put Genevieve at risk. "You and I... Our magic is similar. From the gods. We can both hold off death. I'm hoping you can do something else only I can..."

"Okay..." Evangeline tilted her head.

"When I give someone a piece of my magic, it links us, connects us in a way that allows me to see through their eyes. If you can give me the smallest kernel of yours, I can do the same for you. When I need you, you'll feel a tug—like a rope in your hand, but connected to your chest. Just follow it, and you'll see. If I could show you where he is, somewhere in the Wicked Wood, do you think you would recognize it?"

"I know the Wicked Wood like the back of my hand. I hid within it for years."

"Then you should be able to find me when I need you. When it's time, come to me through the portal."

Evangeline pressed her lips together. "Are you certain this is the path forward?"

"It's the best option we have. The only option," Lea said, her fingers drifting up to the crown of vines wrapped around her head. "Alaric is growing stronger."

"You'll have to escape Gray," Evangeline said. "He won't let us go alone willingly."

"I know. I have a plan for that, too." Lea's heart sank, but she pushed the feeling away. "Your magic. Will you try to give me a piece?"

"Of course. What do I do?" Evangeline walked forward, gliding around the small footstool as if she could see it clearly.

"Find your magic and isolate it," Lea instructed. "Imagine a blade or fire, something that can slice through it. Cut away the smallest piece you can, push it into my skin, and try to merge it with my own magic."

Evangeline nodded, clenching her jaw and clearing her throat. Lea's heart thundered in her ears as Evangeline's cold fingers touched hers. She forced herself to take slow, deep breaths, opening herself up to Evangeline's magic. Lea's stomach swirled with anxiety, hoping with all she had that this would work.

She sighed in relief when, after less than ten seconds, she felt it. Evangeline's power.

It was so familiar, yet different from her own—dark mixed with light, sunset mixed with sunrise, cold water on a hot day, and fresh-baked bread combined with a fiery need for vengeance.

Lea felt a flash of warmth the moment it slipped inside her skin, flowing through her limbs and settling in the vast expanse of her chest.

Lea squeezed Evangeline's hands. "Thank you. Thank you for doing this for me," Lea said.

"I would do *anything* for you," Evangeline replied. "Which is why I need to say something. Something you're not going to like, or agree with."

Lea's lungs squeezed with panic, sweat breaking out on her neck and palms. Was she going to say she wouldn't help her after all? Her entire plan hinged on keeping death away long enough for her to kill Alaric.

"Please don't change your mind. I need you." Lea's voice was full of panic, but she couldn't seem to calm herself enough to lower her tone.

"It's not that. It's..." she trailed off, and Lea was overcome with the sudden urge to shake her. To force her to spit out whatever she was trying to say and end the torture.

"I tried taking someone's magic," she began, wringing her hands. "From Thomas. He agreed, after I said it was for you. But I couldn't do it. Couldn't even get past his skin. It's clear that you are the only one capable, the one fated to battle Alaric. Good versus evil, once and for all. But I have seen the future. You do not survive it, Lea. You don't survive taking it all, because that is how you return it to the earth. Through death."

Lea's heart sank. She knew this already, of course. The goddess had said as much. But she'd also said it was possible. That there was a way for her to survive.

"You can't change my mind," she said firmly. "If it's the only way—"

"Give the magic to me," Evangeline interrupted her. "Please."

Lea opened her mouth to answer, to tell her she was out of her mind, but her words were thick in her throat.

Was this what the goddess had been hinting at? Was it possible this was the answer she'd been searching for? Lea rubbed her forehead, a sudden ache pounding behind her eyes.

"It would kill you. I can't," Lea said, her voice finally working, but coming out shaky and unsure.

"It will kill *you*. I have done terrible things, my sweet girl. All of this, Alaric even getting to this point... It's my fault."

"That doesn't mean you deserve to die!" Lea threw her arms out. She couldn't believe what she was hearing. She'd hoped for another way. But not this. Not killing Evangeline.

"And you do?" Evangeline raised her voice, almost shouting. It was so unlike her that Lea jumped back in shock. Evangeline sighed. "Please." Her tone softened. "Please, just think about it."

Lea remained silent. Could she do it? Pass the burden on to the woman who had given birth to her? Who had sacrificed her very soul to keep her safe?

"You should go," Evangeline said with a sad smile, as if there was nothing more to say. "I need to start on the portal. And it seems you have a decision to make. But Lea," she said, reaching out to her, and Lea allowed it, taking her hands. "I *want* to do this for you. Let me do something good. Let me make this right."

"I don't know if I can," Lea whispered, the backs of her eyes burning with tears.

"That's better than a no. Stay safe," Evangeline said, letting go of her hands.

Lea nodded, unable to speak, but knowing Evangeline would sense it, regardless. She turned to walk out the door, her brain spinning and her heart aching.

"Lea?" Evangeline stopped her, wringing her hands in front of her stomach. "I love you."

Lea choked back a sob. "I love you, too," she said, the words feeling right as they fell from her mouth and sank into Evangeline's skin.

She wasn't sure what to do. What her decision would be. But one way or another, this war would end soon, and she was glad to know she was walking into battle with no regrets or things left unsaid.

Without another word, Lea hurried back to her room. But as she closed the door behind her, her heart felt lighter than it had in months.

CHAPTER 49

ERIK

Erik opened himself up to the sun as he climbed on top of Cinnamon and prepared to leave Auropera, positioning himself snugly behind Janelle. He allowed the sunlight to stoke the fire inside him, filling him with righteous fury. It had been a gift from the gods themselves when Janelle had gasped at the mention of Alnwick. He'd known immediately what had caused such a visceral reaction from his wife, had felt her shock and apprehension as strongly as he felt his own heartbeat, and when she'd confirmed that Alnwick was where Jakob and Stefan had been stationed, he'd known immediately that he had to be the one to scout the outpost nearby.

It was the first opportunity that had presented itself to find and kill the men who had hurt Janelle since she'd told him of her past. The first time his dreams of breaking their bones one by one and plucking out their eyes had become a concrete possibility.

It felt like a morbid version of his birthday, but Erik didn't show it. It caused Janelle pain to think about what had been done to her. And who knew if they remained there? Who knew if they even still lived? Erik hoped with everything he had they did, if only so he could confront them about the horrendous decisions they'd made during their worthless lives... and end them.

He hadn't told Gray of his plan to search for the men who hurt his wife, but he knew his best friend would understand. Erik wouldn't allow it to distract him, would make sure to dispose of the men quickly and return to his primary objective of searching for Alaric, or any information that could help them find him. And who knows? Maybe the bastards would lead them straight to the false king. Maybe men like that were drawn to one another, joining forces to amplify their evil.

Janelle had been hesitant when he'd told her what he was planning, but he assured her he would keep her safe. That there wasn't a chance in this world or the next that he would ever allow them to touch her again. Just the fact that he had to do so made his fury almost boil over. Even after all these years, the memory of what Jakob and his brother had done to her was so vivid, she was still deeply afraid of them on a base level that haunted her subconscious.

Erik pulled Cinnamon in line with the other horses just inside the portcullis. Four different groups, ready to split away on their different missions. It felt wrong separating from their friends. Unnatural.

Not to mention that the last time they'd done it, Lea had almost died of the Lonely Death. Even then, it had been Emma who sensed something was wrong, and Emma was staying behind, unable to warn them of the things they couldn't see or feel. For them to all be apart...

Dread swirled in Erik's gut.

"Send word if you discover anything," Gray said. "If you find Alaric, do not engage. Do not forget that Lea is the one who has to kill him. We do not approach until we have our entire army. They're ready. Once we're all together again, we end this."

"Gods bless and protect you all," Vincent said, placing a hand over his heart.

"Until we meet again. Be safe," Tanad said, his lips pressing into a hard, grim line.

"And for the love of the gods," Janelle added, looking at Lea pointedly, "don't do anything stupid."

CHAPTER 50

LEA

They'd been riding for days, barely stopping to use the bathroom and refill their canteens. Two more moonflower petals had fallen from Lea's crown as they rode, and each time, Gray had gritted his teeth, kicked Obsidian's sides, and pushed him harder. The relentless riding left Lea not only exhausted, but without the opportunity to speak to her father about his part in her plan. She needed a moment alone with him—and soon.

Luna leapt over a fallen log, and as she jostled up and down in the saddle, Lea didn't even have to pretend to feel nauseous. Water sloshed around in her empty stomach, and she swallowed, leaning to her right to clear Luna's side in case she did actually vomit.

"Little Flower?" Gray said, catching her attention. His shadows reached out to her, caressing her cheek as he tilted his head, his eyebrows lowering in concern.

"I'm fine," Lea said. "Just an empty stomach." On cue, her stomach rumbled.

Frown lines bracketed Gray's mouth as he slowed Obsidian to a trot. "You look weak," he said. "And pale."

Lea pulled Luna's reins, slowing her. "Do you think we could stop? Just long enough for you to hunt something fresh? Maybe you could take the others, and Dad and I can build a fire to cook it on?" Lea's stomach growled again, but she pretended to change her mind, shaking her head. "No. I'm sorry. We should keep pushing forward."

"Stop," Gray told Obsidian, who halted immediately. "Of course we can eat. You need strength to fight. A quick stop won't hurt us." The lines around his eyes deepened, and guilt slid into Lea's empty stomach, coating the walls and making her even more nauseous. She knew how it made Gray feel when she was hungry. When her most basic needs weren't taken care of. He'd always taken responsibility for taking care of her, and anything short of that felt like a failure.

Gray looked around at the landscape. "There's a fresh stream not far from here. Can you wait a few minutes?"

Lea smiled gratefully, another, sharper stab of guilt almost making her look away. But she ignored it. She was only doing what she had to in order to save her kingdom.

Gray wasted no time once they reached the stream, helping her down from her horse and making sure she drank some water.

"Henry, make sure she rests. Cole? Patrick?" Gray inclined his head toward the woods, then stalked off, dagger in hand. Lea felt a quick bolt of panic. She didn't have much time. Gray would work quickly to find something for her to eat, worried that she was wasting away. But Daniel was still around, and she couldn't risk him overhearing what she was going to ask Henry.

"Daniel?" Lea asked.

Daniel jumped to his feet, rushing over to her, and Lea was once again reminded that she was no longer a girl from Bearswillow, but a queen.

"Would you move the horses over to the shade down there? Let them drink from the stream where they're out of the sun?"

"Of course," Daniel said, practically tripping over his feet to do what she'd asked.

"Dad?" Lea tilted her head, signaling him to come over. He dropped the pack he'd been rummaging through and came to sit beside her, leaning down and kissing her forehead. It was a glimpse of the affection and attention she'd so desperately wanted after her mother's death, and right now, it felt too late. But she couldn't hold grudges. Not anymore. She had no more time or energy to waste on such things.

"I need to ask you to do something for me," Lea said. "And I want you to let me get it all out before you argue."

Henry's eyes narrowed, but he nodded hesitantly.

"I have a plan to defeat Alaric, but I can't do it without your help. The goddess said I have to be the one to kill him. But Gray can't be with me when it happens."

Henry's shoulders rose toward his ears, but he didn't interrupt.

"When we get closer, when we find Alaric and scout out the camp, I need you to freeze time so I can slip away. Alone. Without Gray following me, at least not immediately."

Henry's mouth dropped open, and he shook his head slightly. "Alone?"

"The goddess said only I could defeat him. I can't do that if I'm worried about keeping everyone else safe. Evangeline has seen it," Lea said. "She's seen me going alone to battle him. Seen me ruling a peaceful kingdom afterward. But only if I go alone. I'll be okay, *if* you help me."

Henry's eyes darted around as if searching the sky for some excuse, some flaw in her logic. "Evangeline's seen this working? You'll be okay?" he asked.

"Yes." Lea lied. "If you help me, I can defeat him. She's seen us all, happy and safe. But only if Gray doesn't follow me."

Henry remained quiet, thinking, but Lea couldn't afford to waste time allowing him to consider the different options.

"It feels like fate, doesn't it? This began with me—with us—when Evangeline sent me to grow up with a father and mother who loved me, the only ones who could keep me safe. This is part of that, Dad. It ends as it began. You helping to take care of me, freezing time so I can go defeat Alaric. We all die if I don't. This is the only way."

Henry took her hand, squeezing it tight. "You are the strongest, bravest girl," he said. "My little girl." He cupped her cheek, his eyes searching her face, but he wouldn't find any hints of innocence or childhood there. They had been burned out of her, tragically and violently.

"Okay," he said. "If you say it's the only way, then I'll help you."

"Thank you," Lea exhaled in relief. She'd been prepared for more pushback, but how could he argue with her when she told him it had already been seen? Maybe it wasn't a lie. Maybe by now, it had been seen. Maybe she'd find a way to survive taking Alaric's magic and make Evangeline's vision of her and Gray ruling beside each other come true without killing Evangeline.

"Thank you," Lea said again. "I'll tell you when it's time. Don't say a word to anyone."

"I understand."

Gray appeared just then, a foobil in hand.

"Care to cook it for us?" he asked.

Before he could even drop the animal, Lea held out her hand and engulfed it in flames, keeping her fire going until the hair had burned off and it was cooked through.

"Look how domestic I've become." She gestured to the cooked rodent, and Gray laughed.

"She cooks, *and* she kills," he quipped before ripping off a leg for her. "And now, she *eats*."

Lea rolled her eyes at his protectiveness. He was as stubborn and worried about her as always, and it only confirmed to Lea that she was doing the right thing. Even if Gray knowing her plan didn't carry the risk of Eudora seeing it and alerting Alaric, even if Evangeline hadn't seen them failing with Gray around, he'd never allow her to go through with taking Alaric's magic, knowing it would kill her. He'd take the magic himself somehow, or force her to pass it to Evangeline. To anyone else. He'd allow the entire kingdom to fall before he'd let her risk her life again. But that wasn't fair. This was her battle. Her burden. Written in the stars by the gods themselves.

Lea lifted the meat to her lips, taking a bite. It had already cooled, and she ripped off a large chunk to make sure it had actually cooked all the way through. Relieved to see there was no pink inside, she popped the piece into her mouth.

As they ate in silence, a hawk soaring in the distance caught her eye. She waited to see if it would turn toward them, wondering if Genevieve was trying to reach her again, but it disappeared back in the direction they'd come from.

Henry stared after it, his jaw set in a firm line, his eyes full of worry.

It will be okay, Lea wanted to tell him, but she couldn't. Until they were alone again, she would just have to hope that Gray didn't notice that while he was gone, something in the air had changed.

CHAPTER 51

JANELLE

The heat was stifling. Absolutely incessant, and the longer they traveled, the more Janelle worried she might die of heatstroke. And not even in a dramatic way. She truly was concerned about surviving this trek to Alnwick. But then, just when she thought she couldn't survive the heat anymore, a lake appeared in the distance. A gift from the gods themselves. Or maybe just the goddess, since it was the god of the sun who was torturing them like this to begin with.

Before she even asked, Erik steered Cinnamon straight to the glassy body of water, and within seconds, Janelle stripped down to her underclothes. With a deep breath of anticipation, she dove into the crystal-clear lake. She hoped she was right that it was deep enough, but it was hard to tell when she could see straight down to the bottom. Each rock and twig were clearly visible, as if she were looking through a piece of glass.

The water was gloriously cool as she submerged, holding her breath and staying under for as long as possible before finally popping her head back out, her lungs burning. She groaned dramatically.

"Stop enchanting the area and get in. We're fine. If Alaric shows up, we're dead anyway. Might as well save your energy and cool off."

Erik dropped his hands to his sides. "It's just to alert me if someone's coming. Give us a head start."

Janelle rolled her eyes but stayed silent, floating on her back and staring up at the blood-red sky. It was disgustingly hot, and she wished they could just stay in the water until the war was over and the sun god calmed the fuck down. Seriously, he was like a child throwing a temper tantrum. He didn't get his way, so now he was trying to smoke them out? Cook them alive? It had been over a week of nonstop heat, with no end in sight.

A zipper scratched open, and Janelle lifted her head, her body warming as Erik stripped down to nothing and waded into the water from the shore, choosing the more cautious route over diving headfirst from the overhang. Once Erik was shoulder-deep, Janelle paddled over to him, wrapping her legs around his waist.

"See? It feels so good, doesn't it?" she asked, wiggling against him.

Erik's enormous hands slid from her shoulders down her back to cup her butt, tilting her against him. "It'd feel better without your underclothes still on. Is there a reason you didn't take them off?" he asked, fingering the strap of her bra.

"Well, I didn't want to distract you, of course."

"You always distract me," Erik said, leaning in and brushing kisses up the side of her neck. "You could be wearing a wool sack that covered you from head to toe, and I would still be completely distracted."

"Well, if that's the case..." Janelle's hands moved to the hem of her tank top, peeling it up over her torso slowly, her best attempt at being sexy. "You know, we haven't tried to see if the mate bond will snap into place again. We haven't done it in the water. Maybe that's what was missing. Maybe my magic is tied to the water—my mom always told me I swim like a fish."

Erik laughed, that beautiful, booming echo that made Janelle fall deeper in love with him every time she heard it. "I don't *need* the mate bond, but I'm certainly not opposed to trying."

He raised his eyebrows, helping her slide the wet bra off her arms. It had just cleared her fingertips when the earth beneath them groaned—a low, ominous rumble that seemed to come from deep within the ground. The water surrounding them rippled violently, distorting the reflection of the sky above them. The trees swayed with unnatural force, their leaves shaking and floating to the ground like it was the changing of seasons.

Janelle's breath caught in her throat, her heart hammering in a sudden panic as she turned to Erik. "What's happening?" Her voice trembled, barely audible above the growing roar beneath their feet. "Have you felt anything like this before?"

Erik's expression darkened, the playful gleam in his eyes replaced with something grim and uncertain. "No," he said, shaking his head as he scanned the forest. He clenched his jaw, his cheek muscles bunching. "But I've heard of it—an earthquake. There was one several years ago in Calir. Half the castle had to be rebuilt. We need to get out from under these trees. Now."

Without another word, he pulled her out of the water and onto the trembling ground. Janelle's hands fumbled as she threw on her leggings and top, her fingers clumsy with panic. She could barely think straight, her mind spinning as she tried to process what was happening. The earth trembled again, harder this time. Branches cracked and groaned overhead, threatening to crash to the ground and block their escape.

Cinnamon reared, her eyes widening as she bucked nervously, spinning in circles, and Erik rushed to her, grabbing her reins to soothe her.

"Whoa, girl," Erik murmured, his voice calm and steady despite the fear on his own face. He yanked hard on the reins, and she stopped rearing, pawing her feet at the ground as if begging them to mount her so they could escape.

Janelle's heart raced as she stuffed their shoes into the saddlebag, her mind screaming at her to run, but her feet were rooted to the ground.

The world around them was falling apart, and she couldn't move. Couldn't think. Erik had always been her rock, a constant steadying presence, but right now, even he seemed shaken.

As if she were made of feathers, Erik picked her up and threw her onto Cinnamon's back, climbing up behind her in an instant. A tree branch split, crashing in a cloud of dust beside them, and Cinnamon reared again, twisting in circles in utter panic. She'd been trained for battle. Trained to ignore loud noises and to run without rest for days. But she'd never been trained for the earth crumbling beneath her feet.

Before they could be thrown from the saddle, Erik pulled them both off, his muscular arms steady despite the earth shattering beneath them. "We have to run," he said, his voice urgent as he grabbed Janelle's hand and yanked her forward. "There's a clearing nearby, I think. We'll be safer there."

They barely made it a few steps before the earth lurched beneath them again, this time with a violent jolt that sent Janelle stumbling. A fissure cracked open ahead of them, a jagged scar in the ground that seemed to stretch endlessly in both directions. The dirt buckled and bowed as if it were being ripped apart.

Janelle didn't even have a chance to scream as a massive tree tilted dangerously to the side, its roots snapping violently as it toppled toward them.

"Move!" Erik shouted, his voice sharp with panic. He yanked her back just as the tree crashed to the ground, missing her by mere feet. The impact was so violent that the earth around it exploded, sending dirt and debris flying in every direction.

Janelle's breath came in ragged gasps, and her heart pounded so hard it felt like it might burst from her chest. For a moment, she couldn't move. Couldn't breathe. The terrifying force of the earth's anger, the way the ground trembled beneath her feet—it was like nothing she'd ever experienced before. Erik climbed on top of the fallen tree, searching for a way to escape.

"Erik, watch out!" she screamed, her voice raw with fear as another tree tilted dangerously toward him.

Erik dodged to the side, barely avoiding the falling trunk. He turned to her, his eyes wide and filled with a terror that mirrored her own. For the first time, she saw fear in him—real, gut-wrenching fear—and it sent a fresh wave of panic surging through her.

"Janelle!" he screamed, his voice hoarse with desperation. But it was too late.

She hadn't seen it—a thick branch, as wide as her torso, falling from above. It crashed into her back and hip with bone-shattering force, the weight of it sending her sprawling to the ground. Agony tore through her body, stars dotting her vision as a scream ripped from her throat. It felt as though her bones had splintered into tiny slivers that were stabbing into her bloodstream and circulating through her body.

Erik was at her side in an instant, his face twisted in horror as he ripped the branch from her body. His hands were shaking, and there was no trace of his usual calm as he pressed his palms to her broken ribs, his magic surging through her. "You're going to be okay," he said, his voice breaking as he poured healing energy into her. "Just hold on. Please, just hold on."

Janelle's vision swam with tears, the pain so intense it blurred the world around her. She wanted to beg him to take her away, to carry her out of the chaos, but all she could do was sob as wave after wave of agony crashed over her. Erik's magic eased the pain, but it wasn't enough. She couldn't move. Couldn't even think.

"I've got you," Erik whispered, his voice tight with emotion. He scooped her into his arms, holding her close as branches crashed all around them, the earth still trembling beneath his feet, and ran. Faster than she had ever seen him move, Erik leapt over fallen trees, dodging craters as the world crumbled. His jaw was set with fierce determination, his muscles straining as he held her tightly against his chest, trying not to jostle her body.

"Just a little further," he murmured, his voice barely audible above the roar of the collapsing forest and blood pounding in her ears. "I've got you. You're safe."

And somehow, through the haze of pain and fear, Janelle believed him. She believed him, because Erik had always been her protector. Honest and steady and true. Even now, with the world unraveling around them, she had no doubt he would find a way to get them out of it.

Branches continued to crash down as they neared the clearing, but Janelle could feel her grip on consciousness slipping. The edges of her vision blurred, darkness creeping in as her body gave in to the overwhelming pain and exhaustion. Erik's voice grew faint, distant, and he cried out in relief at the sight of a clearing ahead.

As Erik laid her gently on the ground, her vision dimmed completely, and she surrendered to the sweet, merciful pull of unconsciousness. He cupped his hand against her cheek, tapping it, trying to wake her, but it was no use. The last thing she heard was his voice, full of love and fear, whispering her name.

CHAPTER 52

LEA

Lea's anticipation built the closer they got to Pontor. But instead of getting more nervous, she felt relief. All this would be over soon. Another petal had fallen, and now only five remained. She was one tick closer to being separated from her mate for eternity. She couldn't allow that to happen. Eudora and Alaric were close, and in a few hours, they would find the encampment and have information to report back. And more importantly, she would find Alaric, and end him.

Lea watched Gray's back as they rode, his strong, broad shoulders that had carried the weight of this kingdom for a century. For him, it would be over soon as well. She thought once again about her birth mother's offer—to give her the magic Lea would steal from Alaric. Allow her to pay the cost of stealing so much power. It was so tempting, but Lea knew deep down she couldn't do it. Even if she wanted to, Evangeline had suffered enough, and a painful death wasn't something she could add to that list.

Obsidian slowed, his head swinging around as he pawed at the ground.

"What's going on, boy?" Gray asked, leaning down to pat his mane as he sent his shadows out, searching for whatever his horse had sensed. Lea commanded hers to join him, and together they spread throughout the trees.

It was only a few moments before they felt what had caused Obsidian to pause. Lea and Gray met each other's eyes as the earth began to tremble, the trees shivering and shaking.

"Run," Gray ordered, and Lea didn't hesitate. She bolted forward, the others following behind her as tree branches began to groan overhead.

A massive branch cracked above them, crashing into the ground with a boom that made Lea's ears ring. Her horse jumped over the branch as she drew her sword, pulling its magic into her body and amplifying it outward. Lea formed a hard shield of air around them, gritting her teeth as she forced it to remain solid while they moved. Gray's shadows reached out in front of them, picking up branches and throwing them out of the way. Branch after branch crashed against her shield, splintering it with every blow.

She threw more magic into it, clenching her jaw harder with every crack.

A fissure opened in the dry earth in front of them and Daniel's horse tumbled, throwing him to the ground. He fell out from under the shield, only for a moment—but it was a moment too long. An enormous branch crashed down, falling from directly above him and hitting him in the head, killing him instantly.

"No!" Lea cried out, but Gray's shadows urged her forward. She wanted to return to Daniel, to find a way to heal him, but it was too late. She didn't need Emma there to know he was gone.

"We have to stop!" Lea cried, pulling her horse to a halt.

"No!" Gray shouted. "It's too dangerous!"

"I can't keep us all safe if we're moving," she said.

Gray's eyes flashed, his shadows surging forward as if they could pull them to safety, but instead, he pulled Obsidian up next to her, and the others followed suit. Lea tightened the shield around them, the strain far less intense now that they were no longer moving and in much closer proximity to one another.

"Daniel— Can we get to him?" Cole asked.

A mix of pity and guilt settled behind Lea's sternum, and she rubbed it, trying to soothe it away. "He's gone," she said softly. "I'm sorry. I know he was your friend."

Cole's face turned white, and he looked back, craning his neck to see his friend's body. Lea commanded her shadows to wrap around Daniel, blocking the sight of his body. Cole didn't need to see his friend's brain splattered across the ground.

"I'll burn him," Lea said. "It will have to do for a burial. Okay?" she asked Cole.

Cole cleared his throat, nodding. Still holding the shield in place, Lea let her fire trail out from her feet, inching toward Daniel until his body was engulfed in black flames.

"May the gods hold you," Patrick and Cole muttered together while Lea recited the prayer silently in her head.

"Do you think this is the god of the sun?" Gray asked.

Lea shook her head, anxiety swirling in her gut. "The goddess said the universe would try to correct what has been taken from it. The sun? That was him. But the wildfires.... This..." Lea trailed off.

What else would they face before they found Alaric? And if the universe was intent on killing her, and the god of the sun was punishing her, how far would they go to keep her from winning this war?

CHAPTER 53

JANELLE

Janelle had thought the pain would never stop, but as she woke up in a soft bed, she was pleased to discover she'd been wrong. Though still sore, her back and hip aching and her body tired, she could actually breathe. Deep inhales that didn't send searing agony through her ribcage.

"Janelle?" Erik's voice cut through the stillness. A chair scraped as Janelle opened her eyes.

"Thank the gods," Erik breathed, leaning forward and touching her cheek. His thumb gently trailed along her skin, causing goosebumps to pebble on her arms.

"Where are we? Did we make it to Alnwyn?"

"No," Erik said, handing her a cup. "We're in a little town called Bacar. I needed to get you somewhere safe to heal."

"Have there been more?" she asked.

Erik shook his head. "Just aftershocks. Small tremors, but nothing like before."

Janelle exhaled a sigh of relief. "How long was I out?" It wasn't as if she could look at the sun to see how many hours had passed.

"About a day. The healing was extensive. Your body needed the rest." Erik ran his hands down her arms, the lines on his face relaxing as she wiggled up against the pillows, moving without agonizing pain. "How do you feel now?"

Janelle twisted side to side, then swung her legs gently over the side of the bed. "I think I'm okay," she said, tentatively standing. The soreness remained, but it was nothing like what she'd experienced when the branch had hit her. She took a few cautious steps, moving to the cracked window to look outside. The town was tiny, maybe ten squat houses around a small village square with a garden at its center.

"We should go," Janelle said, considering that they were taking a room in a house that was likely needed by those living here. "Whose home is this? I'd like to thank them."

"The village is abandoned," Erik said. "They probably went to a different town on our army's orders, to avoid the wildfires."

Janelle looked back outside, her eyes flicking to the garden, then between the houses near it. "Are you sure?" she asked. She wasn't sure why, but it didn't feel abandoned to her. The homes hadn't quite settled into neglect, and a vague scent of bacon and eggs hung in the air. "And, did you make food?" Janelle asked.

A blush crept up Erik's neck. "I know it's technically stealing, but it was just some bread. It would've gone stale by the time the villagers returned, anyway. And some crackers." He looked away. "Okay, and I took some dried fruit to bring with us. But I think what we're doing for the kingdom is enough of a repayment, don't you?"

"Not judging," Janelle said, holding up a hand. "Just thinking."

"About what?" Erik asked, his shoulders straightening as he caught onto her apprehension. Fire gathered in his hands, and despite it raising the temperature in the room by a few degrees, Janelle felt reassured that he had it at the ready.

"I don't feel like we're alone," Janelle said.

As if she had summoned it, the sound of horses' hooves clacked from the stones leading into the village. Janelle ducked, hiding herself as Erik jumped to look out the window.

"What are you doing?" Janelle asked, but Erik ignored her.

"Royal soldiers—deserters, maybe?" Fire spread up Erik's arms. "They have Cinnamon. They must've heard her and gone to investigate. That's why they weren't here."

Relief washed over Janelle as she peered through the window to see Cinnamon returning with the soldiers. They wouldn't have to continue on foot now.

"Let's go," Erik said.

Janelle winced. "Don't we need a plan or something? You're just going to go out there and demand our horse back?"

"I have a plan. If they help us, I won't kill them," he said.

Janelle's stomach twisted as she counted the men—ten against two.

"Do you doubt me, wife?" Erik asked, his eyes mischievous.

"Of course not," she said, but her voice faltered. Were these soldiers still loyal to Alaric? Or had they seen how evil he was and fled?

Two more men appeared between the trees, and Janelle stiffened. Her head swam and her breaths became shallow as they approached, their features becoming more clear with every step. But even from a distance, Janelle would have recognized them easily—these men were the reason they had specifically chosen to search Alnwyn.

She pressed a hand against her sternum, trying to force her heart to slow. It didn't help. Her heart continued to slam against her ribs, each beat coming faster than the last.

Erik's brows lowered as he rushed to her side, his eyes flicking back to the window and his hand going to the hilt of his sword. "What is it?" he asked.

Janelle tried to speak, but only air escaped her lips. She cleared her throat, meeting Erik's eyes, and he leaned closer, cupping her face.

"Is it them?" he asked, his voice like gravel. His eyes were dark, dancing with flames, but his touch remained gentle. Steady and strong.

She nodded.

Erik didn't move for several seconds, staring into her eyes with a look that said everything he wasn't. That he loved her. That he was sorry for what had happened to her. And that he was going to fucking rip them limb from limb.

Janelle had spent years dreaming of this day. Of getting revenge against Jakob and Stefan. But now that they were here, just feet away, Janelle felt the urge to run. To take Erik far away from the terrible men who had hurt her and make sure they could never hurt either of them ever again.

But the tension in his posture told Janelle that nothing would deter him from enacting his revenge. And even if she could convince him to run with her, she loved him too much to deprive him of his vengeance.

Erik finally stood, his flames growing until they began to singe the curtains by the window.

"Hey! Who's there?" someone yelled from outside as smoke escaped through the small crack between the panes of glass.

"Your worst fucking nightmare," Erik growled as he wrapped his hand around the hilt of his sword, lifted his chin, and stormed toward the door.

CHAPTER 54

ERIK

Janelle said something to Erik as he left the room, though he wasn't sure what. He could no longer hear her over the roaring of blood in his ears. Kicking open the front door, he raised a hand in front of him and plastered a smile on his face.

It was the most difficult thing he had ever done, pretending that he wasn't ready to rip each of their hearts out and force them to watch as they stopped pumping, but he took a deep breath. His fury was still there, simmering and ready, but he needed the men to put their guards down, and to do that, he had to at least appear calm.

"Weapons down. We're no threat to you," he said, hoping that they couldn't hear the fury in his voice.

The men narrowed their eyes, scanning the area as if searching for the rest of the rebel army hidden within the ten tiny buildings.

"Hey, I know you," one of the men said. "You're the commander's second."

Erik tilted his head, assessing. "And you are..." he trailed off.

"So glad to see you," the man said, lowering his sword. "We wanna join the rebels. The army Evander is leading."

Erik crossed his arms and tilted his head as if confused, but he knew exactly why the man was so happy to see him. It was because they were cowards. Men without enough conviction to stay in the fight when the tides began to change. Not really men at all. Still, he didn't answer, waiting for the man to say more.

"The rebellion?" he finally said. "Alaric is crazy."

Erik lifted his chin. "Ah. I see. So, you're ready to pledge yourselves to your new king? You'll bravely fight at our side?"

"Of course." The soldier nodded his head emphatically.

"You believe in a better kingdom where Fae and humans can live together?"

"Oh, for sure. Absolutely."

"I'd like to hear it from all of you, if you don't mind."

Three of them quickly agreed, and Erik roved over the men, meeting each of their eyes and staring at them until they looked away. None lasted more than a few seconds, exactly as he had anticipated. They were weak.

"You," Erik said to the fourth man from the left whose face had bent in a scowl when he'd mentioned Fae and humans living in peace. "What's your name?"

"Stefan, sir," he replied, bowing his head slightly. Erik's gut rolled in disgust, and his blood warmed to near boiling.

"Stefan," Erik said, fighting against every fiber of his being that begged him to incinerate the man on the spot. "It appears you all found my horse." He tilted his head toward the terracotta mare straining against her lead to get back to him. "She got spooked in the earthquake. Would you bring her to me?"

"Of course." Stefan slid off his own horse, grabbed Cinnamon's reins, and walked her over to Erik.

"Thank you," he muttered, the words tasting bitter as they left his mouth. "The rest of you," Erik said. "What are your names?"

Stefan turned to walk back toward his friends, but Erik shot a line of fire in front of him.

"Stay where you are," Erik commanded.

"I'm not sure what's going on here, but—" Stefan stammered.

"Shut up," Erik spat. "Better yet, name your friends for me. Jakob, perhaps?" his eyes narrowed on one of the men, and he stiffened, his face going pale. He assessed the boy—thin and tall, with wide shoulders and a strong jaw. Still, he was no match for Erik.

"There's no Jakob here," Stefan protested. "I don't know what you're talking about, or who you think you are—"

Erik encircled Stefan with fire, and he froze.

"Don't. You. *Dare.* Lie to me," Erik seethed. "I already think you're a coward. Try to find a shred of dignity, you worthless sack of filth."

Stefan's mouth gaped open as his eyes flicked from the fire to Erik, up and down like a bouncing ball.

"What do you want from us?" the man Erik had identified as Jakob finally asked.

Erik lowered his chin and stared him down. "The rest of your names. As I have already requested."

Jakob swallowed, looking around at his comrades. He rattled off the names, Parker, Trey, Shawn... Each man's eyes narrowed as he called them out. "Now, if you don't mind, I think you should go."

Erik laughed, but there was nothing jolly in the sound. "I'm not going anywhere."

"Hey man," the man Jakob had outed as Trey said. "I don't know what's going on here or what you have against these two, but I just met them like a week ago. So whatever your vendetta is, I'd like to be left out of it."

The others chimed in, agreeing—all except for two men who shared a nervous look, Oliver and Liam; Stefan's friends. Erik was as certain of it as he was his own name, as certain as he was that his heart beat for Janelle, and that finding the men who had hurt her was his purpose in life.

"Fine," Erik said. "Everyone can go except Stefan and Jakob."

The men wasted no time turning their horses to leave, but Erik stopped Oliver and Liam with a blast of fire that made their horses rear so violently, they were almost thrown to the ground. "Oh, and you two. Stay. Let's chat."

The other soldiers couldn't leave fast enough, sprinting away on their horses without looking back, but Erik didn't care where they went. He wouldn't let them join the rebellion—they certainly couldn't be trusted when they had fled from their comrades. But his quarrel wasn't with them.

"What do you want from us?" Liam asked, his voice so nasally it made Erik want to punch him in the throat.

Erik looked over his shoulder to see if Janelle was still hiding within the house, and she was nowhere in sight. It didn't bother Erik. If she didn't want to make herself known, that was her decision, and he would respect it. But whether she wanted to watch or not, these men were going to die.

"You hurt someone very dear to me," Erik said, flicking a finger and sending trails of fire to surround the men.

"What are you talking about?" Stefan stuttered. "We've never met you before. We've never hurt anyone. Not anyone who didn't deserve it."

Absolute rage surged through Erik's chest. "What about in Bearswillow? A girl named Janelle? Did *she* deserve it?"

Jakob stiffened, but Stefan threw his head back, cackling. "That bitch? We did the world a favor by—"

Erik couldn't control himself. He blasted a wall of flames at Stefan, so hot that he was only able to scream for a moment before his skin melted off, and he collapsed to the ground, nothing more than a bloody pile of muscle and bone.

Erik sighed. He'd wanted to drag an apology from each of their throats *before* killing them, make each one admit to what they had done. Stefan certainly couldn't speak now. He was as dead as they come, but he supposed he still had a chance to get apologies from three of the four. It would have to do.

Erik turned back to the others, inching the fire closer to them. Taunting them. Jakob was shaking, his face pale as a ghost, his jaw open in shock. "What— Who are you?"

"He's my husband," Janelle said, her voice strong as she stepped out of the doorway. Erik smiled as she lifted her chin and met Jakob's eyes. Beautiful. She was so damn beautiful and strong and brave. Pride swelled in Erik's chest, unlike anything he'd ever felt before.

"Janelle," Jakob whispered. "Please," he begged.

But Janelle held up her hand, shaking her head. "I begged like that—for you to help me, for you to stop them from mutilating me. Do you remember that? My voice breaking as I screamed for your help? You left me to die." She swallowed, lifting her chin. "And I think it's only fair that I do the same." Janelle turned to go back into the house, and Erik raised his hands.

"Maybe an apology would help?" he said. "I'll allow you to beg for your life."

The ground began to tremble again, a slow rumble that quickly escalated into a quake that rocked the earth. The house groaned, and Erik twisted as stones tumbled from the roof behind him so abruptly it caused him to lose hold on his trails of fire.

"Janelle!" he screamed, racing toward the doorway and yanking her backward as the house collapsed completely, dust and dirt billowing into the air in massive waves.

"I'm okay," she said, her hands shaking as they moved from her head to her chest. "I'm okay. I— Erik." She pointed, and Erik followed her finger to where Jakob and his friends were disappearing into the forest.

"Dammit!" he hissed, pulling Janelle into the garden and away from the trees as the ground continued to buckle and rumble. His anger built, the smoke from his flames mixing with the dust from the house. He couldn't follow them. Not now, when it seemed the earth was going to break into a million pieces beneath their feet. When a single wrong step could lead to another accident.

Not when it would put Janelle at risk.

As if confirming his thoughts, the other houses followed, collapsing as a wave of tremors rocked the ground. "We'll find them," Erik whispered into Janelle's hair, hoping the earthquake wouldn't kill the bastards. He wanted to be the one to end their lives. Slowly. Agonizingly.

As the final horse disappeared from sight, Erik cast out his magic, wrapping a thread of power around the men and refusing to let it be severed. He didn't know if it would work—he'd never tried such a thing before—but it was all he could do. The only thing he could think of to help him track them as they fled.

"I'll see you soon," Erik spat under his breath, hoping they believed they'd gotten away. Their deaths would be that much sweeter when he found them again, and he would savor the look of terror in their eyes when he pinned them down and forced that apology from their lips. They may have thought they'd escaped, but they didn't understand that they could never escape what they had done—and what he now would do to them.

CHAPTER 55

EMMA

The potion never left her person. Anytime she set it down, her lungs would constrict until her breaths grew shallow, and her heart would race until she picked it back up. She wasn't sure if it was some sign from the universe that she should keep it with her, or just a deep fear that she'd need the potion and not have it. That she'd let everyone down; be the reason they failed. It rattled her enough to make sure it was in her pocket at all times, checking and double-checking every few minutes to a degree that was almost obsessive.

Days had passed since Lea, Gray, and the others had set out on their journey, and Emma felt absolutely useless. There was nothing she could do but wait—a task that was not her strong suit—but she had no choice.

Thomas had kept his word, staying busy making weapon after weapon, reinforcing existing ones with new magic. He worked himself to the bone daily, his effort even greater than when it had been eternal night. Emma knew the waiting was weighing on him as well, but still, he stayed. For *her*, and it made her feel warm from her toes to her nose every time she thought about it.

She finished making his lunch—not anything fancy like her mother would have made— a hearty sandwich with thick-cut ham and fresh cheese—and went outside to find him, certain that, just like every other day, he was forgetting to eat, so engrossed in whatever he was working on that even his rumbling stomach didn't remind him of his need for strength or sustenance.

Just as Emma had suspected, she spotted him sitting beneath the tree he'd taken to working under, leaning against its thick, scaly bark, hoping for a stray breeze to provide relief from the heat. His brow was furrowed, his gaze locked on a bow and quiver full of arrows in his hands. Emma examined the pile of weapons next to him as she approached—at least a dozen—and a pang of worry settled behind her sternum.

"Hey," she said as she drew near, not wanting to startle him.

As soon as he saw her, Emma felt an odd sensation roll off him in waves, a feeling that both scared and fascinated her. It felt like snuggling beneath a blanket by a warm fire, with your favorite book in hand and a cup of honeyed tea—soothing and familiar. And remarkably close to love.

Thomas set down the bow and arrow as Emma plopped down beside him, handing him the plate.

"It's not lunchtime yet, is it?" Thomas asked. Right on cue, his stomach growled, and Emma pinned him with a look.

"It's almost dinner, actually."

Thomas grinned, picking up his sandwich. "You don't have to make these for me."

"I know. I like it, though. My mom always made me special food when I was tired or having a hard day. Though I can't make anything nearly as good as her sandwiches and soups—"

"It's perfect. Absolutely delicious," Thomas said through a mouthful of food. "Come here," he added, wrapping an arm around her, still holding his sandwich in the other hand. She snuggled into the crook of his shoulder as they leaned back against the tree, looking up at the sky.

"Are you holding up okay?" he asked.

"I worry about everyone. And I miss them, of course. But I do think this is where I'm supposed to be."

"So do I," Thomas said, resting his cheek on her head, the feeling of his jaw bunching and relaxing as he chewed tickling her scalp.

A flush crept up Emma's face, but she didn't pull away. She was getting used to Thomas's affectionate words and his physical touch, craving it even.

"A few more days," Thomas said. "They should find Alaric soon, and then we can put all of this behind us. We can move forward."

Emma squinted as the sky darkened on the horizon, enormous storm clouds drifting above the trees.

"Thomas, what's—"

A bolt of lightning crashed into the ground just outside the castle walls, followed by the sound of fat raindrops hitting the dirt.

"It's raining!" He sat up, his eyes wide and a smile spreading across his face as he held out an open palm toward the sky. "Thank the gods. Let's go inside before it ruins the weapons. I don't want them to rust."

They scrambled to their feet, gathering as many of the weapons as they could hold before sprinting toward the castle. The breeze blowing off the storm kissed Emma's cheeks, cooling the sweat dripping down her neck, and she sighed in relief. A storm would be glorious, and Emma considered dropping the swords and daggers inside and returning to stand in the rain, her arms outstretched and her face toward the sky. She imagined the water hitting her skin, washing away the sweat, dirt, and grime that seemed so permanent these days.

"We'll come back out, I promise," Thomas said, as if sensing her thoughts.

Emma smiled, following him up the stairs. Rain. She couldn't believe it. Did this mean the sun god had forgiven Lea? That this reprieve was his way of saying he hoped they succeeded?

They reached the top of the steps, but Emma stumbled backward, throwing her arms in the air as a hawk swept down in front of the doorway. She shrieked, teetering dangerously backward on the edge of the step. The weapons crashed to the ground as she reached her arms out, trying to regain her balance, but Thomas caught her before she could fall, his own weapons clanging against the stone steps.

Emma's heart pounded as he pulled her close, the bird soaring away as if it hadn't just tried to break Emma's neck.

"What the hell was that about?" he muttered.

But Emma didn't answer. Couldn't answer. She was too focused on the scroll at her feet, about six inches long and dotted with raindrops. There was no seal, no bow or writing to indicate who it was for or who had sent it, but she was certain it hadn't been there before.

With a shaking hand, Emma reached down to pick it up.

"Is it a message?"

"I think so," she said, unrolling the scroll.

Thomas,

Lea has told me her plan. She assures me that it will work, but I fear she isn't being forthright with me. Call it a father's intuition. I write to you in hopes that you can pass this message to Evangeline. Lea has promised me her success has already been seen by her birth-mother. That it is already foretold. Please, ask Evangeline if Lea is telling the truth. I need to know if, by helping her, I am giving her a chance to defeat Alaric, or sending her to her death.

All I want is to protect my daughter.

Henry.

Emma's hand came up to cover her mouth as she passed the note to Thomas, her mind racing too fast to allow her to speak the words out loud. She knew Lea had been up to something, hiding her true intentions, but Emma had hoped it'd simply been to throw Eudora off. They'd *all* avoided talking about their plans and their thoughts regarding what they should do and when they should do it, so as to keep the possibilities open in Eudora's visions. But now, knowing Lea had asked for Henry's help, her plan was clear.

Lea had divided them on purpose, choosing to bring Henry to freeze time so she could get away—alone. Lea was planning to battle Alaric by herself, and she was willing to give up her life to do so.

"Oh, Lea," Thomas rasped, his voice heavy with emotion, waves of anger, terror, and frustration radiating off him. "We have to follow her. We have to bring the army. What if he brought his soldiers with him? What if this was his plan all along? Does she think she can take on a battalion of thousands?"

Emma's mind continued to spin. She didn't know what Lea was thinking, but she *did* know someone who might. Grabbing Thomas's hand, she snatched the letter from him and ran through the corridors, up the stairs, down the long hallway, past the red tapestry and straight to Evangeline's room. She didn't knock or announce herself, bursting through the door so hard it slammed against the wall with a crack.

"Lea needs our help," Emma said, out of breath. She leaned against the wall, reciting the letter to Evangeline.

The witch's mouth pinched as she turned away, not saying a word, placing a hand on her chest.

"You knew," Emma breathed, her heart dropping into her stomach. "She's going to sacrifice herself, isn't she? She's going in there alone so no one else gets hurt."

"Dammit, Lea," Thomas muttered, starting to pace.

Evangeline held up her hands. "Lea's plan can work. I *have* seen it. There's a reason she's kept it a secret from you all. The goddess told her she has to be the one to kill him. She's the only one who can. Gray can't do anything other than distract her. And Eudora is watching you. You know this. She *couldn't* tell anyone. Not unless she wanted the future to solidify and alert Eudora and Alaric."

"But how can she take that much magic? She's never taken more than enough to light a candle," Emma asked.

"With my help," Evangeline replied. She closed her eyes and waved her hand in the air, muttering something incomprehensible. Within seconds, a shimmering blue door appeared, like water rippling down a brook.

"A portal," Emma breathed.

Evangeline nodded. "I can hold back death. That is my gift. I'm to meet her when she calls for me. I can give her the time she needs to take Alaric's magic, and end his life."

Thomas was still pacing, ten long, sharp strides each way, his hands fidgeting. "You're a witch, right? Witches can take magic too, can't they?" Thomas asked.

"I'm a witch, in that I hold magic of the witches. But it is not who I am. I can't take magic any more than you can. I've tried."

"So Henry's right, then? This will kill Lea? You said you can hold death back, give her time. But you can't keep it away forever."

Evangeline nodded. "I've asked her to funnel his magic into me. To allow me to pay the price."

Emma's breath whooshed from her lungs. What she was offering her daughter... it was unthinkable. And yet, Emma knew without a doubt that Elise would do the same for her.

Thomas stopped his pacing. "What? You... Even if that was a viable solution, Lea would never do it."

"I've *seen* her alive. She must be at least considering it. I will convince her when it's time. I'm confident I can."

Thomas shook his head. "There has to be another way. And even if we find it, Alaric still has an entire army at his disposal. And who knows how many more from the villages he's recruited. Men and women willing to join him to save their families' lives. You two could be walking into a trap to be slaughtered."

Evangeline smiled, and Emma froze as she sensed a wave of relief washing off of her. "All of this... it was your plan, wasn't it? You knew we'd come? You saw it?"

Evangeline nodded. "To speak it aloud was to risk the fates changing. But yes, I knew you would come. I've seen Lea live. I've seen all of you live, but you're right. We must bring our army. In every vision we succeed, our soldiers are with us. I've been working on this portal for some time, knowing we would need it. It's capable of allowing them through," Evangeline explained.

"I'll gather them now," Thomas said, determination pounding off his skin and against Emma's. A plan of action. That was what he needed to calm the absolute terror he'd been feeling moments ago.

"No. Not until Lea is there. The army will need to be behind her, so they don't alert Alaric. But it will be soon, I think." Evangeline closed the portal with a wave of her hand. "Ready our army, and meet me outside. Emma, do you have the potion?"

She nodded, her hand going subconsciously to her pocket.

"Keep it with you. If we are to fail..." Evangeline swallowed. "If for some reason Lea doesn't survive taking his magic, she *still* has to be the one to kill him. We need you tethered to the other side to allow her to make that blow."

Emma's voice felt far away as she whispered a quiet, "Okay," her body suddenly numb. Was she in shock that it was actually time? That she was so close to once again taking the potion that had almost ended her life before?

She pushed a shaking hand into her pocket, her fingers touching the cool glass of the potion. She *would* take the potion, had decided that long ago, but as she squeezed the vial tightly in her fist, she sent up a prayer to the goddess that Lea wouldn't fail, and that she could kill Alaric before anyone she loved would need to use its power.

CHAPTER 56

LEA

Thunder boomed in the distance, and Lea's head snapped up, searching between the trees for any hint of what had caused it. It couldn't be a storm... Surely the god of the sun wouldn't allow them reprieve from the punishment of trying to cook them alive. Yet, above the tree line were deep gray rain clouds. Massive and intimidating, flickering with lightning and billowing toward them at an unnatural speed.

"Look. Up ahead," Henry said, pointing toward the darkening horizon.

Lea didn't know whether to be upset, frustrated, or thrilled. After all, she would do anything for relief from the stifling heat. But they were nearing the army encampment, and her panic about what she was about to have to do was easing in.

Every few minutes, Gray looked over at her, counting the white flowers on her crown. But Lea didn't have to look to know they were running out of time. Only two remained. It didn't mean much—it could be hours, it could also be days. But one thing was for certain.

They needed to hurry.

Lea urged Luna to run faster, leaning down and sending healing magic into her body as her muscles worked to their limit to get her to Alaric.

Just south of the town of Pontor, Genevieve had said, but even that was vague.

"We can't keep up!" Cole shouted. "Our horses need rest."

Lea turned her head to see them lagging behind, their horses clearly exhausted, but she couldn't stop.

"We have to keep going, Gray," she said.

He nodded, his eyes dancing over her crown once more.

"Meet us there," he shouted over his shoulder. He understood the urgency, and Lea was grateful.

Patrick and Cole stopped riding, disappearing out of sight, but Henry remained right behind them, his horse struggling to maintain their rapid pace.

Please, gods, Lea prayed, slowing just slightly to ensure Henry could keep up. *I know you're angry with me, but please, without him, this plan doesn't work,* she added silently. *Please,* she begged again and again.

They crested a hill, and several miles in the distance, smoke appeared.

"The camp!" Lea shouted, relief and fear pounding through her blood. Gray's chin lowered in determination.

Fat raindrops began pelting their faces, soaking their clothes in seconds as the sky darkened further. Maybe it was a blessing. Maybe it would help provide her some cover, make it harder for Gray to find her after she fled. She had no idea how long Henry would be able to hold time for. She just had to hope it would be enough.

They didn't bother hiding their approach as they descended upon the encampment. Gray called on his shadows, and Lea on her flames, a massive wave of darkness heading toward the royal army, intended to intimidate and terrorize. Obsidian led them straight into the middle of camp, and royal guards scrambled for their weapons as Gray jumped to the ground.

"Don't bother trying to fight. Tell me where he is, and I won't kill you," Gray ordered, rain pounding against his shoulders and shadows exploding as far as Lea could see.

The soldiers froze as long tendrils of darkness shot from Gray's arms and around their bodies like snakes, reaching for their throats, ready to snap their necks in a second.

"Tell me! Where is he?" Gray roared, and his own thunder and lightning joined the storm overhead, matching its ferocity, every scrap of his power buzzing around them a testament to how much he loved her.

Lea slid off her horse, following close behind Gray, her eyes searching for danger.

The soldiers remained silent. "You remain loyal to him?" Gray lowered his chin, snapping a nearby soldier's neck, and he crumbled like a tree in an earthquake.

"What has he done for you? Left you here to fend for yourselves?" *Snap.* Another soldier fell. "One of you will tell me." *Snap.* "Or do you all prefer death?"

Gray threw his arms out, and lightning crashed in a white-hot flash of fury. Six more soldiers fell to the ground.

"Wait!" a young soldier called out, raising his hands in the air and falling to his knees in the mud. Tears streamed from his eyes, snot dripping down his nose.

"Please, I'll tell you. I hate him. I never wanted to support him. I swear it. Please, don't kill us. I didn't know about the rebels, or I would have tried to join you."

Lea felt a stab of sympathy for the boy, *and* for Gray, knowing he would blame himself forever if he'd missed someone who'd wanted to follow them. But maybe this was how it was supposed to be all along. Fate.

"Tell us where Alaric is," Gray said. "If you lie to me, I will know. She will know."

Lea raised her sword in front of her, gripping the hilt tightly.

"And I won't snap your neck," she added coldly. "I will skin you alive."

Gray stepped forward, his shadows squeezing tighter.

Lea ran a finger along the blade of her sword. "And after that, I will remove your veins one by one, plucking them out like weeds until you bleed out in a slow, horrifically painful death."

"I won't lie!" the boy cried. "I won't lie. He's in the Wicked Wood... just south of here. He comes every few days, takes a few of our men." The boy shivered. "I think he drinks their blood, I don't know... but you have to stop him. Please, you have to stop him." The boy pulled at his hair. "I'm sorry," he sobbed.

Gray looked to Lea, and she closed her eyes, focusing on the sword's hilt. Nothing. It remained cool and stagnant in her hand.

"He's telling the truth," Lea said, turning to the young soldier. "You're saying the rest of your men are with him? There should be hundreds more of you."

"He's been steadily taking us little by little for weeks. I haven't seen the camp, but he was very clear—if something were to happen, if he calls—he's directly south. Ride until you reach a lake, the only water source in the Wicked Wood. That's all I know."

Lea nodded at Gray, confirming the boy was telling the truth.

"You, I will allow to live," Gray said, releasing the boy from his shadows. With a flick of his hand, he snapped the necks of the remaining soldiers. As one, they fell in a synchronized dance of death, mud splashing her legs as their bodies hit the ground with a thud.

Lea sucked in a breath in shock, but quickly pushed the feeling down. They deserved this. Every last one of them who hadn't stepped forward. They were no longer a threat. Though there were still more of Alaric's men they would have to kill. The other encampments were close enough to ride into battle when Alaric called.

"My threat stands," Gray said to the young soldier. "You remain here. I don't trust you enough to let you follow. Stay, and I'll allow you to live."

The boy gulped, sitting back on his heels.

"Let's go," Gray said, grabbing Lea's hand and hurrying back toward Obsidian.

But Lea dug in her heels. She reached out and cupped Gray's cheek. Her heart felt like it was being ripped from her chest, the agony spreading between her ribs and into her stomach almost unbearable. Gray tilted his head at her, eyes filled with concern.

"What's wrong? Are you hurt?" he asked, his shadows instantly wrapping around her, caressing her from head to toe.

"No. I just needed to tell you how much I love you," Lea said, tears filling her eyes.

"Why are you crying?" Gray's voice was panicked, and he tried to pull back to look at her, but she refused to move.

"We still have time," he looked at her crown. "There are two petals left. We have to go, if we hurry—"

"I know," she said, her voice breaking. "I love you, Gray. You are the love of my life. After this... Please, please try to forgive me."

His eyes widened in panic as he grabbed her arm and yanked her toward him, his fingers digging into her arm with bruising strength as he twisted toward Henry, but he was too late. Henry did as he promised—freezing time with only seconds to spare.

Gray's hand was outstretched toward her father, shadows suspended just feet from his fingertips, hovering in the air like ice. His mouth was open in a snarl, his eyes full of shock and fury and betrayal.

"I'm sorry," Lea whispered, sobbing as she disentangled herself from Gray's arms. She reached up once more and stroked his cheek. "I'm so, so sorry. Forgive me," she said through her tears, then jumped on Luna's back.

She didn't turn around, *couldn't* look back as she raced toward her fate. She couldn't bear to see Gray's face again, the hurt in his eyes. Not if she was to do what needed to be done.

The sky grew darker, and without slowing down, she looked up to see the moon rising from the horizon and rapidly moving toward the bright red sun.

"Gods above," Lea whispered, shivers running down her spine as the sun was completely eclipsed. Within moments, she was pitched into complete darkness, the only light the occasional crash of lightning that brightened the sky every few seconds.

Lea used the brief flashes of light to navigate her way south, feeling, for the first time, like maybe the goddess was helping her after all. Because in the pitch black of night, there was no way Gray would be able to find her once time moved forward again.

Not as the heavy rain turned the ground to mud, washing away her horse's footsteps. Washing away everything but her lies and betrayal.

CHAPTER 57

LEA

The Wicked Wood loomed before her, no less intimidating and terrifying than the last time she'd braved entering it. The grass still turned to mud and rot at the border, the trees black and spindly, swaying as if inhaling and exhaling like a sentient being. But there was no time for fear. Not a single second to lose. She urged Luna closer to the trees, their long fingers reaching toward her as if beckoning her to come inside.

A chill shivered through her entire body as she crossed into the boundary of the Wicked Wood.

She looked around, daring any demon to approach her as she urged Luna to move faster. She had no idea how long her father would be able to stall Gray. It could have been minutes, for all she knew. Gray would surely be trying to find a way to get to her by now, and he knew where she was going.

She could almost *feel* him coming. The pounding of Obsidian's hooves matching Luna's. His fury surging forward as it searched for her, so intense that even the trees would recoil from his approach. Gray would stop at nothing to find her before she reached Alaric and Eudora.

Lea couldn't let that happen.

A twig snapped to her left, and Lea held out her hand, long black flames at her fingertips. She narrowed her eyes to peer through the trees, part of her mind searching for death's cold approach as the other half ran through the possibilities. Was it Alaric or Eudora? Had they seen her coming, and were waiting to ambush her? Or maybe it was the soldiers he'd taken from the camp?

Another snap sounded, this time behind her.

She called on her shadows as she spun around, her heart racing. *Please, don't be Gray,* she prayed, spreading her fire toward the sound to illuminate the darkness. Luna took a single step, when all at once, hundreds of palm-sized yellow eyes appeared, surrounding her completely.

Fenrir, more than she could count.

Lea threw up a wall of black flames, adrenaline coursing through her veins as she tried to steady her breath. She had fought them once, before she'd known of her powers. Gray had defeated them. Erik had killed one. She could do the same. She had to, because if she was going to die, it would not be between the jaws of some giant wolf.

No. If she was leaving this realm today, it would be because she had taken Alaric's power and returned it to the universe.

She was gathering her primary magic in her chest, coiling it into a tight ball and preparing to destroy the entire pack in a fiery explosion when an enormous silver wolf walked to the front, stopping only feet away. The creature met her gaze for a long moment, and Lea paused. She'd expected to see hunger inside those massive, yellow eyes. A predatory glint betraying its drive to kill, but instead its eyes were soft—understanding and knowing in a way that made Lea's skin erupt into goosebumps. The fenrir arched its back, extending its neck toward the eclipse, and let out a long, sorrowful howl that sent chills skittering down Lea's spine. She met the enormous wolf's eyes again and cautiously lowered her hands. This animal didn't want to harm her. He wanted to *help* her. She was as sure of it as her own name.

The wolf bowed, deeply and reverently, then twisted its head to the side, exposing its throat. She dimmed her flames, calling them back to her as a chorus of howls echoed against the dead trees. As one, the fenrir bowed, then moved out of her path, creating an aisle for her as if saying, *we will be right behind you. We are here with you.* She could feel the promise in their movements, in the way they stared at her.

Lea was breathless, in awe of the beautiful, terrifying creatures. Had they really come to protect her? Erik had said that long ago, the fenrir had been drawn to the most powerful beings, guarding and protecting them with their lives. Following their orders, even to their own deaths. Did they know that not only her life, but the lives of every person in the kingdom were at risk?

"Thank you," she whispered, not fully understanding what had brought them to her, but grateful to not be alone as she made her final journey. A lump formed in her throat as she urged Luna forward, and they followed, their steps eerily silent as they trailed close behind her.

As one, they descended further into the wood, her heart thundering and bile rising into her throat. She swallowed it down along with her fear and guilt, her singular focus making it to Alaric, until through the dense, dark trees, she caught a glimmer of black water. She pulled on the reins, raising her hand to stop the fenrir. As silently as possible, she turned Luna around and led the fenrir back a few hundred yards, out of sight and earshot from Alaric.

Lea climbed off her horse, every sense on high alert as she spread her magic out toward the lake, her shadows mapping out the terrain as she searched for Alaric and Eudora. But no matter where she pushed her darkness, she couldn't find them. Couldn't sense any life until—there.

A flicker of *something*. Not life, but power. Pure, horrifying power that vibrated through the air, taunting her. He was here.

Without wasting another moment, Lea reached inside to find the tether to Evangeline. She tugged on it—three sharp yanks—then opened her eyes and looked around.

"There's a lake in the Wicked Wood," she said after a few moments, "about an hour's ride from Pontor. He's here." She repeated the words several times, showing her surroundings to ensure Evangeline understood.

"There's a lake in the Wicked Wood, about an hour's ride from Pontor. He's here. Hurry."

CHAPTER 58

EMMA

Emma's hand was slick with sweat as she gripped Eudora's potion, her fingers trembling slightly around the cool, smooth glass. This was it—the very thing that would bring her so close to death that she would straddle the thin line between the land of the living and beyond the veil.

The thought made her stomach twist into knots, an anxious churning that wouldn't subside no matter how many deep breaths she took. Her free hand pressed against her abdomen, trying in vain to still the waves of nausea that rolled through her. But they didn't stop. Didn't subside a bit as the weight of what she was about to do settled heavily on her shoulders.

She couldn't back down. So many lives depended on her being brave. And besides, Thomas would keep her safe. She was as certain of it as she was certain that Lea was going to be furious to see them walk through the portal with Evangeline.

The courtyard buzzed with the low murmur of their gathered forces, the soldiers' emotions mixing and pounding against her skin in a way that made her feel as if she was covered in bugs. Shivering at the thought, she glanced at Thomas, his face a mix of determination and concern.

The army had been alerted. Thomas had made sure of that, and Gray's generals had agreed to his plan without hesitation. They, too, had risked their lives to join this war and fight against the tyranny and wickedness poisoning their world. They owed Gray more than could ever be repaid. He'd sacrificed so much for them—for *all* of them. It was absurd to think they would allow him or his mate to face this battle alone.

Emma's gaze shifted to Evangeline standing at the center of the court-yard, her lips moving in a quiet, relentless chant. Her hands were raised before her, trembling slightly as she summoned the ancient magic she'd been working so tirelessly to master. The air around her shimmered, and a portal began to take shape, flickering in and out, wavering like a mirage until it solidified with a *click*. It was both mesmerizing and terrifying, a swirling vortex of light and shadow suspended in the air like water frozen in time.

Emma couldn't tear her eyes away from it. The portal was beautiful. Bright with an ethereal glow that illuminated the darkened courtyard and casted strange, shifting shadows across the grass. The sight sent a chill across Emma's skin, and her heart pounded faster, her grip tightening on the vial as if it might slip through her fingers.

Evangeline's voice grew louder, her chanting more urgent, and the portal began to expand, widening until it was large enough for six men to pass through shoulder to shoulder. Her magic hung heavy in the air, a palpable force that hummed against Emma's skin, making the hair on the back of her neck stand on end.

Finally, Evangeline dropped her arms, exhaling a long, slow breath as the portal stabilized. She wiped her brow, then the back of her neck, her movements sluggish and exhausted. The effort it had taken to create the portal was obvious. It had drained her—taken something from her that she couldn't easily replace. Evangeline had been pouring herself into creating this portal, using power that wasn't even hers to do it, and it was clear it was taking a toll on her body.

"Emma?" Evangeline's voice broke through the tension, shaky but determined.

Emma stepped forward, her legs wobbling as if they might give out. "Right here," she answered, her voice sounding small and scared, even to her own ears. She reached for Evangeline's hand, basking in the confidence and strength radiating off of her.

"Good," Evangeline said, squeezing her hand. "Our army is coming?"

Emma nodded, her heart lifting slightly at the thought. "They're lining up around us now."

"Good. I can hear them." A faint smile tugged at Evangeline's lips. "There are many."

"There are," Emma agreed, her eyes scanning the courtyard as pride swelled in her heart.

Evangeline squeezed her hand. "You and I will go first. Thomas should stay back, for now. We don't need the army until Lea and I have found Alaric." But Before Emma could respond, Thomas stepped forward, his voice firm.

"I go where Emma goes."

Evangeline pursed her lips, her brow furrowing.

"Lea will be suspicious if he's not with me," Emma reached for Thomas's hand, suddenly desperate to have him beside her. She didn't want to be alone as she took the potion, couldn't bear to not have him with her as she allowed herself to be brought to the brink of death. "He's stayed by my side through everything. That wouldn't change just because I'm coming now. We'll tell her I'm the backup plan. I'll take the potion so that if she—" she took a deep breath. "If she fails to kill him before—" The words caught in her throat, and she had to swallow hard to force them out. "If she fails, she can still kill him, so long as she dies with a weapon in her hand. We'll tell her I had to come, and that Thomas wouldn't let me go without him."

The weight of those words pressed down on Emma's shoulders, her chest tightening painfully. The possibility that Lea might fail was too real, too terrifying, but they had to be prepared for it. Emma couldn't let herself falter. Not now.

Evangeline studied her for a long moment before nodding. "Very well."

"When should the army follow?" Emma asked, trying to focus on the logistics of the battle instead of the growing knot of fear in her stomach.

Evangeline sighed, her shoulders sagging slightly. "I don't know. I've seen our soldiers with us, but not when they arrive. They need to be ready, though. Knowing Eudora, I don't believe for a second she won't have extra forces waiting."

Thomas squeezed her hand. "I can let the army know when to come. Once we see more than Alaric and Eudora."

Evangeline tilted her head. "How?"

"I've placed a warning system on certain weapons—Gray's, Janelle's, the generals'. I've been working on it for weeks now, as a backup. A way to communicate when we're apart. When we need them, I can send a signal. Their weapons will hum, vibrate, until I make them stop."

Evangeline gave him a small nod of approval. "That was wise. And I think it will work. The army will stay back unless we call for them. Tell the generals they are not to come until they get your signal."

Thomas wasted no time, darting to the generals lined up behind him as Evangeline grabbed Emma's hands again. "Lea is waiting... we can't delay any longer. I won't let her face Alaric without me."

Emma swallowed, the movement painful. Her throat felt tight, like it was closing in on itself, and her skin itched with anxiety. "Evangeline. Do you think... Tell me you've seen it. Tell me it's going to be okay," Emma said, tears pricking the backs of her eyes.

Evangeline looked away, her attention shifting back to the portal, her expression unreadable. "I've seen many, many things. Now, we must act, and see where the last petal falls."

"I... I'm afraid," Emma admitted, her voice barely a whisper. The fear had been clawing at her for days, but now, standing on the precipice of what might be their final stand, it threatened to overwhelm her.

"Do you have the moonflowers?" Evangeline asked.

"Yes," Emma replied. "Thomas made sure everyone has one. He has an extra for you, too."

"Good," Evangeline said softly, reaching up to cup her cheek. "As long as you have the petal, you'll be fine. I've seen you alive after the battle."

But Emma's fear ran deeper than just for herself. She wasn't afraid of dying—at least, not for her own sake. It was for her friends, for her mother, and the kingdom that hung in the balance. For the souls of those fighting on both sides. Even those under Alaric's control. Death's promise pressed down on her like a boulder, the certainty of it pushing on her shoulders until her body threatened to buckle beneath it. She could feel it creeping closer, dark and inescapable.

"Emma?"

Emma turned as Elise squeezed through a group of soldiers and rushed to her side. She grabbed Emma's arms and pulled her into a hug.

"Mom!" Emma cried, her tears spilling over at seeing her mother. She'd tried to find her in the kitchens, but had to give up her search once the soldiers had begun gathering in the courtyard.

"It's true then?" Elise said into her ear as she squeezed her impossibly tighter. "You're leaving to fight Alaric?"

"I'm not fighting. I'll be okay," Emma said, but her voice broke.

Elise finally pulled back, her eyes full of tears. "Will asking you not to go change anything?" she asked, searching Emma's eyes. Emma knew what she was looking for: any hint of doubt or uncertainty. Any reason to try to convince her to stay.

Emma shook her head. "I'm sorry, Mom—"

"No. You have nothing to be sorry for. I am so proud of you. Of the woman you've become." She reached out and cupped Emma's cheek. "If I thought I could change your mind, I'd take you far away from here in an instant. But I will never be angry with you for doing what you think is right. I could *never* be disappointed in you for following your destiny."

Emma couldn't speak, her words stuck behind a sob she was struggling to hold in.

"I love you, Emma. I have faith you'll be okay." She paused. "Where's Thomas?" Evangeline said, looking around to find him.

"I'm here." Thomas appeared just behind them, and Emma's heart slowed as he slipped his hand into hers. His touch was warm. Steady. And she savored it, allowing it to ground her.

Elise kissed Emma's forehead, then hugged Thomas tightly. "You take care of my girl," she whispered in his ear.

"With all I have," Thomas promised, squeezing Emma's hand.

With a sniffle she tried to hide, Elise turned away. "Be safe. I'll be right here," she said, moving just to the other side of the gathering soldiers.

"We're going to be fine," he said softly, his voice filled with a quiet conviction that made her heart ache. "I promise you, I'll keep you safe."

Emma forced a smile, though it felt hollow. She wanted to believe him. *Needed* to believe him. Desperately. But there was no room for certainty in war. Especially not when Alaric and Eudora were involved.

"Ready?" Evangeline asked, her voice suddenly shaky with anxiety.

Emma nodded, letting go of Thomas's hand to grab her dagger, the other still tight around the cold glass of the potion.

Thomas gave her a nod of approval, and Emma's chest warmed. "Ready," she said, the words gritty in her mouth.

But before they could move, Thomas stopped her. His hand cupped her cheek, his thumb tracing a soft line along her skin. "I just need to tell you that I love you," he said quietly. "I do."

The world seemed to pause for a moment, and Emma's breath caught in her throat. Tears welled in her eyes, stinging and blurring her vision as Thomas's emotions pulsed against Emma's skin—the feeling she had sensed from him all this time.

It was love. Not something close to love, but true, unconditional love. Deep, selfless love. The kind that made her heart swell and break all at once.

She wanted to tell him she loved him, too, that she had always loved him, but the words were stuck in her throat, tangled up with the emotions radiating from all around her. Terror and fear and anger and anticipation and... love.

Before she could speak, Thomas pulled her forward, pressing a soft kiss to her lips, full of promise and hope and, once again, love. Emma kissed him back, a whimper leaving her throat as a tear trailed down her cheek. Thomas pulled back, brushing the tear away before leading her through the portal to the place where, one way or another, the war would end.

Walking through the portal was no different from stepping through a doorway. There was no gust of wind, no flicker of light to mark the transition—just a single step forward, and suddenly the world shifted. Emma blinked, trying to adjust her eyes to the freezing rain and sudden darkness of the Wicked Wood, an oppressive gloom settling over her like a thick, suffocating blanket. A shiver ran down her spine as the feeling of icy fingers brushing the back of her neck made her stomach turn. Every nerve in her body went taut with tension, her senses instantly alert to the danger that lurked in the shadows.

A low rumble of growls sounded as Lea turned, her eyes narrowing as Emma and Thomas appeared. A pack of fenrir surrounded them, their glowing eyes narrowing in on Emma and Thomas as they bared their enormous teeth. Thomas pulled her backward, and she tried to make herself smaller.

Lea held up a hand, and the fenrir paused, but it did nothing to ease Emma's nerves. Saliva still dripped from their massive teeth, and their muscles were still tense, as if just waiting for permission to attack. Fire crackled through the grass toward them, stopping only inches from their toes.

"What. Have. You. Done?" Lea's voice was like the crack of a whip, her gaze locking onto Evangeline. Flames grew all around her, wrapping up Lea's body and reaching toward the trees. "This wasn't the plan."

Evangeline suffocated Lea's flames and stepped forward with her hands outstretched. "I'm aware of that," she said calmly, but Emma didn't miss the exhaustion in her tone. "Things change. Visions change. We need them here, Lea. We need Emma. Because…" Evangeline trailed off as if to speak her fears was to risk them becoming the truth.

Lea's face went pale. "Say it." Her words cut through the air like a flash of lightning, her eyes blazing with an intensity that made Thomas step in front of Emma.

Evangeline pressed her lips together, her shoulders hunching forward. "It's just a precaution," she said, her voice shaking with the threat of tears.

Emma could feel the desperation washing off Evangeline. The way she hoped Lea wouldn't blame her for what was to happen. Her fear that she wouldn't listen, or that one of her unspeakable visions would come true.

"I'm just here to help, Lea." Emma stepped around Thomas, meeting Lea's eyes. "If you get hurt—"

"If I die," Lea interrupted, her voice cold, but resigned. The fenrir once again began to growl, a terrifying chorus of predatory power. "You can say it. We all know it's a possibility."

The words hung between them, heavy as the air in the Wicked Wood. It wrapped around Emma's chest, threatening to suffocate her as the weight of Lea's words settled on her shoulders. She wanted to speak. Wanted to tell Lea that everything was going to be okay, and that she was certain she'd succeed, but her voice wouldn't work.

"If the worst happens—if Alaric overpowers you—you will still be able to deliver the final blow if Emma is tethered to the other side. You'll still get eternity with your mate, Lea. Even if you don't get to live," Thomas said, his voice so sad it made Emma want to cry.

Lea's throat bobbed as she swallowed, her fists clenching and unclenching at her sides. For a moment, her face softened, a flicker of vulnerability passing over her features before she steeled herself once again. "I won't fail," she said, her voice low but filled with determination. "I can't." She glanced at Emma, her eyes briefly softening. "But thank you. For this... precaution."

Emma could feel the tension in Lea's words, the weight of what was coming etched into each syllable. Her heart pounded against her ribs, and she forced herself to relax her grip on the vial in her hand, worried it would shatter.

"Do you have your petals?" Lea asked, meeting each of their eyes.

"Yes," Thomas confirmed. "I have several." He patted his hip with a small, reassuring smile, though it didn't quite reach his eyes.

Lea nodded, her jaw tightening as she squared her shoulders. "Good. Then let's not waste any more time." She looked at each of them in turn, her eyes lingering on Emma. "I'll see you soon," she said, her voice breaking. "Stay safe. Stay hidden."

Emma stepped forward, her heart hammering harder by the second. "Wait," she said, holding up the potion. "You don't know where Alaric is. Let me take it first, before you leave. I don't want to risk you stumbling upon him before I'm tethering the worlds."

Lea paused, her eyes flickering between Emma and the vial. There was a brief hesitation, a moment of silent understanding between them, before Lea nodded. "Okay," she said, her voice quieter now, laced with something close to fear, though she hid it well. "Do it quickly."

Emma pulled the stopper from the vial, her hand trembling as she brought it to her lips. The smell of the potion was familiar, and it made her subconscious revolt as it remembered the last time she had taken it. She leaned into Thomas's arms, seeking comfort in his familiar warmth. He held her close, his hand resting gently against her back and his heart pounding furiously, his breathing rapid.

"Finally. You've found us at last, Azalea." a voice echoed through the trees, cold and mocking, bouncing around the branches so that it was impossible to know where it came from.

Eudora.

Lea's head snapped up, her eyes narrowing dangerously. Within seconds, shadows spilled from her body like ink, twisting through the trees and wrapping the four of them in a thick, protective shroud of darkness. Thomas pulled Emma down into the mud, pinning her against the rough bark of a tree, his body shielding hers from whatever danger lurked beyond the shadows.

"Show yourself," Lea growled, spinning in a circle, rain drops flying from her hair as she whipped her head around, searching for the witch.

"Where's the fun in that?" Eudora answered—a cruel, mocking cackle that sent shivers down Emma's spine. A puff of smoke appeared in front of them, swirling in the air before a heron emerged from the haze, its wings cutting through the shadows like a blade. It soared over their heads, disappearing behind another tree.

"I could be anywhere," Eudora said, her voice disembodied, slipping through the shadows like a snake. The heron reappeared, circling above them before swooping down, its wings nearly brushing Emma's head. She ducked instinctively, her heart pounding as she pressed herself tighter against the tree, praying the shadows would be enough to hide them.

Lea flung a ball of fire at the heron, but once again it vanished into thin air, leaving behind only a whisper of smoke.

"You want to end this?" Eudora's voice called out from all around them, somehow everywhere and nowhere all at once, her laughter echoing through the trees. "Then end it. You know where he waits."

Lea didn't hesitate. She stalked forward, her eyes blazing with determination, her every step filled with purpose. Evangeline followed close behind, a trail of fire flickering in their wake, the flames licking the tree's dark roots before sputtering out in the mud and rain.

The fenrir remained behind, blocking Emma and Thomas from following her, but it didn't matter. They had no plans to try to get to Alaric. That wasn't their part in this battle. Her part was cold in her hand, almost vibrating as if begging her to drink it before it was too late. Emma looked up at Thomas, her hands trembling as she raised the vial once again. "Please," she whispered, her voice barely audible. "Be safe. Be smart."

Thomas cupped her cheek, his thumb brushing gently across her skin. His touch calmed her racing heart, and he leaned down, his lips brushing against hers, filled with unspoken promises. It was over too soon, but his love lingered on her lips, flooding her body and wrapping around her like a protective shield.

"I'll see you on the other side," he whispered, his voice thick with emotion.

Emma had no words. There was no need for them. Thomas knew how she felt—she could see it in his eyes, feel it in the way his hand scraped against her skin, in the way his heart seemed to beat in time with hers. Together, they were a force, stronger than any magic or darkness that might try to tear them apart.

She stared into his eyes for a moment longer, her heart thundering in her chest, before tipping the vial back. The potion was bitter, coating her tongue and throat with a metallic taste that made her stomach twist. Almost instantly, her vision blurred, her limbs growing heavy as the world around her tilted. She tried to speak, but consciousness slipped away too quickly. The last thing she felt was a strange, unfamiliar aftertaste—a warning, and the only sign that this was not the same potion as the one Eudora had given her before.

CHAPTER 59

GRAY

Gray shot his shadows from his extended arm, roaring at Henry to stop, his voice raw with desperation and fury. He tried to pin Henry's arms to his sides, to prevent him from twisting his fingers and freezing time, but it was already too late. In the blink of an eye, Henry was gone. Before Gray could even finish his command, he'd disappeared, taking Lea with him.

The sight of her vanishing, his mate, his *life*, shattered something deep inside him, and his shadows exploded in a rush that made the ground beneath his feet tremble. Who knew how long she'd been gone? How long had time been stopped? Who knew how far she'd been able to travel while he stood there, unable to move or breathe or even fucking think.

Fury unlike anything Gray had ever felt before surged through his veins like molten fire, searing every nerve, every muscle, until he could hardly breathe through the anger, so intense it threatened to consume him entirely. His shadows continued outward in a violent wave, black tendrils reaching in every direction, desperate and frantic, searching with a mind of their own. They hunted for Lea, their other half, as if they shared the same agonizing loss that was tearing him apart from the inside.

"Lea!" he roared, the name tearing from his throat with such intensity it echoed across the woods, mingling with the wind and the rain pouring from the sky.

Above him, storm clouds gathered, the physical manifestation of his wrath and terror. They darkened with his every breath, growing and building until they were almost black. His gray lightning crashed through the sky, splitting the night apart with each crack of rage.

It wasn't enough. None of it was enough to dull the agonizing terror of knowing Lea was gone. "Find her!" he commanded his shadows, his voice thick with the promise of violence. He didn't wait for their answer, couldn't afford to as he launched himself onto Obsidian's back. The stallion reared, sensing his urgency, his fury, and surged forward as fast as the lightning overhead.

"Lea!" Gray roared again, the sound vibrating through the air, a haunting mix of absolute rage and the deepest, rawest fear he'd ever known. How could she do this? She had betrayed him. Not just him—she had betrayed their love, their bond. She had gone to find Alaric on her own. Gray wasn't a fool. There was only one reason she would do something so reckless: she was going to sacrifice herself to end this war. It was the only reason she would ever leave his side, would ever put herself in such danger knowing that it would completely destroy him. Gray's heart twisted painfully in his chest at the thought. She was planning to trade her life for his.

Again.

"No!" He nearly choked on the word, his chest tight with the weight of his terror. Gray knew there was a chance either of them could die in this battle—he had accepted that long ago. But he refused, with every fiber of his being, to let her *choose* death. Not this time. He wouldn't let her slip away like a ghost to sacrifice herself to save the rest of them. No matter what Lea wanted, they *would* face this together. They would fight together, live together.

Or, they would die together.

His shadows stretched out farther and farther, a tsunami of black, inky darkness that crashed through the trees, uprooting them from the ground, but there was *nothing.* No sign of her. No proof she'd ever been there at all. She was gone, disappeared into the pitch-black void.

"Please. *Please,*" he whispered, his voice cracking, his plea directed to anyone, anything that might listen. "Protect her." He prayed to the goddess, to the universe, to the stars above. He would have prayed to his own enemies if it meant keeping her safe.

Obsidian's hooves thundered against the earth, each beat in time with the frantic pounding of Gray's heart. Rain battered against his face, mingling with the tears he refused to shed, and his lightning—his fury—crashed around them, illuminating the forest in bursts of blinding white light.

In that moment, Gray made a vow—a vow stronger than any he'd ever made before—a vow etched into the very fabric of his being.

"I will find you," he whispered, his voice hoarse, his throat raw. "I will find you, Lea, *before* you find him." He would not let her face Alaric alone. He would burn Alaric's entire army to ash if he had to. He would rip the world apart if that's what it took. And when he did find Alaric, when he faced his brother at last, Gray would prove to him that no matter how much power he had stolen, he was the weaker Nestruir. He would trap Alaric inside his shadows, pin him down with every ounce of hatred and fury that had been festering in his heart for years, and he would hold him there. Helpless. Only then, when he was there at his mate's side, would he allow Lea to deliver that final, killing blow—the blow that would free them all.

It didn't matter that Alaric was the strongest Fae in the kingdom, that his power could shake mountains and bring down the sky. None of it mattered. *Nothing* was stronger than Gray's love for Lea. Not the gods. Not destiny. Not the universe itself. And certainly not his fucking brother.

Gray clenched his jaw, his heart thundering painfully against his ribs as he urged Obsidian to go faster. Lightning flashed, thunder rumbled, and still, his shadows spread out in every direction, hunting, searching. He could feel them yearning, just as he was, desperate to find that one flicker of light that was Lea.

"You will not take her from me," Gray snarled at the storm. At the darkness. At the gods themselves. "Do you hear me? You will not take her from me!"

Because she was his mate, his life, his everything. And he would tear the world apart, piece by piece, if it meant getting her back.

CHAPTER 60

ERIK

Erik waited, his muscles tense and his magic thrumming, until he was absolutely certain every last tremor had finally rumbled away into nothing. The quake felt like a cruel joke, as if the gods were taunting him. Testing him. They had practically delivered Stefan and Jakob into his hands—set them before him on a silver platter, ready to be cooked alive, gutted, and roasted to the temperature of his choosing. And then, just when he was about to claim his victory, the earth had fought back. A massive earthquake, shaking the ground and stealing away his moment of retribution.

Erik could feel Jakob escaping, the tether connecting them growing tighter with each passing minute as he fled south. Yet Erik hadn't been willing to take the risk of following him in case the quake started up again. Not when doing so meant putting Janelle in danger of being hurt. He couldn't bear the thought of her being injured, so he'd remained frozen, crouched low as he waited with every nerve on edge.

"I think it's over," Janelle said, her voice soft and tentative as she carefully rose to her feet.

Erik remained in his crouch, eyes on the ground, listening and waiting. Any slight movement could set off another quake. For all he knew, another would start at any moment. But the earth beneath them held steady, unmoving, as solid as stone. Slowly, Erik straightened. He took one careful step forward, then another, adrenaline building in his chest until the impulse to move became overwhelming. In one swift motion, he scooped Janelle into his arms, carrying her as he sprinted toward Cinnamon, who stood pawing the ground just beyond the clearing as if waiting for them.

Erik settled Janelle atop the horse, then grabbed the reins. Closing his eyes, he stretched out his senses to find the trail again—the string of magic connecting him to Jakob. He pictured the kingdom in his mind, mapping out an image as he tracked Jakob's location—south, but then west, moving in the direction of Pontor. Erik tightened his grip on the reins.

He pointed Cinnamon toward the trail and kicked her sides to urge her forward, plunging them deeper into the woods. "Where are we going?" Janelle asked, looking up at the canopy of trees above them as if terrified the branches would rain down on them again.

"I don't think there'll be another quake," Erik murmured, more to himself than to her. "Not now. I'm not letting them get away." He pulled Janelle closer against him, his hand brushing across the familiar scar on her hip. It sent fire through his veins, and he grit his teeth, fighting to hold in his flames. He wanted to save them—every last flicker—to incinerate the men he hunted.

Janelle took a shaky breath. "We should just let them go," she said quietly. "Move on to Alnwick. We need to find the camp and Alaric. We can focus on Jakob after the war, Erik. I'm alright..."

Heat surged in Erik's chest, his anger and desire for vengeance further stoking the fire inside him. "I'm not letting him go," he said, trying to keep his tone gentle, but the edge was unmistakable. Janelle leaned back against him, as if she understood his resolve, and Erik exhaled in relief, grateful she wasn't arguing with him. Because there was nothing she could say to change his mind. Revenge burned in his blood like a wildfire, and there would be no dousing it. Not until Jakob was dead.

Once more, Erik turned his senses to his magic, isolating the long, invisible thread that connected him to Jakob. He was moving further south, directly toward the Wicked Wood bordering Pontor.

"Is he close?" Janelle asked, glancing back at Erik, her voice tense.

Erik shook his head. "Maybe twenty minutes ahead of us. We lost time waiting for the quake to pass, but they're not too far."

Janelle stiffened.

"It's fine. We'll catch up to him—"

"No." She shook her head, reaching to grip the saddle. Her head swiveled around, and she leaned forward to peer ahead of them.

"What is it?" Erik asked, his instincts immediately heightening, every sense on high alert.

Janelle hesitated, her gaze darting to the trees surrounding them. "Are you absolutely sure we're going the right way?" she asked, her voice barely above a whisper.

Erik followed the thread again, tracing it as it tugged further away. "I'm certain," he said. "They're heading southwest, toward Pontor."

Janelle's eyes went wide. "That's where Gray and Lea were headed, Erik. But there's danger there. I can sense it. We need to turn around. Or..." She paused, her voice urgent as she added, "Or go faster. If Gray and Lea are there..." she trailed off, her mind clearly racing as quickly as his was. "What if Alaric's waiting? What if it's a trap? Or they're in trouble somehow?"

Her words came fast, tumbling out of her mouth as her worry and fear spilled over. Erik's stomach dropped, a heavy realization settling in. He'd been right—the gods *were* toying with him, dangling his need for revenge as bait, luring them into danger.

Janelle's magic was never wrong. If she sensed trouble ahead, and Gray and Lea were at risk, they couldn't ignore it.

Erik slowed Cinnamon's pace, twisting Janelle in the saddle to face him. He cupped her face with his hands, his gaze intense. "I have to go after them, Janelle. This could be our only chance. But if you'd rather stay behind, I can take you back. You could wait for me. Wait until I come get you—"

Janelle cut him off, leaning forward and pressing a kiss to his lips. "Until my last breath leaves my tired body," she whispered, her eyes fierce. "I meant every word of our vows, Erik. If this is where we take our last stand, then we do it together."

Emotion surged through his chest, his love for her washing over him so completely it took his breath away. His brave wife. His best friend. The love of his life. He had no words, couldn't speak through the tears threatening to escape his throat. So he simply pulled her closer, kissing her with bruising intensity, not stopping until a tug on the string reminded him that the man they hunted was getting farther away, and his king and queen—their best friends—were in mortal danger.

Erik tore himself away from the kiss and tightened his hold on the reins. He spurred Cinnamon forward, navigating her toward Pontor, praying with every ounce of strength he had that they weren't too late to reach them.

Gray and Erik had started this journey together. And, whatever awaited them in the shadowed forests of Pontor, Erik knew it was only fitting they face it together, until the very end.

CHAPTER 61

LEA

Lea *felt* Alaric before she saw him—his cruel, maniacal energy radiated through the air as if his madness were contagious. It was a low hum, a rumble beneath her feet and deep inside her chest, a nausea that worked its way from her belly up her throat. The intensity of his magic was undeniable, as was the immensity. *How many had he killed?* she wondered.

How many people had he stolen magic from to amass such power? The thought made her sick, but she swallowed down the nausea, the taste of bile thick in her throat. Nothing could change the past, and Alaric's actions could never be undone. But Lea *could* stop him from doing more damage, killing more people, but only if she stayed focused.

Lea stopped for just a second, motioning for Evangeline to stay back. She didn't want her any closer than necessary, and hoped Evangeline could remain hidden, keeping death at bay from afar so Alaric would never even know she was there. Evangeline had urged her to reconsider her offer as Lea had stormed toward the lake, infuriated by Eudora's incessant taunting. She'd begged Lea to allow her to take on the burden, to pay the price for holding so much magic.

But despite the temptation to agree so that she could live, Lea knew there was no world in which she could forgive herself for making that choice. She would spend the rest of her days regretting it—hating herself to her marrow. It would consume her, just as her primary magic had once threatened to do before she'd accepted it as part of her.

Her death was something she had to accept as well. She very well may leave this world by the end of her battle. The goddess had warned her that never again would the universe allow anyone to hold as much magic as Alaric. *Especially* not her. Not when she'd had the chance to rid Alaric of his power already and failed. Not when she was living and fighting on borrowed time.

But if her death was what it took to defeat Alaric and end his reign of terror, Lea would go beyond the veil knowing she'd done her best, and that she would be together with Gray again in the afterlife. That had to be enough.

Lea crouched down as she approached the tree line, peering into the dark, searching for the man she was here to slaughter. She tucked her shadows around herself, shielding her body from detection, praying it would be enough to keep Eudora from seeing her coming.

"Finally found me, my Little Flower?" Alaric's voice slithered to her ears, layered with the voices of thousands of men and women whose magic he had stolen. It hit her like a stone, an electric shock to the chest that jarred her into standing. She cursed under her breath, furious at herself for letting him rattle her so easily, so quickly.

Slowly and silently, she shifted toward the voice to her right, her stomach dropping when she saw Alaric sitting atop a makeshift throne by the water's edge. The reflection of the enormous throne, built of narrow black tree limbs and yellowing bones, danced in the water's reflection, making it appear larger and more imposing. Lea shivered, her heart pounding hard and fast against her rib cage. She thickened her shadows, stepping forward silently as she inched closer.

"I know you're out there in the darkness," Alaric said, leaning forward in his chair. His head slowly tilted to the side as his gaze swept the area around him. "I can feel you, just as you can feel me." The throne creaked as he stood and stepped off the platform onto the dead soil of the Wicked Wood. "I can smell your fear, *Little Flower*."

Lea forced her breathing to remain even and silent, easing herself around the lake's edge in an attempt to position herself behind him. He turned toward her as if he could sense her presence, and she froze, her heart dropping into her stomach as she took in Alaric's appearance.

He looked far from weak and broken, like she'd hoped. But the description she'd heard from the villagers had been accurate—he was taller, more formidable, and somehow even more depraved than before. The veins beneath his skin were black, spreading like spiderwebs throughout his entire body.

Lea stared back, calling his bluff. Alaric couldn't see her, not in the pitch-black night, not with her shadows around her. But still, did he know where she was?

"I dreamed of this, you know," Alaric said, turning away from her in a slow circle, and Lea exhaled in relief. "The things I would do to you. How I would make you beg, how I would make you confess that you are weak. Vile. Disgusting. A traitor." He spat the words, and Lea flinched. Hearing a monster say such things about her made her nauseous. After all, doesn't it take a monster to know a monster? But in the end, it didn't matter. She would gladly become a monster if that's what it took to save the people she loved.

She had lied to her mate and friends—betrayed their trust. She had already made those choices, and she would do much worse if that's what it took to defeat Alaric.

Lea crept forward again, ensuring her footsteps were silent as she kept her eyes peeled for Eudora. If anyone was likely to spot her, it would be that witch, likely searching from above with a bird's eye view.

"I dream of it *Every. Night.* Little Flower," Alaric continued, his voice dripping with contempt. He laughed—a humorless, harsh, and violent sound. "Of how I would make you bow to me. Force you to beg for my mercy." He sighed. "We could've ruled together, you know." Alaric snapped his head to his left, lowering his chin. "You and I. Finally, a king and queen equally matched. But you fell for the weaker brother," he sneered, stalking forward with his back turned to her.

Lea drew her sword silently, gathering her power inside her chest and preparing to strike. She extended her magic forward, readying herself to take Alaric's and praying Evangeline was able to see her from where she hid, that she could sense her intent and would help keep death away.

"But in the end, *you* are the weak one. Did you think yourself to be clever?" Alaric asked, twisting to his left and staring into the darkness. "Did you think you had me fooled?" He pointed into the darkness, and Lea took another step, grateful he seemed to think she was a hundred yards in the wrong direction. "I know *exactly* what you are. *Who* you are. You are nothing," he spat, raising his arms above his head. A massive ball of fire ignited above him, rising above the trees and spreading across the sky. The heat hit her instantly, the lakeside lighting up in a bright orange glow as he spun, his eyes pinning her in place. He smiled, never blinking as he raised a finger to point in her direction.

"Found you," he whispered, the sound scraping up her spine and making her shiver.

Lea swallowed, jutting out her chin as she tried to hide her rage. He'd known where she was all along, allowing her to creep closer as he played with her like a cat does a mouse before killing it in cold blood. But she refused to let him see her fear. Absolutely would not let him know she was rattled.

The familiar smile that haunted Lea's dreams crept across his face, cruel and twisted, his sharp teeth gleaming in the firelight. So slowly it was unnatural, he tilted his head to the side, the angle so sharp it looked as if his neck might snap as he examined her with dark delight.

As his smile spread, so wide it looked painful, Eudora emerged from the trees—young, vibrant, and beautiful. Not a trace of the old witch Lea had known remained in her healthy, strong body. But Lea knew exactly who she was—could feel her essence as clearly as if the old, wrinkled witch she'd met in Calir were standing before her. Lea clenched her jaw, fighting back the curses begging to burst from her throat. It wouldn't help. She wasn't here for a verbal battle; she was here for one singular purpose.

"So angry, Little Flower," Alaric taunted. "Are you mad?" He tilted his head the other way, then pressed a hand to his mouth, feigning shock. "Oh—is it because she betrayed you?" He cackled, throwing his head back dramatically in forced laughter before stopping abruptly and going completely silent.

In the glow of Alaric's fire, Lea could see his eyes—eyes so black, not a scrap of color remained in his irises. She shivered.

"You're surprised she'd work with me, aren't you? The true king of Desia? The most powerful Fae in the world?" His volume grew as he spoke, his voice coated with a bitter edge, and Lea gripped her sword, preparing for him to strike. "You've always underestimated me," he continued, his tone laced with venom. "You, Gray." He paused. "My mother..."

Alaric snapped his fingers, and Eudora waved a hand in front of her. A haze of fog spread through the air, and Genevieve appeared out of thin air, her hands bound and her eyes wide with fear. Blood coated her face and dress, and her mouth was gagged with a thick, once-white cloth.

"How naïve do you think I am?" Alaric roared, throwing his hands to the side and sending flames shooting into the ground at his feet. "Did you think I'd fall for your little plan? Your pathetic trap?" He enunciated each word, the *P* popping in a way that felt like an explosion. He gestured to his mother. "Like this bitch would ever give up on her perfect, golden son?"

Lea's body buzzed, her feet urging her to run, to find a way to reach Genevieve and cut her free, but she couldn't move. Could barely even breathe.

Eudora smirked, twisting a finger in the air, and Genevieve's arms were wrenched backward. She cried out in pain, her words muffled by the gag in her mouth.

"She deserves what's coming to her. Just as you do," Alaric sneered, pointing at his mother while staring Lea down. "And your death will be all the sweeter, knowing you played right into my hands."

CHAPTER 62

THOMAS

Lea hadn't been gone for more than ten minutes before a rumbling in the distance alerted Thomas that something was coming. He'd barely had time to pull Emma away from the portal and into the relative safety of the darkness before royal soldiers descended upon the woods—hundreds of men in blood-red uniforms—maybe more—marching through the wood in the direction Lea had gone.

Gripping his sword, Thomas channeled the power he'd infused inside that would alert those with weapons he'd enchanted back at the castle. He pushed his magic down the thread, hoping the swords in the generals' hands would vibrate and alert them that it was time. That they were needed.

Thomas's stomach twisted into knots as he waited, sending the warning again and again, praying he'd used enough power. He'd never had the opportunity to test the weapons at this distance before, or anywhere near it. But he had confidence that it would work. It *had* to. Without the help of their army, they were as good as dead.

As more soldiers stormed the forest, Thomas carried Emma's still, nearly lifeless body to hide, moving within the shadows until he found a hollowed out fallen tree. Crouching down, he tucked her safely inside, the rough, dark bark shielding her from sight except for a small sliver of her torso. It was the best he could hope to find here in the Wicked Wood, where the trees were narrow and spindly, many too small to hide a full-grown human.

Thankfully, Emma was tiny, just slim enough for him to slide her into place. He tucked foliage over the opening, wet, macerated leaves and branches that covered most of the hold, then gripped his sword in his muddy hand. There was nothing left to do but watch, and wait.

A bright light flashed overhead, fire spreading through the sky and raining down as far as he could see. It illuminated the woods in a way that reminded him of monsters from his childhood nightmares—long, twisted arms reaching out for him from the darkness. Reaching for Emma. He pushed away the thought, focusing on peering over the log to watch the royal army.

In the distance, a group of soldiers branched off from the others, scattering through the trees. The more soldiers that arrived, the more they spread out, inching closer and closer to Emma's hiding spot.

Thomas's skin buzzed with worry, his breaths short and sharp, but he stayed put, crouched down with his sword in his hand. He couldn't move her—not without being seen—and even if he did, there was no guarantee he'd find a better place to hide her. He ducked down lower, every sense on edge as he prayed they would stay away.

The clash of swords rang out, and the sound of battle spread like a disease—cries of pain, clashes of shields, and the pounding of horses' hooves against the ground echoing throughout the forest.

Thomas let out a breath he didn't realize he'd been holding. It had worked—their soldiers had arrived. He was sure of it as the fighting spread and the roar grew louder. His shoulders sagged in relief.

With the army fighting against Alaric's and Emma tethered to the other side, they had a chance. Lea had a chance. If their army could keep the royal soldiers from reaching her and Alaric... A breeze kissed his cheek, interrupting his thoughts. He leaned into it, savoring the warmth it carried in the now cool night. The touch slid to his shoulder, and he swore he felt a squeeze.

A twig snapped behind him, cutting through the air at the exact moment he heard a ghost of a voice whisper, "Behind you!"

Thomas spun around, his heart racing as a battalion of soldiers approached—at least fifteen men with swords in hand and a dark, blank look in their eyes. Eyes focused directly on him.

CHAPTER 63

GRAY

Gray's heart pounded, its rhythm growing faster with every passing minute. Obsidian navigated through the dark as though he'd been born to run at night, effortlessly dodging trees and racing through the forest, not even hesitating as they reached the border of the Wicked Wood. He charged forward as if his own life depended on it.

"Keep going, boy," Gray urged, feeling Obsidian's muscles strain beneath his thighs as he moved at a speed Gray had never seen before.

"An hour south," the soldier had said. But Gray didn't have an hour. He had no idea how long time had been frozen for him, how far of a head start Lea had gotten before Henry's magic had worn off.

His storm clouds followed close behind them, rain splattering the ground and lightning flashing overhead, striking the long, spiny branches of the dead trees in the Wicked Wood. Small fires caught, then quickly extinguished, lighting his way. With as much strength as he could find, he urged his storm forward, mixing it with the rain already falling, hoping it would slow Lea's progress. If he could just reach her before she got to Alaric, everything would be okay. It *had* to be. They were stronger together.

Rage bubbled within Gray's chest, but he forced it down, unwilling to get lost in hurt and anger. His focus was singular: find Lea as quickly as possible. Everything else could wait.

In the distance, the sound of fighting reached him. Obsidian's ears perked up, and his gallop somehow quickened. Gray's heart sank, adrenaline making him feel as if his skin was buzzing. Was he too late? Had Lea already reached Alaric?

Up ahead, three royal soldiers darted in front of him, cutting through the trees and racing south.

"Stop!" Gray commanded, throwing a long trail of shadow out like a lasso. It caught the soldier at the end around the throat, ripping him from his horse.

The soldier screamed, "Help me! No!" But Gray would show no mercy. He bolted toward the man, sword raised, desperate for information, ready to take an arm or a leg if that's what it took to get him to talk. But before he could reach him, a terracotta mare burst through the trees, and in the blink of an eye, the soldier's head was severed from his body.

"Erik?" Gray asked, his shadows retreating in surprise as Obsidian jumped over the decapitated body.

"Why aren't you with Lea?" Erik asked, continuing forward. Gray followed him, the two other soldiers on horseback barely visible in the distance.

"What are you doing here?" Gray asked, ignoring his question. "You were supposed to be in Alnwick. What changed?" he pulled Obsidian up next to Cinnamon, his mind racing as fast as the black stallion. How was it possible they were here? Had they known of Lea's plan? The thought made his stomach twist, but he pushed it away. They couldn't have known. Not Erik, at least.

"Janelle sensed trouble," Erik said, as if that was enough of an explanation.

As they dodged a copse of trees, the sounds of fighting grew sharper, more distinct. Gray peered through the branches, where royal guards and his own army were locked in a fierce struggle to the death. It was a battle unlike anything he'd ever seen before. Bodies lined the woods, slumped on the ground in piles—more than he could count. He searched them for familiar faces.

"How are they here?" Gray asked Erik as they raced toward their soldiers. "How is the fucking army here?"

"What?" Erik narrowed his eyes, his chest heaving and his face going pale. "This wasn't on your orders?"

Gray shook his head, his lungs constricting. Who had brought them here? How had they known where Alaric would be before he did? Gray's shadows struggled to stay contained as his rage grew. What was he missing?

"Is this what you were sensing?" Erik asked Janelle, who gripped the saddle so hard her knuckles had turned white. She shook her head. "No. I mean, part of it—but something worse is waiting for us. Further that way." She closed her eyes and pointed south.

"Lea," Gray said, her name a prayer. "She left me behind, used Henry to freeze time. We have to find her."

Erik gripped his sword tighter and nodded, his face grim. He stopped Cinnamon, just long enough to help Janelle clamber behind him. "Hold on tight," he told her. "And use your dagger." Janelle pulled her weapon from the sheath on her thigh.

With a war cry that made his throat feel raw, Gray roared at the sky, his sword raised as he charged into battle, cutting down soldier after soldier as he fought to reach his wife—his mate—even if the gods no longer considered her as such. His eyes scanned the woods as he tried to piece together a plan. The path of least resistance. The battle stretched as far as he could see, thousands of soldiers blocking his way.

He tried to push forward, but the fighting was so tightly packed that Obsidian couldn't maneuver through. Not quickly enough. Gray jumped off his back, and Erik and Janelle did the same.

"Go around, wait for me on the other side," he told his horse, and Obsidian didn't hesitate, kicking up mud behind him as he galloped out of the madness.

Gray stalked forward, gripping his sword in his fist. His shadows were weapons in their own right, snapping necks and breaking limbs.

"You!" Erik shouted from his left.

"What do you want from me?" the man cried out. "I'm sorry, okay! Janelle! Tell him—"

"No," she said, stalking forward. "You're not. You never were." Janelle lunged, swiping the man's face with her dagger as Erik darted forward, slamming his sword through his hand and pinning him to the ground.

Janelle's jaw clenched as she pressed the tip of her dagger to his chest. Gray spun in a circle, chopping off a soldier's hand as he fought his way south, his eyes flicking back to Janelle every few seconds. She leaned down, saying something into the man's ear, then pushed her dagger into his chest, a sharp shove that cracked his ribs. The light left his eyes and Janelle stood, her own eyes full of tears as Erik embraced her, just for a moment, before stalking toward another man attempting to flee.

Gray continued onward, and a cry for help sounded to his left—a voice he knew. Mark, one of his generals, was begging for his life. Out of the corner of his eye, Gray saw a sword descending toward Mark's neck. Gray sent out a trail of darkness, seizing the sword from the soldier and turning it back on him, running it through his gut and twisting until he dropped to the ground, lifeless.

The general scrambled to his feet, his face bloodied, eyes wide with shock. "Thank you," he said, grabbing his sword from the forest floor.

"Have you seen Lea?" Gray asked, flipping a soldier onto his back with a swift kick to his knees and plunging his sword through the man's eye socket.

He shook his head, jumping back into the fighting. "No. Thomas told us to come, and when we got here, there were soldiers everywhere. No sign of Lea, Alaric, or the witch."

"Thomas?" Gray asked, the revelation making him stumble in his block, and a sword sliced across his forearm. Gray's shadows snapped the attacker's neck before he could strike again. Blood roared in Gray's ears. Had Thomas been in on the plan all along, then? The pieces weren't adding up. Gray sidestepped a disemboweled body as he pressed forward. "*Thomas* told you to come here? Tonight?"

"Yes—" Mark ducked, narrowly avoiding a blow to the head as he rammed his sword through the attacking soldier's belly.

"Where is he?" Gray snapped, unable to process what Mark was saying. None of this had been part of his plan. *None* of these things had been discussed or approved by him or Erik. How far had Lea's betrayal gone? How many secrets had she kept?

"I don't know," Mark replied, wiping the blood off his face.

"Find her," Gray ordered. "Tell the others. We *have* to find her."

Gray's ears rang with the clash of swords, his boots slick with mud and blood. Soldier after soldier, he slaughtered them, swiftly and violently, fighting his way further and further south. He couldn't stay to protect his army, couldn't remain behind to keep his soldiers safe.

Not with Lea out there somewhere, alone with Alaric and Eudora. The guilt threatened to crush him, each step forward feeling like a stone cast against his soul. But if he didn't find Lea, they would all die. Every last one of them.

Erik and Janelle continued to fight near him, staying close and guarding him from behind. They moved as one—forward, forward, forward—until the fighting became more sparse and the sounds of battle faded to a dull roar behind them. Gray broke into a sprint, able to reach full speed now that he wasn't dodging attacks and corpses.

But he didn't make it more than thirty feet before he was thrown to his back in a violent crash. Two massive paws landed on his chest, pinning him down, and his heart nearly stopped as the gaping maw of a fenrir inched closer to his throat, its teeth already dripping with blood.

CHAPTER 64

LEA

Alaric's eyes bulged, capillaries bursting as he thrust out a hand and tightened his fingers into a tight fist. Instantly, Lea's throat squeezed closed, a rope made of air wrapping around her neck and tightening until she couldn't breathe. Panic bubbled through her chest, so potent she almost missed it when a cold chill ran down her spine.

Death, she recognized, was already coming for her, before she'd even had the chance to try to take Alaric's magic. Stars dotted her vision as her body fought for air, but she forced her heart to slow, trying to conserve oxygen. She gathered her sword's energy in her chest and, with a grunt of effort, shot it forward—a gust of wind that threw Alaric backward. It was just enough to cause him to loosen his hold, and she sucked in a hungry breath, oxygen returning to her bloodstream and her vision becoming clearer.

She cast her shadows around herself, as thick and dark as she could make them, only stopping once she was unable to see her hand in front of her. She didn't need to see. Her shadows had already mapped out the woods around her: the lake's edge where the water slowly lapped against serrated rocks, the makeshift throne, the narrow trees.

Alaric cackled, a truly unhinged sound that sent chills down Lea's spine. "It's so fun when you fight back," he said, his voice light. "It's been boring just killing again and again and again. It's been too easy, you see. But youuuu…" He drew the word out, his pitch lilting up as if starting to sing. "*You* give me a challenge."

A pop of fire exploded to her left, dirt and mud flying through the air and splattering her face. Lea jumped, sucking in a sharp breath and wiping her eyes. As silently as possible, she crept toward Genevieve. *Pop!* Another explosion, this time ten feet ahead of her.

"I can smoke you out, I guess," Alaric said, and Lea pictured him stroking his chin, pretending to ponder. But she knew him better than that. He loved the hunt every bit as much as he loved the kill.

Genevieve screamed as another explosion cracked only feet behind her, and Lea darted forward, sensing her opportunity. With a flick of her wrist, she severed the ropes holding her wrists in place. "Run," she whispered in her ear, still mapping out the forest around her with her shadows.

Alaric had wandered in the opposite direction, still taunting her, still teasing her and describing the horrible things he planned to do once he caught her: plucking out her eyeballs, pulling out all her teeth one by one, peeling her fingernails from their beds before chopping up her hands knuckle by knuckle.

Genevieve's breaths were ragged as she twisted toward the tree line, ready to follow Lea's orders and run to her escape. But in the blink of an eye, the map in Lea's mind changed. With a snap of his fingers, Alaric was in front of them, his sword already stabbed through Genevieve's gut. Lea launched at him, swinging her own sword in an arc in an attempt to get him to back away, but it was too late. Genevieve fell to her knees, blood oozing from her mouth and nose, a horrible gurgling sound sputtering from her throat.

Alaric didn't take the time to savor his kill. Instead, he ripped the sword from Genevieve's stomach and lifted it to Lea's throat. Lea ripped his arm back with her shadows, Genevieve's blood flinging from the sword and across her face as she knocked it away from her neck, but she wasn't strong enough to dislodge it from Alaric's hand.

She backed up, trying to get some distance from his sword so she could take his magic without the threat of him jamming it between her ribs. Rolling his eyes as if inconvenienced, he twisted a finger, a ring of fire bursting around them, trapping Lea inside with him and Eudora.

Lea tried to lunge toward him, to swipe her sword with enough force to cut through the tendons of his legs, but he was too fast, too powerful, sidestepping her with ease. "Such a disappointment," he sighed. "I expected more of a challenge than *this*," he said dramatically, but a smile twisted his already cruel features.

Lea stepped back, her sword still tight in her fist. She'd hoped to injure him, in some way first. To distract him with a painful wound, in the hopes that she could make him drop his defenses and distract him as she wormed her magic inside him, but he'd grown too strong. She was no match for him. Not physically.

Praying that Evangeline would still be able to help her from wherever she hid, Lea tunneled inside herself, forming a thick shield of shadows and air around herself to block Alaric and Eudora's attacks. Alaric's eyes went wide with rage, and he leapt forward, crashing his sword into the shield, but it held firm. Planting her feet, she gripped her sword in both hands and isolated her primary magic, once again picturing it as long moonflower vines creeping toward him, spiraling up his body until they pierced through his skin and inside Alaric's chest with a snap.

She pictured her shadows morphing into chains and draped them around Alaric, holding him in place as she grasped at his magic. She wrapped her vines around a piece, the feeling of his power unnatural and foreign. It wasn't Alaric's magic she held, but someone else's. Magic he had stolen, but it didn't matter whose magic she took first. She had to take every last drop. She branched her vines out, wrapping them around as many pieces as she could, and began to pull.

Alaric paused his attack with his sword, his face turning blood red as he grit his teeth and lifted his chin. He roared toward the sky, his magic exploding outward in a mighty wave that broke the chains of darkness holding him in place.

With inhuman strength, he lifted his sword over his head before once again bringing his weapon crashing into her shield. It vibrated so hard her teeth rattled, but somehow, it held strong as she continued to pull Alaric's magic inside herself. Pain seared behind her eyes, a pounding, throbbing agony that spread into her forehead and through her temples, down her throat and into chest. Still, she pulled harder, spreading her vines and grabbing more and more of his magic.

Eudora stepped forward, her calm exterior faltering as her eyes widened, a hint of panic crossing her face. She clawed and banged against Lea's shield of shadows and air, trying desperately to break through, but Lea funneled more power into it, determined to keep them out. She just had to get Alaric's magic. Had to last long enough to drain him, and then, as long as she died with the sword in her hand, she could kill him. She wouldn't fail this time.

Alaric screamed as she ripped more power away, dropping his sword and holding his hands out to throw a stream of fire into her shield, so hot she could smell her skin and hair burning. But even the pain of her burning skin was nothing compared to the agony surging through her body as she pulled another surge of Alaric's power inside her chest.

Lea felt Evangeline's shield around her life force strengthen, holding back death as he clawed at her heart. She could feel death squeezing, pulling and ripping and tearing, but never hard enough, never with enough force to break through Evangeline's protection and take her soul. She reinforced Evangeline's shield, keeping death from sinking its claws into her flesh, then pulled harder, a chunk of Alaric's magic snapping off the mass of power inside him and clicking into place with a sickening thud in her chest.

Lea doubled over, retching onto the ground as pain enveloped her. Blood dripped from her nose and ears, and her vision went blurry, but she forced herself to stand. Eudora screamed, something Lea couldn't hear through the blood roaring in her ears. Her eyes were wide with panic, and she continued banging against the shield, then raised her hands, muttering something incomprehensible.

Lea worked faster, pulled harder, another piece of Alaric's magic severing from his body and shooting inside her. Alaric's mouth dropped open, his face paling as Lea stole more and more from him. Piece by piece, it melded with her own in agonizing waves, the pain growing more intense as Alaric grew weaker. He turned his head, meeting the witch's eyes.

"No!" Eudora snapped, as if reading Alaric's mind, knowing he wanted to flee. "We end this. Here and now!" she ordered, closing her eyes and resuming her chanting.

Lea pushed another tendril of darkness inside Alaric, grabbing another string of stolen magic and tugging it toward her. Alaric resumed battering against her shield, small cracks forming beneath his stream of fire, but it did not break. Not as she felt the last piece of foreign magic leave Alaric's chest. And not as she began taking his own magic.

She was exhausted, tired to her bones, but she dug deeper into her never ending well of darkness, stretching Alaric's power tighter and tighter until a piece of it snapped. His magic surged into Lea, and she screamed, the searing pain spreading through her body so rapidly, it made her retch again.

She wiped her nose, the blood running from her nostrils so heavily now that it was choking her, but she couldn't give up. She collapsed to her hands and knees, closing her eyes and focusing solely on pulling the rest of Alaric's power from his chest. He bellowed again, sending his flames into the ground and beneath her shield.

Her pants caught on fire, but her charred skin barely registered as she suffocated the flames. Alaric threw funnels of fire at her again and again, but his attacks were growing weaker by the moment. He picked up his sword, ramming it into her shield over and over, but Lea pushed on, pulling more of his power inside herself.

Death screamed in her ear, his claws raking against her ribs and his fists pounding against the shield around her soul, but Lea persisted, pulling away Alaric's power bit by bit, each surge rocking through her body with such agony that it caused her to heave up bile.

She pulled another chunk of power inside her, screeching as the pain became so severe her vision dotted, the edges going black.

Alaric struck her shield, a thick fissure appearing in the thick, shadowy darkness. She gasped, death's fingers squeezing around her lungs and heart, as if it could crack through Evangeline's protections. Alaric howled, baring his teeth in a bloody grimace as he struck again, the fissure in Lea's shield growing longer, widening. A gap formed, just large enough for him to stab his sword through, and Lea rolled backward, the pain so intense it felt as if her bones were shattering.

She tried to push more magic into her shield, but Alaric continued his assault against it, her strength fading as he crashed the heavy metal into it again and again. Eudora stuck her hand through the fissure, ripping apart the shield piece by piece, her hands bloody and ribbons of skin hanging from her palms.

Lea coughed up blood, but she pulled at Alaric's magic again, feeling it draining, but there was still more, always more. She screamed, severing another piece from his chest, and her shield faltered again. With the strike of Alaric's sword, it cracked like broken glass, shattering around her in a blast of fire.

Lea pulled herself to her feet, gripping her sword firmly in her hand as Alaric stalked toward her, his teeth bared and his chest heaving. "You will *never* be more powerful than me," he spat. "Never!" He threw his head back, his arms out to the side, the ground beneath their feet shaking and Alaric's fire spreading closer.

But she couldn't stop. Gritting her teeth, Lea continued her assault. Disassociating from the pain as she yanked bits of his power inside herself. She could feel death chipping away at her mother's shield, so close to claiming her. Her body burned as if it was on fire, as if every bone had been ground into dust, but still, she pushed forward, dragging her sword behind her as she approached Alaric, too weak to raise it until the final blow.

She yanked another stream of Alaric's magic into her chest, almost collapsing to her knees, but she forced herself to remain steady. She was so close. She could *feel* it.

Alaric threw another blast of fire in her direction, much smaller this time, and she dodged it, crying out in pain at the jarring movement. She blew the fire away with a gust of air, but Alaric sprang forward, arcing his sword down toward her throat. She raised her own sword, her muscles shaking as she blocked his attack, but he was so strong.

Inch by inch, he gained ground, the sword coming closer and closer to Lea's neck until it was mere inches from her skin. She pushed back with all her strength, desperate. She would not fail—refused to die for nothing. She had to get the last of Alaric's power.

With a surge of strength Lea didn't know she had, she pushed back against his sword. Grabbing the last dregs of Alaric's magic, she screamed, her vision fading as she ripped it backward as hard as she could. She was close. So very close.

"Stop!" Eudora said, stepping forward with her arms outstretched. Lea's eyes widened in terror as Eudora began to chant again, moving closer and closer, her magic pricking at Lea's skin. With every word, Lea's pain grew, the agony intensifying until it was unbearable. She wanted to fight back, *needed* to fight back, to kill the witch before she killed her, but Alaric pushed his sword down harder, once again getting closer to her neck.

As the cool metal kissed her throat, Lea felt death's fingertips break through her mother's shield, just a crack, but it was enough. Eudora chanted louder, shouting now as she pulled the magic from Lea's grasp before she could sever it from Alaric. "No!" she cried. She couldn't do this, couldn't win against them both—not if Eudora could keep her from taking the final pieces of Alaric's power.

But as Eudora smiled, her chanting now deafening, Lea crumbled under the weight of Alaric's sword. The weight of knowing there was no chance she could continue to fight them both.

CHAPTER 65

ERIK

Janelle screamed—a piercing screech that caused the fenrir to look up in surprise. The distraction only lasted a second, but it was all Gray needed. With a grunt, he rolled to the side, swinging his sword sideways to plunge it between the giant wolf's ribs. The animal whimpered, struggling to rise to its feet, but Erik didn't allow it to stand up again. With all his strength, he brought the sword down over its neck, severing its head from its body in one fell swoop.

Gray picked up his sword and rushed forward again, Erik close on his heels, but a growl ahead made them freeze. His hair stood on end as he peered through the trees, his heart pounding harder with every second that passed. A line of fenrir spread to block their path, and Erik grabbed Janelle by the arm, shoving her behind him. There were more than he could count, all nearly the size of horses. All of them with their teeth bared and their hair standing on end.

Gray raised his hands in front of him. "Let me through," he rasped, desperate. "*Please*. I don't want to kill you," he said, as if the animals could understand him. "But I will—I'll kill each and every one of you, without hesitation, to get to her."

A deep gray fenrir stepped forward, meeting Gray's eyes for a long moment before raising its head to howl, its body language unmistakable. *We will not let you pass,* it said.

Erik searched between the enormous wolves, looking for a path of escape as Gray tightened his grip on his sword, lowering his chin. His shadows whipped around him like long trails of vengeance, and Erik followed his lead, calling flames into his hands. His blood whooshed through his head, but even through the roaring in his ears, he could hear Janelle's heart pounding behind him, a furious rhythm of uncertainty and fear.

"Please," Erik whispered to Janelle, speaking without turning around, afraid that any sudden movements might make the wolves launch into their attack. "Please, run. Hide," he begged, allowing his desperation to seep into his voice. He didn't care. Not if it convinced her to flee. There was no surviving this. They were outnumbered twenty to one, the wolves' heads lowered in determination and their teeth bared.

Janelle stepped forward, placing her shaking hand into his. "Erik," she said softly.

"Please," he begged again, his voice cracking, but he knew it was futile. That she would never leave him, just as he knew there was no way he could dissuade Gray from trying to fight his way through these monsters.

"Together," Janelle said as the fighting behind them grew closer, the clash of swords suddenly clearer, louder. Erik's stomach dropped, but he squeezed Janelle's hand tighter.

"Together," he replied. "Always."

"This is your last chance," Gray said, raising his sword.

The gray fenrir looked up at Gray, its eyes sad, and Erik paused, uneasiness swirling in his stomach. The wolf tilted its head and took a step back, as if trying to communicate with them. *We don't want to fight you,* he seemed to say. *Don't make us.*

But, why would the fenrir not want to fight them? Why were they here, if not to help Alaric destroy his enemy? And yet it was clear the beasts would find no joy in killing them. From the way they stood statue still, waiting for Gray to make the first move, it was obvious that complete carnage wasn't their goal. Erik's mind spun as he searched for their reason, but he didn't have time to solve the riddle.

Gray sent his shadows forward, bringing eight fenrir to their knees immediately, their eyes bulging from their sockets as he strangled them with darkness. He stalked forward, sword raised in the air as the others launched, teeth bared and claws exposed. Erik kept Janelle at his back, fighting in a circle with her as the fenrir surged upon them.

Wolf after wolf tried to push them back, their eyes pleading as they approached. *Don't kill me. You don't have to do this...* they said.

"Gray," Erik shouted over the din of battle.

"I know." Gray said, his eyes pained and his face covered in blood. "I know. But I have to get to her," he said, stabbing another fenrir through the heart. He didn't have to say more. Erik knew exactly what he was feeling. What was motivating him. Something was wrong. Nothing was adding up. These animals didn't want to kill them, and they didn't deserve to die.

But that didn't matter. Gray would do anything to get to his mate, even if it killed him. Erik understood, because he would do the same.

CHAPTER 66

EMMA

The darkness didn't last long. Emma peeled her eyes open, her grogginess easing as if pulling off a thick, heavy blanket. She stood—or at least, her soul did. Panic flooded her veins as she looked down upon her unconscious body cradled in Thomas's arms. He tucked her close, carrying her off into the depths of the Wicked Wood to hide.

Heart pounding, she chased after him, her dagger still tight in her hand. She'd made sure to hold it tight while drinking the potion, hoping that it would keep the dead away from her as she slept, but now, looking at her body, she was grateful for an entirely different reason.

It was alarming how vulnerable she looked. How flaccid her limbs were, her head lolling back and feet swinging with every step Thomas took. She held her breath as he tucked her inside a fallen tree, crouching down to tuck the hair back from her face. She shivered as she peered over his shoulder, searching her body for signs of life.

The anxiety swirling between her ribs eased a fraction as she watched her chest rise and fall with ease, the deep, rhythmic breath of sleep obvious. Her pulse jumped beneath her jaw, and Emma reached out her shaking hand, pressing two fingers against it to feel the steady thump of her heart. Is this what the new potion had done? Allowed her to interact with the world while tethered to the other side?

"Thomas?" Emma said, following him as he moved to hide behind the thickest part of the trunk. He didn't answer, totally unaware of her presence, his head scanning the forest as he searched for threats. She reached out to him, cupping his cheek, and he leaned into her touch, exhaling softly.

"Thomas?" she asked again, moving her hand down to his shoulder and squeezing. Could he feel her? Did he know, somewhere in his sub-conscious, that she was here with him?

"I'm here," she said, looking around to search for the souls of the dead, wondering if they would come to find her while she lingered in the in-between.

But there were none. Not a single soul. None of the men who had haunted the Wicked Wood before. Not a single soldier who had fallen in the battle raging so close to where they hid. Normally, the dead were drawn to her like a magnet, but Emma wouldn't second guess their absence. It was a blessing, to not have to experience their agony and suffering.

She turned back to face Thomas, her heart sinking as a group of very much alive soldiers appeared behind him, creeping forward with their swords ready. Their eyes were blank, almost unseeing, as if they'd been put under a spell, and Emma wondered what kind of enchant-ment Alaric had cast over them. She couldn't sense their emotions or motives—just... emptiness. Was it because she wasn't fully a part of their world as she straddled the in between? Or were they being so deeply controlled by Alaric's power that they had no thoughts or feelings of their own?

"Behind you!" Emma grabbed Thomas's shoulder again, this time shaking him. "Behind you!" she yelled louder, willing with everything she had for her voice to be heard. This time, he turned around, jumping to his feet and holding out his sword. Thomas's hands shook as he positioned his body in front of Emma, still hidden within the trunk of the tree.

"He said you'd be hiding," the soldier in the front sneered. "Where's the girl?"

"What girl?" Thomas asked, his eyebrows lowering. He tilted his head. "I don't know who you're talking about."

"Of course you do," the soldier mocked, stalking forward, his eyes as black as night. "He said we'd find a man with brown hair, a *human*, hiding away like a coward. Guarding the girl that allows the worlds to join together." The soldiers spread out, surrounding the tree trunk, their eyes examining every inch. "He said you wouldn't be far from her. So where is she?"

Emma moved to stand in front of her sleeping body as if, somehow, she could help hide it from their view.

"I said, I don't know what you're talking about," Thomas said.

The soldier's jaw clenched. "Make this easy, human. Tell us where she is, and I'll let you live."

"There's no one—" Thomas began, but the soldier cut him off, jumping forward with inhuman speed and pressing the edge of his sword to Thomas's throat.

Thomas retaliated without hesitation, raising his own sword to press it against the soldier's stomach, just above his belly button.

The soldier laughed as if Thomas was holding a dull butter knife. "You think you can defeat me?" he challenged. A chuckle spread between the soldiers, a mocking echo dancing through the trees. "You?" He pressed the tip of the sword harder into Thomas's throat, and a drop of deep red blood welled beneath it. Emma's heart thundered, and she wondered if her body could feel it, still resting only inches away.

The soldier assessed Thomas, his gaze slowly raking down his body until his gaze dropped to Thomas's foot, and Emma followed his line of sight to where a sliver of her dress peeked out from the log. The soldier stiffened, and Thomas ducked to the side, thrusting his sword upward. The sword against his neck drug sideways, and he hissed in pain, but there was no time to check how severe the injury was or try to stem the bleeding. The other soldiers lunged forward, grabbing Thomas and wrenching his arms behind his back while another callously pulled Emma's body from the tree, ripping her out by her arm.

Thomas kicked at the soldier, connecting with his nose with a crunch, and he dropped Emma's arm, his hands flying up to his bloody face. "Fuck!" he screamed as Thomas dropped to his knees, yanking his arms forward as quickly as possible to break free from their grasp.

"Thomas!" Emma screamed, but even with her voice so loud her throat felt raw, he couldn't hear her, didn't so much as flinch at the sound of his name. The soldiers cursed as Thomas rolled away and picked up his sword, swinging it at the soldier dragging Emma's body deeper into the woods. The men moved forward in unison, and without thinking, Emma darted forward, jabbing her dagger between one soldier's shoulder blades. He fell with a scream of agony, giving Thomas room to sweep his sword at the others' legs. They jumped back, their eyes darting around nervously at the surprise attack.

Emma kicked the fallen weapons away, then turned back, closing her eyes as she slit another soldier's throat.

"What the hell?" one of them exclaimed, stumbling back. Thomas took advantage of his shock, lunging forward and stabbing the soldier just below his left shoulder.

As if they'd practiced fighting together a thousand times, Emma ducked under a soldier's arm, thrusting her dagger upward through a man's sternum as another soldier charged toward Thomas. He dodged the attack, but stumbled as a soldier came at him from the side, and together the men fell to the ground.

Emma ran after him, looking for an opportunity to attack without harming Thomas as they grappled, flipping over and over as they fought for the soldier's dagger. Thomas disarmed him, turning the dagger on the royal soldier and swiftly slicing through his throat, throwing the soldier's spasming body off him.

As Thomas scrambled to his feet, the final soldier stalked toward Emma's body, a cruel smile on his face as he raised his sword overhead and swung it down towards her exposed throat.

"No!" Thomas roared, diving toward her. Emma's heart stopped as Thomas threw himself on top of her, shielding her with his body as the sword came down in a furious arc.

Emma sprinted toward him, launching forward and stabbing her dagger through the soldier's back with all her might, but it was too late. The soldier's sword was a second too fast, slicing down and cutting through Thomas's throat with ease.

Emma screamed, a blood-curdling wail that shook the trees as she collapsed at Thomas's side. "No, no, no," she sobbed, pressing her hand to his wound, but there was so much blood. More than she'd ever seen, hot and sticky on her hands as it bubbled from his throat. "Thomas!" she cried. He lifted his head, and in one final act of strength, wrenched the sword from the dying soldier's grasp. Emma reached into her pocket, grabbing the moonflower petal with bloody fingers, but Thomas's eyes had already glazed over with death.

"No, no, no," she begged again, pressing the petal between his lips. He lay still, unmoving, and Emma threw herself across him, her tears soaking into his bloody shirt as sobs racked her body.

"Please, no, Thomas!"

"Emma?" a voice said from behind her.

She sniffled, closing her eyes. "No," she whimpered again. "No. No. No."

"Emma, it's okay," Thomas said, his hand now resting on her back, and even in death, his touch sent butterflies racing through her stomach.

"No!" she sobbed, refusing to turn. Maybe if she didn't see it, it wouldn't be real, but Thomas grabbed her shoulder, turning her and pulling her into his arms.

Emma threw her arms around him, not caring about the blood. Not caring about anything but holding him. "No. No. No!" she cried. The same word again and again, as if she was stuck in a loop. But she couldn't break free from it. Because that would mean she believed it was happening—that Thomas was really dead.

"It's okay," he soothed, holding her tight in his strong embrace.

"How?" she cried. "How is it okay?" She sat up, not bothering to wipe away her blood or tears. A zap of electricity bolted through her chest. "The moonflower…" she trailed off, patting down Thomas's pockets. "Where is it?" she asked frantically, her hands shaking.

Thomas shook his head, sadness in his eyes. "It won't work, Emma. I'm gone."

"No," Emma cried again. "Just try. Please!"

Thomas exhaled, pressing his lips together and pulling the petal from his pocket. He placed it in his mouth, his throat bobbing as he swallowed. Emma held her breath, waiting. She was tethered to the other side. It had to work. And yet… he remained kneeling beside her, his throat torn open, blood coating nearly every inch of his torso.

"You shouldn't have done that," she whispered, collapsing into his arms again, sobbing. They were supposed to have time. This was only the beginning.

Thomas lifted her chin, his touch so gentle it made her heart hurt. "I would do *anything* to protect you. I love you, Emma. I want you to live a good life. A long life. Okay? Don't feel guilty for this—it was my choice.

I told you I wouldn't let anything happen to you, and I intend to keep that vow."

Emma sniffled, her body shuddering with each gasp for air. "There has to be a way..." Thomas's head snapped up, and Emma trailed off, following his gaze to where more soldiers approached, the same dead look in their eyes.

Thomas pulled back, wrapping his hands around her biceps. "We have to fight, Emma. You have to live."

And even through her grief and pain, she knew he was right. If Alaric's soldiers were still coming, Lea still needed her. The kingdom still needed her.

"I love you," he said again, pulling her to her feet. "Forever," he whispered, wiping the tears from her eyes.

"I love you, too," Emma replied, gripping her dagger tighter as the soldiers advanced, unaware of their presence. They were searching for her, had been told what she could do. But they couldn't let Alaric's men kill her. She still had a job to do.

As the men closed in, their eyes fixed on her sleeping form, Thomas's body laying across it in his final act of sacrifice, they raised their weapons.

"I'll see you on the other side," Thomas said with a sad smile before charging forward to fight to protect Emma—even in death—just as he had promised her.

CHAPTER 67

GRAY

Flashes of fire flickered in the distance, lighting up the sky again and again in bright orange bursts of immense power. With every flash, Gray's heart stuttered, wondering if it had been aimed at Lea. If she had dodged it. Or if... No. He couldn't even think the words. She had to be okay. Surely he would feel it if she were hurt. That his body would echo her pain.

The clatter of swords made Gray pause, and he dodged left to avoid a group of soldiers locked in battle, their fighting spreading to where he fought the fenrir. The giant wolves fanned out, just as determined to keep the soldiers away from Lea as they were to keep Gray from getting to her.

He used the chaos to his advantage. Again and again, Gray sliced through their necks, desperate to get to Lea, blood spattering across his face and clothes until he was certain he looked as if he had bathed in it. But still, they continued their attack, just as desperate to stop him. His shadows fought alongside him, pushing the wolves back until a gap appeared between them.

He raced toward it, a smaller, tan wolf snapping at his heels. He grabbed it by the scruff of its neck with his shadows and ripped it away, venturing on as more soldiers appeared, taking his place and continuing the fight.

"That way!" Janelle called, catching his attention. He scanned the battleground, his soldiers locked in intense fights with the fenrir all around him, until he saw a flash of purple hair sticking out in the chaos. "Around that way!" she said again, gesturing to her right.

Gray wasted no time. He surged forward, dodging the fighting and slipping into the trees, somehow avoiding detection. Another bright flash of fire lit up the sky, and in the flicker of light, a lake appeared in the distance. He raced toward it, certain that if he could just make it to the fiery battle he was witnessing glimpses of, he would find Lea.

His heart raced as he got closer, his skin prickling with electricity, confirming that his mate was near. He could feel her fury—her power. She was alive.

The trees thinned as he neared the lake, and through them, Gray saw a wall of fire towering at least thirty feet high. Gray shot his shadows forward, pushing them through the massive flames, reaching out with all he had as he searched for his wife. His everything.

"Lea!" he roared, his heart hammering so hard his ribcage hurt, but he didn't stop. He pushed more magic into his shadows, commanding them to part the flames. Through a gap in the fiery wall, Lea appeared, Alaric's sword pressed against hers as he pushed it down toward her neck, and standing over them was Eudora, her mouth moving in an incessant chant as Lea crumbled beneath the weight of Alaric's force.

"No!" he screamed, panic surging up his throat as he tried to close the distance, but he was too far to reach her. "Lea!" he screamed again, his voice amplifying as it spread over the lake. Eudora's head snapped toward him, her eyes flaring with fury as they met his. As if they were nothing, she shoved his shadows parting the flames away, snapping the wall of fire closed once more.

CHAPTER 68

LEA

Lea's back arched as she fought for the strength to push back against Alaric. She was nearly drained, her whole body in agony, but still she reached inside, desperate to find shadows lingering in her chest to fight off Eudora.

She searched her chest—between every rib, in every vein, but there was nothing left. The pain was too much, and her head swam, her vision going black as she fought to stay awake. To fight.

And then, so suddenly it shocked her searing lungs into taking a deep, sharp breath, her pain eased. Lea kept fighting, pushing back against Alaric's sword, wondering if this was what death would feel like this time around—if her pain would ease until she faded away into nothing. It didn't matter. She would fight until her final breath, and then, she would continue fighting.

Once again, Lea sent up a prayer to the goddess that Emma had taken the potion in time, that she was safely hidden away and tethered to the other side.

Alaric pushed down again, somehow harder than before, but this time, she was able to gain ground, the cool metal of the sword leaving her throat. Her pain eased further, her strength growing as adrenaline pumped through her body.

She pushed back again with a surge of strength, and the sword flew out of Alaric's hand, soaring across the circle and disappearing into the ring of fire. Alaric's face went pale as Lea dragged herself to stand, her movements growing less shaky by the moment. Eudora's eyebrows furrowed, and her words became strangled, but Lea ignored her. There was no time.

She reached inside Alaric once more, grabbing the final scraps of his power. He turned to run, but Lea grabbed his hair with her shadows, yanking him backward and holding him in place. She pulled on the last thread of his magic, bracing herself for the surge of agony that would follow as she severed it from Alaric's body, but it never came.

Alaric fell to his knees, throwing up into the grass as he grasped at his chest. "You— You fucking bitch!" he shouted, struggling to get to his feet. "I'll fucking gut you—"

Lea didn't hear the end of his threat as Eudora collapsed beside her with a thud. Blood spurted from her nose and ears, bubbling from her mouth as she continued to chant. She met Lea's eyes, and Lea sucked in a sharp breath as she took in the fear and desperation in them. Blood seeped from between Eudora's teeth as she ended her spell, and with those final words, Lea's pain faded away completely.

It was as if she was looking into a mirror for the first time, seeing herself and the world around her with absolute clarity. Suddenly, everything made sense. Her heart ached as she looked down at the witch. The one who had deceived them all, but not in the way Lea had thought. Eudora wasn't fighting against them, wasn't helping Alaric, or trying to weaken her or prevent her from taking Alaric's magic. She was taking it for herself.

Lea had no time to ask questions. To confirm her suspicions. As Alaric fought against her hold, she wrapped her fingers more firmly around her sword and threw Alaric to his back in the mud. She spread her shadows out, pinning him down at the wrists and ankles, and stalked toward him like the queen she was—head held high, body covered in blood, mud, and ash, and vengeance radiating off of her in waves. A petal fell from her crown, dancing away in the wind, but she didn't care. Didn't need more time before the last, and final petal still in her crown fell. She was ending this. Now.

Without ceremony or final words, she plunged her sword into Alaric's chest, blood spurting from the long wound with every beat of his black heart and splashing against her already crimson-soaked clothing. He roared in pain, in fury, and then, he began to laugh.

Lea's blood ran cold as his laughter grew maniacal, blood trickling from the sides of his mouth in a caricature of a frown.

"You think you can kill me?" he laughed again, but even through the laughter, his voice was low and full of menace. Lea shivered as he cackled again, then stopped abruptly, meeting her eyes. "I have no soul left to kill," he said. He tried to sit up, the sword still in his chest, but Lea kicked him back down. With a strength she hadn't thought possible now that he'd lost all his magic, Alaric fought back, pushing himself upward. The blade slid deeper and deeper into his flesh, through his bones and out his back, but still, he fought, as if he no longer felt the burden of pain.

"I *am* death," he said, blood flying from his mouth as he used both hands to grip the sword's blade. His fingers were sliced to the bone as he pulled on the sword with inhuman strength and slowly drew the blade from his chest, inch by inch. "And death," he pulled again, another sliver of sword sliding free, "cannot be killed!"

A sudden gust of wind blew, whipping Lea's hair around her face, and a memory danced through her mind—her mother, Adelaide, speaking as she hung a wreath of moonflowers above her bed. *Wait until they're ready, Wildflower. Picked by the right person with the right intentions, at the right time, the flowers from these seeds can stop death himself.*

Lea sucked in a sharp breath, Thomas's voice replacing her mother's as the image in her mind shifted to the locket in the hilt of her sword. *I want you to place a moonflower there, when you learn how to harvest it. Because I know you're going to do it one day, Lea. You're going to cure the Lonely Death and find a way to stop your husband-to-be's father from destroying our kingdom.*

Blood racing, she let go of the sword with one hand, using the other to keep the blade inside Alaric's chest. Her fingers tingled as she pulled a moonflower from her pocket and popped open the locket. Alaric threw his head back, laughing. Howling and cackling as he gripped the sword harder, fighting against her. Blood pooled around his teeth, his eyes and veins still black.

"*I* am death," Lea growled, shutting the moonflower inside the locket and snapping it closed. The sword glowed white, but remained cold in Lea's hand, and Alaric's eyes went wide, his laughter replaced by a sudden gasp for air.

The black of his veins spread, thickening and branching out until his entire body was as dark as the night sky, and bit by bit, he began to crumble, his body turning to ash just as she had seen the moonflower petals do hundreds of times before.

With a flash of silver-blue light and a gust of wind, Alaric was gone, nothing remaining but black, dead earth, and her sword plunged into the bloody ground where his wicked heart had last beat. The fire blinked out with the flash of light. The rain stopped, and the sounds of battle in the distance faded away into nothing but a soft breeze.

Lea scrambled over to Eudora, her hands hovering over her body as she tried to heal her. She reached out to Lea, blood bubbling from her mouth as she pressed a scroll into her hand.

"Tell him"—*gasp*—"it was the only way." Eudora coughed, more blood spattering on Lea's face, but she didn't even blink.

"You knew. The whole time, this was your plan?" Lea asked, tears pricking the back of her eyes.

Eudora nodded. "To speak it aloud... is to change the fates. Tell him—" Blood gurgled again from her mouth, her breathing pausing for several seconds before she managed to take another short, raspy inhale.

"I'll tell him, I promise," Lea said, squeezing Eudora's hands and pressing them to her lips.

A howl sounded in the distance, then more, coming closer and closer as the fenrir sang out a melody of grief and sorrow. Lea turned toward the sound to see Gray only feet away, his mouth open and his chest heaving, covered in blood from head to toe. His sword was gripped in his shaking hands, and behind knelt Evangeline, a hand pressed to her heart and tears streaming from her scarred eyes.

An old, gray Fenrir raced past them, lowering its head to nuzzle Eudora's cheek.

"Hello, old friend," Eudora said to the beast, her eyes growing heavy. "Thank you," she whispered, a small smile gracing her lips before her breath stilled completely and her eyes went dark.

The fenrir howled at the eclipse, and suddenly Gray was at Lea's side, his shadows caressing every inch of her body, his hands cupping her cheeks as he forced her gaze away from Eudora's body and to his eyes.

"You did it," he whispered, his voice gruff and thick with emotion. He crushed his lips to hers, and the dam holding back her own pain broke. A sob wrenched from her throat as she kissed him back, collapsing into his arms.

"I'm so sorry," she said.

"Shhhhh," he soothed. "We're okay, Little Flower. Everything's okay."

"Because of her..." Lea finally tore her gaze from Gray, lifting a hand and closing Eudora's eyes forever, breathing a silent prayer to the gods.

May the gods hold her in the light of day and serenity of night. May the magic of the wind carry her, the kiss of rain cleanse her, and the promise of eternity soothe her weary soul, until beyond the veil we follow.

CHAPTER 69

EMMA

Emma had promised herself that she would never kill. She hadn't thought herself capable of it, but it turned out she was wrong. She fought with Thomas at her side for what felt like hours, soldier after soldier falling to their invisible attacks. She realized about halfway through their fighting that she wasn't seeing the spirits of the soldiers they were killing. Wasn't seeing any spirits at all. Except, of course, for Thomas. But there was no time to think about why that was. Only enough time to hope, for just a moment, that maybe it meant there was a way to save him.

They didn't speak as they fought, their breaths heavy and their limbs tired. Emma avoided looking at where her body lay, Thomas still on top of her, protecting her with his body even in death. That image would be burned into her mind for the rest of her life.

A bright flash of light lit up the sky, and suddenly, Emma's vision went black.

Emma awoke to a bright light and a crushing pressure across her rib cage, the weight of Thomas's death as heavy on her body as it was on her soul. She knew before even opening her eyes that he was really gone. She couldn't sense his emotions. Couldn't feel even a speck of life within him.

As gently as she could, she rolled out from beneath him, flipping him over and cradling his face.

"Come back. Please," she whispered, grabbing a petal and pushing it between his lips. Emma knew it was futile. But it didn't matter. She had to try.

Holding her breath, she waited. Ten seconds. Twenty. But he didn't stir. He was gone.

Gone. Emma's heart beat harder as she twisted around, jumping to her feet to search for his spirit. She should be able to see him, shouldn't she? She could see the dead. Thomas could stay here. Remain on Earth. So where was he?

She collapsed back down at Thomas's side, shaking his shoulder. "Come back! Where are you? Please, come back," she sobbed, shaking him again. A vial rolled from his pocket, clinking against a twig and settling into the mud.

With trembling hands, she picked it up, noticing a thin roll of parchment inside. Had it been there when she'd taken the potion? She wasn't sure. Hadn't had time to look inside after she'd swallowed it down. Emma uncorked the vial and shook the note free, taking a deep breath as she unrolled it. A sob burst from her throat as she read the words scratched out in black ink.

You will not find him again, nor any others. It is better this way. No one deserves to carry a burden so heavy as yours...

He will wait for you.

—Eudora.

Emma squeezed the letter in her fist, throwing herself on top of Thomas as a raw sob tore from her throat. His body was growing cooler by the minute, another reminder that he was really and truly gone, but she couldn't pull herself away.

As her grief crashed over her, threatening to consume her entirely, the sky grew brighter, the sun slowly sliding from behind the moon and toward the horizon, illuminating the bloody battlefield around them in a wash of red—all the men she and Thomas had killed. Bile rose in her throat. There were so many... so much death. But the potion—was that why she hadn't seen them? She read the letter again, her body shaking as she read and reread the words.

Never again would she see the dead.

"Emma?" Erik's voice broke through her haze of grief. She sniffled but didn't look up.

"He's gone," Emma whispered, the words burning as they passed through her throat. Someone choked back a sob behind her, but still, she couldn't look away from Thomas's face.

"He loved you," Lea said, her voice shaking with tears.

"I know," she said, squeezing Thomas tighter, rocking back and forth. They didn't rush her. Didn't beg her to stand, to come with them. They simply stayed there with her in her sorrow, allowing her to mourn. And she was grateful.

Emma didn't know how much time passed, but finally, she stilled.

"It's over?" she asked, turning her swollen eyes to her friends. "Alaric's dead?"

Lea moved to her side, placing a hand on her back and nodding. "It's over."

Emma swallowed, allowing Lea to take her hand as she knelt next to Thomas's body. The others joined them, lending her their strength in silence as the sun continued to set.

When the last glimpses of the sun's rays began to disappear, Emma leaned forward, pressing one final kiss to Thomas's cheek. She stood, choking on a sob as Janelle and Lea held her up, supporting her as she took her first steps away from him.

Emma paused. "Will you bring him back? To bury him?" she asked Gray.

"Of course," he said, bowing his head, and Emma nodded. She couldn't stand the thought of him lying out here alone for even a moment, a cold body amongst the hundreds scattered through the wood.

Stars blinked into the sky as the last of the sun fully set, the horizon turning into a tapestry of pinks and purples and oranges, a wave of shimmering magic washing over the land with a force Emma had never seen before. The trees bent and bowed as it rushed past, magic returning to the earth as it had always been intended to be, and as if breathing life into the very soil, the trees of the Wicked Wood began to bloom.

Tiny green buds appeared on the branches, popping open into bright green leaves and small yellow flowers. Before their very eyes, the dead, rotting ground transformed, wildflowers blooming beneath their feet as far as the eye could see.

Emma cried out as the skin above her heart began to tingle, then burn. The sensation took her breath away, and she looked down, gasping as she examined her skin. With a sob, she turned back toward Thomas, reaching forward with shaking hands to pull the corner of his bloody shirt away. And there, on his blood-stained skin, was a new mark—a moon, the twin of the one now tattooed on her breast.

Proof that she had been loved by a man who had sacrificed everything, including his life, to keep her safe.

EPILOGUE

LEA

The wind blew softly across the rolling hills of Bearswillow, the long stalks of grass bowing toward the three freshly dug graves as if in deference to their memory. Gray stood between them, a prayer tumbling from his lips and tears shining in his eyes as he eulogized the dead. Genevieve, Thomas, and Eudora. The final three to be buried.

So many had been lost—too many—but their sacrifice had been honored back in Auropera. A tree had been planted for each of them, Lea funneling her light into their roots and helping them grow deep and strong until the garden was bursting with life. The garden sat between the castle and the town, full of bright, fragrant flowers and uninhibited sunlight, a resting place where families could honor the ones they'd lost. But for these three, Lea had chosen somewhere different. Somewhere closer to her heart.

For them, she'd chosen home.

Emma had agreed wholeheartedly. Had wanted Thomas's final resting place to be the place he'd loved, near his family, and in the beauty of the mountains he'd grown up in. Lea didn't think Emma would leave this place anytime soon, but she couldn't blame her. Thomas's family would take her in, give her a place to stay and make her one of their own until she was ready to return back home. If she was ever ready.

Emma knelt next to the fresh mound of dirt, Elise just behind her, her own face wet with tears. Emma had dressed in all white, her dress now stained with dirt as she whispered softly to the headstone bearing Thomas's name: *Brother. Son. Friend. Soldier. Mate.* And beneath the dates of his birth and death—his mate mark—etched into the stone with the same finality as the one marked on his body.

Lea's heart ached as she looked at the mark. Emma would mourn him until the day she died, but Lea knew he was waiting for her. Likely sitting just over the hill, relaxing in the gentle breeze, allowing time to pass until they could be reunited.

Or maybe, he was here. Sending the wind to comfort her, just as Lea's own mother had. Watching her, hoping she would find a way to be happy.

Someday, she would be. But the wounds they'd sustained on their souls would last far longer than those that scarred their bodies.

Henry and Evangeline stood behind Gray, their heads bowed in reverence to the ones who had given the ultimate sacrifice. The three beautiful souls who had risked their lives to allow the rest of them to live. A lump formed in Lea's throat as she looked at them standing together, her birth mother and her father, both of whom had lost the other half of their souls. Hopefully, they, too, were waiting on the other side for their mates—Adelaide and Ryland. Lea smiled at the thought of them keeping eachother company until it was time for them to greet Henry and Evangeline beyond the veil.

Lea looked to the third grave, Eudora's name and place of birth chiseled in the middle. And at the very top of the stone was the mate mark they'd found on her body as well, a twin to King Tanad's.

They hadn't been the only ones to find mate marks upon their chests once the wave of magic had crashed across the kingdom, restoring magic and peace as it had always been intended. Erik and Janelle had been branded with proof of their love, as had countless others. More couples than Lea could keep track of, suddenly blessed by the gods with a gift they'd all but thought would never happen again.

Lea and Gray's skin remained blank, only the scars of their past bond remaining, but Lea wasn't sad. At least, not about the mate mark. The fact that she was alive was a miracle. That she would get this life with Gray, as well as the next. They had both survived. They had been given a second chance and had lived to see their kingdom flourish. It was impossible to feel anything other than grateful, especially when so many others hadn't been so lucky. When so many others had been separated from their mates by death's cold hands.

Tanad had allowed Lea to read the note Eudora had left for him, and she'd learned that, on the night of her birth, Eudora had not only seen The Daughter of Suns and Stars defeating the Black King, she had seen Lea's entire life.

For years, she'd helped set up the events that would help Lea to defeat Alaric, allowing herself to be the villain, if that's what it took to save Tanad's kingdom. *It was the only way,* she had written. *I wanted to stay with you. I tried to find something else, anything, but every time I changed the plan, we failed. I couldn't watch your kingdom fall. Couldn't bear to see your people die, and you, along with them. I hope you can forgive me for all the secrets I was forced to keep. I love you.*

Tanad had forgiven Eudora, of course, but as Lea looked at his sad, haggard face, his hands gripping the top of her grave so hard his knuckles were white, she wasn't sure if he would ever forgive himself for believing she would serve Alaric. Especially now that he knew every decision she'd made had been a piece in a moving puzzle that had allowed the next to fall into place.

It still gave Lea chills to think about—that Eudora had been the one to send the fenrir to her village, exposing Thomas's magic and setting their journey into motion. *A favor,* she'd said, *to another with magic as ancient as their own. They belong to Lea now.*

She'd explained that the fenrir had been waiting for centuries for a Fae worthy of serving. Eudora had told them of her vision—that Lea would restore peace and magic as had been intended—and they'd answered her call.

As Gray said the final words of the service, Lea knelt down, pushing a single seed into each grave, hoping it would say all the things she couldn't find the words for. Her gratitude. Her sorrow. She rose to her feet, the wind blowing softly around them, and turned away, wanting to give Tanad and Emma their privacy to mourn, but stopped when long rays of sunshine peeked out from the clouds, scattering across the hill. Small green sprouts popped out from the seeds, multiplying and growing until the entirety of the graves were covered, with seedlings spilling into the grass.

The skin above her breast began to tingle, the scar of her mate mark burning. Her hand drifted to her sternum, her heart pounding beneath her fingers as she traced the lines she knew by heart. She looked to Gray, meeting his eyes as a slow smile crossed his face. Her heart fluttered as his love flooded through her—heavy and passionate and all-consuming.

Little Flower? His voice rang out in her mind, crisp, clear, and strong. Lea couldn't speak, not even through their bond as she basked in the feeling of his devotion coursing through her until it filled every inch of her body. She nodded, tears pricking her eyes, and held out her hand. He pulled her into a silent embrace, pushing every emotion he was feeling down their bond—love, forgiveness, sorrow, pride, grief. They were all there, an orchestra plucking the strings of her weary soul.

Lea didn't know what would happen next. After the mourning, the grieving. They would have to learn to rule. To take care of their kingdom. She hoped they could build a home here in Bearswillow, with a garden brimming with her favorite flowers. A place tiny feet could run and feel the joy of open skies and soft grass and unconditional love.

But for now, *this* was enough, and she closed her eyes, committing the moment to memory. As Gray finally pulled back, his hand sliding into hers, the sprouts that had spread across the graves like clover began to bloom. Bright red poppies opening above Genevieve's final resting place, bright white lilies above Thomas's, and above Eudora's, soft pink peonies. Her mother's voice echoed in her ear as a gust of wind passed by, the flowers gently swaying.

A rhyme for the grieving. A promise of better things.

Lea smiled, lifting her chin to the sky and letting the sun kiss her face before reaching down and picking a single stem of each flower.

Lilies, for peace.

Poppies, for sorrow.

And peonies, for hope of a better tomorrow.

THE END

Acknowledgements

To everyone who read this series, **THANK YOU.** The support I've felt has been life-changing, and without you all, finishing this series wouldn't have been possible.

If you enjoyed this book, consider helping me get the word out by leaving a review on **AMAZON** and/or **GOODREADS** and follow me on Facebook, Instagram, and Tiktok @meganshadeauthor

To the greatest beta readers I could ask for—Shannon, Kerrie, Tiffany, Mary, and Anna—you all give the best feedback and I'm so grateful you were willing to spend your time helping me make this story shine.

Sarah McFarland, thank you so much for your proofreading and horse riding expertise.

Sara, as always, thank you for reading and rereading until we thought everything was just right. I feel so lucky to get to work with someone who gets my vision and my voice, and helps make it shine.

Lindsey Staton (@honeyy.fae on IG), thank you for your beautiful art, support, and friendship. Everyone check out her work!

To Stef, my cover designer, thank you for nailing it every single time and being an absolute joy to work with.

To my husband, my number one fan and biggest cheerleader. You'll never know how much your support has changed my life.

To all my family, for their unwavering support.

To my friends, both those who have read my books and those who have been my cheerleaders, thank you so much for everything you've done to support and encourage me. I love you all.

Also By

A Wildflower in the Wind
A Sun Scorched Bloom

Be on the lookout for my latest projects, to be announced soon!